I0611058

BACK TO CUBA

The Return of the Butterflies

ELIO F. BELTRAN

BACK TO CUBA

This book is written to provide information and motivation to readers. Its purpose is not to render any type of psychological, legal, or professional advice of any kind. The content is the sole opinion and expression of the author, and not necessarily that of the publisher.

Printed in the United States of America.

ISBN   978-1-64552-053-5   (Paperback)
ISBN   978-1-64552-054-2   (Digital)

Lettra Press books may be ordered through booksellers or by contacting:

Lettra Press LLC
30 N Gould St. Ste N
Sheridan, WY 82801, USA
3035861431 | info@lettrapress.com
www.lettrapress.com

CONTENTS

DEDICATION

This book is dedicated to the memory of Eloy Sardiñas, my childhood friend, and to the lands I love, which are many. Above all, to Cuba.

ACKNOWLEDGEMENTS

My first acknowledgement is to my wife Aurora McIntosh Beltran for having endured the long ordeal of my absentmindedness while I was immersed in writing. I also acknowledge my brother-in-law, Carlos Rojo, for having provided me a computer to work with while I was in Andalucia, Spain, where much of the book was written. Since I hardly talked to anyone about this endeavor, there are few that I could mention at this time except for Mr. Peter block, delegate of the French Academy of Art, Sciences and Letters in New York who read the initial manuscript and offered great encouragement for its final publication. Another acknowledgement is to my friend and professor at Keen University in Elizabeth, New Jersey, U.S.A. – Dr. Francisco Feito, for being a good listener, and for providing encouragement without asking many questions, and a special acknowledgement to my good friend Dr. Elio Alba buffill professor emeritus of The City of New York, and executive secretary of the Pan-American Circle of Culture who together with Dr. Feito were the custodians of documents related to the story during my trip to Cuba in May of 2001. I also extend the thanks to everyone who has shared a part of their life with me, and in one way or another had a participation in the story. To them, wherever appropriate, I wholeheartedly ask for forgiveness if my story did not bring them gladness or do them justice.

* * * *

I Herein, acknowledge my appreciation to my readers, and to Ms. Anna Cortez, Lettra Press chief editor, for her valuable assistance, with the final book review, and successful editing, as well as the new cover details for this Special 2019 updated edition.

The Author

PROLOGUE

The author embodied in Michael carries no quest in search for the usual literary recognition as the result of the work surrounding this story, such endeavor most surely could prove to be inadequate in this case but also elusive at best. The story, as it unfolds, is more related to the experience of living and loving – Love of people, love of freedom, and love in the highest degree of vulnerability when such feelings are surrounded by, and exposed to the whims and ambitions of men within the circumstances of political turmoil and through all of it, the anguish created by deceit and separation from country and between love ones in every possible hurtful level.

Michael's journey (as he sets out to look for the reasons and the lessons that can be learned from the many angles and experiences) takes us through it all including the beauty he tries to rescue from otherwise being probably lost. beauty that lives in childhood memories of the years of innocence that he recreates before he enters the intricacies of life in the scenario of circumstances surrounding the events of the last fifty or more years in Cuba and life as an exile where he searches for ways to deal with all of it, and in it entering into the mysteries of guiding forces that appear to come from the memory of a gifted childhood friend who died at an early age, opening the door perhaps to a better understanding of our awesome human nature.

In the search that unfolds he is able to find beauty in the deteriorated, but eloquent facades of buildings in Old Havana, and in the people that have been, and those that still are, enmeshed in its fiber of life and waiting to be free from the negative consequences of abuse of power, lies, neglect, and the fear that lurks in the realms of terror. A kind of terror that, as well as beauty (however apart} is not noted when looked at from a far distance and away from the epicenter of the action, Most importantly, the author wants the readers to be able to share in his travels through the entire spectrum that, in sum, should shed some light on many historic events and the perspectives that surround his experiences as well as that of many others in back to Cuba, while we all, at the end, are looking for solutions to more than half a century's old tragedy than should, by necessity, and the open question continues to be: How?. By reading thru the story, and throughout the end, some clues can be found, like a puzzle that signals to how it may come to its conclusion.

All persons, and characters of the story are real, however, some names may have been changed to protect some possible compromised identities, or perhaps real names have been blurred in the memory. Any similarities with person or persons dead or alive would be mere coincidences.

The Author

CHAPTER ONE

Realization

**Today I really grasp
that time and age are not the same at every stage.
Years on your temples not only make the snow to glow,
but things that become so dear
never looked the same – just yesterday. The enjoyment
grows with every day when you know that you and them
are not always here to stay.
You know so very very well, you have only today to
give, to take,
and not to let it uselessly run away. Friendship is only
one of them.**

Midnight: Two people walk through the elegant entrance hall, behind the maître d', who is walking in front of them,. The mariachi band is playing, . the trumpets are loud, and the young woman singer, dressed in a bright Mexican *"charro"dresst"* delights the crowd with the last notes of "El Rey." The plush nightclub is full of guests from the hotel and of people from the four corners of the world.

They casually met at the airport three days earlier, as if fate had intervened,. he traveled from the east while she boarded the aircraft in Texas after a flight from the Midwest; the plane had just moved off the gate when she arrived, running towards the attendant, at the entrance of the ramp. "Oh! Have I missed the flight? . . . My connecting flight was late on account of the storm."

"We are sorry Miss; you just missed it for one minute . . . Oh wait, the pilot is coming back to the gate. Someone has told him that the 'missing passenger' has arrived just as he was pulling away."

"Wonderful!, something told me that I could not miss this flight after I had run so much." The attractive, shorthaired brunette on a light pink jumper suit stepped in, and practically threw herself into the comfortable first seat of the semi-deserted first-class compartment.

He didn't notice her until they were at the baggage claim section of Mexico City Airport. Five feet away, he noted her air of frustration at the delay of her suitcase. His eyes rolled by the fair, porcelain-like skin of her face – so alive in expression with her high cheekbones slightly blushing, as if reflecting the pinkish blouse. He could not repress from his thoughts a strange inner feeling of amazement and of a great incomprehensible attraction, like something inevitable was going to happen, particularly when he saw her bright eyes that felt like a caressing smile – so full of self-confidence and of joyful life;. Somehow, as though, without knowing exactly how it was possible, he felt that he didn't want to part from her sight from that moment on . . . His astonishment was total when he heard her voice and her clean musical Castilian accent answering his question after she had blown the hair from her forehead with an air of near but contained rage.

"Are you missing your luggage?"

"I don't know,, this is the first time I come to Mexico. It is taking too long,, . is that possible? *"Sera possible."* The gracious woman in her mid-forties said, striking a typical expression showing that her upbringing was unquestionably from Madrid.

Michael was more than amused during the short conversation; eventually, he picked up his suitcase, offered her a ride to the city in the same car that was picking him up.. but, in the end, he didn't wait. She had to fill out a missing baggage claim. He had business to attend so he shrugged under his light gray suit and went on his way, rapidly crossing through the mass of people. He checked through customs and went on to meet the short bearded young man dressed in a black three-piece vested suit waiting next to an equally black and shining European sedan.

He sat next to the driver's seat and heard himself say something he had never heard himself say before: "I have been struck by an arrow" and then sat down without saying anything more. He pulled a travel card from his pocket and wrote her name, the way it sounded in her voice at the brief introduction. Later, he would spend two evenings after business hours, calling various hotels trying to locate Aurora Abril McIntosh again and again without success. He could feel a sense of loss invading him; mysteriously and even far-fetched as it may have been, somehow in his heart he knew and felt the loss of something he never had, and that which he may never again encounter, even if it was just a strong and little-understood intuition, he wondered if he has been waiting for it, alone a long way, like reaching the end of a subconscious long search; a search for the kind of love that suddenly appeared inexplicable and only possible from her total sudden presence. A feeling he had never felt before. It was only a vision he had seen, as if the two days before at the airport was only a mirage in a desert. The thought that he only had a glimpse of that woman for once, before she was gone, was leaving him with a deeper sense of nothingness, like his sense of betrayal had to continue; and worse yet, that this type of feeling was not going to present itself ever again.

After all, those thoughts, and sense of loss appeared to tell him, "Let go of it. It is useless." He still decided to make one more call to the one hotel he had called two times before; among others he had called during the last two days since the flight, but this time, he gave a description of the woman's personality and the pure Castilian accent of her voice to the clerk rather than a name. "Wait a minute, I think…. That the person you are looking for is staying here." A few moments later, her unmistakable voice sounded at the end of the wire. The search had suddenly stopped. . .

Her eyes, sparkling in the darkness of the nightclub, exuded the joy she was experiencing at the moment, bouncing the reflection of the stage lights where the trumpets kept floating with the triumphant sound of the well-known '*corrido*':

"Rodaaary . . . rodaaar . . . rodaaary . . . rodaaar . . ." The singers and the public chanted with delight.

His mind, traveling like in a dream while he received the impact of her total attention, was only thinking of the magic of the moment brought by the unexpected encounter of a few days before at the airport. There was no previous experience that could equal the enjoyment of a moment such as the one he was living. Few words were said by both; he was silent and unusually introspective for longer than usual while bringing his thoughts to an earlier conversation when he had talked briefly about his life – his job, his being married, and about having two daughters that he loved dearly; his life in the U.S., on his earliest years as an exile; his passion for art and painting, the excitement of a recent successful gallery opening, after a prolonged agonizing and disappointing year . . . She brought his thoughts to a halt when she softly asked, after an apparent long pause . . . "Do you love her?" "*Si, mucho*" he answered. He took a deep breath while bringing the glass to his lips as he slowly lifted his head and remained looking silently at the stage.

His thoughts were wondering why he felt so strangely attracted, not only to a woman who was obviously attractive, but as to why he was feeling so self-assured; that it was not just the natural thing to feel, but that this time there was no fear of reaching a point of regretful guilt, as if for all reasons this was to be avoided at all cost, like in many other occasions before this; and feeling the need to find a way out of any such possibilities, and soon find it with elegance, before anyone could feel any regrets.

The walk back to her hotel was more stimulating than a walk alone in the city he knew so well. This time, the night-lights seemed to have a special reflection on the pavement, and the walks along both sides of La Reforma. A look at the angel left in the back, above, demonstrated that this was a special night, for some unknown reason yet. The glow, coming from the famous monument, gave the impression that its shine was never before like it was this night – the sparkling gold coming out from a transparent silver-like halo, evolving around the winged figure with its extended hand offering its gift of a laurel crown in burning zephyr. The sudden good night kiss on her chic, she surprised her with at the hotel lobby was the result of a genuine desire to tell her: "This is the rendering of my deepest admiration of your lovely presence in my life tonight." This was his only intention, but he didn't think she would have believed it if he told her that this was the true meaning, and perhaps more. The only thing of a personal nature he thought, at that moment, was the only thing that he could give her, being at the same time like a goodbye to what was like a beautiful dream, without any true possibilities in the real world. Three days later, he returned with the conviction that he will see her again someday but that only time, after much soul-searching, would be able to find out, if this unexpected encounter was capable of changing the course of his life forever, or perhaps was best to forget it altogether.

She went about her tourist mission in Mexico after giving him a telephone number and her home address where she lived as a widow, almost two thousand miles away from his home in New York City.

The airplane took off on a clear Saturday morning. Michael's eyes looked at the large city buildings getting smaller and smaller, and gazed at the main avenues packed with vehicles, moving at a constant even speed, like blood cells in an artery,.. Insurgentes avenue seemed longer than the horizon line.. He thought of the seemingly smallness of one soul in the midst of twenty million dwellers and travelers. One soul that he felt so sure he knew better than any other, in spite of the short time they had spent together. Every word that was said, every expression of the eyes and hands were coming to his mind and being analyzed over and over. He also thought of every feeling that was expressed, even about the unimportant things that appeared to spark. A multitude of feelings of gladness, however overwhelmingly significant. Suddenly, he realized that he had not felt this way for a long time before. He closed his eyes, reclined in his window seat, and introspectively started to review his mind in an effort to understand why he had been feeling so unhappy most of the time, for a long time, and most of all coming back again, in his mind, to a greater feeling of frustration that competed with a feeling of guilt, blended with a sense of failure like he never thought possible in his life but that confronted him with its harsh reality, this time more challenging than ever. but the love for his family came as usual to his rescue, as a sure greater meaning. All other thought vanished, leaving however, a deepening sense of dishonesty that he needed to suppress as usual, so as not to betray the need of happiness of others over his own.

For a moment, his mind took him away from the stormy thoughts and closer to a desire of becoming disconnected from everything he was coming back to. Soon, he was floating farther and farther away from the speeding jet plane – a flight of his mind to the happiest times of his life, his childhood. Perhaps there is a clue somewhere to be found; something useful to discover about the why and the how; something that will indicate a path to what was now so far from being conceived, but now, undoubtedly, like some kind of utopia. An unattainable path to happiness, in all kinds of fashions.

Michael's thoughts came to the mid-'thirties – perhaps the most peaceful years that the world could ever remember in the twentieth century. At the time, a world worried with emerging from the Great Depression – financially sick, and plagued with hardship for most, but nonetheless, a peaceful time just before Mussolini's war in Ethiopia (the tragic prelude to the bloody Spanish Civil War and the Second World War). Grown up people worked hard to provide and worried greatly about the most important immediate things like having a job, a roof, and some food on the table.

Children did not have lots of toys; instead, the lucky ones could only play with homemade toys or some other "toy" that they will invent and play with. It is apparently a fact that children can make their own happiness, as long as there is peace and love in their midst. So was Michael's case in those years. He had only one older brother, who was seven years older. The differences in age made him play by himself most of the time until he grew up to go to school and share with children closer to his age. by then however, he was used to thinking and doing things in his own individual way, but most of all, he was observant of everything that surrounded him. Like anyone else, the mind was there to be opened to the great experience of our very existence – life with all its possibilities, good and bad, fate and nature, all to play its part to make some thing or nothing from perception or from indifference to it. As he grew up, he was less than indifferent to what life was like around him – in his hometown and its surroundings.

In Cuba, the political scenario had also entered a peaceful period after the ousting of Geraldo Machado by an early 1930s people's revolt, supported by the army in what was called the "Sergeant's Revolt" headed by Sergeant Fulgencio Batista. Batista ended up as the strongman, but not after the death of Guiteras, a popular socialist student's movement leader who was not known to be an extremist revolutionary leader but somewhat of being a respected progressist, who was shot down on a hideaway near the northern coast of Matanzas in a place called "El Morrillo",, where he was waiting to escape.

Machado had been an elected president who was credited with much of Cuba's industrialization during the good and prosperous years of the mid-'twenties, but his party forced a change in the constitution in order for him to be reelected, and that, together with the abuses of power of some of the authorities and the secret police, whom the people deceptively called *"esbirro"s* during his second term, angered the people to the boiling point. Michael was barely three years old then but at six, he had already heard enough about the preceding period and he somewhat remembered the election that brought Batista to the presidency by popular vote in 1936 and more so, he remembered Batista's reelection to a second term in 1940 because that time, was shortly after the end of the bloody Spanish Civil War, and the worries brought up by the beginning of the Second World War in Europe.

In thinking about that period, Michael remembered when, during those peaceful years of the mid – to late 'thirties, the Havana harbor received the visit of the battleship Texas. He remembered how enormous and powerful it looked from the high point of *La Loma de los Cocos* ("Coconuts Hill") that overlooked Havana from Regla. It was a site he would never forget. Somehow, it reflected the strength of the neighbor, ninety miles to the north. However, its presence, although supposedly friendly, may have had a symbolic reminder that Cuba was still under the ominous Plat Amendment, that reserved for the United States the right to intervene in Cuban political affairs. (An unfortunate treaty that gave to many, the fuel to vilify the powerful country of the Stars and Stripes and its so-called intentions to rule the island for their own "imperialistic interests"; in a way, planting the seeds of anti-American sentiment in a country that was above all very fond of the American way of life and its reputation as the bedrock of liberty.)

For Michael however, at the time of the famous battleship visit, all he remembered was the beauty of its lines and how, for his childish mind, it practically seemed to overflow the bay just as if it was a small bathtub, and that image remains to this day. Overall however, he related in his mind to the characteristic of his people. The Cuban people during his growing up years was a people, not indifferent to political developments anywhere, but also, were zealous guardians of their independence from any foreign force whatsoever as they were always very conscious of the sacrifices made by its people during its long struggles for independence.

Michael, as all the freedom-loving Cuban people, can't forget the long struggles and sacrifices to gain freedom from Spain as well as the ingrained ideals and fundamentals of independence and the principles of the right of people to rule their own destiny in dignity and self-respect, as well as the respect of others. Principles that were deeply instilled by enlightened leaders and philosophers of freedom like Padre Varela, Jose Antonio Saco, Jose de la Luz y Caballero, Jose Maria Mendive and José Martí for more than two centuries. Even when the principles have been manipulated by self-imposed dictators throughout the short hundred years of independence for shamefully prolonged periods of time, he was sure that they are so strong as to survive and flourish far and beyond such dark periods.

It is shameful, and insulting that for more than fiftyfive years during the Castro regime, the principles of freedom have been used to manipulate and enslave the country under a false pretension of defending such principles.

From a very early age, he remembered how his hometown had enjoyed the growth and economic boom of the roaring 'twenties. The country as a whole had experienced the flow of investment in industry, probably more than the other countries in Latin America, because of its proximity to the United States, and the strategic positions and adequacy of its ports. Cuba was primarily an agricultural country, but its sugar industry experienced its great development after the colonial years, providing great wealth to investors; tobacco and other exports contributed to promising, and attractive foreign ventures in the island. The aches and pains suffered by a very young republic produced successive failures in government, democracy was practiced in very few spurs between foreign interventions, dictatorship, and the military coups that ensued, during different periods after 1933. The momentum for economic progress was apparently unstoppable in spite of the political instability. The progress however was not necessarily notable at all levels; while jobs were developed around the port cities, it was not enough to satisfy all the needs of a growing population. There has been a tradition for a good quality of education that was also growing in the number of schools. Quality in education was a tradition that had its origins in the colonial years, and extended into an ever-present drive for progress of a good part of the population. This was apparently a characteristic, intuitive or inherent, in the Cubans – descendants, or not from the motherland Spain, and in an admirable degree in the Afro-Cubans – descendants of the Africans that were brought as slaves but were culturally and orderly blending in extraordinarily well under the circumstances of this very young experiment to form a wonderful country whose characteristic was to be reluctant to accept anything without questioning it. Most significant characteristic, of those years was the relentless desire for change and progress.

The "Dance of Millions" that preceded the Depression left an indelible mark in Regla, the colorful town across the bay from Havana, the capital. Its railroad terminal was one of the largest and busiest of any country in Latin America, and close in importance to those of the major industrial cities of the northeast of the United States. Large sugar and tobacco warehouse terminals crowded the town's shoreline; nearby underground tanks, where molasses were stored and pumped into tanker ships docked alongside, not too far from a major coal depot and gigantic steam-operated hauler cranes. From that coal depot via the railroads, the country feeds its industrial power belly, prior to the advent of the electric power in the sugar industry. It also had its first trial run right on this town with a first-class electric generating plant that used coal as well for its operation. The same electric plant powered the first trolley car that rolled over the cobbled-stoned streets of this town, which some said was the first time that happened in Latin America. Michael's family always talked about his grandfather, from his mother side, being the conductor at that historic moment. The beautiful trolley cars later on became the pride of the beautiful capital city in the near horizon. Havana, the city that was already, blossoming, as a major tourist attraction. The city that could be seen from almost five miles away from the top of the massive quartz,-filled rocks hills that surrounded his colorful hometown of Regla, on the southeast of the beautiful bay.

The industrial activity, and the port provided jobs to a large number of stevedores, longshoremen, railroad men, and factory workers as well as the municipal slaughterhouse on the outskirts of town alongside the railroad terminal from where the cattle were unloaded. All of these produced a rich mesh of activity that included cowboys and horses – that were the thrill of youngsters, particularly when the bulls escaped, creating quite an excitement in the nearby neighborhood. The area enjoyed, from time to time, the colorful public celebrations of the brotherhood of the Abakua's – descendants of the first African slaves, those that participated in that secret brotherhood that was mostly formed by black males, port and slaughterhouse workers who lived in the outskirts of the town. It was quite a rich, and colorful cultural outpour in the sound of drumbeats and chants, as well as costume, in real authentic display, unchanged, by any means, traditionally,. during the years, away from the eyes of modern developments and trends,.Michael remembered the exuberant demonstration of that rich African inheritance during the yearly celebration of the town's patron saint La Virgen de Regla, that took place during the second week of September, when thousands of people came from everywhere by means of the famous *lanchita* – from the capital at the other side of the bay, and by buses and all available means of transportation crowding the streets near El Emboque, as the old ferry terminal and bus station was called then.

The solemn procession of September the Eighth, was a well-known event that brought many faithful people from all races and nationalities to see the sacred image taken out of the church at the edge of the water at the small Santa Catalina beach, in an impressive display of devotion. The next day was the day when all the organizations related to the various African traditional organizations professed their beliefs, brought by the Africans popularly known as *Santeria.* they would go to the streets in what was called a *Cabildo* – a tumultuous parade. A display of joyful chanting and rhythmical dancing at the sound of the *bata* drums, as an offering and the honoring of the deities or *Orishas;* particularly to *"Yemaya",* which, according to traditional Yoruba beliefs, rules the waters, and is the mother of all African deities. Michael and his friends would watch the *Cabildo,* sitting on the edge of the hill that reached the top of *La Loma de la Ermita* – "The Hill of the Hermit" – where the ruins of the old colonial church overlooked the southweastern branch of the bay.

The day and night celebrations that continued for about ten days included many attractions and games along the crowded main streets of the town, and fair areas near the church, by the arriving boats, where fireworks would illuminate the night sky blue and where people would also enjoy the most tasty lobster *enchilada, tamales* or Cuban sandwiches and a cold beer for only seventy-five cents.

One year, his brother and a friend decided to set up a kiosk to sell beer, refreshments, and the famous *enchilada de langostas,.* But Michael was not allowed to work at the counter by his brother and friend but he remembered, how he completely wore out his shoes to the point of destruction just by bringing the refreshments, the ice, and the food from his brother's girlfriend home, located one and a half miles away, all day long for over the entire week, through the bumpy back roads of the town to avoid the crowds, and for most of the way using only a wheelbarrow; it happened every day until the end of the festivities and, of course, the end of his shoes. It was hard work indeed, plus the frustration for not being let to be inside the kiost, attending the public, like his broither and friend, enjoying his time.

After the celebrations concluded, there was not much money being made to amount to anything worthwhile, and he remembered telling his brother:

"Please brother, don't think of any more businesses like this. Please!!"

CHAPTER TWO

Scared Intruders And The Ghost Of The Pirate

It was already dark that evening in late of July, 1939. Michael and his father were usually close to the radio after dinner, as they have been doing for the last three years of the bloody Spanish Civil War that started in 1936. For those four or five years they had listened together to the reports on short wave that broadcasted news from Spain, with its anguish-ridden civil war.. Thinking about this period, and the sound of the classic Spanish song *"Las bodas de Luis Alonso"* as the radio station started and finished the program, brought back vivid childhood memories.

Sitting on his window seat flying from Mexico back to the U.S., Michael was still hearing, over and over again, in his mind, the majestic Spanish piece, like it was still sounding in the airspace he was flying across. The night he was now remembering with the reports, as usual, had a mix of anguish and novelty, hardly an entertainment. As the 1936 Spanish Civil War was a prelude to more tragic events in the European continent; the events as they were happening in Europe, by the early 'forties, were frightening; strangely far away, and yet so close. It was for him, who was in his tenth year of his life, a sign of early maturity, with the worries that clashed with his childhood fantasies – notions of a paradise that could soon be lost, and that which needed to be absorbed and lived to the maximum, if possible. That kind of urgency was constantly present in his mind. He was thinking now about that unforgettable night: the plan that he and Eloy had talked about with another friend that afternoon. He could hardly wait until the end of the broadcast, and immediately after, he went to his room at the back of the house. His father had left for a fraternity meeting, and his mother would stay another hour or so in the front porch talking with the next-door neighbor, his beloved would-be godmother.

He felt the blood rushing and his heart pounding when he climbed and let himself down from the tall wall behind the house. It was a very dark night and he had never ventured outside his house at that hour of the night and more so because, he never left his house without permission from his parents. but how could they have allowed such an adventure to take place ever, at his age? Going to secretly watch an initiation ceremony of the Yoruba secret society –" *Otan Efo*" at the far end of the "Hill of the Hermit" – *La Loma de la Ermita* – as the place was known, would have been out of the question. The back of his house was two houses away from the back of Eloy's house, at the same spot where a year before, he and his friend watched over a burning firewood oven under the traditional pile of dirt where they were able to make vegetable coal, a process learned by his friend as well as many others, which the resourceful and enterprising friend experienced while he was growing up in the country. Eloy was already there in his backyard with Coco, the thin and dark complexion little neighbor who, occasionally participated and worked with the two boys in some of their activities. Michael was greeted by Coco with his white teeth and eyeballs shining in the dark. The three of them walked, and crawled at times until they went over the third fence, and into the semi-dark end of the yet unpaved and bumpy street that climbed up to the top of the hill. The lights were few and separated by one block each, so that most of the walk up through the three-hundred-yard long, thirty-degree climb was done in half-shadows. There were less than ten houses on the first block, the rest was bare hillside with narrow paths and a dangerous deserted rift that needed to be crossed, in order to get to the top, where they were to turn right into the darkness to pass a large.... corner house – where people were probably sleeping, judging by the darkness surrounding the entire house. Only one light in one of the back windows was not enough to throw any light towards the back – a very steeped rocky and slippery side that overlooked the secret spot. It was an area that was impassable at night and was only used as a shortcut to the slaughterhouse and to connect to the entrance of *El Callejon del Sapo,* a long and narrow dirt road alley, full of mystery, that was primarily used to bring cattle unloaded from the trains almost a mile away. Only few people would venture to go down that way through the very difficult and slippery path during the daytime. Steps had been precariously cut out on a narrow, three-feet-wide passage on the left side of the rift, made by a deep opening on the southeast side of the hill. This night, down below – thirty yards away from the edge, where the three boys climbed down to hide behind the tall grass and small bushes, on the small ledge at the hillside, they could watch without being seen from the bottom of the pit; where the light of the bonfire would flash swats of red and yellow, undulating flashes that dramatically projected shadows of the dancing celebrants of the ancient secret ceremony, and of the small group of drummers together with the *yoruba lucumi* ritual singers chanting in authentic African Yoruba words.

The air was suddenly filled with the mysterious sound of a very powerful secret ritual instrument never heard before by the three scared intruders. Such an instrument, and how the sound was produced was not known by many, outside the brotherhood leaders. It came from the secret room of *"Famba",* as the secret room was called; a small cabin at the bottom of the hill. The loud sound ran continuously for about eight seconds in three-second intervals, at the same time with the drumbeats, which gave way to an eerie feeling, and a strange hypnotic sense that was only broken by fear.

The visual impressions the three trembling hidden observers had from their vantage point, were no less frightening, as: the rhythmical ceremonial dancers, two tall-hooded figures dressed in black – with bells tied to their waist, wrists, and ankles, casting shadows against the blue-gray rocky hillside – was something to behold, amidst the choir chants of a dozen dark, bare-chested men standing near the old rusty barrel that was being used to keep a fire going, about twenty-five feet from the two dancing ritual figures.

After about seven minutes of almost breathless tension, the three intruders ran back uphill and away from the site at a speed that only scared children know about, just like running away in the face of a life-threatening fear. The three knew that they had intruded into a secret, ancient and forbidden ritual that they had violated, just as they had violated the sense of obedience earlier that night.

The three parted at the same spot where they had met less than an hour before. Michael reached the fence behind his house and went to the lowest spot of the brick fence and pulled himself over. Standing there, he reached for the ledge of the tiled roof and swung a leg over, and then the other leg, until he was on top, walked down the steps of the ladder into the small courtyard of his house and entered through the back door and went immediately to his bed. He was still trembling. This was a night that he will never forget.

He had, from time to time seen the daylight public ceremonies performed by the brotherhood of the Abakua in front of his house, looking through the blinders of the French windows as he remembered since he was six years old, but nothing like the secret rituals in the darkness of the night,. he had seen the impressive strength of the ritual dancers, and heard the chants of the participants that still used the native tongue of their slave ancestors, praising their African deities or *Orishas* at the beat of the *bata* drums. Ancient rituals kept by a very little understood and feared society composed mostly of the male peasant workers of the bay and slaughterhouse, performed at the edge of the town and away from the authorities that most of the time prohibited such public manifestation of these ritual celebrations; a colorful cultural heritage that had little to do with voodoo or *santeria*, and much to do with a culture that exuded color in costume, uniqueness in music, rhythm and movement in dance that was different from anything the Europeans' culture had brought to the colonies or found in them; a powerful influence that already was, and for a long time grew to become the fiber and bedrock of one of the greatest influences in music and other art forms in Cuba and the Western World thereafter.

The excitement of that night's adventure was one of the first experienced by Michael with his new friend. He didn't have, at the time, any idea of how the visual impressions of that night's secret rituals would so vividly lodge in his mind, and how or why they would emerge some thirty years later as an important piece in the puzzle of his mature life. For the moment it was just another day in the life of an eleven-year-old boy. More adventures followed after that. For unknown reasons, he kept his mind occupied on his childhood memories during his flight from Mexico, as if time had suddenly run very fast in his thoughts; it continued to go back and forth over happenings that offered him the enchantment of life that was real, without being as painful as life's realities have a way to be on occasion. Time however was running at its usual predictable way as not more than one hour of flight has passed, while more than three years have come as a cavalcade through his brain and inner sight.

back again in his thoughts, it went to the time when he and the surprisingly sharp marble player that had just made his debut in the neighborhood left the game site to walk around the three blocks at the foot of the hill known as La Loma de la Ermita and to the old park above it. The walk around the few blocks was like a ritual new friends go through, in which they can get to know each other. Eloy, very fast told him about his life in the town he came from, near the southern city of Cienfuegos. He had grown up in rural surroundings and had learned many things related to trees and hunting. He could recognize any kind of bird and he knew what plants had good medicinal qualities or what to use it for and where to find it, and which plants we had to avoid being in contact with. Michael found this to be interesting as they did not pay too much attention to the variety of plants in the surrounding area; being closer to a larger city, with large industrial activity, the attention to plants and creatures of the countryside was somewhat secondary, except that his eyes had always been very impacted by color, and he spent time admiring in amazement the many variety of birds, the multicolored tropical fish found on the nearby brook, and the myriad of butterflies that came flying just in front of his house during the short tropical springtime when the April sun advanced the intense heat to come in mid-summer days. In his contemplative, early years, even without moving away too far from his house, he not only enjoyed all the wonders that nature offered in such abundance, but also was able to admire with the eyes that suggested artistic interests, all the impressive activities of the public rituals and festive celebrations of the Yoruba descendants with its rich authenticity of color, costumes, movements, drum beats and chants.

He told all of this to the newcomer and went on to tell him about his friend Julio, and the haunted house he used to live in. It was the oldest house in a town, outside of town. The old frame house was at the corner of a much older citadel dated back to the late 1500s. The walls of the citadel were more than twenty inches wide, made out of a kind of flat red brick that had been placed flat, one on top of the other alternatively, only the difference is that, the old Spanish construction consisted of a larger and flatter brick about one and a half inches wide held by mortar., other areas of the walls, away from doors and windows were composed of limestone which was very available in the Caribbean and could be seen on the spots where plaster had fallen off. All this was new for the lightly freckled kid that appeared to be enthralled by his newly found friend's description, as they walked in front of the old citadel, only half a block away from Michael's house. The citadel was about one square block with two interior yards; one of them was also square in the center, of what were probably the living quarters. A number of subdivisions not larger than two hundred and fifty square feet each and which some fifteen families had partitioned conveniently into a living area of bedroom and kitchen for which they paid a minimal rent to Enrique" "El Turco" who owned most of the rental property for poor people in the area.

"El Turco" could be seen once or twice a month, slowly walking and sweating, holding a fat leather handbag with his two large hands behind him as he walked. A few feet away, his fourteen-year-old junior followed, like a shadow who attempted to be a replica of the half-bent figure of his father; possibly a misunderstood soul that most people in town perceived as a wretched usurer. The man was one of the notorious characters of the town.

The eastern side of the citadel had the same housing distribution along a rectangular patio that ran from the south side front to the back. The east wall had a wide door like the ones used for carriages connecting into *El Placer de los Piratas*, a large, lightly sloping field that flattened out where the natural grounds for baseball started to run, and where *manigua* baseball was played right across La Finca de Vicente. Manigua meant "countryside brush and fields" where baseball was played at its purest form. No uniform, no spikes, and sometimes no gloves except for the catcher. but as the story goes, many great professional players saw their first light of hardball game in that somewhat wild field as well as at El Arenal near the riverbank two miles away after passing by La Finca and La Loma blanca.

At the front entrance to the citadel there were two curious Roman-like bridges about four feet wide and ten feet long connecting to La Calzada.

At this point he and Eloy were standing right in front of the old frame house. It had a front porch elevated five feet over the street, a frontal central door and two side windows. The western, left side of the house had a window in the center, and a smaller window near the roof and a small side door near the spot where the house connected to the wall of the citadel.

Michael said: "This is the house where the pirates used to live, as the old story is told… They usually moored their ships on this side of the bay by the river. Everybody here talks about ghosts and midnight sounds of dragged chains and how a few years ago they found pirate weapons, swords and knifes in the old attic. There is the suspicion that this house is being rented now by a woman who will open it up as a bar, for the merchant sailors who are starting to come to the nearby docks. The people here are afraid that this is going to be a problem for the neighborhood if it will be turned into a brothel, that is, if the rumor about the new tenant is true and it comes to happen. This house is where my friend Julio used to live with his older brother, mother and father, as well as his grandmother – a very old lady who was always on her rocking chair, and who spoke to herself in what people said was Flemish. That was something very rare around here, more so because she had come from Spain with her son, Julio's father, and his mother., Julio's father was very poor, but an enterprising man who made tin pot and pans as well as toys that he used to peddle from his Pushcart, all over the adjacent towns, exchanging his craft for bottles that he would later sell to pharmacies and other patrons. His earnings were very limited and, as Julio told me, most of the time there was no food to put on the table but some bananas and cornflower meal and, not always, some bread. "The family was talented," Michael said; he followed by telling Eloy about the stage that this humble man used to set up in the middle of the citadel, or on the yard across Michael's house where he and his family would perform old plays and getting people involved in singing and comedy every year during the town festivities and up to the time of Julio's disappearance.

"Where is Julio now?" Eloy asked.

"The family moved across the street in front of my house after the death of his grandmother. but Julio has disappeared and nobody knows where he is. I have his picture as it came out on the front page of a newspaper with the story of his disappearance. Most people think he is dead but I don't believe it."

"Why? Do you know where he may be?"

"No, but I will tell you why I don't think he is dead. I visited and played with Julio a couple of times on the large and almost empty living room of the house. We played with an iron locomotive toy that he had; it had no wheels, and we moved it around over the worn-out old wooden floor. The floor was not leveled on both sides and it had a hump across the middle, a few yards from where his grandmother was sitting in her rocking chair. There was no other furniture in the room and this looked very somber, but once you were there, you could feel a great peace in the quietness of the place with all windows closed and very little light. I never thought of any ghosts while we played in that room. The old lady always looked as if she was just waiting to die while she mumbled words in her strange language. Julio cared for her and brought her water if she coughed . . . You could tell that there was a strong bond between them. I think he felt very lonely when she died. It is possible that this is one of the reasons why he left."

"I hope you are right, Michael." Eloy said.

"In any case I wanted to find out more about the secret tunnel; people said that it started from the basement of the house all the way down to the shore, about half a mile away. This was a tunnel that the pirates used to move the booty without been seen, and where they could have buried their treasures . . . I armed myself with an old lantern loaded with very weak batteries left over from the last hurricane of the year before, and convinced Julio to lead me down to the basement, and we both went towards the back side of the house. There were no steps to go down, and we had to crawl from a hole they opened on that side of the house. Once under the house we could see the bottom of the deformed floor held by rustic wood pillars, except in the middle, where the floor separated from the central pillars and seemed to be held only by the pressure from the two sloping sides. We came to the front, right underneath and at the edge of that porch" said Michael as he continued telling Eloy about the experience. "... Julio signaled to the wall that was made out of heavy boards all around, and we both removed one of them to one side. It was all very humid; we heard the sound of water which happened to be the water that came from the spring that ran under the sidewalk of that side of the street from 'El Solar del Rubio', a nicely kept two-floor wooden tenement, about three blocks up the street. The water at the spot where we were running was under the porch of the house.

"We removed the spider webs out of our way and entered what looked like a tunnel indeed and walked for about three or four yards following the direction of the water. Then we saw the light that filtered from a narrow tube about a half a block away from where the water would come out and run along *El Placer de los Piratas*," Michael continued.

"So, there is no mystery to the pirate's tunnel?" said Eloy.

"Well, we didn't know because the upper part of the tunnel where we were was made out of the same kind of old bricks from the colonial times, just like the ones you see on the small Roman bridges on the other side of the house connecting to the citadel. So it seemed that some passage might have been hidden with the little that we saw using the dammed old flashlight. I could tell there were two or three spots where the old bricks seemed to veer in the direction of the shore but it was all covered by heavy rocks as if a wall was made to cover any tunnel entrances many years ago. So the mystery continues to be unresolved...

"You see, this house is more than two hundred years old but the citadel where the tunnel runs across its front is more than four hundred years old, dating back to forty or fifty years after Columbus' journey to these islands. The town people believe that the spirits of the pirates, and in particular one with a wooden leg, is still roaming around in that house. Frankly, we were scared to hell when my flashlight finally went off and we had to work our way back in the darkness just following the water back to where we started from. There were rocks on the bottom, here and there." He went on.

"I can see that you must have been afraid at that point," interrupted Eloy.

"The greater scare was when I came across a large land crab with a big claw that suddenly locked unto my left foot. Fortunately, it was just over my sneakers and I had to thank Julio for his fast reaction – grabbing the crab by the head and jiggling its claw out of my shoe . . . He is very brave, you know. One day he will be back; he probably left out of sadness because of the death of his grandmother, and also to look for a better fortune."

"How about the ghost?" Eloy asked.

"Well, it was not all about being scared by the crab – that was probably as afraid as I was at that point; it was all very dark and mysterious down there after the flashlight went off so we decided to head back to the basement of the house . . .

"When we came out of the tunnel and started walking under the floor of what was the large living room, Julio then hushed: *'Listen, listen.,'* Roosh . . . knock . . . roosh . . . knock . . . the strange noises sounded as if someone was dragging a heavy chain on his ankle, followed by another sound which was like a short and dry knock with the same alternative rhythm: roosh . . . knock . . . roosh . . . knock . . . roosh . . . knock . . . We could hear these sounds softly but with a sort of echo coming from the floor above our heads.

"'That is the pirate's ghost,' Julio said then, 'I hear him late at night many times; he had a wooden leg and the other was chained at the ankle. He died as a prisoner in this house, according to the old stories I have been hearing from older people.'

"We rushed out of the cellar in a hurry and up into the main room but we only found Julio's grandmother fast asleep on her rocking chair . . . For now at least, both the tunnel and Julio's disappearance will remain a mystery; and for the ghost, who knows!" Michael said.

Eloy was silent for a while until he suddenly said: "Well, there are many things that nobody knows about, but we won't get stifled thinking about it; we have a lot to do. Let's go."

A few weeks later Michael would understand much better what his new friend had meant.

CHAPTER THREE

Children's Enterprises And Memorable Town People

Michael was sorting out in his mind all the activity that he and Eloy got involved together since the beginning of their friendship – from the games, to the serious business they were constantly active with, and to the relaxed moments when they would stand by the porch of his house and chat with their two admiring girl friends on Sunday afternoons.

As time passed, the memories of his childhood adventures became a source of inspiration. As in most cases, good childhood years leave an indelible impression. Somehow he has kept them as a sort of special space in which he would enter with his inner mind and aside from the impact of the memories of the landscape, the skies, and the sea, there was always a strong presence of his friend Eloy standing there with his freckled rosy face saying: "Let's go; see that mountain? Let's climb it . . . Look at that rift, let's jump over it." No matter how difficult or daring, they did it, and did it well, almost like magic. Michael and his new friend always had things to do. For the last three years, since his friend had come to live in his neighborhood, he had had a most unusual experience for a child their age. Eloy was like a fast-moving bouncing ball that appeared to be not only fast, but also to have specific direction and purpose, and most of all, with unbelievable precision. Michael was more contemplative at the time, although not less self-propelled in terms of initiative. He was certainly not a follower although he probably lacked the appearance of self-assurance that his friend immediately showed at any situation. This quality in the country boy's character amazed and attracted his interest in Eloy's personality, soon contributing to bond their partnership. Michael found himself to be a sort of moderating force as much of a conduit through which the positive energy that Eloy generated was channeled in all sorts of creative endeavors.

He could never forget the day they went for a walk around the neighborhood after they met at the marble game across from Michael's house. On the first day they were inseparable. They were going across the park at the top of the hill when a small-framed kid suddenly challenged Alfredo, the tall and strong black youngster who was well known to him. They used to play first base in the baseball team that happened to be one of the contending teams against the Pirates which was the neighborhood team that Michael came to direct a few years later. The slightly freckled-faced kid made the challenge to a fight; this kid was taking a boxer stance and uttering some offensive remarks to the surprised Alfredo who was walking in the opposite direction but on the same side where Eloy was walking. It was something that was not customary in the provincial town from where this highly spirited kid came from. Michael defused the possible fight upon his intervention, and by Alfredo's gentle reaction to this unexpected encounter.

It took him a good part of that afternoon to explain to Eloy, or at least for the spirited kid, to understand that in this town just across the bay from the capital, they all grew up in harmony with all nationalities and all races and that they all shared the same schools and the same friends in play and games and that there was nothing wrong with that, and that it was not only fair, but that it was good, and everyone respected everybody else and that was the way it should be.

He started to feel protective to this new comer. He wondered what would have been the result of a fight against such a stronger built opponent, who was at least eight inches taller and thirty pounds heavier than the small-framed, not more than five-foot-tall boy whom everyone called Eloycito. The result was not likely to be favorable to his new friend. Certainly not a good beginning and instead something worse.

Ever since that day, he and Eloy would be seen together everywhere other than school time, since they were going to different schools. The projects and activities they became involved with ran from bird hunting and trap placing in the mangroves, to buying empty wooden boxes from the fruit shopkeepers; wood that they would use to make woodcraft that they would later sell. On other occasions they would be cutting trees on the nearby woods in order to make vegetable coal for cooking, which was scarce during the Second World War. During playtime they would confront challengers at the marble games, or exchange collectible cards with other kids..

While some of these activities can be considered normal in almost any active youngster between the ages of 10 to 13, Michael had the impression that somehow the activities, in which they became involved with most of the time because of Eloy's initiative, were absolutely unique; he realized that children their age didn't worry about anything else but playing, while his new friend's time was used seriously and efficiently on any activity whether playing or not.

They spent the time creating and meeting challenges, but if Eloy was to do something it was done usually in a surprisingly effective way. If it was at marble game time he would be unbeatable, as Michael had seen for the first time that morning, hat was a kind of unforgettable experience that came to him time and again through the years. Eloy's aim at the game was magical. Challengers came from out of town to play against him for hours without ever being able to beat him in the end. He learned the best techniques of the game too, but he didn't have to play much; as partners they ended up with all the marbles in the neighborhood and as usual, were able to sell some back to the other kids..

The same thing happenned with the card collections; they were able to exchange many with other children because of the fact that they owned most of the marbles that the others needed to be able to play. One of Michael's aunts worked at one of the major cookie factories that featured collectables, such as the "battleship of the World", "Gulliver's Travels", "Snow White", "The Lone Ranger", and others. Not only was he able to always complete his albums, he also had an extra supply of the most difficult cards, both of them had a shoebox full of cards. They were the bankers to which others had to come for exchange and purchase.

Their partnership brought them into many other small enterprises. They designed, and created woodcraft and artifacts of various household, as well as decorative uses. Eloy would cut them and he would polish and paint decorative motifs on them and then varnished them. They would later go and sell them door to door around town. Every hour outside the school was used creatively; both being the sons of self-made engineers who earned a modest but fair living. So they did not, as children, have a need to work for money, but those were the years after the Depression, and toys and other children's frills were not in good supply. Family money was tightly controlled. Michael's father had lost all his savings and even though he still held his job as a master builder, at the coal terminal where he had helped build the largest steam coal hauling cranes in the Regla side of the Havana harbor, his financial condition was not as it used to be. Eloy's father had recently moved to the area and after a long time without steady work, he had taken a new, more promising job mounting radio towers, both families had good prospects for the future, but that was all there was at the time;. in any case their zest for productive enterprises appeared to be unusual to children of their condition and age; it was all fun nevertheless,. they managed to make money out of all their activities. Money that they would use to buy more material and tools, or to go to the movies, or buy ice cream without having to ask their parents for any money at all.

On many occasions they would get up early in the morning and walk for three or four miles in the misty and cool morning to go hunting with their homemade traps and other hunting gears so they could get enough quails or any other seasonal fowl to cook and eat with fried plantains in the hidden encampment they had built in the midst of the mangroves. Next, they go to the four square miles of tropical forest by the coastline, and beyond the large industrial railroad yard and terminal, and near the docks where they would fish for abundant bass and blue crabs, always in the company of Michael's dog Sibiri, who served as playful company and some protection. Many of the adventures they lived through were in such beautiful playgrounds. Not much different than what any other children their age did, except for the apparent magical dexterity shown by Eloycito in everything he decided to do. He could hit any target with a small rock thrown with his slingshot in just one single throw,, no matter what the distance, or the speed of the target. He could jump the widest gaps as if his small body was floating in the air and apparently with very little effort. Michael was larger and heavier, and although slim and muscular, he seemed to put a greater effort in jumping long distances. both of them jumped from moving railcar to moving railcar with great ease and did it frequently, with carefully practiced precision.

He saw his friend as someone with quasi-supernatural abilities, not only at children's games but also at every activity they became involved together., it was hard work too. On late afternoons they would plant traps for 'hurones', a species of very wild ferret with sharp teeth and long menacing claws that had its habitat at a tall but spotted grass and dry ground next to the thick mangrove-filled area. The two friends would get up very early in the morning, when the first sun rays were only a prelude in the horizon, behind the hills at the west, and then they would walk the three or so miles to the hidden trap sites to see their catch. Many times they found that the catch was stolen; other times they would find that their catch was not a wild huron that could be sold for five dollars to the tobacco warehouses by the docks, but sometimes they would find a large crab instead, which was not a desirable catch. All in all they would always enjoy the morning walk in the mist and over the fresh dew that was slowly melting in the grass.

The two boys were enjoying the morning walk along the long road that crossed La Finca de Vicente, the farm at the edge of their neighborhood. The summer months with its many birds and butterflies flying around have all been left behind, and this time they were enjoying the white *Aguinaldo* flowers that grew all over the fences and the roadside bushes. The flowers opened up as the first ray of light cut the mist – to look like snow. The optical illusion overwhelmed the two boys as they walked up the dirt road that lay along the farm while they carried the traps in the mildly cool morning.

Later that same morning, like many other days off from school, they went jumping over the wagon trains, and finally after a while, they ran away from the pursuing railroad police, and then disappeared into one of the many secret entrances to the tunnels, carved out of thick brush, bushes, and medium – to tall-sized trees that formed like a jungle, thirty o or fourty feet deep – separating the railroad yard from the lagoons and tall grass areas, next to the mangroves, running all the way to the docks by the east and the riverbanks on the south.

On this occasion, he remembered, that they had separated and at some point he found himself at the edge of one of the lagoons with his dog Sibiri, the trees there were tall and inviting. He could not resist playing "Tarzan" as he climbed the tallest mangrove tree to look from above and try to find his friend. His dog started to bark playfully as dogs always do when kids climb trees and their pets had to wait below.

The tree was at the edge of the thick vegetation of *"El Mangle"*, as they called the area. Michael breathlessly looked over the treetops from his position on the top branches. At the southeast he could see the highest part of La Loma blanca, with its white limestone side beaming under the bright sunlight, six hundred yards away. Looking directly southwest he could see the silver-like sands of *"Los Arenales"*, extending flatly far away towards the mouth of the San Martin River, and the waters of the bay at a point that was called *"Arellano y Mendoza"*, the names of the sugar cane tycoons from the "Dance of Millions" era, . but now, with its abandoned docks by the riverbanks, millions of small crabs would surely be sunbathing as usual near the small Arellano beach.

Looking directly east, he marveled at the brightness of the waters clashing with the rusted hulls of the two old sunken ships that capsized during the infamous hurricane of 1926, approximately fifteen years before. As Michael turned his head northwest, he looked at the massive cranes, "Los Aparatos" as the twin three-hundred-feet-high iron structures were known, and where his father and uncle had worked for many years. The cranes had been idle since the late 'thirties but it still offered its imposing presence. The gigantic figures rested next to one of the lagoons of that side of *El Mangle* next to the railroad spur that ran toward the docks. He was now looking the northeast, where above the rooftops of the houses of La Calzada he could see La Loma de la Ermita, and the ruins of the old colonial church.

In between the eight-hundred-yard distance he could see the locomotives moving along a trail of wagons loaded with all kinds of scrap metal, constantly moving through Fesser Station and eventually shipped to the United States where the metals would be used in factories that produced all kinds of weaponry for the Second World War.

The barking of his dog intensified suddenly and Michael had to look down, with the hope of finding Eloy, but after a few minutes, the dog kept barking loudly and fiercely. He soon realized that a policeman, was standing only thirty feet away from the tree and his dog. When he looked closer, he saw a shining gun on the policeman's right hand; he immediately let himself off the tree and landed close to Sibiri, and grabbed the barking dog while he shouted to the surprised policeman:

"You don't need a gun. Are you crazy or what?"

He saw the policeman's action with the gun as an irresponsible act and became quite angry, but felt no fear. He became furious and incredibly demanding, just as if he was already a grown man while he yelled to the policeman to put the gun away, which the policeman did with a nervous movement. Michael detected this as he started to tell him that it was not proper to draw a gun to a boy who was barely twelve years old, and who was just playing. Surprised with the boy's unexpected reaction, the officer, almost apologetically told him that he was new in the yard, and that kids should not be playing near the trains,. but Michael insisted that he was not at the yard but that he was anly playing in the woods and that he will complain about his drawing the gun on him.

The policeman blamed the dog for his drawing the gun and left as fast as he had appeared on the scene, at which time his friend Eloy showed up after having been watched from behind the thick brush.

On their way back home, they encountered the well known chief of police officer of the local railroad station, and complained about the incident.

The chief looked at him a bit puzzled and said: "Perhaps it was wrong, for the newcomer to draw the gun, but it is also wrong for children like both of you to play near the yard because of the danger that it represents, and I will talk to your father about this." After the incident, Michael did not see the new policeman anymore.

His father told him a few days later that the policeman had broken one leg while running after some kids at the edge of a moving train. He also said that the chief told him that once he recuperates from his injury he would go back to his previous assignment as a guard in another town. He could not hide a smile that his father also shared, but not without pulling him aside and talking to him about it.

"You have to promise me that you will not play on the trains anymore, Michael."

"I don't know how we are going to do that father," he said. "We have to cross the railroad yard every time we go hunting in *El Mangle*, or when we go to swim."

"I understand that you have to cross the yard to go swimming or hunting, but that does not mean that you have to jump on the trains as I know you have been doing."

"but we were not on the trains when that policeman came and pulled his gun."

"I am sure you are telling me the truth, but I know how dangerous it is to be around the moving trains and you have to promise me that you will stay away from them."

"but Father, we walk many times along the tracks to go and look for mangoes and other fruits on the farms near Santa Maria del Rosario. We also have to go and get pieces of soft cedar boards from the mill in the same area. How can you expect for us to give up all of that?"

The senior Mr. Beltran started to get quite frustrated with the conversation as he said:

"You heard what I said, didn't you?"

"Yes, Father, of course, but I hope you will understand . . . I promise that I will not jump on the trains and will be very careful when going to all the places we go to play and hunt around there."

The usual persistence apparently paid off, when his father finally said, "Well you be careful, and don't let me find out that you jumped on trains anymore."

Michael had promised that he would not jump on moving trains, but he was able to, at least play and go to the places he liked, and that was all around the trains anyway.

He and Eloy had many other adventures that kept them busy without having to play on the moving trains. One of the most memorable experiences Michael enjoyed remembering was when Eloy decided to buy a newborn pig with part of the money they earned selling the vegetable coal – the ones they had made after a long month cutting mangrove trees and aromatic bushes full of thorns and that grew around La Loma blanca in the back of La Finca de Vicente. They spent as much time bringing the firewood and the thick branches they had cut, to build the cone-shaped oven, the they had to put to fire after covering it with dirt. Eloy and Coco kept watch all night so that the oven would not open up suddenly and be blown away by the open fire. That night, he looked in frustration from the rooftop of his house, towards the backyard of Eloy's house where the oven was erected a day earlier. He had come down with mumps and was not let out of his house. He was only allowed to momentarily go to the roof to greet his friends from there before nightfall.

'Choncho' was the name Eloy gave to the funny-looking pig.. The original idea was to fatten the little pig and raise it in the backyard and then sell it later on; however, they soon decided that the pig would make a perfect pet. Eloy placed a pink bow on his head and tied a light chain to his neck and took it everywhere he went. Soon the little pig would follow them as if it was a dog, becoming an attraction everywhere they went.

Choncho also became an attraction at the circus that the boys opened in the summer. Michael would bring small crocodiles, twenty to twenty-five inches long; that he borrowed from the nearby tannery.. Part of the act consisted of hypnotizing the crocodiles and chickens. The chicken's act was a very funny one since the chickens were easily hypnotized and once they came out of the spell they would run all over the place. It substituted the old act of two tarantulas fighting to death, which they decided to eliminate from the show because of the cruelty to the lizards. These lizards were used in hunting the tarantulas, and other large repellent spiders. A boy walked on a wire and a dance was performed very nicely by another kid from the neighborhood. The improvised circus was mounted at *El Placer de los Piratas,* at a corner of the large esplanade. It was a cooperative effort that included boxing matches. Children paid a few pennies for entrance and they all enjoyed the fun. The show ended by early evening. He made some cardboard figures representing characters from comics and movies then projected the shadows on a screen at night using the light from a candle. He made the figures move and mimic a dialog. It was like going to the movies with lots of action from cowboys, Indians and the cavalry coming to the rescue in the end, with appropriate music and all. It was an uproar as the entire show ended.

The odd pet story didn't have a happy ending. During a hurricane that hit in October of that year the already grown Choncho disappeared, not to be found any more; the boys were saddened about the loss but they soon went on with their usual activities. The neighborhood where the two boys were growing up had many interesting characters that amused them; some of the characters were very colorful and funny such as the music players that came to the corner stores or *bodegas* that was run by Spanish immigrants. The establishments were well stocked with every conceivable foodstuff and some housewares and were serviced by three efficient and affectionate personnel including the owners. The wandering musicians and singers would come to the *bodega*, sing, and play guitars, harmonicas or bongos depending on the specialty of the visiting performer. It was fun to watch. On occasion the mayor of the town also visited their secluded neighborhood, as well as during political campaigns.

The most memorable personality among the politicians was that of the most endearing mayor the town ever had. He was a great politician who was mayor for three consecutive terms. Octavio Cabrera was indeed a very popular man. "He would sell ice to the Eskimos," some people used to say; he had the ability to listen to any complains and he frankly imposed his not too tall but large enough figure that he managed without showing too much of his being lightly overweight. He made his presence felt every time and anywhere as he accompanied his charismatic personality with a thundering but handsome voice. He was a great speaker who would give a speech at any time, including every funeral at the town cemetery, and he was very good at it. He was always very elegantly dressed with finely tailored English fabric suits. His rosy cheeks glowed most of the time, possibly because of the habitual cup of fine cognac he had at every corner store bar of the town, where he would stop. Best of all was that this beloved mayor was a man of his word. He had promised to pave the streets just as La Calzada which was the street where Michael was born and where the story unfolded. He had the streets paved in less than two months from his promise. I believe Octavio Cabrera still does not have a monument in the town of Regla, but he will someday because, he lived and worked with and for the people. He was not only a popular politician, he was very sympathetic, that he would embrace everyone that would come to the corner stores where he stopped, and would also greet, even his political opponents. ..The town was known to have top rate, among Cuban school system, started during his tenure, and there was great pride instilled in the town's students, most of whom were able to pursue a higher education in later years.

Everyone, that may have lived there, in those years would always remember, the fine and emotional eulogies that the popular mayor spontaneously, and without any written notes used to give at the town cemetery, whenever there was a funeral. Most outstanding is the one he gave for the five playing small kids that died when lightning struck them at La loma de los Cocos. It was a very sad happening, in the town recent history, happenning in the early 'forties. In his mind, to this day, from his memory, Michael remembering Octavio Cabrera's powerful style, is able to compose such an emotional and momentous speech:...

> **"We are not here today," his voice thundered as he repeated . . . "We are not here today, to pay tribute to any citizen of this town with merit of age and deed. We are not here because of a farewell, and not only for comforting the relatives who have lost a dear one after a long, fruitful, and honorable life. We are here because we all wonder, and we all cry in sadness for five beautiful angels that have been called back to heaven by that divine force we humans can't ever begin to understand, but respect. It is not possible to think that life has been in vain for those who have had but a few years to bring the gifts of love that little ones can only bring . . . In resignation, we can only think of five little children playing in paradise. Let us not forget the gladness of their tender life, and let us walk out of this small sacred piece of land where we have placed their remains but not their angel wings, which**

there is no doubt they have . . . Let us all, mothers and fathers, brothers and sisters, let them live now in their sweet children dreams, but not without all of us feeling blessed for the time they spent with us, and for that lasting gift of love and faith that they have placed in our hearts."

All during that short emotional eulogy Octavio Cabrera's roundish face was red and wet with tears or sweat, because of the intensity and sincerity of his delivery. He made every such moments totally unforgettable, and then everyone slowly walked out of the cemetery in silence and with a glowing feeling of acceptance and serenity.

The town was a colorful place, and so was Michel's neighborhood of La Calzada, also known as *Patilarga* because of the long walk to get there from the center of town. La Calzada also had a very lively atmosphere all year around. There was not only the "tin man" who made many tin utensils and sold it in exchange for empty pharmacy bottles. He would remember him and his family with admiration as he had told the story to Eloy when he first met him. The "tin man" was a poor man but he was an educated man before he immigrated to Cuba from Spain. He was the father of his friend Julio – the one that used to mount the stage and made a representation of "Don Juan Tenorio," on the celebration of All Saint's Day, every second day of November every year. Everyone in the "tin man's" family would dress in appropriate costumes and surprise everyone with a high quality of theater acting.

These were the days when there was no television and it was the time when people did their own entertainment; it was all very interesting to watch. It was also a learning experience for everyone. It was the same street where Pancho Majagua lived with his wife. Pancho Majagua was one of those old *troubadours* of the turn of the century that used to have parties where they sang the old ballads that Michael liked so much to hear; even when most of the other kids in the neighborhood laughed at the "oldies," as what they called the odd-looking group. They were great singers and guitar players. Most of the songs were not heard of and probably died with them, a few short years later, but no doubt, they were popular at the turn of the century, and many songs returned to popularity many years later in a very unexpected way.

He liked to watch over the domino playing at Don Pancho Majagua's porch. The old singer would not tolerate losing at the game and would end the games in a fury, vowing that he would axle all the ships, table, and all while his wife would yell at him from inside the house; a few hours later the good man would set the game up to play again. Michael was able, as he was growing up, to participate in some of the games when there was no older person to cover. He enjoyed every minute of it, particularly when he would play to lose and hear Pancho Majagua's loud laughter over and over again – all of which were preferable to him, instead of hearing the man swear and rave when he lost and would have to see the game abruptly stopped.

The street always had visiting vendors that used their *pregones,"* or songs to announce their presence in the area. There was the traditional "El Manicero", an immortal and world-renowned song made famous by Maestro Lecuona. There were also the candymen and all the other typical vendors including the fruit and produce vendors, all with their peculiar call. The sounds of their announcing *pregones* were as exciting and memorable as the change of seasons in the year. For Michael, the sounds of the town were like the music of paradise.

On festive days, the morning sound of trumpet, drum, and cymbals calling "Retreat" was heard when most people were still in bed. Children would start to run out into the street just in time when the first bengal light would fly and explode high up in the air. The festive atmosphere was infectious, with all kind of races for kids and adults, including horse races at midday along the entire four or five long blocks. At night, the singing contest would last until very late – to the disappointment of kids under eight years of age, like Michael, who was that age at the time. He tried to sing a popular song and his father did not want to let him wait until it was so late. He would not have done well anyhow, because his voice was certainly not that of a prodigy; but who knows, he may have missed one of his first callings because he was convinced that he could do well (but that was perhaps one of the first signs of being an optimist, more than a singer). Memorable sounds were everywhere, wherever they were vendors for mangoes, oranges, papayas, and whatever else. The traditional whistling of the fat fellow with the sided Spanish beret and his scissor-sharpening wheel, and the combination of sights and sounds made you feel alive and in a place that throbbed at your heart in every corner without you having to go too far. The sights and sounds keep resounding in your mind, like the night call of the famous peanut vendor or the one with the hot and not-so-hot *tamales*; a missed blessing in the intricacies of time and distance, from a warm and loving country where many of the loveliness have been left behind – perhaps forever.

CHAPTER FOUR

The First Homeless And The Marble Player

The early winter morning walks in La Calzada going towards La Loma blanca, at the end of La Finca de Vicente (the only dairy farm in the outskirts of town), with its blue-green pastures on the left and the railroad tracks not very far away on the right, came to Michael's mind. both sides of the unpaved road looked like fences covered with white snow instead of just the tropical *Aguinaldo* flowers; as beautiful as Christmas cards from a New England State or any other idyllic winter wonderland of sorts. This memory seemed to come to him again and again – perhaps to soothe his spirit at a time of distress. He could almost feel the light sweet smell of the white *Aguinaldos* as his mind recreated the visual effects the make-believe illusion of white snow sprinkled on top of bushes and over the tall weather bitten picket fences the climbing plant would produce during late December and early January, a very pleasant kind of "white Christmas" for anyone walking on that road. The magical effect was ever more striking with the early-morning mist. The coolest mornings would leave frost over the grass, but never snow, yet it was as if snow was covering each side of the old dirt road for the full length of the long, straight passage.

Michael was enjoying the thoughts and visual memories of those morning walks and his senses could feel the breeze, bringing the *Aguinaldo's* soft scent; the voice of the flight attendant asking him what he wanted to drink before lunch brought him back to the reality of the moment. He was still on his return flight from Mexico City to Newark. Suddenly he found himself asking: "Why was he thinking so much of his happy childhood years in his beloved country?" He had lost any perception of time; his mind had flown away from the jet plane, where visual impressions were flying at a greater speed through his mind. He realized how powerful the mind can be; almost two years of the happiest times of his life had gone through his mind in probably less than thirty minutes of flight, over the turquoise mantle of the Gulf of Mexico.

Lunch on the jet plane was the usual beef or chicken choice. He chose chicken because it was usually served with rice that he had not eaten for the duration of his visit to Mexico. Mexicans have a distinct way to cook rice to which he had not yet developed a taste – such as the hot peppers or tasty chili. You have to grow with it or take it really easy if you are to survive your stay there, without literally burning yourself inside out.

As he finished his meal, his mind had gone back to the uneasy thoughts he left Mexico with. He could not control nor place in order the conflicting feelings he had, as there was nothing to decide except to forget the last few days in Mexico as if they were unreal. but he could not take away from his thoughts, eyes, and ears what they have come to enjoy as a promise of lasting joy – which was very difficult or impossible to deny, let alone forget, even when he was compelled to try to. He could not resist the thought of that predicament, and looked out the window into the blue sky over a bed of clouds, as if he could find the answer somewhere in the open space; the answer he could not find in the four walls that seemed to enclose his mind otherwise.

The open space before his eyes brought him back to his childhood thoughts, but this time not on the pleasantries of the walks down La Calzada. His thoughts were with the first homeless he ever met. Perhaps the thoughts of "El Indio", as the dark-complexioned strong man dressed in burlap drabs was called, were more appropriate to the seemingly hopeless feelings of his own mind.

He could suddenly see the supplicating, very bright black eyes of "El Indio" and the perfect white teeth showing a gold-crowned tooth that suggested years of past prosperity. He remembered the impressive tall and strong figure the sad man cast when he walked towards him with his outstretched right arm holding an empty old tin cup in his hand. Michael would take the cup to the corner store to get a piece of bread and fresh espresso coffee with plenty of sugar that "El Indio" loved. The *bodega* owner would not charge for the coffee or the occasional Cuban sandwich they would prepare for the poor man. This happened every morning before Michael would leave for school.

"El Indio" was well liked in the neighborhood, but he showed no visible emotion except for his intense bright eyes that Michael could interpret as a mix of gratitude and unmitigated sadness. He never spoke a word. After sleeping in the railroad yard all night, he would come to sit at the edge of the veranda in the middle of the block, two houses from Michael's house where he waited for the opportunity to have his daily coffee and bread which was his breakfast most of the time.

The poor homeless man would lie down on the ledge on the porch of one of the houses in Michael's block until the sun would be so hot that he would have to walk slowly down towards the railroad yard where he would find a shade to lay down (between the aligned wagons) in the areas where he usually spent the afternoon hours after coming back for his customary lunch sandwich and coffee. It was a sad life indeed. It contrasted with the stories of the man that he once was: a very handsome and elegant rich man, before he turned into what he had become. He still had an eighteen-carat gold-crowned tooth that was visible when he lightly opened his mouth – as if he wanted to speak but he never seemed to be able to utter a single word.

"El Indio's" life had been an interesting one. He was born to a poor family but became an orphan before he was twelve. A wealthy family that owned a large tobacco manufacturing company then adopted him. The newly found family gave him a good education that eventually helped him to become an enterprising businessman. He was able to become rich on his own right. The story goes that "El Indio" was later on able to help his benefactors to regain the fortunes that they had lost during the Depression.

The generally accepted story about "El Indio" was that he had been a successful businessman who fell in love with a beautiful woman – a very well-known and beautiful singer who had many artistic engagements in the country and also in Europe. The woman he loved, in spite of her glamorous life in which many suitors surrounded her, loved him dearly but they lived separate lives due to the demands of her career that required extensive travels.

"El Indio" was always seen with her in the best and most elegant places during the late 'twenties and early 'thirties, that was, if they had the opportunity to be together. He lavished expensive jewelry on her, as well as the finest Parisian fashion of the1920's. As one version of the story goes, just when she was at the height of her career, she suffered a sudden mysterious death. "El Indio" lost his mind and gave up all his businesses; he lost his ability to speak and became a homeless wanderer. Other versions by some superstitious neighbors (who feared witchcraft and its struggle between good and evil) said that he was suffering from a curse placed on him, as if someone had placed a potion on his drink or cast other forms of malevolent sorcery typical of some African traditional beliefs where supernatural forces play the roll of protective deities. Other evil-minded practitioners use a black magic's destructive forces or voodoo to cause the kind of misfortunes like the one the broken-down man was suffering from. It was possible that a jealous rival who was trying to conquer the heart of the beautiful woman placed a malefic witchcraft's curse on him. Some other stories spoke of the woman being given poison by one female jealous rival, or that she was killed by another suitor who could not see her loving someone else. Undoubtedly she loved "El Indio" so much that she would not pay attention to any other man.

Michael's father, a most practical man not used to accept any doubtful theories without a reasonable explanation, made a different comment:

> "The poor man probably lost all his faculties; his
> mind lost in a sea of denial, abandoning himself to live
> like a tree without leaves or flowers in the lonely winter
> of the rest of his life."

Michael could imagine how this poor man's mind may have gone on a terribly unbearable spin and anguish, perhaps having been present at the time of the tragedy, he could not endure seeing the woman he so loved suffer and die in his arms without being able to save her. He could not understand then, as a child, the drama of this solitary man. but as the memory came back during the flight, he wondered if the soul of this homeless man had found its peace and comfort by forgetting even his name and feeling no pain in his accepted misery rather than facing a painful struggle to erase the realization of the irremediable loss. It must have been difficult, he thought, to let everything go and accept defeat without a struggle to survive – unless it is not by choice. Too much is lost when a man, or a woman for that matter, accepts total defeat and won't try to survive change in search of some undeniable success in overcoming difficulties and pain – however hard or far-fetched it may seem. He felt better thinking of "El Indio", not as the man who lost his love and enviable life but as the man abandoned by life itself.

While "El Indio's" love story had an unhappy ending, Michael could not help but find his remembrance of this man to be fascinating, mostly because it spoke to him of the passion of this interesting figure who for a short time appeared in his childhood; and somehow at this point in time, more than forty years later, it told him something about the deepest feeling of a man for what he obviously perceived as the passion and love of his life, without which his existence as he knew it was worthless. Such was "El Indio's" life, so much so that he only found consolation in his silence and solitude, as his life languished like a blot of a man walking away in the morning mist covering the road to La Loma blanca. Michael, for a long moment during his flight now, could not take his mind from the short but intensely fulfilling moments he had lived before he boarded the plain, thoughts that keep him wondering about the possible significance that were making him shiver.

One summer day, he realized he did not see his silent friend anymore on the usual place where he waited to get his morning coffee. The neighbors did not have a sure answer as to his disappearance. Some said that he might have been taken to an institution; others weren't so sure. They suspected that he may have fallen asleep on an empty wagon at the railroad yard and that he may have ended up very far away, as it happened a few months before. Only somehow, at that other time he managed to ride on another wagon and return a week later to what was his home, the Fesser Station, the large industrial railroad terminal about half a block across Michael's house. In whatever case, "El Indio" was not to be seen again. His disappearance was as mysterious as his state of mind.

Michael missed the sad-looking figure for some time. Something missing, something found, his thoughts told him as he began to look over the clouds on the horizon as his plane advanced thirty-five thousand feet over the ocean. Memories of Eloy, his childhood friend, came to him again; this time with more details, as if his memory was stimulated to do so like never before in his adult life. A month after the experiences with the disappearance of the first homeless person he had ever known was the time he came to remember again, the time when he was playing marbles in front of his house and he saw another kid standing at the side, intently watching the game. The lightly freckled kid appeared to be shy, but soon, without stopping to talk to any of the other players, walked straight across the group of kids and came directly to him and asked:

> "Can I borrow seven marbles from you so that I may join the game? . . . My name is Eloy, and I shall pay you double after the game."

He could see in the boy's eyes a hint of self-assurance he had not seen before in any of his playmates. He extended his hand with the seven marbles saying: "I am sure you will, my name is Michael . . ."

"Let's play another round," he told the other three boys he was playing with.

On his previous recollections of the beginning of this momentous friendship in the life of the two boys, Michael had overlooked the details that he was now enjoying in a very special way; since very soon, as he often did, he would be thinking about the sad and abrupt end of their unforgettable friendship.

The newcomer placed six marbles on the sixteen-inch ring Michael had drawn on the ground, and so did the other three boys and Michael. They all took turns throwing their main playing marble to the line, which lay about fifteen feet away from the ring.

The game consisted of each player throwing his main playing marble at his turn; the marble catapulted from the hand by the thumb after the hold on the middle finger where the marble was placed before the throw was let go. This action was always taken with the back of the hand resting on the ground. The rosy-cheeked newcomer was the third to throw from the line, and Michael the last one.

Each of the first two kids had been able to draw two marbles out of the ring. Eloy drew only one which allowed him to take his next throw to hit one of the opponents. Michael was surprised to see how this small-framed, sharp-eyed kid had decided to try to hit the opponents' main playing marbles because each of them was about twenty feet from his marble. He was more surprised to see with what ease his marble had lifted up in the air and went on to strike the first one. It looked like magic. This meant that Eloy had won the opponents' marbles on the ring. Then, on the third allowable throw, he hit the second playing marble of the opponents. There were only nine marbles left on the ring. Eloy's marble was rather far from the ring by then and his next throw was to get closer to the ring. Michael's turn came. He hit one of the marbles in the ring but his playing marble rolled with great speed, more than twenty feet away from the ring. The newcomer's turn came again and with five throws he expertly drew each of the remaining marbles out of the ring, winning twenty-two marbles, without waiting for the other kids to come out of their astonishment, he turned to Michael and said: "Here take the fourteen marbles I promised you . . . . Now I can play again with my own marbles." The freckled boy added.

This quality of character as well as clarity of thought mixed with uncommon self-assurance made Michael wonder about what was going to be next with this newcomer and newfound friend, just as when the first homeless person he had ever known, and his friend Julio, the son of the "tin man", had suddenly disappeared from his life. Somehow he immediately had a strong intuitive feeling that the intelligent marble player was also to play an important role in his life. His instinct was absolutely right even when during the three years that followed there was always the sensation of all of it being unreal.

The zest for achieving excellence, the multiple activities and business partnership, the unbelievable abilities of the kid with the penetrating eyes, and his tireless and boundless initiative gave an impression to Michael that his new friend had to live whatever life he had in a hurry, although strangely enough he looked very calm most of the time, as it obviously emanated from the self-confidence the smart boy exuded.

At this point, as he brought back these childhood memories while still on his flight from Mexico City, he also had to bring back to his mind the ending of that magical period, together with the momentous encounter at the marble game.

Fate has a way about it that leaves no doubt of its indubitable nature of being inevitable and intrinsic in the development of life itself. If you get to understand it, you will grow in confidence that all that is to be significant in life would not change or happen in vain.

> **"For I have learned**
> **To look on nature, not as in the hour**
> **Of thoughtless youth; but hearing oftentimes**
> **The still, sad music of humanity,**
> **Not harsh nor grating, though of ample power**
> **To chasten and subdue."**
>
> **– William Wordsworth**
> **Lyrical Ballads (1798, 1st Ed.)**

CHAPTER FIVE

Cuban Cowboys/The Forbidden Path (The Sudden Farewell)

Michael's memory again went to the happy times spent hunting and playing in what he saw as the paradise where he grew up. Wild, but beautiful grounds surrounded him and his friends – the industrial railroad station near the then clean waters of the bay where they enjoyed, swam and fished aplenty. In those years, the water of the bay was full of eatable blue crab, tropical colored fish by the fresh water brook that ran into it, red snappers and all kinds of tropical fishes that he spent hours looking at from the small mooring dock built by his father. The clear waters allowed anyone to see the bottom, fifteen feet below, just before increased bay activity spilled oil and polluted the waters in the middle of the Second World War.; he remembered the day his older cousin Paco threw him from the higher deck so that he would learn to swim as it was customary with small kids. He came out to the surface and did swim for his life while his cousin laughed and jumped to help him; he reached out to him as he held himself on the nearby rowboat that was anchored five feet away.

His eyes looked at the horizon over the clouds, still visualizing the mangrove jungle near the San Martin riverbanks with its *arenales,* "silvery glittering sand", and muddy edges where millions of minute baby earth crabs would sunbathe and could be seen running all at once to hide on small, half-inch wide, deep holes they had dug in the sand if anyone approached their natural habitat. On the warm spring mornings he would be watching the myriad of multi colored butterflies numbering in thousands that flew across the front of his house; so many that it would practically make it impossible to see through without squinting. He could see himself again, running with his friends and his dog Sibiri to hide from the railroad guards by entering into a series of secret passages from any of the five different brush covered entrances into this labyrinth of tunnels which were originally dug by cows through many years of walking under the thick maze of bushes, tall grass and trees, away from the hot summer sunlight (wild as it could be in these tropical surroundings).

Entering those tunnels they would come to their usual central encampment they had built, still under the thick brush next to the running brook where he and his friend kept fresh water and a few cooking utensils which they would use occasionally to cook the catch of the day which could consist of either fish or some fowl, product of their hunting abilities. His new, and eternal friend, who became his partner in work and play ever since that memorable marble game, was an expert in these endeavors. It was not all playing though. The memory went back to their walks along the railroad tracks to reach the mill, twenty miles away, where large cedar and mahogany timber were sawn to make the finest strips of wood boards and lumber; they would pick enough pieces of wood that would last them for a couple of months, which they would use to make the finest crafts at Eloy's father's shop.. The most sought after by the ladies in town were the bag handlers that became very popular and fashionable, particularly when used with plain raw burlap. They would sell all the production in just a couple of days. While their basic needs were met at home, the money also came very handy for going to the movies occasionally, or for buying ice cream for them and their girl friends, who gathered by the porch of Michael's next-door neighbors to chat with them on Sunday afternoons.

The boys of La Calzada were the luckiest in town; they had everything that could stimulate their imagination and adventurous nature. It was where the cowboys lived; the only place where they had rodeos every year on the grounds of the so-called El Placer de los Piratas, a large span of natural lawn with spots of green and aromatic short *artemisa* bushes on the edges. It was a great playground for him and his friends. The small-framed and agile cowboy, Pancho "El Ganadero"(The cowboy), with his white well-trained Arabian horse was one of the children's heroes. There was also the cowboy known as Pepe, the thin but ruggedly tall cowboy. They were part of a cowboy crew of five that moved the cattle from the railroad unloading stop about a mile from the slaughterhouse next to La Finca de Vicente coming down El Callejon del Sapo. Many times, the youngsters and teenagers would run in front of the cattle, or behind it, just like it is done at the traditional "run of the bulls" through the narrow streets during the festivities at Pamplona, Spain; something that the neighborhood kids didn't know anything about it being an old Spanish costume at the time in which they were doing it, but enjoyed it just as much – with the intrinsic danger of being trampled by the herd of forty or more beautiful-looking, young Cebu bulls running at full stampede pace. Fortunately, getting badly hurt was something that never happened in those exhilarating events because the kids were extremely fast running and got quickly out of the bull's way by climbing the fences or trees that lay along both sides of El Callejon.

On many occasions a few of the bulls would escape from the herd and it became a more interesting event yet. Michael saw Pancho and other two cattlemen lazing and working a wild bull out of a deep trench by the bend of the road, right where the children used to gather multicolored tropical fish in what he considered the most beautiful ravine in the world.

They spent hours playing there during the summer months; it was at a deep rift by the bend of the road to the slaughterhouse. Pancho "El Ganadero" worked almost two hours to get the bull out of the virtual hole. He saw Pancho falling from his horse near the bull, and he saw how Pancho's horse immediately went between him and the angry snorting animal, to protect his master and give time to the thin, lightweight cowboy to jump up to his saddle again and pull the bull out of the deep trench in the end.

It was all high adventure to be able to enjoy the work of the Cuban cowboys. El Callejon del Sapo would be a deserted place otherwise. People didn't walk through it; they considered it a frightful place with its side trees and bushes closing on top that looked like a tunnel. Only a few sunrays penetrated the thick foliage on top, and everyone spoke of the haunted house half a mile up from the slaughterhouse corrals. They spoke of the woman that was axed to death in the abandoned house on the left side of El Callejon coming from the foot of a deep rift of the southeast side of La Loma de la Ermita, right where the *"Nanigos"* celebrated their secret evening rituals of initiation with their *Diablito* costumes that he, Eloy and Coco had witnessed as scared intruders that frightful and unforgettable night.

A few days, after the hurricane in which they lost their pet pig, Choncho, on a hot summer afternoon in broad and bright midday light, Eloycito said to him: "Lets go up El Callejon, all the way the two and a half miles to the railroad tracks, where we can hunt the largest wild ducks and quails that come to the far end open field to nest alongside the end of El Callejon." His eyes were sparkling between his narrow, frowning eyebrows to insinuate without saying, "Let's dare, won't you?" Michael looked at his friend with intense silence and with a final smile as if saying: "Here you go again." He took his slingshot from his back pocket and finally said: "Yes, I always wanted to go that way but just didn't dare. Nobody has. Let's go to the forbidden path." "Let's go, my friend," he thought as he started walking behind Eloy. He could not help but feel as if his incipient hair was standing on his back, and he experienced a feeling of uniqueness he had not felt ever before; a feeling that this was a path that they would take together before their roads would forever part. They went all the way through the shadowy path – Eloy at the front followed by Michael about twenty feet behind. In a few minutes, they went by the infamous house.

It was separated from El Callejon by a thick layer of brush and cactuses that grew alongside, but they could still see the topside of the abandoned old house about sixty feet away. They stopped to look from a distance without saying a word, and after a moment that seemed very long (as though they were paying respect to the memory of the poor woman they never knew), they continued their walk towards the end of El Callejon. It was a surprisingly uneventful adventure. They didn't see a single bird.

Those happy growing-up years were to end abruptly, not by any dangerous ghosts or the bulls at El Callejon, or by any moving train during the dangerous games they used to play running over and jumping between the moving wagons, but by an unknown and never-understood design whereby the most intense and brightest of the stars is consumed by its own force in the shortest of time, leaving an indelible light traveling eternally through the spaces that we have not yet visited.

One day, unexpectedly Eloy fell sick. The doctor said that he had to be hospitalized to check what caused his head pains and dizziness that he was suddenly experiencing.

A week went by and he was still at the hospital,. Michael and his mother visited him a few times. There, they would talk for an hour or two, conversations that Michael would never forget. His twelve-year-old friend would tell him stories of his hometown near Cienfuegos, as if he wanted Michael to relive with him the years before they met; all the years before their ninth birthday, and of the recent three and one-half years of their fast-moving adventurous pace of the past. Now, they were about thirteen, and the hours seemed to end too fast, but each one counted as precious drops of life.

The decision was made to operate a growing dangerous tumor on the brain of the boy; this condition earned for Eloy the love of the nurses and the admiration of the doctors attending him. He showed a lot of courage and his eyes did not stop shining for a moment from between his encroaching eyelashes, with its usual smartness as if saying he always knew more than what he was able or wanted to say.

The surgeons opened but then hopelessly closed the brain's membrane. His friend had his head in bandages the last day that he visited him, . both mothers left the room, in tears that were barely hidden from the two boys. Eloy half sitted on his bed, while Michael sat at the side in a position where they could see each other face to face. The pale and lightly freckled boy, who had suddenly lost his usual rosy cheeks talked about the things the two of them used to do during the last three years of what appeared to be, until then, an inseparable friendship . . . Michael had not been told of the failure of the operation until he left the hospital that day. Eloy talked all the time, while Michael only interrupted occasionally to tell him about things they could do when he got better, trying to bring a hopeful and happy outlook and feeling to his friend.

For a long moment Eloy smiled while he lifted his bandaged head in an air of apparent quiet contemplation from the light on the open window high across the room. His shining, penetrating, still full-of-life eyes came down to look into his friend's eyes and then said to him:

"You know, I will never forget you. You have been my best friend.;" his eyes were clear and it showed much peace and an inner smile; it revealed no fear at all.

"Remember we will play and win again. I am not afraid, so don't you ever be afraid." Then using one of his favorite expressions he said: "We won't get stifled about anything . . . I will see you soon."

Michael never saw him alive again. His life went into a kind of vacuum and he became full of doubts about fairness.

> **"There was a Boy; ye knew him well, ye cliffs**
> **And islands of Winander! – many a time,**
> **At evening, when the earliest stars began**
> **To move along the edges of the hills, Rising or setting,**
> **would he stand alone,**
> **Beneath the trees, or by the glimmering lake . . ."**
>
> **– William Wordsworth**
> **Lyrical Ballads (1801, 2nd Ed.)**

There was none he could find at this juncture of his life; his father saw it in his saddened eyes. And for the last two months that he had to live, he took many long walks with Michael.

In a warm spring day at dawn, they walked past the tall warehouses by the Fesser docks. La Loma de los Cocos' sharp, upward sloping ridge stood at their right, and cast its early-morning shadows across the entire road, just to let the warm sunlight partially shine on the fading yellow-orange thick walls of the old building and on a few sections of the unpaved road. He so loved to walk by the tranquil Fesser area, mostly because of its peaceful atmosphere that was a constant penetrating presence in those surroundings, which no one could ignore, or fail to feel deep down – like fresh water from a running brook slowly flowing inside your body and around your soul, washing away all that could be useless, as you walked through the entire three-block-long road that was covered with sparkling, partly sunny, and partly shaded golden gravel, next to the tracks. All of these, together with the unique light and shade effect of the high slope made it look as if you were walking inside a cathedral, where you're entirely alone and feeling inside all of the soothing forces that its majesty could command.

That morning, Michael was following his father, silently walking on the right-hand side of the railroad towards the other side of town and beyond for about four miles, until they came to the hills that ran along the rocky northern shore of the Morro Castle towards the fishing village of Cojimar.

As they were moving up the hill in what was a narrow path among the bushes and reddish rocks, halfway between Casa Blanca and Cojimar, he saw a beautiful small bird that was flying freely and which suddenly came to his hands as if moved by a magical soft breeze. He ran uphill with great excitement going, towards his father, showing him the beautiful bird. "Look at this father! what kind of bird is this? I have never seen a bird like this."

The bird was very small with wings of bright green feather and body, with a red collar and a long beak protruding between its small, shining black eyes.

"Yes I know about that bird, son. There were many of them near the mountains, by my hometown of Manzanillo, in Oriente. We used to call them Carta-Cuba, it is almost like a hummingbird but a bit larger.; contrary to the hummingbird that feeds only on flower's nectar, this bird also feeds on bees and other small insects; it is very rare to see them here. This bird loves to live in freedom and will die if placed in captivity. You should set it free.

"It may die very soon if left alone because, it seems to have hurt one of its legs." The startled boy said and added: "I will care for it. I will feed it with sweetened water and it will live. You will see father . . . If you let me have one of the paper bags where we have our snack I can put the bird in it and then I can open some holes for it to breathe from until we get back home."

Miguel Beltran Gonzalez, looking at his son from over his eyeglasses, could see how happy he was. He had not seen his son as happy since before the death of his friend Eloy, so he smiled and said: "Fine, do what you want, but remember what I said about that bird needing to be free in order to live. I agree that the poor bird may die anyway, but I don't want you to be heartbroken."

"Don't worry father, I understand."

As usual, they had a good time swimming in a spot at the reefs, just a block west from "La Poceta de los Curas", which was a popular spot on the bare reef seashore not too far from a salt factory on the outskirts of Cojimar. His father liked to bring the family there now and then every summer, usually in the mornings, and then they would return home before the sun would be very high and hot. He liked the spot because it was more private. Michael liked it too because it gave him a feeling of ownership, while his older brother would go where the crowd was – a block away, towards the town.

Depending on the tides and the winds, the spot was either hit with wave after wave of the deep blue Caribbean Sea or the surf would be moving softly and gently with the tide, going above the sharp reefs most of the time. Swimmers had to know how to go in, and better yet, how to come out of the water, particularly when the waves were hitting hard, and almost constantly, one after the other.. He had seen people being thrown over the reef and getting pretty mauled and bleeding with serious wounds. He loved the challenge that swimming there represented. He learned and memorized all the sinuosity of the bottom around the shoreline where he used to swim and knew very well the few spots where he needed to get out without being thrown over dangerous "dog teeth", as the reefs were popularly named. He knew where the bare rocks and corals had to be avoided and where the soft bottom was when he wanted to stand on it.

Under the clear sunlight there was a clean and crystalline quality to the waters that made an optical illusion of the bottom, even when looking at it from the edge of the shore. He amused himself by watching the white bellies of the sharks turning and showing up in the transparency of the waters near the wave's crest, only thirty yards from the shore on the same spot he liked to swim. Five – to eight-feet-long sharks came to those relatively shallow surroundings now and then. Cojimar was known to have enough sharks to keep busy a nearby "Sharkery" which in this case could be the name that should be most fitting to "Tiburonera" as they called the place where the sharks were stripped and processed for the different industrial uses. As he remembers, in those years Cubans didn't like to eat any shark meat at all. "La Tiburonera" was located in El Cachon, on the same part of town that so stimulated Ernest Hemingway when he wrote *The Old Man and the Sea*. In those years, the sharks were brought to the "El Cachon Sharkery" for final processing of its many commercialized products; luckily the sharks apparently became self-conscious of the sharp reefs and used to come to Michael's preferred swimming spot on a kind of ritual during a certain time of the year, but without having attacked anyone. It was of no doubt then that only the small ones, called *Cazones*, that Michael remembered seeing since much of the larger ones, from ten to fifteen feet long, were being brought in daily by the fishermen from the catch that was usually done in deeper waters, a couple of miles from the shore.

After an interesting day at Cojimar, father and son returned to Regla by bus, and he placed the bird in a small cage with the hope that the bird would bring him some joy in this sad period of his life. He took care of the little bird every day, before and after school. The bird seemed to adjust to its new environment; its feathers were ever brighter, and it was apparently getting used to the sugary water he was letting it suck from – an eye-drop dispenser he had taken from his mother's medicine cabinet.

Three days later, after school, he came to check on his bird as usual, only to find that it had died. Michael later thought about the events of the beautiful bird that had come straight to his hands in such an unexpected way on his way to the beach. As if the bird had taken a symbolic flight to find the ultimate freedom, but not before showing him the full splendor of its vitality, and the bright colors of its feathers, under the tropical sun and clean, free air that gave reason to its existence, and perhaps, in a mysterious way, accomplishing its mission to the fullest meaning, because he was suddenly able to understand how important freedom was for the beautiful bird as his father had said, and with the turmoil and transition that his own life was going through, he was able to grow out of sadness and into the awareness of the meaning of life: that you can't violate the rules that make life valuable and significant in a real sense just to satisfy an apparent personal need, at the expense of other beings, no matter how insignificant they may seem. He was able to learn the valuable lesson that translated into his own love of freedom forever.

Less than a year later, his father passed away after being hospitalized with a complication from anemia and kidney failure. He was sixty-three years old. During the entire year since the death of his best friend, Michael and his father had been inseparable, and had many conversations during their long walks. They could be seen at the docks, fishing or walking by the shore along the short beach, next to the docks that his father had built, or when walking down La Calzada, or taking the long walk along Fesser and across town towards the faraway Cojimar through the same passage road where he found the small beautiful bird.

They also used to take the motorboat or *lanchita* that crossed the bay and ride the trolley cars as they did when he was a few years younger (when he went with his father to visit friends and family in Havana), or just for sightseeing in the city. He was going to miss all of it – all of what he had lost within such a short period of time and at such an early stage of his life, and somehow, he was determined not to lose it from his heart and mind. In the end, his mother became a tower of strength and inspiration. These were among the many things he remembered, looking out from his window in the plane in which he was traveling that afternoon. He made a great effort to contain tears, as the memory rushed through his mind.

With very few words his father had consoled him when he lost his childhood friend, before he himself would also be gone. During the walks they had together, his father had taught him about the discipline of life, telling him, "Accept the things that you can't change but meet the challenges and change the things that you can. Achieve, build a strong individuality; it is better to be alone than in bad company," he said many times . . . "You will probably never again find another friend like Eloycito, but his memory will always be with you. It is a strong spiritual force. He was so gifted; it didn't seem natural at times. It is something that can't be explained but it is like visiting angels immersed in light – they come infrequently and leave fast. Those that come in contact with them are very blessed."

Michael appreciated the effort and sensitivity shown by his father in trying to console him, and he had to accept the death of his friend as something that he could not change, but the encounter with such a radical finality and defining of the word impossibility, at such an early time in his life, gave him the strong sense of persistence and perseverance that became one of his characteristics for the rest of his life, and perhaps it became the very reason that he never accepted any situation to be hopeless and kept going up to the very defining end.

He meditated about his father's comments for many days, and he felt himself suddenly growing in maturity. After the death of his father he was mostly by himself, and was always on the move. He acted as if time was not enough. Not to waste it became an obsession. It will be something that will not change during his entire life. He was always looking for something more meaningful to fill; some unseen gap that would otherwise be loss forever. He was for the first time impacted by the cruel and sad reality of the end of an ideal world. He grew up with the conviction that life was the real illusion in our eyes as long as it lasts – not to be repeated, not to be replaced; a total apparent loss except for the experience in memory. And his memory grew stronger for his inner soul's enjoyment. This was the real gift, a gift that he would carry with him and reenact in his mind, the only real joy that could last for all of his life and touch others with its glow as the bright feathers of the prodigious bird that touched his.

The visual impressions of everything that surrounded him on his temporary paradise were kept printed in his mind. He learned now that man is owner, only of his days and hours, as long as they are provided by fate – with all its circumstances, opportunities, and difficulties that only he himself should overcome, with hard work and perseverance. He also learned that life would only have a significant meaning when something good can be made out of it; something perdurable and something that could not die. Michael remembered how he accepted all of this and grew up. He was mostly by himself during the first high school years of his life, for the most part, except when he was using his leadership inclinations organizing the neighborhood junior baseball team for a short while after the death of his father. Later he turned to being on the move all the time; he became a competitive swimmer, training in between his school activities that also included special evening classes. He used his time used to the fullest.

During the growing-up years he looked for things to do to be able to earn some money to help his mother meet the family budget, for what they only had was a small widow's pension from his father and some income from his brother working as a maintenance man with the Havana Coal Company, where his father used to work as a crane operator and engineer. The first opportunity came when one of the girls next door, knowing that he had abilities with drawing in school came to him and asked: "If I pay you for the materials to paint me a dress in oil, would you paint it for me?"

"Sure," he said, "but it may cost you twenty to thirty dollars. We can go together to buy what will be needed."

"That is fine," Carmen Fernandez said, smiling and opening her big chestnut brown eyes. She was the oldest daughter of the Galician couple that was part owner of the corner store . . . "I will give you thirty dollars tomorrow and you go and buy what you need. I want some Chinese motifs on a mustard-colored dress that my dressmaker is sewing for me," she finally said.

It was the beginning of an interesting period for him, a period in which he painted many blouses and dresses that became very popular in those years. People would come from all over town looking for him to paint – from dresses, to furniture for newlyweds, and for cushions, pictures and other decorative items. In all, he was not only able to have a flow of money to buy books, school materials, drafting tools, and tables for his mechanical and architectural drawing classes, but he was also able to develop his natural skills with colors, which exercised his own creativity as well.

His constantly being on the move between school and athletic activities did not help on his feeling of loneliness, and on his late teen years he already longed for a family and children of his own. His mother was the force behind his constant longing to achieve and become goal oriented. Her independent spirit and guidance after his father's death, as well as her stern dedication to all matters pertaining to the need to protect what was a very modest way of life with a limited pension and life insurance fund, found ways to support her son without having to compromise her younger son's education and eventually helped and stimulated him to find a job once he mastered the English language. He remembered how his mother sent him to learn English with an American lady from Arizona who had moved to town, just when he was only eight years old. Later on, she sent him to another half a dozen private teachers, so that by the time he was thirteen he already qualified to get into a program of higher education that eventually earned for him an English language-teaching license from the Ministry of Education. He never used it to teach, but it certainly helped him to find the career opportunities that his mother had envisioned for him.

"You work hard, and have goals for higher achievements," his mother would say. "There will be nothing to stop you from it, wanting is power; squeeze the lemon," she affirmed, using her very own personal vocabulary. "You will be lucky only when you have knowledge. Don't fall asleep on the laurels . . . It doesn't matter that you succeed, you have to keep working to do even better; don't just be complacent." All these inspirational advice and her sensitivity, through her faith in a Superior Guiding Power which undoubtedly provides protection and strength through prayer in a world not always friendly and sympathetic, was just part of her invaluable legacy. While Michael's father was a tower of strength in character and practical wisdom, he was however a somewhat distant figure (even when he never went away except to work), he surely departed too soon for him to be fully understood by his younger son. Perhaps the strong image of his father projected over those lonely growing-up years created a yearning to fulfill the role of a father to his children as soon as he could reach that point in his life. The thought of it was more than that; it was like he had to be able to create something of his own – something to care for in a world of uncertainty. He had to find a meaningful reason to the struggle that life imposed and to the disappointments from all the deceptions and adverse irreversible turns of fate that could kill or separate with apparent infinite cruelty. There must be a reason for all of this. Nothing happens for anything at all, and it should be good in the end for it to be of a sublime divine nature in a little or not at all understood grand design. There should be no other way. For him, in simple terms, life had to be made worthwhile.

First,, Michael was faced with the responsibility of acquiring enough practical knowledge that could assure him of a job that would allow for subsistence. He remembered the stories about his father when in his time children had to start to work as apprentices to develop a mastery of the trade. His father did so by learning carpentry and later on, structural construction and then developing an expertise on steam engines. He studied at night under a kerosene lamp, teaching himself enough, to work and later become a foreman in the construction of new sugar mills (some of which were near the areas where only a few years before the decisive battles by Cubans to gain independence from Spain, and later the Spanish-American war had been fought.). One of the mills was the giant Preston sugar mill that was a model of modernization, and industrialization in a country that was already becoming the greatest producer of sugar in the world by the end of the century.

He thought of how his father had sailed on the steemship *Orotava*, an old steamer, he took from the bay of Nipe, in the northern coast of Oriente, province in Cuba, and disembarked in New York. Soon after that, he settled near Philadelphia where he worked in the construction of railroad bridges; there he continued his independent studies and became the manager of a crew of one hundred and fifty workers that included master construction personnel – many of them tough and hardworking irishmen, which presented him with real challenges that he managed to endure and still be successful at a very demanding and difficult job. He returned to Cuba nine years later as a self-made engineer who could build anything – from a house, to the enormous steam engine-operated cranes in Regla (that managed to unload all the coal that fueled all the sugar mills and every heavy industry in the largest Caribbean island from 1915 to the late 1930s). but the mid-'forties were not like the turn of the century; the Second World War had swept Europe and the Far East and had the entire world on its feet working in the world effort. The good man who lost all his savings on the financial crash of 1929, was never able to recuperate from it in time to rebuild a solid economic base for his family before his final departure.

Michael was faced with tough decisions in regards to his own education. There was no possibility for a long career, whichever it could be; there was the need to become proficient with a trade that would allow him to start working and help his mother financially and alleviate his older brother's burden and decide to go for an education in technology and be licensed in industrial technology within four years. He did and was able to get a contract in the design and supervision of the entire electrification of a new factory before he was twenty years old, and although he was able to earn enough money to fulfill his purposes, he was not totally happy since his heart was with a career in Visual Arts that he had to postpone, as he told his uncle Luis that day a few months after his father's death. His uncle wanted to help financially during his years in art school and his uncle also felt that it would be easy for him to win scholarships and grants given his natural inclinations and ability to paint,. but he felt that his career in the arts would have to wait, as he told his uncle on his thirteenth birthday:

"No, my uncle, don't worry. I will do my own art on my own way once I get older and have raised a family, and I will do it well. Most people that go to San Alejandro School of Art end up frustrated and changing their own instincts to cater to the established norms of the academy – and many of them, including those that have become great artists, leave it without finishing their education. At least I will be free from that."

The answer he gave his dear uncle Luis haunted him throughout the hard years of his self-education as a painter (when he found himself struggling in every front, not only to learn the hard way on his own, but also to reach recognition, which he had to do by participating in tough competitions and enduring the difficulties that needed his perseverance). Above all, it was a great pressure and challenge that he had, nonetheless enjoyed, in spite of the price he had to pay; but it was something that he would not recommend anyone to do, if he can help it, unless they would have similar circumstances and the same determination that he had, and even then, he may still not recommend it.

Yet, there still was some time for Michael to also play in those developing years after the death of his best friend and his father. Playing baseball was something he always liked; better yet, he had wanted to direct his own group of kids ever since he was eleven. but playing was very difficult for younger kids in those years mostly because the few available fields were controlled by the older teenagers most of the time. As captain, he managed to get his group in the game by bringing some of the older kids to play in his team and by contracting games with the older teams from nearby neighborhoods. In that way, by the time he was thirteen, he had a great deal of practice in the art of organizing and directing.

He tried pitching but he was very wild; although he was a strong hitter and was able to play first base well, he preferred to let the big Alfredo play first base and instead put himself on the right field. He and Alfredo were the stronger hitters and also the largest and strongest of the team; the rest of the team was made up of very fast, lightweight players. "El Negro" Alfredo and Michael had developed a good friendship ever since the time the lightweight Eloycito had challenged him to a fistfight which, thank God, never happened.

baseball was a very competitive endeavor even for junior players in those days, and more so in his hometown – a town that had produced a few big leaguers such as Gilberto Torres with the Washington Senators, Adolfo Luke with the Yankees, and others that were famous players during the late 'thirties and into the 'forties. A good number of Cuban big leaguers had at one time or another sharpened their skills playing in the fields around Regla, particularly in "Los Piratas."

Michael finally overcame his frustrations of his earlier years of not being able to play as much as he would have liked by growing up strong and by becoming an able team organizer. The year he always remembered was 1945. He had managed to form the strongest group out of the neighborhood kids and contracted a few good players from nearby areas. They called the team the Pirates, because their home base was the famous natural field next to *La Loma de la Hermita* known as "Los Piratas" where the old haunted house and citadel of the notorious wood-legged ghost was located. Through the years he had always liked to tell the stories of the adventures related to the team; and as he was bringing back memories during his flight, this one came up to lighten his spirit as it contrasted with the presiding sad period of his life.

It was very difficult for most kids in those years to have good gloves, appropriate spike shoes and the like, but as it was, they all had tennis shoes, old as they may have been. They managed to collect some money from the neighborhood to buy black caps and had some of the mothers sew the "skull and bones" pirate's logo on them. They bought black T-shirts and some professional Spalding balls. They would make their own bats on an old lathe at the shop of Michael's uncle. Michael and the catcher's gloves were made out of canvas, and somehow they also managed to get some old gloves for the fielders. The balls for practices and many times for playing were also handmade (with a piece of rubber inside, surrounded with layer upon layer of tightened strong fiber and fastened in the end with hospital tape). They were very hard balls indeed; great to hit hard with and which flew far away. The protective mask for the catcher was a rather old one that needed constant repair but still, it served its purpose.

Enthusiasm grew that year as the team played and won the first nine games. There were no championship games of any kind and the neighborhood and players drew a great deal of pride in winning. Teams from all over town came to contract games in an effort to beat the Pirates. The reputation of the team grew, including the envy and desire of the other teams to beat them, who tried to win but didn't. Finally at the eleventh game, one contending team brought in reinforcement players from out of town, some of whom were considered a bit above the league. The game was a heated one; on the fifth inning the umpire called a doubtful safe on home base that caused a vigorous protest that almost developed into a fight. The game at that point was seven to six in favor of the visitors. The Pirates' pitcher was being hit hard by the most expert players the visitors had brought in. On the sixth inning, the Pirates scored a run and tied the game. The rule was that, if the game was suspended for any reason before the end of the seventh inning, it would have to be played again from the beginning in another day.

There were some dark clouds that summer afternoon. The Pirates' second best pitcher also had to be replaced because he hurt one finger when he tried to stop a hard grounder with his bare hands during the visitors' turn (with only one out and the tie-breaker runner on second base). Michael called Roberto "El Chino"; he was one of the two Robertos in the team. The other one was Roberto "El Habanero", who was also a great hitter. both were of small frame but had big mouths when it came to arguing. between the two of them, they were the terror of the umpires. As "El Chino" finished his warm-up, it was decided to give the classic four-ball to the next batter in order to fill the bases and make the double play easier. but "El Chino" was taking forever – turning to first, and then to second base. He and "El Habanero" called for time at every opportunity. Michael started to notice the dilatory tactics when a loud thunder made everybody run for cover. The rain, which came rather late, was so heavy that the game had to be suspended. On the walk home, they discussed the things that got wrong that afternoon, but the two Robertos insisted that the other team had many players who did not belong. bottom line: The attitude that they both kept angrily repeating was: "We are not going to lose. No way! *De ninguna manera!*"

The next Saturday, after being ahead three to one in the fourth inning, the contenders started to hit so hard on the fifth that the game became ten to three, and all hell broke lose. "El Chino" was pitching again and gave a dead ball with a hard pitch to the left arm of the batter which then started a fight. Michael, who was playing first, moved to try to stop the fight but "El Habanero" had already reached the spot and started blowing punches. In a fraction of a second, the fight ignited like dry grass being hit by lighting. Candy, a tall dark fellow and the strongest player of the opposite team, came to Michael and threw punches in the air. As he dodged the punches, they went on a clinch and both ended rolling on the ground. Soon it looked that only the two bigger guys were fighting while the smaller culprits just watched. Michael was down with his back on the ground but he had both of Candy's hands locked under his armpits that kept Candy so close that there was nothing he could do to hurt him. At that point his older cousin Paco, thinking that he was in trouble, came to his defense and lifted Candy up. Paco was a weightlifter and no sooner had he grabbed Candy, then Michael came between the both of them to avoid the worse as he yelled to Paco, "That's enough, that's enough!" The fight stopped. Nobody was hurt but the game was suspended and the Pirates stood without officially losing any game up to that point.

The team developed a new reputation, so much so that there was again another fight a month later under similar circumstances with another menacing team. Soon they ran out of teams to beat from out of town who wanted to play them.

Under those circumstances, Michael's brother worked out a tentative agreement for the Pirates to play a team from the town of Casa blanca, at the other side of Havana. but he said to him: "Look Michael, two of the sons of my boss are on that team and the only condition is that you guys don't go there to fight but to play. I do not want any embarrassment. I hope you win, but no fights. If that is okay, then I will make the arrangements for next Saturday." "Well, I will talk to my guys tonight and let you know, but as far as I am concerned, there will be no fight. I like to go and play the Casa blanca Eagles," he answered jokingly, inventing the name. His brother smiled and finally said, "I will tell them about their new name. I am sure they will like it."

Michael met with the primary troublemakers and said: "I very much want us to play that game, win or lose. but I don't want any of you to cause any trouble that may disrupt the game . . . If that is okay, then we will go."

They agreed and they went. On the eighth inning, a hard ball that backfired hit the mask of the Pirates' catcher. He was not a regular player but a good catcher and strong hitter that Michael had contracted for that game in an effort to reinforce the team. Since the mask was so old and worn out, the bare metal made a wound on the substitute player's forehead, which needed a few stitches. After his wounds were taken care of, he left on a bus and the game continued. both teams had strong hitters but the unfamiliar field was much

too long, so the Eagle's filders caught a good many would be – home runs in any other field. He himself saw the centerfield of the Eagles come out of nowhere surprisingly showing the ball in his glove (for what he thought would have been an astounding home run). They lost the game – was finally lost thirteen to twelve which was tied to twelve by the end of the ninth inning. Michael's brother Miguel Angel was proud and happy, but all the mothers in the neighborhood were worried to death. by the time they all arrived in town, a crowd had gathered around them, in great anxiety. "What happened? What happened? Are you well?" Over and over, and they all finally started to laugh happily.

Manolo, the substitute catcher, who had the injure in his forehead, had arrived half an hour earlier in the neighborhood with his head in bandages and had told everyone that there was a big fight and that he was the only one that was better off after the fight and everyone else was still being taken care of in the hospital. They almost could have killed the liar literally with the baseball caps as they all hitted him shouting liar, liar and it all ended in laughter while the relatives were shaking their heads in disbelief.

It was the last baseball game for Michael, since the following season, he and his brother trained for the swimming team of Casino Deportivo in Havana. He also was just beginning his secondary education. It was also the last game for the Pirates, marking the end of a period. New developments started to come into the young man's life as he entered his late teen years.

CHAPTER SIX

Beyond Childhood And Back

The airplane in which Michael was traveling was already approaching the Newark airport at a great speed (as jets do), starting the descent from more than thirty thousand feet of altitude – still twenty minutes away from destination. And he was looking in some sadness to so much that he would have to do, in order to perhaps forget any thoughts of frustration and actually immerse himself in work. He has left an exhibition going while he was working in Mexico, and he had to start by retrieving the paintings, and concentrate his thoughts in new works, as soon as possible while dedicating rtime also to his family and ways to overcome unpleasant experiences and finding peace and harmony in his ever busy life instead, away from any negative, but all that would be ensuing pleasant feeling. Somehow, it was like a reminder that there were beautiful things in life that could be enjoyed, far beyond the usual struggle of life – filled with intense, and at times obsessive, work and speed, just as if he was trying constantly to get away from something dreadful, or was riding frantically in the zest to achieve, to imprint if he could, as an artist would do – something for eternity, something worthwhile and lasting like an immortal gift, for the love of people. but that is almost impossible unless you die in the intent, and even that, in dying you need to have had done enough, he thought; or, would it be ever enough? And so, he felt like dying a bit every day and sometimes every hour, his thoughts went to the memories that he so cherished when flying back thinking like a feeling of freedom of a child running in an open field, looking at the big blue sky that so brightened the fields and the surrounding waters of his far away homeland, but he knew would not be possible in real terms, however he made his mind in maintaining his usual positive drive.be.

The liberating feeling, was stronger when he was able to dedicate as usual with his family and the desire to continue to being the protector, the provider, and the shield; the appearance, contrasting however with some emptiness as a sense of guilt invaded him. "Have I failed by not understanding that an attitude of self-sufficiency, may have caused the appearance of the return of expressions of love, he suddenly thought.

Perhaps just letting him be was the ultimate prize given to him, without even a thought for what he could really need. Was there ever a thought or move not to systematically criticize and feel scorned, or to give him something intangible – simply dressed in the beauty of a smile and two open arms without request? Without remorse, without an obvious sense of not having a more likeable alternative. Or, what about some tenderness, or a desire for closeness?, something that could manifest a communion of feelings; a meeting of two souls. It may have been my own fault, or is it not? . . . Questions and more questions like these were like darts piercing his brain when answered because they painfully pressed against him like a reality he either did not want to confront or was a useless fight to resolve. It was like part of a culture that had to be accepted; that had to be not contended, or tried to change because that effort did not seem to have worked in many times before., and in many times being useless, besides being frustrating, to one, accustomed to struggle, and in most cases succeed through perseverance, and patience, and, at some point being.... a limit; a dangerous one. An acceptance of things that cannot be changed, but a silent killer for the soul; a creator of falsehood dressed in apparent truth, a unilateral unconditional surrender.

It was a very uneasy feeling. There have to be more pleasant thoughts. His mind was pulling him back to the waters of the bay – sitting in the open air, under the steps of the wooden deck his father had built (at the northern far end of the dock where large coal and other mineral cargo ships used to moor). In that silent hiding spot, he quietly watched the many fishes that swam by or stayed still against the clear bottom. Caribbean fishes full with all the colors of the rainbow. His thought were again and suddenly into the colors and the quiet beauty of his childhood days.

The bright sun shining all over that part of the bay he so loved, sparking at the distance brought him into the contrasting brightness of a midday walk he had with his mother at the beautiful Villa of Guanabacoa. He was seven years old that time and any venture away from home was of course an exciting and interesting happening. This time, while looking into the waters, he could see himself going with his mother to visit his grandfather's house. The event was more impacting than could be expected of any outing.

First, it was the usual riding towards the main bus station in town. The ride was on an open bus with its side-to-side seats and a roof for a shade; such open buses were a blessing under the balmy breeze of the hot summer months. It looked like an open old Western stagecoach with up and down windows, except for the absence of horses and the ever-present long nose (for the noisy motor coming forward in front of the straight windshield) behind which you could see the driver and all the driving gear without even getting inside the vehicle; this was considered completely obsolete and would be substituted by a closed version by the end of 1938. The romantic era of the colorful open bus was coming to an end.

The second bus from the main station of El Emboque to the far end of Guanabacoa reaching the station at "La Loma del Indio" was already one of the new closed buses, with a not-so-long nose and the typical yellow color with a red bar along the side and a black top; still interesting to see when you think in retrospect, but indeed tighter and uncomfortable inside. The bus would cross by the beautiful center of the colonial town – with its high and square bulky profile of the Church of the Ascension on one side of the tree-shaded main *plaza* (a relatively large one); and then the bus would continue around the church at one end, and on then the other, passing through the old and elegantly ornamented kiosk, where a band would play every Sunday afternoon. It was always an attractive scenery to drive by. The bus finally came to the long road through the rolling hills. His mother asked the driver to stop in front of the huge and solitary *bohio* (equal in rustic construction but much larger than the typical Cuban huts), standing about fifty yards away from the road where they stepped down.

behind the *bohio*, a large *Ceiba* tree offered a soothing shaded, grass-barren area that ran between the *bohio* and the hen's corral behind the outhouse. The shaded area was a relief from the hot summer sun, with an enchanting soft breeze coming from the fertile valley of "La Noria" that ran along the Cojimar River, on the northeast of town. It all made a world with a country flavor – the sound of roosters, his uncle's pigs oinking in the background as he feeds them with *palmiche*, and the palm's fruit coming from the few palm trees at the far side of the small farm just behind the hills next to the valley where the river snakes and flows calmly, about two miles away.

Michael, as usual, went to play inside the cabins of the few trucks that were rusting away in a junkyard, lying just about a block away along the road where many old automotives and tractors rusted away (as shown by the attractive rusty pieces alongside the old farm equipment). He loved to roll up the speedometers and play with the large steering wheels, where he pretended to drive in a dreamworld – where the automobile was king. He tried to emulate Fumero, a locally famous, racecar driver from his hometown (where the car races ran in those years precisely at Galban Lobo Stadium near the shore of that part of the bay called Marimelena at a time that car racing had become extremely popular), and he was also beginning to relate to the exciting world surrounding him. The long and slender racecars of the time had four wheels at the end of the two long axles under the unprotected body located in front, where there was a small hole for the driver's seat. As usual, it was painted with many colors – primarily as much as bright red and yellow, with the white-and-black emblematic flags painted on the narrow sides. The entire body seemed to be quite flimsy when compared with the heavy, cranked delivery trucks that came to his neighborhood corner stores to bring ice and beverages at a time when horse or mule-driven carts used to deliver vegetable coal for cooking, or hay for the cows at the nearby farm. This particular cart, with its high bed and back wheel axles, was a lot of fun since the kids liked to hang on its backside and swing back and forth as the cart moved hurriedly down the still unpaved road.

His mother, calling from the backside of the *bohio*, drew him away from his dream world. There, she was, with his uncle Jacinto, still wearing his bus driver's light blue uniform and round top cap and visor. He was a slim, almost osseous man, in his mid-forties, with a friendly smile and his usual easygoing gestures. He would take his cap off and show his thinning and straight blondish hair as he dried the sweat from his wrinkled forehead, right over his light blue eyes. Jacinto was the father of five children, two to seven years old. On that very afternoon his wife was in the hospital giving birth to their sixth child. Michael wondered how they managed financially, but he easily figured it out; Jacinto was always doing something businesslike. He worked by driving the No.29 Regla-Guanabacoa bus; perhaps he had inherited this line of work from his father, who was also a trolley car conductor who had conducted the first trolley car that rolled over the cobblestone streets of Cuba, precisely at Michael's hometown of Regla, where the first and most modern electric power plant was located at the turn of the twentieth century. When not driving the bus, Jacinto would be selling pork meat once or twice a year. In the meantime, he was also a number's bookie; something that he was very good at because he was constantly on the road driving his bus, so everybody knew him. The official daily lottery numbers was the most popular gambling game at that time and prizes were frequent and fair.

As he approached the two, he noted a sad expression on his mother's usual pearly-white face; as attractive as usual, with her mellow, honey-colored eyes, under her bright and sparkling reddish-brown abundant hair that she always kept in style. This time she had it somewhat loose over her shoulders, with a mesh flowing over half her forehead. We had to go to grandfather's house, closer to town, she said, since he had turned very ill during the last few days and had been taken there to be closer to the doctor who was treating him.

A few minutes later, they took off on the nearly empty bus on the way back to where the road to La Loma del Indio started. Mother and son stepped down and started to walk on a side street, then continued on a dirt road (with only a few houses on the side), passed the curve where the last town house stood, and then descended the hillside. The road was totally covered on the sides with loose and highly bright limestone rocks, where the spiked wire fences separated the fields from the cloistered "Piñas de Raton" plant with its orange-yellow small fruits that were unique to the area, leaning against the side of the fences together with myriads of wild flowers that appear to hide in low profile among the taller grass.

The brightness was almost blinding to the point of being unforgettably striking, on a hot and sunny midday under the high Caribbean blue sky with its spotty white clouds on top; as such, it was not enough to give any merciful shade, except for his mother's ever-present parasol that she had always ready for such occasions. At the far distance near the horizon beyond La Noria valley, the clouds piled one unto one another, forming dense figures that seemed to carry on a capricious and voluptuous tight dance over the hills separating the valley from Cojimar (on the northwest) and towards bacuranao (on the northeast). His eyes were like mirrors, piercing in the distance far beyond as if to shield itself from the brightness that emanated from the long descending road.

They finally arrived at the old lonely frame house where, to his astonishment and indelible impression, he saw his very skinny and pale grandfather sitting on the middle of his bed. The doctor had just finished one of his painful treatments to his legs, severed at the knees and still showing the uncovered flesh and the protruding bare bones. The grand old man softly called his grandson to the bedside, where his mother helped him to come close enough and receive the last kiss from his ailing grandfather. It was a beautiful day with a sad ending for the boy; an early lesson in life's painful ways. His grandfather was a not too old man who had been rather energetic and was now being taken down by gangrene. A sight that was also as unforgettable, in his seventh year, as the bright sun under the immense blue sky over the planes of La Noria where the Cojimar river was gently flowing.

Somehow the memories he was now recreating when daydreaming about his early years were coming to him as if he didn't want to confront with the realities of his own life as a grown man, – those realities that that so haunted him during more than thirty years and the long years in exile. There was so much he wanted to explore in his mind, and much that he needed to place in perspective. Thinking and expressing them helped sort out parts of history and parts of his experiences in a desire to understand them, if at all. Why does his passion for painting everyday until the early morning hours help him to cope with the separation from the country he so loved and also with his intimate frustrations?. While details in his paintings were not in the least what he needed now as they would speak for themselves,. (As many of those paintings do, revolving around scenarios, as if appearing occasionally – like necessary and significant backdrops to a life and its times, and like if he was floating into a painting of his Midday in Guanabacoa when he visited his grandfather by his mother's hand.) He felt the need to have some insight behind his motivations and frantic drive. The only way, perhaps was to explore it without being immersed too much or appearing too embarrassing unto himself. Then, in this instances, his preference has been to feel as if a silent listener would speak about all of it with a foreign and if possible, an unbiased voice as sometimes paintings can do.

He continued to recall the old times, and later, he captured the new and more painful times where, like many other of his countrymen, he confronted the painful separation from his country and loved ones.

The high school years and beyond,. where Michael found active grounds for his drafting abilities. The school was full with posters he and other able students produced for the different celebrations. In the same class, there were only a few with great abilities. There was one whom he considered to be the most talented – Miguelito Fernandez, who later went directly into a career as a gifted illustrator. Michael now and then thought about how Miguelito may have done and where his talent may have taken him during the forty-plus years of the Castro regime, or if perhaps he may have perished, like thousands others, in an attempt for freedom through the Florida strait, or with better luck and destiny he may still be alive and producing all the good art he was surely capable of creating. Miguelito Fernandez had completely disappeared from sight since the last day he met him on a bus ride in Havana in the late 1950s, and saw the proofs he was carrying under his left arm – a tender pencil drawing of a mother and child, intended for a magazine advertisement of Milkmaid condensed milk.

The memory of those anecdotal high school years brought a smile to his mind. He remembered when he and Miguelito made twelve drawings each during the time the test had lasted, run by professor Matilde Single in her drafting class. The assignment was for each of the students to draw a penciled still life of an arrangement of bottles. No sooner had the class of twenty-four students handled the sheets back to Ms. Single, then she put her two hands around Michael and Miguelito's ears and immediately ran the two youngsters outside the classroom while the class was laughing loudly as both culprits were chased through the halls. Ms Single flipped all the papers on her right hand ultimately flying over her head as she shouted: "How can you do this to me? How can you do this to me?" As she pushed the two boys down the hall until they reached the principal's office. Everyone had to do the assignment again and it was regarded as a fun event that even the teacher herself laughed about it for years to come (as some school anecdotes go in time). both students were known to draw all the time – either humorously or seriously, depending on the occasion. but both were very fond and appreciated the guidance of the already aging good teacher from San Alejandro School of Arts that they were lucky to have at that early stage in their life. The work they did with books that they illustrated with stories, and particularly movies they reproduced as comics, were well known by everyone in the school. They worked together in producing comic series of the *Tarzan* movies (which starred Johnny Weissmuller), and Flash Gordon's space adventures – which were some of their favorite stories.

They got along very well with the other artistic students of that class, namely, Antonio Ferra who had great ability as a caricaturist, and Arnaldo Ravelo, a newcomer from Casa blanca who later pursued his career at San Alejandro School of Art and won a Fellowship in Spain and New York. Returning to Cuba loaded with paintings about the onset of the revolution, Ravelo then left the country, less than two years after his return since he was horrified by the limitations and the oppressive atmosphere imposed by the regime. Arnaldo Ravelo diluted himself in many facets of his artistic talent. He was a very independent man who thought of himself to belong to the Renaissance period and lived its part by producing not only paintings (of which he was very good at, particularly palette work), but also jewelry, ceramics and *vitrales* (or stained glass work) in a personal and unique style. He lived very modestly and dressed only in caftans (which he himself made) for his conferences since he was very knowledgeable about ancient cultures and mythology, becoming one of the most sought-after guides at the Metropolitan Museum of Art in New York during the 1960s and '70s.

It was interesting how he and Ravelo met again in a New York subway train in 1968, after more than fifteen years since they last seen each other. Michael would not have recognized Ravelo with his thick beard, if not for his tall and heavy set but athletic figure, and only after he called him by name (when both of them were just leaving the train through different doors); it was fate perhaps. At that time Ravelo showed him many of his recent works. Michael then signaled to his two young daughters and said, "These are my works.", when the two friends met again a few days later in Ravelo's studio, Michael added: "Up to know, at least."

Three years later, he showed Ravelo some of his first paintings from childhood memories. The meditative old friend, who sat on a chair, contemplated on the paintings and could only say a long and pensive "Hmmm!..." The stimulating friendship continued until the unfortunate death of Ravelo from a heart attack while doing one of his favorite things – swimming, in South beach, Miami.

Ravelo was only fifty-one in 1979. About three years later, Michael paid tribute to Ravelo when he exhibited twenty-three of Ravelo's works in oils; dismounting his own works from the walls of his studio in Ridgefield, New Jersey where the event took place. It was a memorable occasion where many artists, friends, press notables, as well as writers and poets, came to pay homage to an artist who, in many ways represented to him, a significant connection and stimulant in the development of his own late career. The need to catch up was born; the need to use the time to do what he knew he had to do. Time was just too short. The obsession and the fear of losing the grip on time started to be more pressing when he thought, "How much time will I be given by fate?" Even when sure of its mandate, you are never too sure of how much, nor how you will be allowed to manage it; and, at that point, you become a tyrant of your own time.

Much earlier, during the college years when Ravelo went to San Alejandro Art School, Michael instead went for what he thought was a more formal and practical education at Fernando Aguado Arts and Trades School – which he decided in order to make a career with immediate financial rewards, contrary to his uncle's desires.

From 1946 to the late forties, Michael came face to face with a very active formative period. He had a strict self-imposed discipline. The classes at the Arts and Trade School ran from 8am to 4pm after which he would go to his training as a competitive swimmer. Later, he would find himself arriving at 8pm. in night school – still with his wet rolled towel and swimming gear. (That, after coming back to his hometown through a long ride on the trolley car and the beloved *lanchita* – the boat that crossed the bay.) His dinner at home would be waiting for him not earlier than 10pm p.m. every evening. His ambitious and competitive drive as a swimmer made him an honorary member at some of the sponsoring clubs in the Vedado and Miramar sections of Havana, the Casino Deportivo, and later on of the Cubaneleco Athletic Club (under Carlos Cubas first and Osvaldo Francisco later – both famous trainers for the Olympic games).

The Helsinki Olympic game aspirant, who was on the top of his form and time (in both the two – hundred – and four-hundred-meter swim – freestyle) succumbed in his dreams when he could not swim in the finals because of a painful ear infection, after winning 1st Place in the preliminary competitions. It was a terrible blow for him after three years of intense training and a great disappointment for Osvaldo Francisco who almost cried when his most promising swimmer gave him his swimsuit on a symbolic gesture saying:

"This is it for me. Sorry coach, it was not for me".

Obviously it was not. There should be something else – something that he knew deep inside but which he was not yet ready for (an elusive but intimate knowledge, more than an expectation). It was something that could wait, as if it was the only sure thing he did not even think he knew – except for knowing that its time would come when he was ready.

Soon he would be entering a new period in his life. It was time when the university and the secondary schools in Havana saw how some student leaders and their followers were somehow encouraged to exchange books and reason for guns. A time when ideals were mixed with gangsterism – far beyond the possibilities of being typecast as a romantic stereotype but more towards undertaking a dangerous path. (A path that would prove to be fatal for the future development of a nation that had less than half a century of republican history and a much shorter period of democratic exercise.)

CHAPTER SEVEN

Summary Of A Prelude To Tyranny (The 1940S In Havana)

As the plane taxied through the Newark Airport that afternoon of May in the late 1980s, Michael was still immersed in the thoughts that had started moments after his plane left Mexico City. For those minutes from the runway to the gate he realized he was still reliving, almost unconsciously, many parts of his own life's recollections. It never occurred to him that he would ever consider it worthwhile in any way except that, at this time, the recollection of memories were unconsciously helping him to cope with all the frustrations that he obviously had to contend with. He was not a man that would escape responsibilities of any kind and it seemed that life had a way of testing such determinations in a very demanding way and in diverse directions to which he had to attend, or otherwise ignore or yield. He was a man that could not do either.

For years to follow after his flight from Mexico, bringing his memories to mind became the most soothing self-prescribed therapy, as much as painting them already was. He continued to remember beyond his happy childhood years and into the crisis that followed in his beloved country. As it was, his memory traveled through his student years – the years when he was a young student in Havana of the late forties. The thoughts came sharply, to correlate with the developments of those years and the most current situation of the last three decades after the coming to power of Fidel Castro. The thoughts and the life that surrounded them were already part of history.

Confusing as it may be for anyone that was not exposed to the background of the political conditions in Cuba to easily understand how all the most recent developments in Cuba came to happen, it was necessary for him to put them all in the perspective of time. As time went by and he became inclined to write about his thoughts, he would at the same time need to shed light on the process itself. He found himself with the inevitable thought that surely many Cubans who left the country to get away from an oppressive and limiting regime had to face and to question themselves about:

"How has this country come to the mess it is in?"

He was trying to find some helpful hints for him to at least have a better perspective and understanding of how or why it may have happened, for whatever it may be worth.

On telling the story even to himself, he had first to avoid falling in rhetorical arguments typical of any politically motivated argument and not to lose sight of the fact that he was not a man with great interest in politics, except to know his rights and to keep himself as the free thinker that he was, and in a small and unpretentious way, help others in the understanding of the process that took us there.

Perhaps it is a part of the process of learning for any nation whose people had suffered so much in order to open a bright window of hope for the future. A future as a free democratic society, that which is not possible without learning something in the process prior to the endurance of the hardship.

There are very few Cubans, he thought, who would not have opinions and a theory on how to resolve any problem the country was suffering from. They are usually very passionate about their points of view, but at the same time losing the objectivity about it for the same reason.

Michael, not even on spelling out his thoughts very superficially, was going to pretend that they could have more objectivity or validity than anyone else's; but nonetheless, they could add to the bulk of knowledge and experience that will be necessary to be considered for a better understanding of the lessons that history is trying to teach all of us, and to avoid tripping at the same rotten rock again and again.

"Don't be sermonizing." His brother would tell him on occasion.

"I know, brother, I am far from perfection, but…" he would answer.

Inevitably persistent as he was, he would make his point again anyway.

In arguing or simply trying to explain some of the events and experiences in Cuba in the last forty or fifty years, may come to run the risk of being considered as if he was involved in a tendentious exercise (but not spelling out his views could be considered to be shamefully equivalent to consent). Since that would be out of the question, he had always hoped that, at least, his point of view would be understood as being honest and constructive, in the final analysis.

To him, persistence always paid. Only that in politics, he preferred not being too judgmental because history has a way of making the wrong look right and the right to look very wrong sometimes, depending on how it is eventually written, and the long-term circumstances surrounding it. but regardless of this, freedom cannot be compromised. Hopefully, time and sobriety can tell it better; therefore, it is not the question of impressing upon anyone, it is more than having a clear mind on what he has experienced, and what is really important – which is, to learn to attain and preserve respect for human rights and true independence. To have others understand this principle was important; but to have his brother understand it was a matter of passion – a matter of high volatility.

He had very bitter arguments with his brother about Cuban political issues since he arrived from exile in nineteen sixty, about a year and one-half after the arrival of Castro's forces to Havana, demanding absolute dedication – meaning, absolute submission to the government (mostly because of the division in the families that have been typical since the first year of the insertion of the so-called people's revolution). Sons and daughters against parents, and brothers against brothers. Their loyalties were only with the state that encourages the division in order to assure its control and deception among the sufferers and sick beneficiaries of the rule.

The arguments with his very dear brother developed into a sad situation that set them apart for more than twenty years. It lasted almost until their final and most definite reconciliation at his brother's deathbed. Sitting by his brother's bedside in the hospital during his brother's final days, they managed to laugh about the funny anecdotes of their younger years. It was some kind of strange happiness; they both cried as well, mostly because of all the years wasted in vain and the suffering of the family because of the prolonged separation. (That also became a rift in his own marriage, mostly due to the unfortunate unforgiving nature of his wife which contributed to more family distress and deep-rooted unhappiness, considering the harm done to love in such a situation would generate along the way.) Very painful thoughts indeed, so he moved away from them and was soon back to where he had started – on his thoughts about the years as a student in Havana of the 'forties.

In 1944 Fulgencio Batista, after eight years in power that included four as de facto and the last four as elected president of Cuba, celebrated a democratic election and an overwhelming majority against the government's elected candidate – Dr. Ramon Grau San Martin. It was the emergence to power of the revolutionary leaders of the 1930s. Michael remembered how multitude of people went to the street in joyful demonstrations, crowding trolley cars and all sorts of public and private vehicles, waving Cuban flags and filling the air with the sound of bells and chants of: "Ramon, Ramon, Ramon". It looked as though the nation had finally reached a point of democratic maturity, and it was something to be celebrated. He thought of how happy his father would have been if he were alive. His father had died in May of that same year.

The Grau San Martin years saw the post-world war era of economic reconstruction and optimistic outlook. During the final years of the batista presidency (of the early 'forties, following the tendency of an alliance with the United States and England with the Russians during the war), the Communist Party in Cuba was legalized and they started to exercise some influence within the organized workers' syndicates with some leaders like blas Roca and Juan Marinello figuring prominently and openly. The party changed its name to Socialist Party but never achieved any degree of power under popular vote since the party never even actually reached five percent of the popular vote in any election, however, they were able to form alliances primarily with the party in power. Oddly enough, one of the alliances was with batista's party itself.

Likewise, the influence inside the student movement was also uneventful and the only noticeable thing was the occasional agitator who carried no apparent label except the aim to disrupt and create turmoil whenever there was an opportunity. It seemed such an aimless effort but as he now realized in retrospect, it was a tactic that would eventually pay dividends. (As they would be somehow intimately tied with the gangster's activities, without presenting a distinguished face but only that which would create confusion and opportunity for behind-the-scene conspiracy, possibly infiltrating any tendency which would offer an opening to power without showing its identification to any foreign interest; a force preparing to dominate the political scene at any cost and with the purpose of eventually placing it under the domination of the true twentieth-century disguised imperialist: The USSR.)

Most likely, many of the communists of those years, whether above ground or under it, were sincere believers that the cause of the so-called proletariat and its way to achieve the ends regardless of the means were perfectly justified and necessary to improve the human condition. That is, without thinking that its dictatorship would eventually treason the very principles of the equality that they so professed.

Needless to say now, there are many regrets on the apparent pursuit of a more just and humane society through the theories of communism, as it failed its highest test. Still, its faulty principles continue to exercise its power in the most oppressive way in a few countries, which unfortunately includes Cuba, as a means to perpetuate a few elite leaders and their lackeys in power (against a majority that is controlled through fear showing some significant parallel to a gangster exercising his extortion to his innocent and helpless victims).

In Cuba, the caldron of political players and their means to achieve their ultimate purposes was taking place in the universities and the secondary schools of the mid – to late 'forties. Only, no one knew for sure who the survivors would be and how they would emerge to claim their opportunity for absolute control and power for perpetuity.

Meanwhile the students, of which Michael was just one of them, were being made ready to be used in the conspiracy (without them even knowing) whenever and wherever possible. All they had to do was to be sincere idealists – something that was easy to be. The ideals of independence, freedom, and justice for all as proclaimed by all the illustrious patriots of the liberating wars of the nineteenth century in Cuba and the progressive ideals of a young democratic republic could not ask more from its youth.

As it was during Michael's freshman years, the students at the Arts and Trades School were very unhappy with the leadership of the Student's Association. A good number of teachers were abusive and unconcerned whether there was or wasn't any progress made by the students in their classes.

The teachers, with some honorable exceptions, would come to class and have a sloppy and fast presentation. The students had to take notes very fast and at the best they could, to make sure that they had as much information as possible (to be able to have some idea when the tests came) because the teachers would not use any well-organized text or system that could give the students appropriate guidance. He developed a shorthand system of his own which helped him; but at first, he could not very well distinguish what he had written, due to the many symbols and fast scribbles that he had done.

The other reason for discontent was that the leadership in power was formed by the people that had long passed in age but had purposely prolonged their stay in school as a way to maintain influence and serve the interest of bureaucrats who funneled monies from the Ministry of Education to the association; money that was not used to benefit the students' interests in any way.

He had come in contact with the leaders of "Accion Civica Estudiantil" when Valdes Muñoz, a charismatic slender young man in his mid-twenties with a persuasive smile under his light bronze skin and who was well-respected by everyone, asked him if he would want to get the spot of becoming the delegate of his class in the forthcoming elections. Michael accepted and started to campaign among his fellow students. He soon became confident of the sure success of his candidacy. There was no question that the Civic Action Movement would win the election and gain control of the Student's Association. It was the third year of Ramon Grau San Martin's government in 1947 – a year when student protests were in high gear, staged mostly by a very politically active University Student's Federation (FEU). Among the most visible leaders of the federation was the delegate from Law School, a tall but somewhat flabby young man of about twenty-one years of age, with an incipient shadow of a moustache. His name, Fidel Castro Ruz.

The famous Alma Mater, "Escalinata Universitaria", with its wide steps that ran from San Lazaro Avenue up to the university grounds, became the battleground for all popular just causes that the students would enthusiastically endorse. The range of protests was wide and frequent in 1947 and into 1948, the later part of Ramon Grau San Martin's presidency.

Among the many student protests, a few were only worth mentioning starting with the protests against the increase of the charge for electric power (when a multitude of students carried lighted candles well into the darkness of the night at the *escalinata*). Others were protests against the police, and protests for the increases in public transportation and the like. Many of such manifestations were to preserve the university as an autonomous entity, and to keep the police from entering the campus. There was protest at the *escalinata* whenever the University Student's Federation (FEU) would call for them.

Among the FEU speakers (that included the president of the federation, Manolo Castro, before he was appointed by the government as the Sports Minister) another voice was starting to be heard. It was the voice of one who was just beginning to try his wings on the political arena of the university. His name: Fidel Castro, the student who barely a year before, had just come out of a Jesuit secondary school – Colegio de Belen. The law student who was never elected to be FEU president, but who still managed to make his presence felt at every opportunity, and who was emerging as a student's leader not only at the university but also among the younger students at the colleges and secondary school circles.

The definition of the *"escalinata"* as the battleground was well deserved. The large stretch of steps in front of the university witnessed frequent brick-throwing towards the police as well as inflamed barrels thrown down the steps all the way to the police cars, half a block away. There was occasional gunfire, provocatively coming from behind the walls near the steps, as well as shots by the police. One of the most fearsome protests against Grau and his allegedly corrupt Minister of Education took place after a young secondary school student named Carlos Martinez Junco was killed during a scuffle with the police. The raging students in front of the university overturned various police cars. The students took to the streets and hijacked the trolley cars that were driven towards the university, with loads of students chanting: *"King Kong que se vaya Ramon . . .* King Kong out with Ramon," over and over again.

The aspiration of President Grau to run for another term was thwarted, thus demonstrating the influence that the constant student unrest and their protests excerpted on the political life of the country. Sadly enough, much of the backdrop of all the agitation was fueled not only by the idealistic desire for reform and justice that the students supported against corruption, but by well-orchestrated so-called revolutionary groups that were controlled by notorious gangsters, and where extremist political activists could find the protective shield under which they could almost anonymously conspire.

Michael and his younger cousin Lazaro, who by then was himself a student at the Institute of Havana, were familiar with the protests from the students' standpoint and had been caught in the skirmishes that followed the manifestations at the university. They learned how to run through the campus between the various faculty buildings and into the side streets, avoiding the police when things got out of hand. Lazaro was knowledgeable of who the leaders at the institute were, and both of them also knew how to identify the typical agitators. They were usually pseudo-students that had long passed the age of the classes they were registered at; they seemed never to graduate and they were never seen in class. Invariably, they were only seen acting their roles at any jointure that would have the potential to create turmoil.

As Michael became a candidate for delegate of his class, he and his cousin exchanged information about the activities in both schools and the university.

Three days before the elections at his school, Valdes came to see him outside his classroom and said: "Michael, we will have a meeting tomorrow night to discuss the strategy and assignments for the Election Day."

"I will be here after classes as usual," said Michael.

"No, we will have the meeting at seven in the evening at the Institute. We will meet at the student association's office. It is very important that you come, not only because we have to determine who will be inside the school inspecting the election process, but who will be outside promoting votes among the students."

"I already know that I will be outside promoting votes all day, I don't have to go to the institute for that. I have my swimming training session in the late afternoon and my English class in the evening as usual."

Valdes' expression became somber with preoccupation as he told Michael: "Yes, but Maso' has inside information about the intentions of our opponents to cheat and to keep control of the association."

Michael had briefly met Maso', the president of the Student's Association of the Institute of Havana; it was at one of the visits he made to the Institute to see his friend and co-student at the School of English Language, Elio Alba Buffil,, who was acting as vice president of the association at the time. Michael knew that Maso' always carried a gun, and he also knew that not all the student leaders were involved with gangs (as he knew his friend Elio Alba well enough to know that even when he worked close to Maso' in the administration of the student association, he was a distinguished honor student and a very meticulously, honest, and peace-loving person, not given to the gun subculture of the time).

"How do they know about the intentions to cheat?" Michael asked Valdes.

"Maso' has some contacts in the Ministry of Education, that's why he knows. In any case, they do not expect that those bastards are going to give up their control easily, and they, our opponents, are aware that they may lose this one if they don't do something about it, unless they win the votes."

"All right, I will be there on time."

Valdes continued: "The meeting is very important since we will have some of the FEU leaders from the university coming to give support to our cause."

Michael came to the Institute of Havana to find that there was no access to the student's association room. He was met at the front entrance by Valdes, who immediately mumbled a complaint and added: "They have closed access to the school today because of an inspection due to recent unrest, so we will just meet at the far end of the building by the sidewalk."

He looked towards the left corner of the beautiful neoclassic building that occupied the entire block and saw about eight other students, some of whom had already sat on the flat cement border at the edge of the lawn, while a few others were standing on the sidewalk.

As the two walked towards the meeting place, Valdes said: "We are awaiting some FEU leaders to come to give support. They are from the Masferrer's MSR people."

Michael wondered what Rolando Masferrer's people had to do with the meeting because he had heard about the man as being the leader of the "Movimiento Socialista Revolucionario" (MSR), which was known to be one of the most fearsome gangs that played a role in gun confrontations with other groups (that apparently competed for participation on graft and corruption and engaged in assassinations among themselves, a situation that prevailed in Havana in the 1940s. Allegedly, some of the gangster's activities were encouraged and perhaps supported by the government, which intended to use the groups as non-military action groups to indirectly help erode the possibility of opposition towards the government, and to exert control in unions or worker's syndicates). Allegedly again, in that environment, groups tended to eliminate each other's enemies.

He had heard that Masferrer had been a mercenary fighter on the side of the Republican against the Nationals during the bloody Spanish Civil War of the mid – to late 'thirties. For much of the outside world, the Republicans had the support and sympathy of the freedom-loving people everywhere,. but, in the end, they were controlled by the communist activists. In Cuba, serious students disliked the gang's activities. Obviously, there were some university student federation leaders who were involved with the MSR and other groups.

before he could ask which leaders from the FEU were coming to the meeting, Valdes said: "Fidel Castro is coming!"

He was surprised to hear that Fidel Castro may be involved with one of the most notorious gangster group since so far, he had seen the student leader in what he considered to be good causes.

The informal meeting started with Valdes explaining: "We have to be watchful of the election process because of the expected cheating. And we have to be prepared to act if that comes to happen."

At that moment, he saw the familiar tall figure coming from across the street on one side of him, the president of the Institute Student's Association – Maso', followed closely by a small and thin young student (that Michael remembered his cousin Lazaro telling him that his name was Regueira, who shadowed Maso' wherever he went. He also remembered, what his cousin Lazaro said about them; they were both always armed. He also said that Maso' usually carried his loaded gun inside a hollow book. Michael noted that he had a book under his left arm that night. Lazaro had also told him that Regueira had a short fuse and was rumored to have been involved in the shooting of a sailor when riding on a trolley car a few days before. Michael could not help but feel a bit uptight about the gathering.

Walking next to Castro, on one side were two thin-looking students, one of whom was wearing very large and heavy black-framed glasses. The smaller-sized companions made the figure of Fidel Castro look heavier and much taller. Castro was dressed casually this time, Michael noticed, because he remembered the student leader dressed in a dark suit on most of his public appearances at the university rallies. The loose beige long-sleeved shirt he was wearing over his slightly darker trousers was very casual indeed by comparison; he looked quite heavier than he thought he was; he seemed to be a bit overweight with a roundish face and with a very light shade of an incipient mustache (that did not get to be groomed or was not intended to be a mustache at all). Michael had seen Fidel Castro many times at the university, but never this close.

Maso' started talking by saying: "As you have already heard, we know that your opponents are armed. They know that you will win and they are ready to take the victory from you under any pretenses. You need to be armed also, and Fidel is here to help us with this issue." Regueira, who looked like a child not yet out of grammar school, meanwhile seemed, with his quiet appearance, to be watching every move everyone in the group was making.

Castro had taken a seat, with his long legs on the sidewalk at the right end of the same ledge where Michael was leaning against. Between him and Fidel there was Valdes and another student candidate from his school followed by Maso', and Regueira after Castro at the far end,. Castro, with the heavy, dark-glassed figure, stood among the students (who were making a semi-circle around him) then said: "All of you already know that we have come here tonight to give you the support you need.. We have weapons for everyone. How many of you do not have a gun?"

As if moved by an invisible spring, Michael, almost jumped away from the ledge he was leaning against and without hesitation looked at Castro and said: *"Armas para que? "* "**Weapons for what**?!", And immediately asked: "What do we want weapons for?" as he continued to face the university leader.

Valdes immediately answered before Fidel Castro could: "If those people are armed, as we know they are, then we are not going to be unprepared."

At the other end, Castro was intently looking at Michael without saying a word (but was probably thinking that the younger, inexperienced sophomore was most likely naive) and he did not make an effort to answer the unexpected question, or perhaps the challenge he was facing was so unexpected that he could not say a word.

Valdes continued: "Well, some of you may not need to be armed with a gun but we will see to it that we get the guns that we need. We will also have the people from the institute, under the leadership of Maso, to show their authentic support and hopefully, those bastards will not dare to pull any tricks on us."

Michael said: "Fine, I do not want a gun."

The air was tense at that moment, but Valdes kept his usual gentle poise and said (looking at Michael and the other four or five younger students that were not part of the leadership yet: "Okay, you guys can go now. We will continue our meeting with Fidel to discuss details about getting the necessary guns."

"Will, see you tomorrow," he said as he started to walk away. ". . . I will be outside the school promoting votes for our candidacy." He left with an uneasy feeling, ran after a passing trolley car, and jumped on it to go in the direction of Muelle de Luz where he was to take the popular *lanchita* to Regla at the other side of the bay.

As usual, he stepped on the motorboat and went right to the back deck where he liked to ride, holding himself unto the handle bar of the roof which was his preferred spot in the evenings, where he could watch the reflections of the lights of his hometown on the waters of the bay as he approached it.) The balmy air of the bay with its soft caresses blowing his usually short-trimmed hair was a welcome relief from the tense meeting he had just left behind at the institute. His thoughts, however, were deeply immersed on the recent events. He had an aversion for guns as he connected it with violence and many times with abuse of power. He remembered the stories about his paternal grandfather who was seriously wounded in Zaragoza, during the revolts against the Spanish Crown during the decades of the 1860s and '70s in Spain.

As a young student in Zaragoza, Spain, Jose' Beltran Manero, whose liberal ideas clashed with the "Carlista" rulers, became involved and was seriously hurt in some of the city's most violently crushed popular protests and ultimately with the revolutionary uprisings. He was strong enough to make it back to his home in the small town of Caspe, south east of Zaragoza in the same province.

By the time his mother arrived home, she found him lying face up in bed, almost unconscious, with his hands pressed over a deep bayonet wound to the abdomen. He was profusely bleeding from it and he also had a less serious bullet wound to one of his thighs.

Luckily enough, his mother was able to look for help and hide him from the authorities in a nearby farm (where he was taken care of and treated from his wounds and began to recuperate with

the help of a knowledgeable Catholic priest who was a friend of the family). In the end, still feeble, he dressed like a woman and was "smuggled" into a boat sailing to Cuba. Michael did not know much of the details on how his would-be grandfather fared on the journey and whether he arrived still as a woman or not (since he was told the story in general terms by his father and other relatives.) but presumably, the young Jose beltran changed his disguised identity as the boat sailed from Barcelona and arrived in Cuba as part of a contingent of Spanish soldiers.

Somehow he made a career in the military and at the end of Cuba's last war for independence and liberation from Spain, he was in charge of the Spanish army's food supplies in Manzanillo, where Michael's father was born. During the terrible times of the concentration camps (imposed by the most hated Spanish general in Cuba – Major General Valeriano Weyler), Don Jose Beltran, at risk of court martial, was instrumental in passing food into the inhuman concentration camps to surreptitiously feed the starving Cuban families of the Mambises – who were in the fields fighting against Spain. When the war ended in 1898, (after American intervention in a war that became known as the Spanish-American War), the triumphant Mambises left Don Jose in charge of the supplies as a civilian. He was respected by all; he was by then married with four children, of whom the eldest was Michael's father.

Michael had grown up during Batista's military takeover, after the Machado regime had been overthrown. He had, with all the factors included, developed an aversion to anything military and in any association that had anything to do with guns and dictatorships (let alone seeing what was happening during his high school years – when guns, in the hands of gangsters disguised as idealist reformers, were being used in assassinations all over Havana).

back in town, he met his cousin Lazaro and told him of his experience in the meeting and his confronting Castro and his gun-carrying friends earlier that night. Lazaro adjusted his heavy prescription glasses against his forehead (as was his custom), and very quietly motioned him to move towards the next corner, away from other friends who could otherwise hear their conversation. Although a year younger, his cousin who was not into athletics as Michael, was however a very strong young man with long strong hands; he probably developed his body from working with his older brothers and father dismounting heavy steel beams from the two large, old cranes. "Los Aparatos", as the old derricks were known in the town, had been idle for more than, ten years. It was a demolition job that Lazaro and his brothers did, lasting for almost two years and finished by the end of the 1940th.

Again, nervously with his large right hand pushing back his glasses into place, Lazaro said: "Michael, you have to be careful. many of these guys are always carrying a loaded semi-automatic gun which they are quick to use at any time, at the service of any group they may belong to at the time, and against anyone who would get in the middle of their agenda, whichever it may be. The guy with the heavy dark glasses whom some students nicknamed Espejuelon, besides being a delegate of his class at the university, had aspirations to become the secretary of the FEU Student's Federation. There is a rumor that he belongs to the Underground Socialist Youth which is now under the control of Masferrer whom you know is among the gangsters."

"Yes, I know. He is the head of the MSR. I am surprised to think that Fidel Castro is involved with any gang."

"Don't be silly Michael. Anyone with high political ambitions in the university would have to belong either to the MSR or the UIR, and Castro is no exception. I thought he was more a member of the UIR (Union Insurreccional Universitaria) which is the group of Manolo Castro, the president of the student federation. It is the group founded by Emilio Tro, an ex-U.S. marine from the Second World War. both groups are one way or another involved in many turf disputes for government graft and are, notoriously or not, involved in extortions and gangster struggles – as much as in their apparent ideological affiliations and in the insurrectional and revolutionary ventures that their organization's name suggests."

Hewas impressed as he realized how much his cousin seemed to know and interrupted him to say: "Then Castro may not be the idealistic and patriotic type he tried to project in his speeches."

"No," said Lazaro. "Everybody in my school thinks that he is a truly sincere leader interested in denouncing all kind of corruption in the government. And I think that it may be true."

"Yes, so do I,. Just like most of the idealistic students in my school are. But, why the apparent association with one of the worst gangsters?"

"Well, it may be because he is trying to become a closer friend to Alfredo Guevara, 'El Espejuelon,' who is a communist, with an affiliation to the Socialist Youth, which enjoys the protection of Masferrer. In this way, he assures his survival. Whatever it may be, you have to be careful when you antagonize any of these people. One way is to be idealistic, in the efforts to create a better democratic society that you surely want, and another is to be a fool and not see the danger of being like an outsider with no known affiliation other than your principles which, I am sorry to say, won't count as much when it comes to deal with a situation where if you are not ready to become a criminal you may end up becoming an innocent victim."

"I wonder if that is the situation that Fidel Castro has been faced with, in which case, since he is still alive, one can surmise what his choice had been. In any case, I am glad that you are so well-informed, cousin."

"Actually I got all this information from some friend whom I would not want to mention and who is on my class. He is rather intelligent and involved in the political scene at the school; besides, his brother happens to be one of the guys that like to carry a gun, although he is mostly interested in illegal gambling. He is a sort of small banker and deals with many of the guys involved in what you could call gun trade."

"Well, good, I was beginning to wonder about your expertise in all of this, when you have only been in school less than a year."

"Yes, but remember, I am not like you. You are always running between two schools and your swimming lessons and you don't stop in any way to look much around you. All you know to do is to keep busy as usual and not allow yourself time to find out about these type of things."

"Well, that is why I have such a smart cousin. Don't you think?" Michael said jokingly as he pulled the heavy, thick glasses out from his cousin's face. They both laughed and headed home.

When they parted to go in different directions, Lazaro said: "I will be there at your school tomorrow. I hope nothing happens and that Civic Action wins. You will make a good delegate."

"I hope so, good night."

He and his cousin met again the next evening by the tall gate behind the main school building and the shops – a massive, high-ceilinged structure behind the main three-floor graystone section that housed the administration and the classrooms. Michael had been inside, voting in the afternoon and working all day to promote the "Accion Civica" candidacy. but as the vote count started, he was already outside the building. It was already dark, about 8.30pm, when they met. Lazaro pulled him aside for a moment and casually signaled to a group of five or six people around a tall, very heavyset man saying: "That big guy is Reinoldo. He is one of the guys who had come with Maso' and his people from the institute."

Michael looked at the group that was standing near one of the trees at the corner of the small plaza across the side street and saw the little guy, Regueira, next to Maso' and the big fellow Reinoldo. He then said: "Yes, I see them. Who is that other dark-haired stocky guy?"

"That is Porto, I think. He is connected with people in the Ministry of Education since he is always getting special favors, like last month's free bus tour to Varadero beach."

"Yes, I remember the tour, but I decided not to go on the last minute after waiting for the bus to leave for more than an hour. It seemed to me that the whole thing was badly organized."

"He was the one who kept the bus humming. He is a bit crazy."

"Yes, I remember. He was sitting in the middle of the bus making all the noises with the drums. But, I can't seem to recognize him in the dark at this distance."

"Well, I am sure they are all armed with handguns."

The group of students outside the gate kept growing in number, occupying the small plaza.

They returned to the gate and were looking at the well-illuminated open corridors adjacent to the patio, noticing that there were a good number of people moving back and forth. Suddenly, Michael saw a few of them running towards the gate yelling . . . "We have won, we have won! but they want a recount . . . they want to steal the elections!"

A tall black man whom Michael did not know stood halfway over the gate screaming: "They want to dispute the results . . . It is inadmissible! We have to seize and protect the ballots. Come inside, come inside all students. Let's all come together and guard the urns and protest this violation."

The gate did not open in spite of the pressure everyone outside was pushing against it, at which point, someone yelled: "Let's go inside from the door behind the shop building."

Lazaro and Michael ran towards the back. Maso', Regueira, and Reinoldo, were already there guns in hand. The large and heavy Reinoldo stepped back fifteen or twenty feet and ran, throwing his entire body against the wide door knocking it down flat. Michael and Lazaro followed towards the door and ran over it as Maso', who was standing on it, lifting his gun up in the air yelled: "Those with guns follow me."

No sooner than he and his cousin were inside the dark area, then shots started to sound loudly. The shooting had begun. He could see the flashing sparks of the gunfire in the dark and stopped to hear Lazaro yell loudly: "Hey, we don't have guns."

"You are right, this is crazy. Let's get out of here." The gunshots sounded like it was inside a dark box where thunder and lightning were being wildly unleashed.

Neither one of them could see where they were going, as the lights had suddenly gone off in the place and all they could see were the flashes made by the guns as it fired. They decided to run back and rushed over the large fallen door as the shooting continued inside.

"This is insane. This is insane." Michael kept repeating as they both ran back towards the gate.

He got to the gate ahead of his cousin. by then, most students had ran away and in a flash, he saw the dark-haired stocky man yielding a frightening large pistol from under his wide-open dark blue shirt while encroaching on the left side of the gate. The man immediately began to shoot straight towards where he could see people running in all directions by the unprotected corridors. He impulsively grabbed the gunman by his shoulders as he yelled: "Stop! Stop! Are you mad or what?" Two more shots sounded loudly in Michael's ears as he felt two strong hands pulling him back violently and away from the frantic gunman, unto the ground. It was Lazaro, screaming at him: "Let's get out of here primo."

"This is crazy!" Michael kept yelling. "This is no way to win an election."

The police sirens started to sound closer, presumably already nearby. The shots still sounded inside the school. He noticed the mad gunman already running away from the gate. His cousin pulled him away, with a strong grasp on his belt and shirt yelling: "Let's get out of here! . . . Let's get out of here!"

Soon they were running away along the already deserted back streets. They ran until they could run no more. Exhausted, they sat on a dark sidewalk breathing heavily. Michael still repeated with a saddened voice: "This is crazy. This is crazy. The shots had already stopped but the sound of ambulances and police cars could still be heard at the distance. Michael, with his arms falling at the side of his body, felt completely demoralized. His cousin, without saying anything for a moment, put his hands on his shoulders. After a long while, he said: "I told you that there would be a problem. I knew it when I saw all these people with concealed guns standing there. That guy could have shot you with that frightening German "Parabelum" he had. You know, he would not have stopped at anything. He is absolutely crazy."

"Yes, this is madness." Michael responded as he looked at the pavement with his forehead resting on his arms, and both of his elbows resting over his knees.

The two young students took the ten o'clock night bus to Regla. As they sat next to each other on the almost empty bus, Michael was still tensed and repeated again and again: "What a disaster! I can't believe that this had to happen!. I am sure that many people got hurt. I think I saw the school principal with his usual dark blue suit moving around the people who were running on the outside corridor in the midst of the turmoil at the same time that the crazy guy was shooting his heavy gun in that direction."

In his young, seventeen years of life he had never been exposed to any experience such as the one they had just witnessed. He could not make sense of what had taken place that night. He was angry and frustrated. As much as he wanted to understand it he could not, and he didn't think that he would ever do.

The press the next day gave an account of the events: as shoot-out in an election dispute. The school principal was seriously injured by a bullet to his stomach. The incumbent president of the school's Student Association had a bullet wound in one of his legs. Other four or five students resulted with minor injuries; one of them had a broken leg when he jumped from one of the windows to escape the shooting. Classes were suspended for three months while an investigation of the incident was going on. The election results were cancelled and "Accion Civica" filed complaints about irregularities by the incumbency. It was eventually more than a year later before things went back to normal.

Fortunately during the investigations, the school principal had recuperated and returned to school, determined to hear all the complaints the serious students had against the abusive teachers and the lack of appropriate texts. The following term, the students saw a correction of many of the problems. The school administration facilitated the mimeographed prints of every subject and made it mandatory for every professor to prepare clear texts and use specific reference books related to their subject matters. Every test had to be inclusive and supported by materials properly identified by and Imparted to the students and none which was outside the established programs. The change made a lot of difference but by the time Michael returned to his classes and until he finished and later received his license and certification, he was not already involved with school politics. His efforts and concentration were directed towards his graduation. Oddly enough, he never saw Valdes any more. It was like he had completely disappeared. About a year or so later his cousin told him that Valdes Munoz was eventually assassinated presumably by some unidentified gunman with multiple gun shots while he was sitting somewhere inside the Institute of Secondary Education. This news however came to Michael long after he has left the school and years after the shooting of that traumatic election night.

It was sad to see the most nefarious results of the gang's activities. The sporadic violence among gangsters continued, as well as the university protests. Michael continued to go to the rallies at the university, especially those that were directed at eradicating corruption in government. While he disliked the gangsters and any extremist groups trying to influence the student's movements, he still considered the need for the students to be very visible in their criticism and denunciation of corrupt politicians.

Protest for the increase in bus fares was taking place. The government-controlled cooperatives were substituting the old buses with new English Lakeland buses. They were beautiful vehicles painted in white. In the process, many old buses were also painted white but it did not offer the comfort of the new ones. Yet, the fares still went up regardless. Michael didn't like the fact that the clean, comfortable and beautiful trolley cars were also being taken out of service. There was something romantic about them and he refused to see the end of them. For him, it was not just because his maternal grandfather had been a trolley car conductor, but most of all because he enjoyed riding on the trolley, regardless. There was something about a ride on a trolley car that was irresistible to him and there was much that, in his view, a trolley car did for beauty in a city like Havana, especially when it would come down the narrow streets of Old Havana sounding its familiar bell; or when it turned in front of Muelle de Luz and went up the elevated short passage overlooking the bay and the docks.

There was also the excitement when, on school initiation day, the sophomores would take the freshman students out of the school, trim their hair down to "Zero", make them hang their shoes from their necks with their tied-up shoestrings, and give them a tour of the city on a trolley car at full speed, with the constant sounding of the bell. The excitement became hilarious with the throwing of small bags of white flour to make the hazing more dramatic and comical. The sudden crowding of the car was so overwhelming that the conductor had to abandon it to the students, who somehow "gently" aborted him from it. In his freshman year, he was able to pass as a sophomore and avoided the rap, perhaps because his body was already more developed than the average freshman. His constant training as a swimmer had something to do with it. He was able to escape the hair trimming, and had lots of fun on the ride. His conscience didn't allow him to do it again when he actually became a sophomore the following year.

Another good memory about the trolleys was when he and his fellow student town mates on going back home, would ask for more than one transfer (to somewhere where the car was most crowded) as they approached the docks. They would usually come out with at least one extra transfer each, which they were able to sell to the stevedores who needed to ride on the famous *lanchita* back to town. On most Fridays of the week, the youngsters would still end up with the nickel that he had since Monday (for his daily transportation fare, to and from school). Those were the days! No doubt the students loved the conductors as much as their trolley cars.

That day, the students decided to hijack the old painted buses they called "Las bien pinta's'" back to the university grounds. Michael was on intensive training for the most important swimming competition scheduled for that year, so he did not participate. The students took a number of buses back to campus in protest for the fare increases but there was great confusion, and of course, police intervention as well as some shooting. When Michael and his cousin met that night, Michael, with the evening newspaper on hand said: "Hey, did you see this?" pointing his finger to the photo on the first page. " . . . This fellow jumping on the bus is you, isn't it?"

His cousin said: "Let me see . . . Oh yes, that is me. I didn't know that I was being photographed."

"Well, there you go. Anyone can identify you with those heavy glasses of yours," he said laughing.

Lazaro was amused to see his picture in the newspaper, and started to tell his cousin how it all happened. The protest only had a psychological effect because the increases were implemented anyway and the old "bien pinta's" were taken out of service within a relatively short time after.

Protests for one reason or another continued and in an act of defiance to the government, in November of 1947 the FEU managed to bring from Manzanillo to Havana the bell from La Demajagua sugar mill (which was a symbol of freedom, as it was the bell that was rang on the 1868 uprising against domination from Spain). The uprising had been led by Carlos Manuel de Cespedes, who, like George Washington in America, later became known in the history of Cuba as the "Father of the Country". The students were protesting the corruption at the Ministry of Education of the government of Grau San Martin. There was a great deal of publicity about the arrival of the bell to the main train station in Havana. A great expectation from the students brought a large crowd to the station. A caravan of cars was formed to accompany the bell to the university.

Lazaro and Michael were there and managed to ride on the rear bumper of the first convertible car, rolling just behind the leading convertible that carried the bell. The FEU leaders riding on the open car supervised the custody of the famous bell. Most visible were Fidel Castro and his invariably close companion in those days, Alfredo Guevara. The others Michael could not identify, as he did not know them. It was a proud day for the students and Michael did not think about gangsters and shooting. It was for him a day in which the students could celebrate freedom; the freedom to openly criticize the government without fear of reprisals. A freedom of expression that in spite of all the ills of a young republic was still possible.

The pace of violent events and assassinations accelerated all throughout 1947 and '48. A police lieutenant was shot dead, and a few weeks later the student leader Maso and his lieutenant, Regueira, were found dead with close-range shots to their faces at a park near the Almendares river. Their picture in the front page of the newspapers was a grim reminder of the sad conditions that gangsters brought to the nation.

At some point, in late 1947, the Masferrer gang, with financial help from some elements in the Cuban government, had managed to organize an invasion to the Dominican Republic with the intention to oust the thirty-long-year dictatorship of Leonidas Trujillo. On the last minute when the invaders were ready to leave Cayo Confites (a key located north of the province of Camaguey). The Cuban government averted the invasion. There were rumors among the students that Masferrer's MSR group was for this occasion allied with their traditional enemies the UIR organization under Emilio Tro. The FEU leader Manolo Castro was known to belong to UIR. The rumors were that Fidel Castro was also doing a balancing act between the two gangs and that he was also in Cayo Confites, at the time. It was known that at the break of the agreement between the two gangs, his life was in danger. He managed to escape from the boat before they could find him.

Shortly after the incident, Emilio Tro and a number of his men were killed in a shoot-out that lasted a few hours in a house surrounded by notorious gangsters (apparently in conjunction with members of a special government force who gunned the gang and its leader since the event was filmed by Guayo, a cameraman, who became famous for his report of the shooting). The entire country was exposed to the crude and graphic depictions of the killings as it actually happened.

Early in February of the next year, the ex-president of the University Student's Federation (FEU), Manolo Castro, who by then was the Sports Minister in the government of Dr. Grau San Martin, was shot to death outside a theater in the suburbs of Havana. There were rumors that Fidel Castro had been involved, since a member of the group that he controlled as captain was captured by the police with a recently fired gun, but Castro was apparently able to get an alibi. Other comments among the students were that, both Fidel and Manolo Castro (who were not related) were somehow at odds with each other and were most likely caught in the midst of the power play Between the two gangs. Fidel Castro, with his political ambitions, was so enmeshed with the gangs that he always feared for his own life. For a number of weeks Fidel Castro disappeared from the university scenario to surface again in Colombia where he went to attend a Student's Congress, again in the company of the ever-present shadow of Alfredo Guevara (with his gangster-style large, dark eyeglasses), who had been elected secretary of the FEU at the time.

Argentina's president Domingo Peron had sponsored the ill-fated Congress in Colombia. The "Peronists" were trying to promote their nationalist ideology and gain influence throughout Latin America. both the Communists and the "Peronists" appeared to have, at that time, some common political interest against what they called the so-called Imperialism. Just before the congress convened, the Colombian socialist leader, Gaitian, was killed. The uproar created by the assassination caused an uprising, which was known later as "El bogotazo". It is said that more than 3,000 people lost their life during the bloody events. The Cuban FEU representatives were caught or were part of the ensuing skirmishes of the uprising and in some way actively participated in the shootings. Somehow and without much of a clear evidence of what they did they were able to come out alive and return to Cuba.

The killings among the gangs continued to be a sad and awesome design in Cuba from the mid – to late 'forties. Corruption had its high price. The country's law-abiding people were tired of the corruption and the bloodshed and freedom was in danger. The political scenario was heated. Ramon Grau San Martin finally desisted in his intentions to run for a second term and his "Partido Revolucionario Cubano-Autentico" was able to have Dr. Carlos Prio Socarras elected to the presidency in the 1948 elections. Corruption appeared to continue amidst the prosperity of the early 'fifties, but the elections scheduled for the second year of the decade never took place. Eddy Chivas, a popular candidate for the presidency in a new "orthodox" party offered the promise of rescuing the principles of the party founded by José Martí during the War of Independence and which had also inspired the generation that ousted Machado nineteen years earlier. Chivas, had emerged as a strong presidential candidate for the forthcoming elections of 1952. He, who had vigorously proclaimed the need for honesty in government and who had proposed to put an end to corruption, ended up shooting himself when giving a speech in a radio station when he could not offer proof of his denunciations of corruption against one of the government ministers.

Fidel Castro who somehow had managed to survive the years of violence as an activist in the University was, since the early fifties, actively seeking a candidacy for a seat in the Chamber of Representatives and he saw the opportunity in the "orthodox" party. He had already graduated from law school and was seen as being close to the leader of the party. (So much that he was standing behind the party leader at the time of his last broadcast and suicide.)

The death of Eddy Chivas, the leader of "Partido Ortodoxo", not only left a leadership vacuum in the party but also in the aspirations of the Cuban people to have an election that would not only represent the consolidation of the democratic principles, but also the opportunity for a new beginning in the pursuit of progress and to eventually put an end to the shameful corruption in government.

A prestigious university professor, Dr. Roberto Agramonte took charge of the party leadership and proceeded to announce his candidates, leaving the name of Fidel Castro out of the list of selected candidates. The reason was later said to be because of the notorious involvement that Castro had had with the gangs in the university, but the elections never took place. Fulgencio Batista, who had recently returned to Cuba saying that he was to be a candidate in the elections, organized a coup with the help of his old army friends and ousted President Carlos Prio Socarras in the early hours of March 10 of the same year just a few months prior to election day; thus frustrating the legitimate aspirations of the Cuban people.

Castro, who was also frustrated for not having been accepted as a candidate, saw the military takeover as the greatest opportunity to foment an underground revolutionary movement to oust batista.

The rest is history – the attack he launched against Cuartel Moncada in Oriente the following year which resulted in the death of more than a dozen government soldiers and almost as many of the attackers who were allegedly captured alive then killed gave name to Castro's "Movimiento Revolucionario 26 de Julio". Castro and his brother were made prisoners, and Castro escaped death again when Batista pardoned him and his brother Raul eighteen months later and both marched into exile to organize their landing in the Oriente province a short few years later. All of these events and the silent conspiracies since the mid-'forties were just the prelude of the worst yet to come to the suffering Cuban people.

''Scared Intruders'''
Oil oncanvas 48<36 inches1981
Newark Museum –Third Biennial Selection 1981-82
Private Collection

''El Callejon del Sapo''
(The Forbidden Path)
Oil on Canvas 66x5r0 inches - 1988

Oil on canvas 48x36 inches-1982
Museum of Art of the Americas Collection,
Washington DC.

Reproduction of childhood memory
drawing of author with
Eloy Sardiñas Eloicito(Arial)

María Antonia Marrero Albelo

Miguel Beltran Gonzalez
Circa 1920
Mother and father of Michael and Elio Beltran

"Midday in Guanabacoa"
Oil on Canvas 28x36 inches - 1987
Editorial America Collection. Miami, Florida

"LaColína de los Sueños"
Author's Oil on canvas 24x36 inches – 1987
Private collection

Vestibule of Havana University
A view from the inside of the student's hall at the top of ''La Escalinata
Universitaria'''
Ovelooking buildings of St. Lazaro Street

Author's Memory oil of San Lazaro Street across la Escalinata

*Armed police during a student demonstration and unrest at the
Escalinata. (Year 1947)

"The Dangerous Wave"
Oil on canvas 20x24 inches- 1994 (FIU Collection)

CHAPTER EIGHT

Untold Stories Around Guerrilla Warfare

The majority of the Cuban people became extremely unhappy about the interruption of the democratic process when Batista seized power in 1952. The fifties as a whole ended up being prosperous years. A prosperity that had started prior to the takeover and continued regardless of the circumstances surrounding the unfortunate political situation. Opposition was mounted openly by the political parties as well as the underground, culminating on the presence of armed guerrillas in Oriente province and the departure of Batista in the early hours of January 1,1959. Altogether, the country was still suffering from the ills that characterize practically every government since the beginning of the Republic, In spite of it, Cuba was progressing on its labor laws and its constitution, which was reformed and finally instituted in 1940, became a model for Latin American republics. There was still, however, a segment of the population that depended on the sugar industry (for those who were not able to have year-round jobs); there were also segments of unemployment, but never a total abject poverty. Cubans were always hard workers and enterprising people and there were a lot of self-employed people who were able to make a living. There was much more to be done to develop the country to more widespread prosperity, regardless of who was in power. As a result, there was a constant desire by the Cuban people to improve their conditions; but the majority wanted it to be within the frame of democracy and not under a dictatorship.

At the end of the 'forties Michael had completed his specialization courses but left his final exams (for his certification and license) lapse for a few more years while he continued to study at night in the English Language Center. It was precisely his proficiency in English that helped him to start a career with Royal Dutch Shell Oil Co. in Havana in 1949. Having started as an apprentice in the office, he soon became the assistant engineer for light fuels and soon afterwards regional manager for operations, distribution and sales. He married three years after he started on his job, in spite of his brother's discontent because he thought he was too young at the time. His mother was also not convinced that it was the best thing for him to do at so early in his life, but she felt contented as long as she saw him happy. She knew that he wanted to have a family of his own early in his life.

He had met Margarita Rivero Ruiz when he was nineteen. She had the poise of a distant and elegant young lady, with an air of quietness about her at the time, which he liked. Her deceased father was an engineer, as his own father was, and the similarities on this aspect seemed to fit perfectly, besides his being extremely attracted to her mere presence, both families were of modest means, and they both had hardworking parents; her forty-seven-year-old mother, already a widow, was a woman with a challenging and suspicious sense of humor. A good woman who proclaimed the virtues of staying single for the last six years and did not consider marrying again at all. The first reason for it that she always talked about was: to take care of her two teenaged daughters and ten-year-old son, and the second reason was because she believed that men were not worth the trouble; in her mind they were all not trustworthy. The fact is that, the harsh opinions sharply contrasted with accounts of her late husband being a good man whom the daughters revered in the highest degree.

Michael understood otherwise the good lady's personality and occasionally enjoyed her sense of humor. She had told Michael many to make a living. There was much more to be done to develop the country to more widespread prosperity, regardless of who was in power. As a result, there was a constant desire by the Cuban people to improve their conditions; but the majority wanted it to be within the frame of democracy and not under a dictatorship.

At the end of the 'forties Michael had completed his specialization courses but left his final exams (for his certification and license) lapse for a few more years while he continued to study at night in the English Language Center. It was precisely his proficiency in English that helped him to start a career with Royal Dutch Shell Oil Co. in Havana in 1949. Having started as an apprentice in the office, he soon became the assistant engineer for light fuels and soon afterwards regional manager for operations, distribution and sales. He married three years after he started on his job, in spite of his brother's discontent because he thought he was too young at the time. His mother was also not convinced that it was the best thing for him to do at so early in his life, but she felt contented as long as she saw him happy. She knew that he wanted to have a family of his own early in his life.

He had met Margarita Rivero Ruiz when he was nineteen. She had the poise of a distant and elegant young woman with an air of quietness about her at the time, which he liked. Her deceased father was an engineer, as his own father was, and the similarities on this aspect seemed to fit perfectly, besides his being extremely attracted to her mere presence, . both families were of modest means and they both had hardworking parents. Her forty-seven-year-old mother, already a widow, was a woman with a challenging and suspicious sense of humor. A good woman who proclaimed the virtues of staying single for the last six years and did not consider marrying again at all. The first reason for it that she always talked about was: to take care of her two teenaged daughters and ten-year-old son, and the second reason was because she believed that men were not worth the trouble; in her mind they were all not trustworthy. The fact is that, the harsh opinions sharply contrasted with accounts of her late husband being a good man whom the daughters revered in the highest degree.

Michael understood otherwise the good lady's personality and occasionally enjoyed her sense of humor. She had told Michael many times that he would make a mistake in marrying her daughter. She gave a number of reasons for her saying it, but he didn't take his future mother-in-law seriously and was happy to marry her daughter, after two years of the usual Cuban-style chaperoned courtship. His young wife detested her mother's style and there were many situations in which her mother and younger brother's attitude created unhappiness and stress in the couple's relationship. In the long term, some of the worst characteristics would come to haunt his wife and exert a negative influence in the way she looked at life as a whole. Michael, on the other hand, usually had a positive and optimistic attitude. He was delighted to be the father of two loving daughters and happy to have formed a beautiful family; he was also determined to make his marriage work. by the mid-'fifties he was transferred from Havana to Camaguey so that from this attractive, colonial, and provincial capital he could be closer to the region that he was responsible for. Having set up their home away and totally independent from any kind of family stress, they made the struggle for happiness possible and also to bring up the children in perfect harmony as could possibly be.

He worked very hard setting up the distributorship and traveled all the roads in Cuba during the entire 1950s. The process of the anti-batista sentiments was progressively developing within the same time frame. While not everyone was conspiring to overthrow Batista, the majority of the new generation, of which he was one, as well as older people who believed in democratic principles, were in favor of changing the situation. He always disliked military intrusions in government and wanted to see a truly democratic government in power. During all those years he was able to support, in one way or another, the efforts of the opposition, mostly the movements of the university students with their "Directorio Estudiantil Universitario" which represented opposition within the inner cities. by then, Fidel Castro was conducting his armed hit-and-run guerrilla warfare in the mountains of the Oriente province.

After 1957, the opposition intensified and Batista's army was not making any progress against the rebels, neither did the great deal of propaganda that was slowly eroding Batista's hold on power. In desperation, he hired the services of Rolando Masferrer who organized a group of armed street militia called the "Masferrer Tigers". This action infuriated the people more as it meant more repression on the streets of the cities. (This one-time gangster was once leader of the MSR whom Castro had an interlude with during some of the university years.) A time when Castro was apparently able to save his head by maneuvering between the two major gangs until Masferrer planned to eliminate him once a truce between the gangs (during the Cayo Confites affair) ended. In any case, paradoxically enough, the mercenary's gang returned to the scene of the action, this time to help batista.

During those years, Michael traveled all the time by car between the cities of Camaguey and Santiago de Cuba where most of the war's activity was taking place. He also traveled to and from Havana with great frequency. On of these times, during a promotion for a gas additive called "Ignition Control Additive" (ICA) – a promotion his Royal Dutch employer called "Shell con ICA" – Michael was assigned the mission of bringing four recently hired young graduates from Havana, dropping each one of them in a every major provincial capital cities along the way from Havana to Santiago de Cuba.

Everyone had their suitcases placed in the trunk of his car. The one man designated to go all the way to Santiago had hidden in his suitcase what looked like a shoe box. The shoe box contained a good number of " "Directorio Estudiantil" bonds intended to raise money for the cause of the revolution, as well as some printed anti-government propaganda, folded under a flexible pair of shoes, he knew that one of the other three men also had activities in the underground and he knew that given the circumstances, it was going to be a dangerous trip indeed.

All that he had was his ID as a regional manager for the oil company which, in case of strict surveillance, served as a sort of *salvo-conducto*. The atmosphere on every city they crossed was extremely tense, with many guards of the army patrolling the streets. but it was in Camaguey that he saw at a distance the infamous "Tigers" dressed in civilian clothes and armed to the teeth. Michael knew the very narrow streets of Camaguey very well and decided to take the route that he thought would possibly be without surveillance (as they continued to enter the city just at the edge of nightfall). According to the normal plan, he would have to drop the last two men riding with him to spend the night at the Grand Hotel in the center of the city, and then go to spend the night with his family in his home (located in a quiet suburban area in the northern part of the city where he used to live at the time). but soon, he noted that at every attempt to approach the hotel area, he could see that armed men were searching every vehicle, so he would turn fast away from the street and look for another alternative access. There were not many alternatives since every one of the streets approaching the center was being practically blocked by the guards. As Michael pulled away (backing up fast to turn behind a sharp corner and get away), one of the guards signaled him to stop. Ignoring the signal, he speeded backwards, positioning his car to escape, making a loud shrieking noise with his tires. At the same time, he could hear the guard's voice yelling: "Stop! Stop!" He saw him lift his gun, pointing straight to his head. The three men heard two shots being fired as they speeded away through a much narrower Colonial time cobble-stoned street. His car trotted jumpily but at full speed over the rough pavement. As he put a large distance away from them, they heard the siren of the military police sounding in the already dark night. Fortunately for them, everything happened so fast that there was not a chance that their car could be properly identified, given the distance and the darkness, or at least so he hoped.

"Don't worry, guys, we will go to my house and make arrangements for you to sleep there." Michael told one of his companions after the two of them had lifted their heads from the floor of the car where they had suddenly dropped at the sound of the shots.

On the second day, only he and the last one of his companions were driving very early in the morning, speeding towards the oriental capital, Santiago de Cuba; luckily, they passed without any difficulty any of the checkpoints coming in and out of Camaguey and the cities on the route passing Victoria de las Tunas, Holguin and bayamo. but after the last town before reaching Santiago (when they had barely driven for four miles), they saw a few soldiers on the road and had to slow down; enough to see the bodies of two dead men dressed plainly and lying next to the fence of a small sugar cane plantation only about five yards from the road they were driving on.

The sight was enough to make the two men shiver. There was no way to tell if the dead men were rebels, underground people, or just innocent peasants. Yet more worrisome was the thought that they may have been young people like themselves being caught in the dangerous web by which the whole area, and the country for that matter, had been entangled in at such an uncertain time (considering all the contending factors and lack of guaranties created by the unrest, and most of all the introduction of civil-clothed militia where it was apparent that any one of the factions had a license to kill randomly if they wanted to).

As the two men came driving downhill into the city of Santiago de Cuba, it looked like they were coming to a state of siege where the major players were the infamous Masferrer "Tigers" dressed as usual in civilian clothes and carrying automatic machine guns. They were very visible and ruthless, ordering every vehicle to stop crossing the main streets of the city, and appearing in the most unexpected places in groups of three or four, heavily armed.

When Michael noticed that they would be asked to stop crossing (which was the street closer to the hotel they were coming to), he told his companion, who still had the anti-batista propaganda hidden in the trunk of his car: "Just be very quiet and let me do all the talking."

One of the three armed civilians came to the driver's side and pressed the point of his machine gun hard under Michael's left clavicle and asked rudely: "What are you two doing here?" Michael with his documents in his left hand, calmly extended them towards the man while at the same time grabbing the gun barrel of the man with his other hand, pushing it slowly away from over his shoulder as he said: "There is no need to point your gun at me, sir. We are just here to work . . . Do you want to search the car?" he asked as he extended his documents more towards the angle of vision of the man. The man made a signal to one of the other two men to follow Michael's car while he briefly looked at the documents. The man's eyes seemed to be looking in every direction as he signaled Michael to continue forward, which he did, not without feeling his right leg tremble as he softly pressed the gas pedal. He did not want to stay there overnight as he used to do when things were normal, so he just brought his companion to the Casa Granda Hotel, unloaded the compromising luggage, took the young man to the local office to meet the district manager – Señor Vicente Novoa (who was to run the company promotion of the new product in Santiago), had lunch with the two men and got out of town that afternoon.

The disquieting sight of the dead men by the roadside was still with him even after a few hours of having seen them. It was, no doubt, a time of great tensions. Any time that he drove at those roads he would hear occasional shooting near the cities, and particularly in areas near the mountains. Michael used to hear more and more close shots as he crossed the mountains coming in and out of Santiago de Cuba. Most of the time he thought that the shots came from the rebels hiding in the mountainside, possibly trying to scare drivers, create disruption from regular activities, and maintain the unrest, or worse yet dying or killing. being as it was, it was not a pleasant experience for him when he passed that way during the last year and a half before the end of the batista government, but this time, it signaled a prelude of worst things to come because he was seeing the bodies of people that had been obviously shot without any passerby being able to know the special circumstances surrounding their death, except for the prevailing conditions in that region.

Towards the middle part 1958, due to the rebels as well as the repression forces' activities on some of the main roads in the island, Michael would occasionally travel by air. In one of these occasions some disruptions happened with the air services to and from Havana and he decided go to the capital traveling by rail. The train was already about one hour on its way when he decided to take a walk towards the back, going from car to car. Much to his surprise, as he entered one of the low-fare passenger cars (which was not very crowded), he saw the familiar face of a tall and strong-built man whom he thought to be in his late fifties. The man was wearing a white polo shirt and his face looked as if he had gone for a week without having shaved; his strong neck and hands easily showed a rather dry and mildly wrinkled skin. Michael immediately recognized him as one of his favorite movie actors from his early youth. The man was none other than Errol Flynn, traveling on that wagon, occupying a seat on the long bench that stretched alongside the windows amidst other common passengers. Michael was thrilled to have found him traveling on the same train that day and could not avoid going towards the famous actor and asking: "... You are Errol Flynn, aren't you?"

"I am glad you didn't ask if I was Robin Hood," the man said. "Just as well, I like him too" Michael said, smiling as he extended his right hand. " . . . I am so surprised and happy to have met one my favorite Hollywood stars. My name is Michael."

Flynn stretched his broad right hand for a spontaneous handshake. Michael felt the strength of the hand and the dryness of the skin. He could not help but think that the actor's notorious heavy drinking had something to do with his hand's dry condition. There were rumors in Cuba about the drinking habits of Flynn and Hemingway. He remembered a similar impression he had with the famous author of *For Whom the Bell Tolls* and *The Old Man and the Sea* whom he had once seen fishing in the village of Cojimar, where Michael used to go frequently during his teenage years.

"I hope you are enjoying your visit to Cuba, Mr. Flynn . . . Are you working on a new movie?"

"Not really. I just like Cuba and enjoy being among the people. And I like to travel by rail from city to city. We are getting off in Santa Clara in a few minutes," he said as he looked at his woman companion who was sitting on his right. Michael acknowledged the petite, middle-aged brunette who was dressed very casually and who sat very silent and quietly next to the actor. She nodded but stayed quiet as if she was traveling alone, with a faraway look in her small eyes. Michael did not recognize who the lady could be. He heard the conductor announce their arrival in Santa Clara train station. He wished both of them well as he moved away and went to his car in amusement, thinking that somehow Flynn really had the adventurous nature he showed in his films and that perhaps he was traveling back from a visit to Oriente province where he would have been closer to the action that was being covered by the *New York Times*.

A few weeks after the interesting encounter, Michael visited his distributor in the city of Victoria de las Tunas. As he arrived at the establishment in the center of the city, his distributor brought him inside his small office and said, "You know Antonio, my mechanic's helper, don't you?"

"Yes, I know him. He is a good kid. What is the matter?"

"Well, it has been known to the authorities in town that he is involved with an underground group. His father has been advised that he better take the kid out of the city if he didn't want him getting in trouble or, worse yet, to be shot and killed."

"I have not seen him for a while now. I guess he is already out of town, no?" Michael finally asked.

"No, he isn't, and that is why I wanted to talk to you to see if you can help take him with you on your way to Santiago when you leave today and drop him in a village five kilometers from the entrance to Holguin."

"Well, don't you think that the guards will see him the moment we come to cross the checkpoint line when we get out of town?"

"Don't worry," he said, "it has all been agreed with by his father, me, and the military chief that will be covering the surveillance on that spot."

"How can you be so sure that we will not be met by the 'Tigers' and have a real problem?"

"Trust me." Alvarez said, looking him in the eye and pressing his left arm. "You know that I would not ask you to do this if I was not sure." Then he continued: " … Once you present your credentials and job order from me for Antonio, they will let you go through without questions."

Michael had known Jesus Alvarez for over six years since, when he had appointed the friendly and very trustworthy Spaniard as his agent and distributor in the area. Michael said: "I hope you are right. Where is he now? I should be leaving early enough to get to Santiago in daylight."

"Don't I know your routine when you visit here or what? I have been ready since you called yesterday, telling me that you will be here and I have arranged everything beforehand."

"How could you be so sure that I would accept this crazy proposition?"

With his loud customary laughter, Alvarez said, "by now I should know that you have a good heart, no? … besides, I know you have a good angel riding with you since the day you told me the story of the time you came out of this town at great speed under a dense fog guiding yourself only with the lights of the truck, rushing fifty yards ahead when your instinct or whatever, . . may be your angel, told you to stop, and not until after you stopped, as if commanded by unknown mysterious forces did you get to see the two drunkards arm in arm as they zigzagged, like a suicidal, in front of your car."

"Well, I still won't try to tempt the devil, regardless." Michael said, adding, "It is fine, Jesus, I guess I will have to trust you and my good angel."

He was able to take Alberto out of town and drop him off before he entered the city of Holguin. As he drove away from the guards in the east side of the city, he could not help but think that in spite of the bad reputation of the people in power, there were still decent people who did not want to do harm to others for the sake of their government; or perhaps it was one of the virtues of a small city where everybody knew everybody else. In any case, he felt good that he did what he had to do for the young man.

During 1958, the situation got worse. Michael started to travel more by plane and had used chartered planes to transport bottled gas along with other necessities to the various cities where normal traffic was no longer possible. The rebels' clandestine radio broadcasted a campaign against Shell Oil Co. because they said the company's president, Mr. Julio Iglesias de la Torre, helped Batista to get war jet planes and bombs from England. They called the campaign *Shell con Sangre,* meaning "Shell with blood" as a substitute to the company's promotional slogan "Shell con ICA".

The adverse campaign was hurting the company considerably, and Michael received a call from Silvio Salinas the cross-eyed manager who was one of the most controversial men in the company's headquarters and with whom Michael had had some confrontations (due to the sharp-shooter *Señor* Salinas interfering with his handling of a troublesome large distributor). The distributor was then trying to abuse his influence on the manipulative administrator by trying to do what he pleased against what Michael considered his company's "best interests". When he answered the call, Salinas said, "We will have a meeting of regional managers here tomorrow. Don't talk to Anyone about the meeting. I can't tell you much about it by phone but it is important that you take the morning flight from Camaguey and be here." His voice, with its unusual tone, of it was like he was preoccupied with something that required strict privacy. That was not in the usual style of the man on the other side of the line who, for the most part, used to be crude and blatant while still keeping a somewhat sarcastic smile. Other than those characteristic traits, the "old man", as they called him, besides the other less appealing nicknames, was considered to be a very effective manager.

Michael flew to the capital the next morning and was picked up by the driver of the company in a Station Wagon. "This doesn't look normal," Michael thought when he saw the familiar face of the driver, particularly when he was the only one who arrived. He would have expected at least the manager from the central region arriving at the same time.

On arrival to the main office, the driver told him that he was asked to tell him to go straight to Salinas' office. He did go, and didn't have to wait since as the secretary saw him she announced his presence and he was rushed inside immediately. Salinas, who was alone in his office, greeted him with an unusual smile. Michael could not help but wonder what the most-of-the-time satirical man had in mind. They were both alone in the large office.

"Where are the other managers ?" he asked.

"There are no other people being called for this meeting. It is just you and me, alone."

Michael didn't like the fact that the man who was considered to be the most intriguing person in the company appeared to have something apparently mysterious which he wanted to have Michael involved. He was not wrong with his apprehensions, and soon he knew that his suspicions were right.

"You know about the negative campaign against our company, don't you?"

"Yes, of course."

"Well, I have a plan to see if we can stop it. And I know you can help with your contacts."

"What contacts?" Michael asked.

"Well, you pass through the areas near where the guerrillas are operating, and we thought that you could help us to make contact with Fidel Castro. I think that if I have a meeting with him we can convince him to drop off this negative campaign."

Michael noticed that Salinas was shifting too many times from "I have a plan" to "we have thought" and back again and he finally asked, "Who else knows about this plan? Does Julio know?"

"This is a high-level plan, of course," he answered, implying but not quite saying that their president, Julio Iglesias, knew about it. but he added, as if to give him some reassurance, "Julio is very worried about the situation and wants to stop it."

Michael owed much respect and esteem to Iglesias, not only for the way the man always greeted him in a fatherly gesture by putting his arms over his shoulders while they both walked down the halls coming into the office whenever they would meet upon entering the place (it happened from time to time, ever since he started as a very young office apprentice), but also because of the way Iglesias acted when he found out through his secretary that Michael's mother was seriously affected with colon cancer. Lelin, the secretary, had spoken to Iglesias about it and he called Michael to tell him that his brother Pachino was probably the best surgeon in the world who specialized in colon cancer. That same day, Julio Iglesias with Michael sitting in his plush office, called his brother by phone and immediately arranged for Michael's mother to visit the famous doctor without delay. Pachino operated on her successfully before the month had ended. Not only did she totally recuperate, but also able to leave for 25 more years after the operation that did not cost mother and son any money but only more of a deep gratitude to the two Iglesias brothers.

After being suggested by Salinas that Iglesias knew of the plan to have a conference with Fidel Castro in La Sierra, Michael, after a silent minute, said, "I think that I can do something about making the meeting possible but I can't say how until I talk with the people who I think could help with this. I do not want to compromise their right to privacy unless they approve of me giving you the right signals to come down for a meeting. I will call you within this week. Would you be able to travel to Oriente once I tell you the time and place for the meeting?"

"Yes, of course." The notorious, shrewish man answered.

"If that is the case, I will give you the date and place. You will probably need at least three to five days, and must travel immediately after the arrangements are made. I will call you and will talk to you myself about our scheduled regional visit to my distributors so as not have anyone eavesdrop and put the plan and ourselves in jeopardy."

The thin man, with his scarce, clean but unkempt white hair, who was about fifty-seven years old (but looked much older), winked his crossed eyes nervously and said without standing from his chair (as Michael got up to leave), said, "Fine, I knew we could count on you."

Michael returned the same day without seeing anyone else to avoid unnecessary speculation about his unexpected visit. On the airport, he made a reservation for the next day for a flight to Manzanillo, in Oriente province, from his home city of Camaguey. He then left the next morning.

Miguel Galiana, a tall, round-faced man with smart, small and friendly blue eyes, and who was his distributor in Manzanillo, was waiting for him at the airport. "What is happening?" He asked immediately. "This does not look like your usual visit."

"No, it is not. I will tell you in the car after we leave the airport." As Miguel Galiana drove away from the airport, Michael finally said: "I remember what you confided to me during our fishing trip down the southern keys two years ago about your farm near the edge of Sierra Maestra."

"I also remember it," Miguel Galiana interrupted. "…I remember how much you enjoyed the abundant fish and everything about the trip except the storm, on the night we sailed back."

"Yes, I know. I will never forget that the waves were so high during the storm that I could hardly see the light on the leading boat. It disappeared before my eyes every fifteen seconds. I thought that we were not going to make it, but thank God we did after four or five hours of battling the storm. Instead of being exhausted by the time we got back to port, I was so happy that I didn't feel it until the next day."

"What about the farm you wanted to talk about?"

"I will tell you what it is. I know from what you told me, that you and some other business people from town contribute to the rebels by supplying them some cows and foodstuff through the heavily wooded section of the mountains that is located very near your farm."

"What do you have in mind, Michael?"

"I wonder if the people you have contact with could arrange for a meeting with Fidel Castro."

Michael immediately went on to explain about the situation to his friend, just before they reached the office.

Miguel Galiana stopped the car momentarily along the roadside and looking directly into Michael's eyes with his penetrating, shining little eyes, said, "Michael, things are getting very difficult lately in this area. We should not talk about this in the office or anywhere else while you are here. I will need two or three days to see if this is possible. I will have to go to the farm personally and talk to some people with my confidence. If the meeting with Castro can be arranged, I will call you and tell you that we are ready for our distributor and sub-distributor's meeting at such a date. You and 'SS' will have to fly here by the day I will tell you, otherwise, it will not work. We will be waiting in farmer's clothes and straw hats, ready to go by jeep first and horseback later, if all goes well."

Michael and his distributor went to their usual business. He was ready to leave for the airport only to find out that the regular flights back to Camaguey had been cancelled. The uncertainty was growing by days, and it was something that was apparently happening with more frequency than usual. He did not want to stay overnight and during their wait at the airport, Michael noted two other businessmen who had the same problem so he went and talked to them. A few minutes later, the three of them were negotiating a flight with a pilot to see if there was any possibility of a charter plane to go back to Camaguey.

They were able to charter a single-engine propeller plane and flew back to Camaguey that same afternoon. Michael could never forget the sight of the largest river in Cuba. When the old and noisy plane was flying over the Cauto River, which is the largest river in Cuba, he saw how the impressive wide river (that his father had described to him so many times with stories from his childhood) was completely flooded, offering a magnificent but awesome view from the air. The heavy summer rains caused by a Caribbean depression had been hitting the area with more than the usual rain, causing the river to rise far beyond its usual boundaries. He took comfort in thinking that the flight cancellations were due to the weather and not to the guerrilla war, but took no comfort being on the small and low-altitude flying old plane, swinging sideways with sudden uncontrolled jitters as if dancing with the strong southeast winds, while the pilot tried to keep his north - western course.

The secret meeting took place close to three months before Batista's departure from power. The manipulative Salinas, in the end, did not let Michael come with him to the mountains, saying, "You look too young and you may put the plan in danger if they stop us. The soldiers will be suspicious if they see you."

"'SS' is right," Miguel Galiana said. " . . . You better take the same flight back to Camaguey."

Michael protested, but to no avail. Miguel pulled him aside and told him, "Let the old man go alone. He is right. besides, I think that it will be better for you not to be a part of this."

In later years, when Michael found out that Salinas had planned everything behind Julio Iglesias' back, he was glad he did not go to the meeting with Castro and would have become more involved with the shrewish old man's scheme.

The bigger surprise Silvio Salinas found at his arrival in Castro's headquarters in the mountain was that he was never allowed to see Castro personally but instead was met by the younger sales manager the company had, Enrique Oltuski, who had been secretly working on the underground all along and who had been summoned by Castro to meet his own boss at the Sierra, or perhaps he had just happened to be there on the sporadic visits he made to bring money collected for the rebels. but looking at it in retrospect, and knowing about Castro's ways now, the mishap had surely been arranged.

As it was, Salinas only came back with the thread that Fidel Castro handed him through Enrique Oltuski. And as it was, the message was that if Castro would catch Julio Iglesias de la Torre when he gets to Havana, he would mercilessly put Iglesias to a firing squad.

CHAPTER NINE

Turning Point

Finally on the early morning hours of January 1, 1959, the radio and TV stations broadcasted the news that Batista had left the country. It meant the triumph of the revolution.

Michael was in Camaguey at that time. The morning was filled with the joyful news. There was still some disbelief and uncertainty including one about the arrangements made by Batista to leave one of his army generals in charge of the transition.

by late afternoon, there were already rumors and expectations that the rebels had started to move from the mountains in Oriente province towards Camaguey and eventually onwards to Santa Clara where apparently some rebels commanded by Che Guevara had been active already. There were also rumors that the "Masferrer Tigers" were ready to prepare their resistance, barricading in the city's army headquarters which was south of Camaguey, approximately two miles from Michael's home in the northern section of the city near the main railroad station.

by evening, the streets were deserted with the exception of speeding cars as if no one wanted to stay on the streets. The next morning already brought news about army personnel in the barracks along the way, already disposing their arms to the advancing guerrillas. Castro apparently had not yet made his move as he stayed on the rear guard, presumably assuring himself of having absolute control along the way.

Camaguey was apparently quiet until the afternoon when shooting started to be heard sporadically, intensifying into the late evening hours. Michael had his two scared daughters go under the bed as machine gun fire was heard closer to the house.

before seven a.m. of the next morning, January 3, the loud sound of someone knocking violently, almost like hammering on the front door, made Michael wonder as to who could it be. The first thought was, of course, that it may be the civilian militia or perhaps the thugs associated with the nasty "Tigers" because the ominous sound could not be anything good. He left his frightened family in the most protected room of the house, away from the living room and as he tentatively looked out his front window, all he could see enveloped in the morning mist was a bearded man dressed in a rebel's olive green uniform and armed with a rifle as he screamed: *"Abran la puerta* (Open the door)."

"Wait a minute, wait a minute, I will open it," Michael shouted back.

He had come out of his initial apprehension, as he could not think of anything that would make him worry about the rebels.

As he opened the door, he found the bearded man standing tall in front of him with open arms and his rifle hanging on his back, loudly saying: "Don't you know who I am?"

As the thin young man embraced him, he could hear a familiar loud laughter coming from a man who just stepped out from behind one of the columns supporting the roof of the porch.

"You don't know your friends anymore, Michael."

Michael immediately recognized his Spanish friend and distributor, Jesus Alvarez, from Victoria de la Tunas.

"Aha! And you must be Alberto." Michael said as he turned to look again at the man he did not recognize and who looked exactly as if he had come straight from the mountains, with his worn-out rebel, army fatigues.

"My God! I would have never imagined that it would be you at my door today; come in, both of you." He said as he put his left arm on Jesus' shoulders and held the young soldier by his right arm, guiding both of them inside the house. "I will let my wife and daughters know that you are my friends. We will get some coffee and breakfast for you. You must be hungry after having traveled so early and without a place to eat, considering the situation ... I am glad to see you alive, Alberto." He added, "I see that you have joined the fight."

"Thanks to you." The young bearded man in his olive green fatigues answered. Taking his cap off, letting his long hair down, and smiling, he said: "I did go straight to the mountains and was there two days after you dropped me off near Holguin two years ago." Then he added with a broad smile: "Hah! You thought that the rebels came for you, no?"

"I did. Man, you look fearsome. You look like a real guerrilla fighter. You must have a lot of stories to tell, don't you?"

"Yes, but we really came for you," Alberto said, suddenly getting very serious.

"Is that right, Jesus?" he asked turning to his friend as he handed him a cup of coffee.

"Yes, we have to do some important business here," Jesus said as he added with a worried expression on his face: "There are about twelve trucks loaded with foodstuff that have been detained here for the last ten days as Tunas was surrounded. I have been named as delegate to come and obtain its release, and I thought of you as the person who can help us on this, since I don't even know where to start."

"Well, as it is now, there is a lot of confusion with all the shooting," Michael said. "but I heard that apparently the rebels are now in charge since the resistance of the army is non-existent in the city and the armed thugs had either been shot or have left. There have not been any more shooting since last night. I will call some of the people that I know who are involved with trucking and find out where we can start."

Half an hour later, Michael drove ahead of Jesus in a pickup truck that took them to Camaguey, heading in the direction of the main highway towards the spot where the idle trucks were. There was a great deal of confusion, and no one seemed to be in authority.

"You are the ones with authority ... He with his uniform and rifle, and you with your credentials as a delegate, so just give the drivers your instructions to move and if anyone comes to stop you, it should be someone with real authority over everything here. The way it is, there are a lot of people already starting to go hungry in Tunas, and there is nothing wrong with the roads, otherwise, you would not be here." Michael said to stress the point.

The determination and authority showed by Jesus and Alberto worked and the caravan of trucks started to roll easterly with the pickup truck ahead of them.

by January 5, the country was like a beehive, only that many of the bees were newly self-indicted revolutionaries suddenly dressed in improvised olive green shirts and pants, some of them with a gun to the side. Many of them were obviously opportunistic people or anyone who wanted to be a part of the triumphant revolution and such people were mixing with the real rebels, but you could easily set them apart. Michael remembered finding that most of the participants in the ridiculous parade were among the most unlikely people to have done anything ever for any cause whatsoever.

As the leaders were advancing, with Castro's forces disarming the army regulars at every barracks on the way, Michael received a call from Silvio Salinas. He could not avoid but feel uneasy about the call considering that most of the time the relationship with "SS" had been unpleasant.

"You know Enrique Oltuski well, right?" The controversial man asked with his usual ironic tone of voice.

"Yes of course."

"There is a rumor that he will be given responsibility for a ministry in the new government, and he is still in Santa Clara, possibly waiting to join Castro before his entrance to Havana," affirmed "SS". "You are the only one in our company besides myself who knows of Enrique having been involved in the underground and I know that you can find him and talk to him before Castro arrives in Havana."

"Where is Iglesias de la Torre now?" Michael asked.

"We don't know. There is a lot of confusion in Havana."

"If nothing else, I would hope that nothing will happen to him when Castro gets there." He said, adding, "I hope that now that the revolution has won, there is nothing to be gained by going after him."

"Yes. That is one of the reasons why you should get to Enrique and make sure that the boycott against Shell products is lifted without repercussions."

"I will definitively try to talk to Enrique about it. I will call him, but if I can't get him by phone, I will leave tomorrow for Santa Clara."

Michael was in the office when the call came. There were four visiting bearded rebels, one of whom was a relative of Rafael Mejias (one of the major gas dealers in the region), and there was a festive atmosphere in the place. A small party was organized for that evening at the younger Mejias' home to celebrate the end of the war and the return of his cousin.

At the party, Michael mentioned to one of them that he was going to Santa Clara the following morning, to follow Castro's caravan to Havana. Later on, the four warriors pleaded with him to let them come along on the trip. He accepted, feeling that it was not a bad idea to have his own "personal guards" with him. They left early the next day.

The trip was quite an adventure. The 1958 Plymouth Fury was somewhat heavily loaded with guns, the rebel's carry-on bags and Michael's own suitcase. The ride started with the car's back fender quite low. The overloading became critical when they had to take detours due to the bridges being down and the ride continued through sugarcane fields in areas where the only road seemed to be the one made by the many vehicles following in caravan. They were not even close yet to the city of their first destination and the going was slow and bumpy. "It was a miracle," Hel will later recaled. "It was a miracle that we did not have a flat tire or a broken spring during the ordeal."

Michael was amused by the stories of the guerrilla war told by the four youngsters during the entire four hours that the trip lasted. They were of the ages between eighteen and twenty-one, and he was already twenty-nine at the time and felt like an older brother towards them. He was surprised to hear that most of the time there was no fighting at all. The four have had little exposure to violence, and they feared more in their own towns than in the safety of the mountains. They told funny stories that made Michael laugh for most of the trip. They also said that Fidel Castro would never directly participate in any action and was heavily protected by his close friends and guards. His headquarters moved around in a way that they did not know where he was at any given time.

In Santa Clara, after leaving the companion rebels with others traveling by open truck, Michael dedicated himself to look for Enrique Oltuski. He drove first to the office; they gave him some information that led him from the municipal building to another house where there was a lot of coming and going of armed people in their olive green uniform. Finally, he spotted the thin figure of Enrique with his characteristic oriental-looking eyes behind his thin-rimmed glasses; he was wearing a short-sleeved shirt, and his hands were full of papers while giving instructions right and left amid the hustling and bustling that was going on in the place.

As Michael approached his co-worker, who was suddenly converted into revolutionary leader in front of his incredulous eyes, Enrique said to him, "I know why you want to see me," without stopping what he was doing but signaling him to go to his left side where they could be closer.

Michael was silently waiting to see if the glabrous young man would stop what he was doing, and Enrique finally said: "How come you know I am here?

"I have been already approached by Emilio Loy, the local manager. I will tell you what I told him – Fidel is going to do whatever he has in his mind about the boycott problem," he continued.

"Yes, Enrique. but I am more interested in the fate of Iglesias. You know, he is a good man, not a politician but a businessman, and Fidel has said that he will have him shot when he gets to Havana." Michael emphasized, adding: " . . . That is not the way to start a government whose leaders have proclaimed to do away with the abuses and the crimes of the previous ones."

Enrique, brushing aside the last remarks made by the frustrated interlocutor, abruptly said: "You don't have to worry about Iglesias de la Torre. He is already out of Cuba. He was already out on a trip with his wife before Batista left the island, and I am sure he is not going to be foolish enough to come back, so don't worry about him, Michael. Sorry, I have to go now," and extended his right hand to give Michael, whose face was already intensely red, a handshake. Frustrated, he saw the would-be minister go out from the courtyard of the large colonial house and into a car with a waiting driver, leaving the place immediately.

Michael would never see Enrique Oltuski again, except for pictures in the newspapers when he was named Ministry of Communications and became the youngest minister of the Revolutionary Cabinet. Years later, it was said that Oltuski clashed with the Marxist Che Guevara and Castro's communist brother Raul and he had been demoted perhaps having fallen in disgrace alongside the majority of Cuba's freedom-loving people when Castro openly embraced the communist camp.

The day everyone was awaiting for with great expectation finally came when Castro, riding on a tank, entered Havana. He had already addressed the Cuban people two days before from some of the stops he made on his way, with an enthusiastic and lengthy presentation of much of the goodness he had envisioned for his country. (Promises that sounded like a politician running for office where most of the thrust was on the multitude of issues.) Issues that he knew would be pleasing to most people to hear, giving little, if any, hint of his extremist inclination. Raising his figure like a shining star over a country that needed as much a lasting peace among its citizens as the eradication of the ills that plagued most of the attempt made by previous governments to run the people's fate effectively and honestly to which most have failed one time or another, or in one issue or another, caused the frustration of the majority.

Finally, Fidel Castro entered Columbia, the military base in the outskirts of Havana. Prior to his entrance to the city, his men and security forces had gathered all the weapons surrendered by the Cuban army and he, in the night of January 8, appeared to give his first major speech that was televised in the entire country. The messianic figure, dressed in olive green uniform was surrounded by the gentle-looking figure of the heavily bearded Camilo Cienfuegos on one side, and the figure of "El Che" on the other, as symbolic white pigeons flew around them, and the crowd roared: "Fidel, Fidel, Fidel."

No sooner had he started his speech when Fidel went on with a strong attack of other revolutionary groups (particularly the one known as "Directorio Estudiantil") on the reports he had that such groups were gathering arms and hiding them in various places of the city. As one of the white pigeons came to stand on his shoulder, he repeated the crucial question: *"ARMAS PARA QUE?! (ARMS FOR WHAT?!)"* Over and over he said as the crowd screamed in disapproval in the action of the more independent groups.

Michael could not help but remember the night, little over ten years before when Fidel Castro had come to meet with the small group of students on the sidewalk of the Institute of Secondary School in Havana to offer support to the students. Support that he translated in guns for everyone in the group that wanted them, two nights before the irresponsible shooting in his school took place. It was a shooting that so much infuriated and frustrated Michael that he had reacted to Castro with the same question . . . "ARMS FOR WHAT?" This was exactly the same expression that Castro was using before the big crowd this night of January 8, 1959 which bore a contradicting resemblance to his own memories of Castro's involvement with the gang's activities during the university years. The memory was just a flashback that did not however make Michael think negatively of it this time, as he never liked arms anyway. He missed the overriding point that became obvious as time passed that. Castro wanted arms only on his side, so much so that there would not be any significant opposition when he made his move away from the democratic principles that the Cuban people so much wanted to have restored. A few short years later in his so-called Ejercito Revolucionario, Cuba would become the most heavily armed institution in the continent except for the U.S.A.

Castro justified the alliance with communist USSR to protect his people's revolution against a possible invasion, but the same arms eventually served the most ominous purpose of oppressing the freedom-loving Cuban people.

The infamous Committees for the Defense of the Revolution were formed, and everyone was afraid of everyone else. The sense of pressure to conform and accept everything without question started to exacerbate anyone with ideas of right to privacy and independent mind – people who would not accept domination or manipulation such as the kind that had started to show its ugly face that, and the firing squads with a circusy aspect to it became a scene of threat rather than an act of justice.

Meanwhile, many demagogic moves that were made presumably to project an image of false assumptions of the new government as that of being equitable and concerned for everyone regardless of the status. but as the government moved to take over private businesses and also control the unions and prohibiting them to strike, condemning it as an anti-revolutionary act, the pressures mounted when moves were made to suppress the free press in the country. Michael saw the turning point in all those signs and the fears of the so-called enemies of the revolution, which Castro proclaimed as the reason for all such moves, moves that did not make any justification at all and became an insult to intelligence, as well as a prelude of worse things to come. Even the poorest people in Cuba didn't want to pay such a high price. It was a country whose overwhelming majority loved freedom and independence above all else regardless of the status, regardless of the pain and struggle to make progress. Its people were used to work hard for their progress and earn it with imagination and dedication. A country that had pride in its individuality and abilities to resolve and overcome its necessities, but without a false paternalistic hand hanging over it and controlling it as if it was a marionette. There were, of course, the exceptions. There were the frustrated, useless and mindless few who saw opportunities in the new state of affairs rather than seeing it as a disgrace. There were the miserable few who embraced hate to spread fear and exact unjustified vengeful deeds on family and neighbors even on the same economic scale (envy and ill-founded resentments played a big role in these individuals who were generally misfits. There were many, of course, who did not see the signs, or were too naive and hopeful, or sadder yet, impotent, that it did not make a difference for them until they had no choice but to reach for a raft and leave at the expense of losing their life in the waters of the Florida Strait).

The day when the Air Force pilots from the old regime were declared innocent in the trial for their participation in the bombing raids against the guerrilla was another turning point for Michael, not because of the verdict but for the action taken by Castro when he publicly denounced the verdict as unacceptable and declared it null and void, ordering another trial where the pilots should have a guilty verdict and a hard penalty imposed. It was unprecedented. There were pilots who in many occasions purposely let the bombs fall away from their intended targets. There was no clear evidence of a population or even encampments of rebels being hit. The pilots ended up with a penalty of up to twenty-five years on the second trial. The most significant lesson the country had ever experienced was Castro's most arrogant disregard for the judicial system.

The point in his mind was that a country where the judicial system was subjected to the judgment of one man outside the court's due process was an indication of things to come – where there will be no justice at all but only the rule of a powerful man representing only one slanted view, whatever it was, and most likely at the detriment of fairness and real justice. The fact is that such demonstration of imposition together with the attack on the free press signaled to a totalitarian regime in the making. This thought a lone made him very uneasy. He thought of having to raise his two daughters in such an environment, as signs of more intrusions in people's lives started to appear like having to adjust to brainwashing in schools where the children would have to belong to specific organizations such as "Pioneers of the Revolution" and whatever else was imposed in order to be signaled politically, was in one way or another repugnant and unacceptable.

Michael started to consider his options. To conform to the existing conditions was unthinkable unless the trend would radically change towards a true democratic system of respect for individual freedom. He, as well as a very large segment of the population, did not approve of the Batista regime, but they would not approve of limiting their freedom of choice either which is the hallmark of a democracy.

The second option Michael considered was a difficult one. becoming a political activist was not in his personality; he did not consider himself to have been born to become a politician; his preference was always to defend his rights for his individuality and his independence of any political persuasion. The only thing left under this option was to fight against the imposition of a totalitarian rule.

The sure thing was that he would put himself in real danger and as a result place his family in jeopardy, particularly his small daughters.

The decision for a third option was beginning to come to his mind more and more. It was that of leaving the country. This particular alternative acquired more relevance when the government decided to takeover the operations of Shell Oil Co. where he had been working for ten years.

The thought of working for the government was not appealing at all, even when the take over started with the demagogic strategy of increasing his salary by more than fifty percent practically overnight. The increases were announced by Fidel Castro himself during a visit to the refineries (built five years before) when he said that all salaries would be adjusted upwards to equal that of the salaries paid by another major oil company, namely, Standard Oil. Michael could not share in the euphoria of many of his co-workers because he saw it as a sign of irresponsibility and intrusion in the name of controlling everything, including the apparent beneficiaries of the decision. In his mind it would not add to anything good in the end; something that would represent the end of the apparent panacea which he saw coming rather soon. by the end of the year, he had started preparations by requesting passports for his four – and five-year-old daughters. The thought of working for a government agent was not appealing to him at all.

by mid-June of 1960, the takeover had been made official. The oil companies were all seized by the Castro government with the promise of payment to the legitimate owners (according to all that was said by the government at the time). He had the passports and also the U.S. visas for him and his wife, but he still needed visas for little Maggie, and Maritza. There was a long delay for processing visas at the American embassy in Havana that Michael made an attempt to go to the Consulate in Santiago de Cuba in an effort to obtain them faster but it was useless. There was a back load of requests; apparently that was the time when many professional people were doing much of the same. Meanwhile, he already had a confrontation with the new management of operations in Camaguey.

Oddly enough, a new local operations superintendent had been placed by Salinas, who appeared to be playing the game of endearing himself with the Castro government by appointing one of the opportunistic people (one who had turned arrogant and despotic against others who have been working in the local operations with loyalty for many years). The workers went on strike and the young leader of the group who was not known to have political affiliations of any kind ended up in jail, as the strike was declared illegal. Michael was not directly affected by the strike nor the new management as he did not report to that sector of the business, nor did he belong to any union either, but he resented the way things where handled by the older Salinas and the new management since the strike was only in protest against the way the workers were mistreated. (Something that, in his view could have been easily resolved.) He found himself clashing again for one reason or another, with the famous "SS" who appeared to be maneuvering again, this time in an attempt to ingratiate himself with the powers to be. He made his feeling public in the office and his attitude cost him a good number of tense confrontations. He wanted to leave all of it behind as soon as possible, as he could not find another immediate solution. His major preoccupation was centered in obtaining the visas. He had lost more than twenty pounds in less than two months. He had never been heavier than one hundred and sixty pounds, so his being that low on weight made him look as if he was sick. Perhaps he was.

He started giving most of his things to his mother and mother-in-law. He had already sold most of his furniture and had moved his daughter's Steinway piano back to his mother-in-law's house; all of these were done during his five-week vacation period. He had practically moved everything and his family secretly to Havana in the expectation of obtaining the difficult visas soon enough. Frustration mounted when he spent an entire day standing in line at the Embassy that already ran for two blocks (where people waited for an appointment in the visa department).

He came back, a third time to the Embassy with his wife and their two daughters, but this time he left them standing in line; he went at the back of the Embassy and entered by the side door which was the entrance to the Cultural Affairs section. He talked to the two ladies who attended the section, and after explaining about his situation said: "I am desperate now. I do not want my daughters to be brought up under this conditions and I want them out of the country with their mother before I present my resignation to the government agent leading the intervention and then I would leave as soon as possible to join them in the United States."

The two American ladies looked at each other and after a short while they both went to the far side of the office; one of them came back to Michael and said: "I don't know what could we do, but let me have your daughters' passports." She took them and went inside, after talking to the younger woman who was already coming back from behind the wide door.

Five minutes later, the older lady came back with the passports and asked: "Can you bring your daughters and wife today for an interview?"

"Sure. They are already here standing in line, about two blocks from the Embassy, and they must be already exhausted from the heat."

"Well go and bring them here. I think that we may be able to arrange for an interview for the four of you."

Michael's eyes illuminated as he thanked the gentle ladies. Then he walked fast to the door and down the steps to the street, looking for his family with a glow in his heart.

As they were escorted inside the long and wide room, Michael noticed that it was full of waiting people; many sat, but a good number of them were standing against the far-end wall. All of them were behind a divider (where the long corridor they passed through was located) which separated the applicants and the interviewers before any of the applicants could get to one of the dozen desks where the interviews were being conducted. Michael and his family were asked to sit in front of one of the desks. There was no one behind it. by then the older lady (who already looked like an angel to him) said: "The vice-consul, Mr. DaCosta, will see you in a few minutes." They sat down and waited for about three long minutes until they saw a man on a wheelchair come towards them. The not yet totally bald man with reading glasses mounted on his forehead greeted them quietly and looked at the little blond and brunette girls' innocent faces and smiled softly. He already had the passports in his hands, and asked, "Are you planning to stay in the United States, Mr. Beltran?"

"Honestly, we are, sir," Michael answered without hesitation.

"I see that you both have a brother and a sister already living in our country."

"Yes, sir."

"We are giving you and your family a three-month visa that you may be able to extend for three more months at the Immigration Department. You should contact an Embassy or a Consulate in a foreign country during that time and apply for a resident's visa. There is a lot of paperwork and procedures you will have to follow, and once you are advised, you will have to leave the country with your family to attend an interview and have a physical examination before you are given the necessary documentation as legal residents and to be able to return to the U.S . . . . I recommend the consular office in Toronto, since it is the closest and most convenient, considering that you will be in New York as you indicated. Good luck," he said smiling, as he extended his right hand after stamping and giving Michael the passports.

Michael would never forget the moment nor the man and the women who made it possible. He saw the good man turn his wheelchair and roll away after receiving his warm handshake.

"There is no time to waste," he told his wife as they left the embassy. "I will get the tickets for you and the girls to leave for Miami tomorrow morning . . . I will stay until I resign from my job, leaving everything on the clear as far as my responsibilities with it are concerned. but first, I will have to get a permit to leave the country."

"I know," she said unemotionally, "but why don't we stay until you make all those arrangements, and then all leave together afterwards."
"No, I am sure you understand, as we have talked about it many times. I am afraid that if they don't give me that permit, it could be a long time until I can escape by boat or any other means whichever may be necessary, and I do not want you and our daughters to have to face all that danger and chaos that is already setting in and getting worse. Most of all, I do not want our daughters' minds to be manipulated as they will be when they are forced to go to youth centers against our

will, and be exposed to all the political brainwashing that they will surely be given. You can all be free, safer and happier with your sister in Miami while I do what I have to do here before I can join you there." He did not say all that had been running through his mind as he was talking; he reserved for himself all his fears about the possibility of being jailed, or even killed as he made his opposition to the insipient Totalitarian regime more evident.

"Now we have to go to the bank and get the two hundred and fifty dollars each that is the only amount of money that the government allows anyone to take out of the country. We will have about seven thousand pesos left after we buy the necessary dollars. It is all we have saved in the last five years. We will give that money to both our mothers for them to use as things get worst in the country. Scarcity of food is already setting in and it will cost much more as the government continues to take over private businesses and increase control over all sources of production. Even eggs that were so abundant are already difficult to get and its price is soaring in the black market along with the vegetables. It is frustrating and unbelievable that it is happening in a country where all these vital items are so plentiful and cheap. Now they are talking about rationing milk with the excuse that it will be made available to more people, particularly the poor, when in reality it is the poor who can't even buy it at all now . . . How many lies do they think they can get away with?" They sat silently for a long while as they drove away.

Next morning, Michael saw himself driving back from the airport alone. Still in his mind were the sad eyes of his little daughters piercing his heart as he lifted each one to kiss goodbye, followed by the Images of his wife walking away with the two of them looking back to him as they sadly waved while crossing through the checkpoint, behind the glass that separated them from him. His eyes blurred as he drove intuitively, without seeing clearly any of the vehicles that moved ahead of his car like speeding ghosts. Ghost that were also the people he was passing by or crossing in front of inside the airport. His senses had been blocked except for his determination to finish what he had started to do. Only the ghostly figures seemed to suddenly surround him.

CHAPTER TEN

Farewell

As he drove his car away from the airport and into the familiar road of Rancho Bolleros to Havana that August 17, 1960, his thoughts were fixed on the short telephone conversation he had with his old fraternity friend the night before. He had been a mentor to Leovigildo Fernandez, during the three years prior to the younger and bright understudy becoming the second president following his direction of the civic youth organization in their hometown. He also remembered how they coincided in their ideology of respect for individual freedom, and how they had rejected the rules imposed by their institution's older sponsors and protested the impediments and finally succeeded in their demands to be left to rule the destiny of the young branch, allowing them to participate more openly in charitable and social activities with other organizations in the town, such as the "Rotary Club", "the Lions" or other civic organizations including the local Catholic church whenever the cause was one of merit – such as the fund-raising campaign to provide shoes and toys to poor children during Christmas as well as other similar charitable activities that the older mentors rejected because of their traditional opposition to anything that had to do with priests and any other organization that would not be to their liking, regardless of the worthiness of the project. The older mentors wanted to keep the organization isolated and do their good deeds alone. The younger, more progressive organization wanted to have an open participation with others even if it meant to share in the credit for it.

Those were small struggles where he found Leovigildo to be an enthusiastic and promising leader in addition to being one of the best public speakers he had ever known up to his young age of twenty-two (when he left the organization under the leadership of his junior colleague) leadership. Logic and sharpness, with a clear diction were the hallmarks of Leovigildo's style – at times poetic, and ever idealistic; a young man who was about three years younger than him.

He knew that Leovigildo Fernandez could never be in favor of any totalitarian scheme. Seven years had passed since those fraternity years and Leovigildo was now First Assistant to a respected minister in the Castro government – prestige that was won when he was a university professor.. Michael had seen him a year before, shortly after his friend had returned from a trade mission in Canada; he was proud and happy of the role he was playing in the outset of the revolutionary government.

The telephone call he made to his old colleague was just to see if he was going to be available the next day, as he wanted to talk to him about very important and pressing matters. He did not say what he wanted to talk about, but he received the usual enthusiastic response from Leovigildo and the appointment was set for one thirty in the afternoon in his Vedado office.

Michael arrived punctually and was immediately received by his friend, who had come to meet him at the entrance hall with his usual frank smile under his neatly trimmed moustache, and with a friendly embrace and handshake.

"You look very thin," his welcoming friend said as they walked down the wide hall. "What happened? I know you had never been overweight and being an athletic swimmer, you had always been trimmed but not that much," he added.

"Well, I don't know. I have lost some weight during the last three months. I think it is only because of being worried too much lately, Michael said, looking at his friend as he forced himself to come out of his tense predicament and managed to show his usual carefree smile.

"I want to show you the minister's office. He is traveling now and we can talk there rather than at my office where we will surely be constantly interrupted by all kinds of calls," Leovigildo said as they approached a tall and wide French door which he immediately opened, inviting Michael to enter ahead of him.

The office was impressive, with fine marble floors and walls that included the top of the large desk and the various elegant pieces of accessory furniture of a Napoleonic style, all under a tall round ceiling. They did not sit as they talked. His friend leaned backwards against the edge of the desk as he explained that it was the office where some foreign commercial dignitaries were received and plans were reviewed before they could go to meet the ministers.

Michael said suddenly, without waiting for his friend to continue: "I am glad that you are happy with what you are doing, and obviously it seems like a great career is opening for you, but I am afraid that this government is going communist."

"You don't know what you are saying. This is the first time that Cuba has a true independent government in its entire republican history," his friend said, showing a degree of antagonism that was not known to Michael.

"I thought as you did on the first few days, then the circus-like atmosphere of the trials and the implementation of the firing squads made me feel quite uneasy. A few months later, Castro ordered a retrial for the pilots who had been acquitted and after Castro's tantrum about it they were given long sentences. Additionally he has broken his original promise to create a climate for free elections within the first eighteen months. Furthermore, the pressure has mounted to control and suppress the press. All along, the firing squads continued to operate far beyond the few cases of alleged notorious criminals, and more people that had nothing to do with batista are being put in jails across the country," Michael said adding: "These are clear signs to me that this is just the beginning of worse things to come, and that is the reason why I came to see you. I am leaving the country."

"Don't tell me you are leaving at this luminous hour of our beloved country." Leovigildo said, raising his voice with emotion.

"This luminous hour you are talking about is not so luminous to me, Leovigildo. I see much more behind the apparent patriotism of the leader who is attempting to fool the freedom-loving people of this country whom I suspect will end up limiting everybody's freedom before long."

"Michael, you have to remember, all we have struggled for and how many people had died to change the old pattern of corruption and inequity in our political life. The revolution has many enemies and if we are going to eradicate all the injustices of previous governments we have to protect it from its detractors."

"Yes, I am already becoming familiar with that jargon, but the only one way this government will find ways to protect itself is to make life impossible for anyone who does not think the same way and eventually jailing or killing them, even those who were never involved with the batista government, including those people who contributed to oust him. Ultimately, they will be taking away all the individual freedoms that you and I, as well as every sensible citizen, had struggled to protect." Michael said with a saddened emphasis as he continued. "... So you will be falling in the same aberrations as all the other dictatorships or worse, by imposing a repressive totalitarian system such as the one in Russia."

The young understudy stepped away from the desk, his face flushed but without saying a word for a moment, as Michael continued, "Tell me if this government will uphold the ideals of José Martí who, as you know, considered Marxism as a source of indignant imposition of one class against another without offering a peaceful future for the world, in spite of the fact that he commended Karl Marx for his apparent concern for the poor. At the time of Marx's death, he made it very clear that he didn't consider Marx's formulas to contribute anything to our ideals of freedom, much less for the kind of independence he wanted for our country."

"Yes, Michael, but Marti also said that he knew the monster as he had lived in its belly, referring to the United States. You would have to agree that if we want freedom from their power, this will be the only way and I can't believe that you would not participate in this just and high ideal of being totally independent."

"No, I won't participate. Not this way, because we have enough of the ideals of all our own national patriots and philosophers who formed our ideals of independence and who had struggled so much for our independence, for us to go and borrow from Russia or anyone else at the expense of our own individual freedoms. You should remember our ideals and the many times that you and I spoke about the need to build a strong individuality through education and civility, one in which every person would be free and able and be prepared to achieve individual progress. In that way, contributing to a better and healthier society. A government should only strive at creating a free, stimulating environment and to deal effectively with the issues of education and health of its citizens in order for everyone to be able to contribute to the goodness of all, at their own free will," Michael asserted and added emphatically: "look at what Stalin did in Russia, jailing and killing anyone who would not bend to his dictatorial ways."

"Yes, Michael, but we were also in agreement that corruption in government had to be eradicated, and this can only be done if we have a strong government determined to do it," his friend said.

"Yes, but it should be a democratically elected government supported by the majority of its people, not a government that imposes a totalitarian rule by force and by fear which is the aim of terrorism. This is what I see developing in Cuba and this is why I want to leave. That is why if I don't, I will have to stay to fight against that happening, and I don't want to do that because I can't see myself fighting against my own brothers. I am a man of peace; I love it as much as I love freedom." Michael said as he could not stop his emotional outpour. He added, "You, yourself may have to shoot me, or I may have to see myself shooting at you. I am already suffering from all these fears, and the fear of having to see my own beloved daughters losing a father at this stage in their life, or seeing them grow up in a controlled and enslaved society rather than in freedom as I grew up in. In spite of all the ills that our society had to contend with, there was still individual freedom, the kind of freedom that we are now losing. That is why I have already sent them out of the country this morning," he finally said.

Leovigildo Fernandez, as he used to do many times during his emotional declamations during the years as a leader of the civic organization they both participated in during their younger years, suddenly raised his hand in the air above his head and shouted: "Ah! This is absolutely insane. You have been definitely influenced by the detractors of the revolution who prefer to abandon the struggle rather than share and contribute to the progress that our country is trying to make at this, the finest hour of our republican history."

"I disagree with you wholeheartedly," Michael retorted, "I think that you have been too involved to see what is already happening out there. Leovigildo, believe me. In any case, I have decided that I don't want any part of it. I want to live in a free society and be able to raise my daughters my own way and not any government's way. This is the most important thing for me now . . . As you know, I will have to get a permit from the Ministry of Interior according to the new regulations whereby anyone with an Engineering degree or license would not be allowed to leave the country without it. I will not be allowed to leave without it, another imposition as you can see. I will have to get a permit since I am licensed in electro-mechanical technology and also since I am specialized in the handling of liquefied gas."

"Well, the government doesn't want to lose any professional people who are needed to build a stronger country."

"That is fine," Michael said, "but how good will it be for the government if I stay here in opposition to it? I hope I will be given the permit, and that is the reason why I have come to see you."

"I will not have anything to do with it. It will be the Department of the Interior as you already know, and there is no influence to be made in favor of anyone. This government allows no special treatment to friends and any kind of influences. Remember, *No Amiguismos,*" Fuentes stressed the remark to paraphrase one of Fidel Castro's favorite expressions of those days, but as he said it, Michael noticed the restrained, not relished signs on his friend's facial expression. "*No amiguismos!*" he repeated, "so, good luck, go ahead and go there as anyone else would. Goodbye, Michael," he said it standing straight in the middle of the large room. At that moment, he felt as if the whole room was gyrating around the two of them standing at arm's length in front of each other. Neither one made an effort to extend a handshake nor an embrace. He turned around and went for the wide French door to leave. He had already taken three or four steps unto the long deserted hall when he heard: "Michael . . . Michael." He turned his head to hear his friend's last remarks to him . . . "Ask for Captain Alvarez when you get there."

Michael didn't say anything and kept walking fast towards the main entrance and into the parking area then drove away in the direction of Old Havana. His head hammered on those last words by his friend as he wondered if he would be taken to a jail or given the permit once he presented himself to Captain Alvarez.

Half an hour later he ran up the six or seven steps of the entrance to the old building where the Interior Ministry was located. He asked one of the guards for Captain Alvarez, and he was immediately escorted inside a busy room where a very thin man in his thirties, dressed in olive green uniform, was standing behind a desk full of papers. The man lifted his eyes as he sat down and read the name on the passport.

"So you are Michael? "Yes, I am."

The man lifted his eyes again towards Michael for a few seconds which appeared to Michael as if time had suddenly stopped.

He saw the man slowly open one of the desk drawers and took out a rubber stamp, placed it firmly in one of the pages of the passport, signed it and finally gave it to him without saying a word and without placing his eyes on him again.

"*Gracias,*" Michael said and left as fast as he had come inside.

It all happened in less than three minutes, since he entered the building and he could not believe it, as his thoughts were fixed in the intense discussions he had with his friend. After all, his friend had apparently grown to become the person he had always thought he would grow up to be – straightforward and with a determined sense of fairness and respect for every human right. The deep baritone voice of Leovigildo resounded in his ears as clearly as the time when he gave a speech about celebrating Benito Juarez's legacy during a reception Michael organized for the youth organization in 1952, for five young delegates from Mexico when they visited Cuba to attend a youth congress. The then very young designated speaker ended his speech, saying with great emotion in his voice ... "Let us never forget the words of the founder of the Mexican republic when he affirmed, . . . 'The respect for the right of others is the peace ...'"

Michael could feel a knot in his throat as if his sudden feeling of happiness was overwhelmed by a feeling of loss. The certain premonition that means he would lose the familiar surroundings he so loved; the sights of his hometown and the great capital city, both by the edge of the bay, with all its memorable corners full of color and sounds; All the other colorful towns he knew so well; the looks and sounds of its happy and expressive people; the many moments and visual impressions he would have to keep alive from a distance and for a long time, together with the bright and shining sun with its many angles of the day, or the reflections of the night over the unforgettable waters surrounding every inch of his beloved island, perhaps not to ever return to experience them again. They will all be left behind, they will all be like the old trolley cars over the cobble stoned streets that came to his mind now, almost ten years since they disappeared from the scene, coming down the narrow streets of Old Havana. They will only remain in the visual images of his mind like an old photo that just stays dangling as if floating before his eyes, reaching out to see beyond a downward hill without bottom and with ghostly figures riding in it like taking the ultimate ride without return.

Immersed in his conflicting feelings of joy for his soon-to-be liberated fears clashing with unavoidable sorrow, Michael drove his car to the headquarters of Shell Oil Co. at the convergence of La Rambla, Twenty-third St. and Calle Infanta, where he was already expected by the government controller – *Señor* Castillo, to whom Michael had already indicated his intentions to resign (from his position as regional manager). *Señor* Castillo was a soft-spoken and somewhat gentle engineer in his early forties whom the Castro government had appointed to manage the transition of its intervention, better yet, takeover, of the Royal Dutch Company from its British and Dutch owners under which Michael had been working for eleven years.

A few days before, when Michael said that he didn't want to work for the government under any circumstances, *Ingeniero* Castillo had tried to convince him to stay with the promise of greater lucrative incentives, and as he had put it: "We need you in this operation. You can count on our complete assurance that you would be left alone to work the way you know how without interference from anyone. The information I have is that you are an effective and independent manager. You are also known to be knowledgeable about the technicalities involved in handling gas, which is also very important for us. There are not many specialized engineers on that field, as you know, so please take your time to think about it." This time, Michael came prepared with his letter of resignation that he presented immediately after being greeted by Castillo.

"I see that you have already made up your mind. No wonder some of the people who have known you for a long time around here have told me how strong minded and persuasive you were when you wanted to make a point," he said as he added. "No persuasion was necessary here except from my part and I see no point on trying. I will have to ask for your final statement and liquidation."

"That will be fine," Michael said, "I would not want to come back for it. I hope that it can be done right away. I have brought my car and the lease contract with the record of payments I have made in the last two years that should be part of the final calculations for my last check. The car is less than two years old and in perfect condition. In the trunk I have brought all pertinent documents and files relating to my job which I want the person responsible to inspect and sign the corresponding release."

Three hours later, Michael rode in the back of a taxi for his mother's house with a ticket for the next day in a ferryboat to Key West already in his coat pocket. He knew how painful it would be for his mother who already knew about his intentions and all about the last few months' agonizing events. Regardless of her apparent stoicism and decisive encouragement, he knew very well of her inner sadness and he wanted to spend as much time with her in what was left of the day and the evening before his departure. He also wanted to have some time to walk around the areas where he had grown up and where so many happy memories could still be captured in his mind as he would again feel the caressing breeze, warm and soft as a prolonged loving kiss. He had not told Mariita, his dear mother adopted sister from him, anything about his going away on exile, as he had not told practically anyone except his mother (who would surely tell her, or perhaps had done so already at some point in her own way). Mariita was already there when he arrived (surely she knew or suspected that it was the farewell visit), but her high sense of love, respect and loyalty made her just a silent, supportive witness. For a brief moment she stayed around, giving him a hug and then left.

"How did it go for you today, son?" His mother asked, putting her hands over his shoulders as she looked at him directly in the eyes.

"Everything went fine, Mother. The girls are already in Miami with their mother and aunt, and I am ready to leave tomorrow by ferryboat to Key West," he said as he moved to sit down by his old desk made by his father. (The same desk in which he spent so many hours working on his school projects, studying or drawing and painting as he did for many years, next to the French door by the rectangular enclosed patio that offered a view of the deep blue skies spotted with the whitest clouds framed by her mother's plants: tall *Araleas*, climbing Asparagus, and potted palms shooting towards the sky on one side and the long, stucco stairway up to the tiled roof on the other; ferns alongside *vicaria* and "Impatient" flowers, better known as *Maravillas* in Cuba lying all around the edges and on the roof of the kitchen and bathroom, six or seven meters away from the end of the embracing, narrow, and partly shaded patio invaded by a soothing peace as usual. Michael sat there silently looking at all of it as his mother went towards the inside rooms where she could let her tears roll down her cheeks without showing him her pain.

Ten minutes passed in silent quietness before he stood up and walked across the patio to enter the backroom that her mother had converted into a dining room since the death of his father. It was an L-shaped room conveniently located next to the kitchen. His mother also liked the privacy offered by the partial wall making a Small l bay away from open view and where she had an old dresser. On top of which she had her shrine: a small bible and prayer book and a burning candle among family relics, a small image of the Lady of Charity on one side and one of Saint Lazarus on the other, a few evenly hanged old pictures of family members and a simple, fifteen-centimeter wooden cross at the center of the wall which was about the same size as the two finely cast images. Maria Antonia heard the steps of her son coming and gently stepped out from behind the room's divider to meet him with a relaxed smile as she took him warmly by his left arm and said: "I have something for you," as she showed him a small leather bag she had in her left hand. She opened the bag that was about half the size of the palm of her hand and started showing him what she had inside. This is a scapular. I want you to have it always with you, and this is a silver crucifix that belonged to my family and which I have had practically all my life. It is an antique but most of all, it is sacred," she said as she showed him the three-centimeter family religious relic, putting it back on the small bag after she kissed it, adding "I have been praying so that you, your brother and all your dear ones will be always protected and free from harm and as happy and healthy as you all can be. God bless you my son."

Michael took the small leather bag and put it on his left front pocket as he said: "Mother, I will carry this with me always as what you want." He remained silent for a moment as if his mind was somewhat wondering about something as he looked down quietly and added: "I want you to come and join us very soon. I do not want you to stay much longer here considering that things would get worse."

"Don't you worry about me too much. I don't think that this situation will last. I don't like to leave my familiar things and the house where you and your brother were born and where I will wait for you both," she said raising her head to kiss his forehead. "Come on, I have prepared one of your favorite foods. I will serve the stuffed green peppers with rice I just made before you arrived. I also have fried plantains and *yucca con mojo* to go with it, and *guayava* shells for dessert."

"Mother, how did you manage to get all of that for this banquet?"

"There is nothing that you could not do when you want it," she said with her usual optimistic and uplifting philosophy. " … Of course these days it would depend on what you will find on the stores, which is becoming less and less. But, fortunately your uncle Teofilo came yesterday and brought me some vegetables that he planted in his yard in Guanabacoa where he grows his small garden. He also brought me some fresh ground beef he managed to barter with the butcher who is his neighbor. My brother Teofilo is as poor as you know him to be but very resourceful and good hearted as usual."

"I know how good he is. Make sure you give him my regards. I hope he and his wife still have the watercolor drawing of his altar I made for him seven years ago on the celebration of Saint Lazarus' feast in December seventeen. I always remember how much he helped me when I built my first house after Maggie was born and it was not finished until about the time that Maritza came to the world. A house where I have hoped to see my two daughters growing up happily but where we ended up being so unhappy. We worked so much for nothing."

"There is no such thing as working for nothing. There is always the experience you gain on everything you do. Perhaps you made a mistake by building that house where you did, right in the backyard of your mother-in-law. but you surely learned something from it."

"You are probably right. One thing for sure is that I enjoyed building it with my own hands with only the help from some of my school colleagues and my uncle who came to do some of the work and brought the famous professional brick-layer *Señor* Candela who had such big hands and tools that he could lay a ton of bricks per hour," he said laughing. "It was something to behold when that big man worked. He looked like a brick-laying octopus." His mother joined in the laughter. "The only problem with *Señor* Candela was that he disappeared for a week and I had to go and look for him all over Guanabacoa every time. It was a good thing I only paid him as he finished every stage of the work."

They enjoyed the reminiscing while they had what was to be, without their knowing it, their last dinner together.

"How soon are you going to see your brother?" she asked.

"I don't want to live in Miami. We will go to New York as soon as possible, so I think that I will probably see him there in about a week."

"I will be happy knowing that you are both near each other. I know you are very independent and you have different interests from him but I know how much you love each other in spite of your differences in character. Remember that there is strength in unity. I will suffer much if I see that you are not getting along."

"Don't worry, Mother. You are right about the differences. Do you remember how I used to argue and press on him every time he seemed to be so unconcerned? It looked as if I was the old man and he was the one seven years my junior instead of the opposite. I remember when I was barely thirteen after Father died and we were waiting for the terrible hurricane of nineteen forty – four. My brother came home with a lot of wooden boards and nails to protect all the doors and windows and then went to sleep in the middle of the afternoon. The expectation was that the hurricane was going to be one of the most dangerous in history, since it was predicted to have more than two hundred kilometers per hour of winds and as it was a very slow-moving storm, the predictions were that there would be a lot of devastation. You had prepared with lots of milk and chocolate along with bread considering that a good number of our neighbors living in weaker houses would surely come to us during the storm as usual."

"Yes, I remember. Sometimes it looked more like a celebration than a dangerous affair. I had prepared candies for the children and many crackers so that no one would go hungry during the long night. I also had a homemade bottle of Ciruelon, the sweet plum wine, to help warm up anyone coming from the storm. You prepared the kerosene lamps and two flashlights because the sure thing was, the electric wires would be on the ground before long."

"It was already eight thirty in the evening and getting dark and very windy already and still my brother kept on sleeping. I came to wake him up a number of times but he kept on saying, 'Don't worry, don't worry.' I finally got impatient and started hammering the boards across the closed windows. He finally got out of bed and was still hammering boards even when the storm was already blowing hard. Our door had to be opened every ten minutes to let people in. It was hard, even for the three of us to close it against the wind. The tree across the street was threatening to fall over the frame house that was used as a kindergarten classroom for the small neighborhood children. Lito got out and joined the three men armed with a long rope that they tied to the tree with great effort against the terrible blowing winds. They wrestled with it all and managed to make a cut on the trunk and kept pulling the tree's heavier branches away from the old building that already looked like it was leaning dangerously. The tree trunk finally broke and Lito and the other men were able to pull it completely down and secure the heavy branches. That was when everyone had to take shelter."

"Yes," his mother said. "I remember when part of the roof of the house next door collapsed and the family of Pancho Majagua came knocking loudly at our door horrified with fear that the rest of the roof would completely collapse and kill them, as it was all made out of concrete blocks like our house. All I know is that we kept doing maintenance e jobs to our roof every two or three years."

"How well I remember the maintenance jobs that we used to do. I remember the last one I did with my cousin Mario on the improvised scaffolding. We prepared to get closer to the five-meter-high ceiling and scrape all the rusted beams bare, paint them with anti-rust paint, put new plaster and later on go up the terracotta-tiled roof and fix every possible crack and ended up by painting the whole house as I did many times with my brother before he left for the States. I have never told you but I got very jealous whenever you said 'Lito did this, Lito did that,' and you never said how much I did for the house too."

"Oh, you did? I am sorry, I never meant to ignore what you had done, but he was the one who had been so far away. I always say how many thing you have done when you are not around. I am very proud of you, as you know. You have always been able to manage your life without me worrying too much about you. but your brother . . . well you know him as well as I do."

"Yes, Mother. I also miss him very much and worry about him as usual. Lito is quite a guy." Michael found himself saying his brother's nickname over and over again during the conversation. After more reflection about those years came to his mind, he continued saying, "I hope he does not have his terrible nightmares anymore. I had developed a way to protect myself when he would wake up screaming and throwing punches in the middle of the night before Father would come to hold him until he woke up. I acted like a spring, getting out of my bed and under it before he would jump with his feet on top of me as it happened from the beginning. It all started after that bastard Chicho broke his head with a piece of steel pipe when they had a fight behind our house. I was looking from the roof and saw the wretched drunkard yielding the pipe from behind the wall where he came to hide, running away from my brother as I yelled, '*Cuidado* Lito, stop, don't go there, stop, stop!' but it was too late. Soon enough he fell to the ground bleeding. My brother had always been very good to everybody and everybody loved him, maybe too much, particularly the women. He used to get in trouble too easily."

"Well, he is now married already and also has two daughters like you. I am sure he is fine. He always writes saying that he does not have nightmares anymore," his mother said.

"Yes, I hope so. I also hope he has better choice of friends. Everyone just becomes his friend too soon. I always remember the day of my seventeenth birthday, on the eve of Saint Barbara's celebration in town, when me and my younger cousin Mario were passing by the large fiesta hall that had been opened for those days in Maceo Street near Cespedes at about eleven o' clock when a great fight started inside the crowded place. No sooner had the fight started when it spread in to the street. I saw my brother being held by a man from his back while another man with a knife was trying to get at him, which the man could not easily do because Lito was kicking like the devil. I could not help but get into the fight, grabbing the man that had the knife and pushing him away from my brother. There was such a turmoil among all the fighting people that the man practically disappeared in the crowd as I saw a woman hit the heads of everyone she could with the sharp heel of one of her fancy shoes," Michael said laughing. "There were so many people in the fight that no one could tell who was against whom, but as I said, when we came into the fight to help my brother, the ones who appeared to be fighting Against him dissipated like magic amid the confusion. but my brother also saw his two friends, Humberto el Chino and the other called Armando who also lived in Agramonte Street and who liked to drink and hang out in the street corner all the time without anything better to do, disappear like magic. I could not believe that they had left my brother alone at such a moment as we saw them running away. I was furious and told Lito to stay away from those two notorious fancy bombs. I wanted to look for them and confront them, and I finally did in the park on the top of the hill near home. I was still furious and told them to stay away from Lito. My brother could not get over my indignation so he embraced me and took me away. He promised that he would part from them because they were not worthy of his friendship, and he did stop going out with them after all. He really listened to me that time. He always thought that I was always complaining, and I know that I was sort of a non-conformist to the norm most of the time. The best times we had together were when we were on the same swimming team back in the mid – to late 'forties before he left. I really enjoyed that time when we came to be so close. I was about fourteen at the time that our competitive swimming started. He was already twenty-one and happy to be able to compete in it since he was such a strong swimmer. but as you know, he spent his most important time by playing basketball. He was the best high school player during those three years as captain of our town's team, having won against important contenders like the schools of La Vibora, Vedado and the Escolapios of Guanabacoa who were the best contenders."

The beaming, proud mother listened with delight as she tried to stimulate more memories. She managed to make a short comment:. "Your brother got sick after the last basketball game."

"Yes, I know. He had to be hospitalized and be rid of his tonsils. The day he was operated, I went to the hospital very early and stayed next to him all day long but at ten P.M. everyone was told to leave since the hospital did not allow anyone to stay. I hid myself in a closet for more than an hour and came out when all the area was already dark and got back to his bedside. He was surprised to see me standing next to his bed but could not talk and only pressed my hands and put them on his chest. I pulled a very hard metal chair with my foot and sat there without letting go of him and I only slept that way the entire night. I wanted to make sure that I was there to help if he did not feel well. I had been traumatized by the memory of my father never returning alive from the hospital just two years before. I really loved my brother!"

"I am sure you still do. I love him too and I also love you," she said as she stood up to run her left hand through her son's wavy hair. "You have had a rough summer. I can see that your hair is not a sun-bleached blond as it used to be every summer. I hope you take some time to rest. You have lost much weight with your worries."

Michael had been so carried away with the memories that he did not start eating the main course after the traditional soup.

"Eat your meal, son, before it gets cold," she said as she placed his dish closer to him with her right hand. "I have enjoyed the stories. I never knew about that fight the day of your birthday."

"Well, there was no need to give you any worry. The good thing was that it all ended well. I don't want you to worry now either. I have some money from my savings and from my liquidation. It is about seven thousand pesos that I want you to have on one condition. Just make sure to use it on yourself. I am sure you will need it."

After dinner, mother and son walked back to the living room where he gave her a large leather bag full with his personal papers, drawings and things he wanted her to keep for him, together with all the other things he had left with her when he got married.

"I will now go for a walk across the railroad tracks and go near the docks, Mother. I want to take another look around for a while."

"Wait," she said. "I will also give you something else. I have saved five hundred dollars since I visited your brother in New York two years ago and I want you to have it. You will need it. I know they don't allow you to get but a few dollars from the bank these days."

Michael warmly embraced his mother as he said: "Don't worry about it. I will do fine," and left her at the front porch of the house. He looked up past the top of the handsome Dorian columns that supported the high roof behind which the yellow-red clouds of a mid-summer sunset started to appear as he went for his farewell walk.

The night had already tinted the timeless *cupula* above with its deep blue Cuban infinity where some stars had begun to sparkle beyond the low, summer cumulus clouds. All its majesty signaled the end of a hot but balmy day, by the time Michael returned to the house. His senses were invaded by the beauty of the surrounding sights – small details that would escape as commonplace for most. The fading lights and gentle shadows on the facade and sides of the old warehouses by the docks, the long and shining rails where wagons and tank cars were lined up endlessly, the reflections of the city lights on the waters of the bay, both close by when he walked along the old docks built by his father, and later far away but still so close to his eyes when he reached the top of the "Hill of the Hermit". (The same that had seen him going by day

after day as he grew up.) All in all, a necessary silent journey that brought him many thoughts – the sad and the joyful, all which gave him the awareness of how lucky he was of having been born in a land that offered so much beauty and so much warmth on its people, in spite of the tragedies surrounding the growing pains of an adolescent republic. He was to take all of that with him in abundance; enough to last him as long as life.

CHAPTER ELEVEN

The Night Of The Exile

Maria Antonia came to open the door and greeted her son with a broad smile as he came from his solitary walk. "I see that you look very relaxed, Michael, I am sure that you enjoyed your walk. Have you seen anyone you know?"

"Not really. Everything looked very quiet. There was no one on the street from the side where I came from. Apparently everyone is inside their houses except for a few people inside the corner store as usual. but I walked fast past it, as I wanted to avoid having to talk to anyone today. A few kids were playing hit ball on the far corner with the usual ball made from cigarette box wrapping. Remember how much I liked to play that game every summer night until my father would call me to come home at about eight thirty every time? I used to make those balls by saving my father's empty cigarette packs. He smoked those strong, oval Partagas cigarettes, as you would remember. I used to cut the outer layer of the small boxes evenly by half and after wrapping a heavy piece of rubber tightly in the paper, I finished the ball with the two layers of the cut cardboard," Michael said as he sat next to his mother.

"Have you packed your things yet?"

"Yes, Mother, I have two large suitcases back in the house. I will pick them up tomorrow when I go to say goodbye to my mother-in-law on my way to the boat. I have clothes already packed, including my swimming flaps," Michael said showing an intended ironic smile. "As if I would have time to swim" . . . I have not have time since last year's vacation in Varadero already more than a year ago, and I would hardly have time, or a place for swimming, but taking the gear gives me a feeling of normalcy that I need at this time. I am leaving too much behind, and that includes you. I hope you will be able to come soon if this situation gets worse as I expect it to get."

"I hope that you will stop worrying so much about that for now, son . . . You will have your wife and your dear daughters with you to take care of. I am glad that we had that vacation last year in Varadero. I really enjoyed to have been a part of it too."

"Yes, that was a great time. The girls loved that beach with its white interminable sand and the multiple colors of its water where they played for hours. It was one of the best times we have had together."

"Except for the frightening moment when Maggie went too far out to go after her ball which floated away. I am sure you have not forgotten it."

"Of course not. I saw Margarita going after Maggie. She was badly swimming towards her and both of them were getting farther and farther away in the open current by the time I got to them. I don't remember swimming as fast, since my years in competition. I finally reached them when they were close to go down and drowning together. I was able to keep their heads above water until that boat came to rescue us, before the current could make it more difficult to bring them back ashore. The apparent low tides in Varadero could be deceiving because you can go from knee deep to shoulder deep and then back to knee deep again for a long distance. but if you reach the currents you can be in danger unless you are a good swimmer. The good thing is that you have to be quite far off from shore for it to become dangerous and most people don't go that far. Maggie liked the ball you gave her so much that she would not stop going after it, even if she got dangerously farther and farther away."

"I was taking care of little Maritza when all that was going on. It was scary, but I felt better when you reached them and started to pull them back and as that rescue boat was getting closer, I know how much you care for your daughters. Those two girls adore you, as you know."

"Of course I know, and I love them dearly too," hel said . . . They are very good. I wish you could hear Maggie play the piano lately. She has made a lot of progress. She takes it very seriously as everything she does. Maritza is more relaxed and less of a perfectionist as her sister and playful, although not as much as she used to be. I want to see them grow happily, away from all of that is happening here."

Michael continued after taking a long, deep breath: "I can't forget the day of the explosion at the munitions depot. Maritza was playing in the front porch and I was watching her there while you were inside showing your plants to Margarita, and Maggie was reading by my desk. There was a large Russian oil cargo ship already quite empty. I was momentarily looking at it when I saw the explosion that looked like it was right on its deck. I saw the expanding ball of flame before the effect of the explosion and large noise was felt by us. It gave me just enough time to grab Maritza, lifting her in the air and jumping towards the living room and yelling to Maggie to drop to the floor. I fell and skidded over my elbows, cutting myself with the glass that had already fallen from the broken windows when I was covering Maritza under me, as the push of the terrible explosion dragged both of us until I came face to face with Maggie already on the floor at the end of the living room."

"I remember that you thought that the explosion was from the ship and became very agitated about it because you said that more explosions could follow as the ship was likely to be full of gas. We could not close the door, and the French window was also out of the hinges, there were pieces of sharp glass that stuck to the walls like knives. It was terrible." Maria Antonia said, visibly showing signs of distress as she spoke . . . "You drove away with us and Antonia, the neighbor from across the street who managed to be close by and frightened. We were near Guanabacoa when you stopped."

"Yes, I was worried about more explosions if it came from the ship. You would remember the explosion of the ship *La Cubre* that exploded a year ago and caused a number of deaths and injured many people in Havana. We did not know until later, that it was the army's munitions depot at the other side of the shore not much more than a mile from the front of your house that exploded, then, I started to worry about Maritza. She was so scared that she did not talk at all for more than five hours. I thought that she had lost the faculty of speech. It seems like a long time ago as we talk about it again but it happened only about three months ago. Our life has changed so much in that short time that it is unbelievable, and it will change even more, Maritza has remained very quiet and talked much less than she used to, and I am concerned with that. Thank God we will be away from all this, and I hope you will be too very soon."

Mother and son did not talk much more that night and the rest of the time that they were together, except for the few words they exchanged before Michael left her at the gate of the dock. Up to that moment, they were both silent and introspective, as if neither one wanted to acknowledge the pain or give an opportunity for any apprehension of finality that could creep in their hearts and minds.

The rest was the image of his mother's face pressing against the wire fence as the boat slowly sailed, getting farther and farther away until he could only see the white handkerchief he had given her before boarding, floating up and down until it was imperceptible, as it blended with everything he was leaving behind in the distance as he kept his eyes on her, without moving them. .

An hour later, he saw the skyline of Havana sinking in the horizon. He was still pegged onto the rail as if to absorb through his eyes all that he was leaving behind, like it was all becoming only water and sky, surf and clouds that speeded away (as if his whole world of the past was going through the narrow ebb of a gigantic and bottomless sand clock in which he was floating into a new dimension of uncertain, but challenging possibilities where the most reassuring expectation was the one of being free and the one of being self-confident.) He counted on nothing else He definitely didn't want to be a burden to his brother – arriving without a job and only enough money to last him barely one month, but he counted on his moral support and guidance to get started in a city like New York, the city that he has known only superficially from a short visit three years before, enough to feel the pull of its cultural milieu and the excitement that its life generated.

The Key West bus arrived at the Miami bus station after midnight. He stepped down to find a large crowd of people calling for their relatives, embracing them in screams and tears. No one he knew, as he had not advised anyone of his arrival that day. There was a lot of confusion at the spot where the luggage was to be picked up. A tall, black bell captain in uniform kept repeating in a loud and purposely squeaky voice: "back to Castro … back to Castro," probably as a way of complaining about the turmoil and confusion around him, or to add to it with his derogatory flagellation that appeared to give him some pleasure. No one paid attention to him, which probably made him more frustrated. Michael picked up his two pieces of luggage, got into a taxi and went to his in-laws' apartment house in the southwest section of Miami, getting everyone out of bed. The two girls clung to him on both sides … "Papi … Papi," was the sweet sound of their voices over and over as he was greeted by his in-laws and tired-looking wife. He was surprised to see how small the apartment was – with two small bedrooms, one of which could fit only a bunk bed at best, a kitchen and dining area, and one small bathroom. It felt quite tight and somewhat uncomfortable, but that was the least of his worries at that point. His sister-in-law, Dulce Maria Rivero, whom they called Dulcita, was as usual very pleasant. Her husband, Pepe Castaneda, has also been gracious and warm in welcoming them in spite of his usual pessimistic outlook in life. He had not been successful at keeping any job in Miami and was planning to leave eventually for California. To Michael, the surroundings, as well as the depressive atmosphere, only added to his anxiety to reach New York, as soon as possible. He had never liked Miami except as a vacation place and did not offer any other incentive to him at this time in his life.

The following morning, Michael looked in the newspaper's public notices section looking for the agencies that requested for drivers to transport cars to New York. He went to one that had some cars to take up north. The only car they had to take to New York was a beautiful and fairly new Sports Corvette, which he drove around the block with pleasure, but eventually he turned it up because it would be impractical and uncomfortable. The other choice was a brand-new Lincoln Continental. He signed the agreement to take it and deliver it in Philadelphia within five days, paying the gas after the first tank was used up. He had assured free transportation for the family at least to Pennsylvania, paying the final leg to New York City which was to be traveled by bus, and one or two nights' stay in a motel along the way.

He was yet to have the first unsavory experience about the heavy cost of driving a luxury car, as a poor man in a rich country;.

he was stopped by a state ranger on one of the main roads entering Philadelphia. The ranger insisted that he was speeding by eighteen miles per hour over the sixty-mile limit. Michael insisted that everyone else on the road was passing him at higher speed. "Why would you stop me, and not anyone of the others?" He showed his credentials and pleaded with the officer, telling him about his having left Cuba, and was driving the impressive new car as a hired driver and as a means to save the cost of transporting his family to New York City because of his financial limitations at this critical time in their lives.

The pleading and his requests were of no avail to the young officer, who was about his age and kept insisting for Michael to follow him to a roadside court. The end result was, with the judge being very lenient in consideration to his special situation, he was given the lowest fine. "Michael heard the opening remarks of the judge with appreciation, but had to sit down on his chair to avoid falling when he heard the amount of fine to be paid was ninety-two dollars. He paid after protesting to the judge and left to get to back to the car that had suddenly become a more expensive one to him than he had anticipated.

The young ranger approached the couple to apologize over and over again, before they could drive away, prompting Michael to say, "Thanks for your apologies but they would have not been necessary if you listened to my plea when you stopped us." After which he drove away completely frustrated. His thoughts were that, to live in freedom, Somehow, you have to learn to know and follow the rules, or pay dearly if you don't.

They finally arrived at the New York bus terminal, past ten in the evening. The heat was extremely intense and the heavy humidity, stubbornly invaded the air-polluted atmosphere of the station, turning it into something not like anything Michael remembered experiencing even in the tropics. The two little girls were sleepy and tired but quietly carried their favorite dolls under one arm as they watched the luggage being unloaded from the belly of the large Greyhound bus. No sooner had that happened when they heard the voice of Miguel Angel and saw him approaching them with his hands up in the air and practically screaming.

"How can you do this? . . . Leaving your good job in Cuba and coming here to this country to start all over again. You don't know what you are doing. You are crazy! You are absolutely crazy." Michael's perplexity did not let him say a word, but he managed to grab his brother in an embrace as he had lifted his hands again to emphasize his spontaneous complaint that by then had already angered his sister-in-law into a solemn silence where she would hide her resentment to never forget, and, let alone ever forgive.

Half an hour later, Michael and family arrived in front of a row of old redbrick buildings, all about five stories high, at Second Avenue of the East Side between Seventy-third and Seventy-fourth streets of Manhattan, getting out of the very tight and crowded old Chevy his brother was driving; loaded with the luggage; later on, they made two trips up to the third floor with it and a few minutes later they were greeted by Edeya, his sister in law and his two nieces, each about one year younger than Michael's daughters.

He had noted that the approximately twenty-five-feet-long but narrow apartment had only one bedroom, and the children's small beds were assembled at the end of the open space where they had a three-seater sofa in front of a small TV set that was resting on a table. These were all that made up the living room area, following the site where the couple had placed a dining table and four chairs next to the small kitchen counter near the entrance to the surprisingly limited living quarters.

Michael had met Edeya in Cuba after his brother's wedding when they had visited the island to become the godfather and godmother to Maggie, his first daughter. Edeya had an easy laugh and a carefree, easygoing character that matched his brother's personality beautifully. Her father had been a prisoner of the Nationalists in the Canary Islands during the Spanish Civil War, and had been killed when she was only three and a half years old, but she remembered him and the upheaval her family suffered before they were able to leave for Cuba and later to the United States. Her mother had, justifiably, a resentful memory of the event.

"Lito," as he lovingly called his brother, had a good paying job that he had gotten, since the prior year with a baccarat glass manufacturer from France that had a major distribution center and store in Fifty-seventh Street. It was a blessing for him because of the lack of good employment during the late 'fifties and into 1960. "This is not the best of times to look for a job in New York," he had told his newly arrived brother. Ever since his arrival to the U.S. in late 1948 his brother had helped his mother by sending her some money orders every two or three months, knowing that the insurance money she received after his father's death was totally gone even before he had decided to leave in search of better job opportunities, in New York. Modest as it was, it represented great help, particularly during the time Michael was still going to school. Michael always appreciated his brother's generosity, but during the later years he became concerned of his brother's inability to save and to be able to buy a house, as Miguel Angel continued to be as careless with money, as when he lived in Cuba after their father's death. They lived rent free in the small apartment due to his being the building superintendent.

Edeya served hot milk and chocolate cookies to the sleepy girls, and the two couples later sat in the kitchen to eat some sandwiches and coffee. The heat was almost unbearable, if not for the stand fan that blew away some of the warm air from one corner of the room.

The conversation was centered on the stories Michael was telling about his reasons to leave and his desire to bring their mother also as soon as it was possible. His brother was not happy about any of the remarks and would now and then try to justify and give good points for the revolutionary government in Cuba, all of which Michael took time to calmly explain that anyone who had lived through it all knew how different it really was from the opinions his brother had – he, being out of Cuba and not knowing all the facts. In the end, Michael felt that he was not convincing enough at this early stage of his arrival so he decided to let go of the subject and change the conversation without showing any discouragement.

"We need to find a hotel. It's very late and we are tired," He said.

"No, you don't need to do that. There is an empty room in the fifth floor of the next building where I am also the superintendent. The owner had sold all these buildings and they will soon be demolished to give way to a new structure. Most tenants are out of that building already."

"Can I see the room?" Michael asked.

"Yes, let's go right now and see how it is. The people that lived there left this morning and I have to see if they left any furniture. You can come with me to take a look." Michael got up and followed his brother and was surprised to see that his brother was heading upstairs instead of downstairs.

"Follow me, Michael. We have to go in through the window and enter from the fire escape." They went to the roof above the fifth floor and crossed to the roof of the next building and down again using the fire escape on the back of the building, one floor down the outside metal stairs. He followed his brother who opened the window and entered in the dark empty room with a flashlight on hand. Michael was totally amazed by it all, but at the same time he was invaded by a depressive feeling when he saw the condition of the small, square room where not even the lights would work. The plaster on many spots of the wall had fallen. The window shades were ripped by the sides and the dusty, hardwood floor was partially covered with loose paper and debris from the broken plaster of the walls.

"We can't stay here, my brother," he said.

"Don't worry. It is too late to go and find another place now. I will bring a kerosene lamp, a broom and some cleaning stuff."

"That may be fine, but we don't even have any bed."

"We will bring a mattress that I have and will set this up as nicely as we can for all of you to rest 'till morning."

"To tell you the truth, brother, I appreciate it and I like the sense of adventure this is offering me, but I don't know . . . I don't know," he said scratching his head as he thought of his wife who would surely dislike the place.

"We will bring the mattress through the window, once we have cleaned this room, because I don't want anyone left in the building to see what we are doing. But we will bring your wife and the girls quietly by the front entrance." His brother remarked without paying any attention to Michael's sudden apprehensive mood.

The two brothers carried the mattress up through the same fire escape staircase and managed to bend it, finally forcing it into the room. They lit the kerosene lamp and dressed the makeshift bed with a clean sheet and a light blanket. A few minutes later, they each brought the sleeping girls in their arms and placed them softly in bed. Michael's wife let herself into the sheets next to them without saying a word and the three of them were in deep sleep within a short while. Michael took his shirt off and sat on the edge of the mattress contemplating on them as he leaned forward, staying static and sleepless for hours, with his arms resting over his knees. The kerosene lamp threw its diminishing light, distilling it into spreads of yellow-orange weak beams among the shadows. He could visualize all the monsters in the nightmares he thought he had left behind, reaching out to get them in the distance, with the horrors of the firing squads (the fears caused by a subtle, and surreptitiously induced terror that was systematically planted to last for a long, long time). He could see all of it like piercing darts entering the narrow spaces in the darkness of what he found himself immersed into – a sleepless, sad night among the many they were going to live through, like so many other Cubans in their long nights in exile that he himself was experiencing for the first time. The long night, of exiled Cubans. A very long night that was not to be understood by many, as time would pass, wearing out any notoriety as commonplace, in a world interested mostly in the spectacular, while many would die waiting for a return, as many would die with their hope of freedom, if not justice, ending deep beneath the Florida Strait.

Michael's sadness of that night was multiplied by having to confront with the reality that his brother was completely convinced that he was wrong; not only wrong in having left his country, and his job, but above all because their political ideals appeared to be through and through incompatible. (A manifestation of the division in the family that he had already seen emerging in Cuba – where brothers were against brothers, and parents against their sons or daughters had already become an essential part of the so-called revolutionary process as the power of a few exercised the domination over the many, not necessarily for the betterment of all.) It was a country where the ideal of its finest founder of creating . . . "A nation with all and for all . . ." was far from being realized. He was so impressed by this night's event that his mind semed to block it for years. Michael would not talk about it at all. Only twenty-seven years later, after having completely reconciled with his brother (who died at the end of 1987) did he pour out his feelings of that night into a large oil painting that a few years later was to become part of the collection of the Museum of Art at Florida International University.

Equally blocked, for many years from any mentioned to anyone was his discussion with the exterior commerce department assistant friend, and the end result of that eventful discussion. Michael did not talk about it until thirty-eight years later when he heard that his friend had died a number of years after having fallen in disgrace with Castro, most likely because of his friend's ideals being far from being met by the totalitarian rule adopted by the government. He was always afraid of creating difficulties for his friend if he would reveal the way that he, and his family was surprisingly helped when in 1960 he needed to go into exile.

Next day after his arrival in New York, Michael took his family to the old Sherman Square Hotel, in Broadway and Seventy-first Street, where his old friend Heriberto Fernandez was working. He had helped Heriberto, by teaching him English, and also given him some money before he left for New York in the mid-'fifties. His friend had helped him in the construction of his house, and now Heriberto was helping him by getting for him a good rate for a furnished room with a kitchen and dining area for only about one hundred and twenty-seven dollars a week. Michael had expected to find a job sooner and be able to leave the hotel for a more economical and convenient living quarters but more than three weeks had passed and he was still without a job. He had come to the end of the rope with money running out. He would buy the newspaper every day and call prospective employers and still without any luck. Likewise, his search for an apartment in nearby Queens was not successful either.

Already in that predicament, he was sitting next to the phone reviewing the classified ads when his brother called.

"Have you found a job yet, Michael?" his brother asked.

"No, I have not, brother. I don't know what I am going to do. The only job offer I had was with a gas distributor in upstate New York which I don't want because I don't want to leave the city. besides, if this is all that the 'Shell' people here can offer me, then I don't want it. I will hold up until I get something interesting in the city. I am ready to go and clean telephone booths in the evenings if necessary, as bad as it may be. I have a friend who told me about it. At least we will be able to survive until I get out of this situation."

"I have told you about how bad it was here. You can see now what a big mistake you have done in leaving everything you had over there to come here. You should have never done it."

"Hold it, hold it," Michael interrupted his brother. "I have told you the reasons many times already and I don't want to say it again. You should know that this is already getting me very frustrated with your lack of understanding. You should have called me to give me encouragement and hope, not anything else. I didn't even want you to help me at all. What I only wanted was your moral support and I am not getting it. Please, brother, don't call me anymore if you are just going tell me the same thing over and over and over again like you have been doing."

By this time, Michael's voice was loaded with emotion, and anger was starting to come over him. As he was ready to hang up the phone, he said: "I have to go now."

His face was red with fury, a fury he was not used to feel, let alone be it towards the brother he loved so much, and the one that he traveled so many miles for to be near to. He paused for a few minutes With his head in his hands as silent tears dripped over the newspaper lying on the table. His search for a job, and an apartment intensified during the last week that he had to stay in the hotel.

In the middle of the fourth week, he returned at the hotel from a long search. It was already the last week in September of 1960. The tail end of a hurricane was passing through New York with heavy rains and winds blowing as he walked around the city, visiting employment agencies only to hear again and again that he was overqualified and then returned to the hotel after a rough and discouraging day. He had dinner and helped his daughter Maggie with her homework. She had been going to the first grade in Saint Joseph School, practically across the street from the hotel and was making progress in handling the English language. Her younger sister Maritza was also going to pre-school and still had that saddened look in her eyes, the same ones she had after the explosion that so scared her a few months before they left Cuba. This time, the little and usually playful girl was probably saddened with her father's worrisome expression which he could not easily hide.

That night, he found himself awake again after his wife and daughters were already sleeping, or so he thought, he could not get out of his mind the serious situation he and his family were experiencing, as he was in bed looking at the ceiling and saying in a low and sorrowful voice: "I don't know what else to do, God. We have to leave this place in two days. I don't have any income. I don't know what I should be doing, but I will go and get a job cleaning telephone booths tomorrow if I have to, and I will not give up, and find a way out of this." His self-encouragement did not do much for the feelings of desperation overcoming him as he tasted the salty flavor of his silent tears, again when he looked at his two daughters sleeping nearby.

He was having breakfast the next morning when a call came in from his brother's friend, Manolo Dago.

"Hi, how are you, Michael?"

"Not so good. Thanks for calling me. I am still looking for a job."

"That is why I called you. One of my clients from the hair salon I work had told me that the young man they have handling their data stockroom, and the customer service department will be leaving in a few weeks for Arizona. She is very distressed about it, because, as she said, he was very good at the job, and it will not be easy to replace him. I have told her about you. Would you be interested in going for an interview?"

"Of course, I am," he answered immediately. "What kind of business is it?"

"It is a marketing research service company that services all the important promotion and research companies in New York like Elmo Roper, J. Walter Thompson, and many others."

"It sounds interesting," Michael said. " . . . Who should I talk to?"

"You have to call Mrs. Philips who is the vice president and wife of Mr. John Philips, the owner."

"I really appreciate that you thought of me, Manolo," Michael said.

"I am only too glad to help. I think that you deserve it … Has your brother called you?"

"Yes, he has, but it was better that he didn't. I am not very happy about what he tells me every time he calls."

"I think I know why, but don't worry about it, someday he will come out of his frustration of you having left Cuba. He is only thinking about the damn political reasons, and is blind to everything else. He will get over it."

"I hope so."

Michael got the phone number for Mrs. Philips and called for an appointment which was set up for next day at 9.30 a.m. Following the call he started to get ready to go out for the morning paper when another call came. It was Heriberto who said: "Michael,, there is an opportunity for you to get an apartment and a job at the same time."

"What?"

"Yes, my father has told me about one of his clients in Astoria, Queens. His name is Jose Leonor, he and his wife are from the Philipines and they are very good and fair, both of them. They have a building with sixteen apartments there, and he needs a new superintendent. If you are interested and he finds that you qualify, you will be given one apartment in the building for free and some other arrangements that I don't know about. I think that you should consider it."

Michael could not believe what was happening that morning. Every door that had been closed appeared to open for him and his family so they can start building their life again.

He remembered when his mother, when she used to say: " … God can press very hard on you, but He would never choke you."

Within two days from his most desperate moment, he had two jobs and a place to live rent free. He thanked God for his sudden bliss and he went after it, invigorated and optimistic that he was on his way to reconstruct his life and educate his two daughters the way he always wanted.

Living in New York City represented a significant change in lifestyle for Michael and his family, but he enjoyed the challenge and the exposure to the cultural life of the city. Having two jobs kept him busy all the time which was something he was used to, but one of the things he dislike was not having a car and having to depend on public transportation. While the subway system was an absolute necessity to go to work in the city, whether he had a car or not, still he missed having one. He saved some money and bought a car after their first year in New York. The used Ford Station Wagon made it possible for him to take his family for rides away from the city in what was the beginning of a real life in freedom.

He enjoyed the change of seasons, and most of all the colors in fall, and the snow in winter as a substitute for the bright sun of the Caribbean. The beauty of the exuberant vegetation of upstate New York, Connecticut, New Jersey and Pennsylvania with its Nordic newness entering his retina, felt like the appropriate substitute and at the same time, one that nicely soothed his nostalgic feelings. He also enjoyed his job where he was exposed to the American way of life, particularly to the courteous and caring way he was being treated by everyone – from his employers to his associates, all of whom made him feel not only welcomed but respected and appreciated. Within two years, he had made contact with executives from various oil companies that had offices in the metropolitan area and he was able to have a third job which consisted of traveling in the Caribbean as a private consultant making market studies for what he was paid as an independent contractor. His other two employers were gracious enough to allow him to take a week or two off for his consultant job from time to time, all of which was very unusual and encouraging for him.

The one activity he really wanted to do but had been forced to put away every time since he got married was his love for art, but it had been his choice to raise a family first, and he knew that once he was ready he would get to work with oils again. This dream he fulfilled when he traveled on special job assignments away from the country. Many times he would carry drawing paper, pencils and charcoal on his trips, but he soon found out many times that paper from the hotels was sufficient enough to work in, especially when drawing from memory (where he would recall the surrounding areas where he grew up in, like his hometown and around Old Havana). Most of the drawings were of poor quality except for their idea and composition, he had always thought, but it was a way to exercise his memory and prepare the base of the inspiration to work on his childhood memories oil paintings in later years.

New York City offered the opportunity for the self-development he always wanted. Every day from Monday to Saturday he spent his lunchtime and some evenings in the library across the street from the Museum of Modern Art which was very close to where he worked, and in the library near Steinway and Broadway Ave. in Astoria, which was around the block from his home. He read and studied Art History as a whole with special emphasis on Modern and Contemporary Art. He also used his free time to visit every important art museum and gallery in the city. Living in New York City was a very valuable experience, of which he did take complete advantage in learning, as much as he could; the kind of knowledge he was hungry for, as his time in school had been good to prepare him to attend to the needs of his family but little to do with the need for his most natural intellectual inclination and vocation. His technical education offered him knowledge of mechanical drawing and the application of perspective in relation to construction, and partially to architecture but nothing related to how the world of art had developed and where it was in relation to his own time. It has been his choice to forego art school when he thought that his inclination and natural abilities would be sufficient, and he also thought that it would be an asset by being strictly a self-made man with only his own perceptions and expressions without rigid academic influences, as he had told his uncle. A misconception that he would pay dearly in his developing years, when he became very sensitive about not being readily recognized by his own people, particularly the ones entrenched in the so-called establishment as absolute infallible judges of what was good art, some of whom he thought to be snobbish, perhaps unfairly in some cases, but nonetheless constituted a powerful blocking wall that made access to acceptance extremely difficult. He would eventually have to work very hard and well in order to break such barriers, as the only way to accumulate enough merits toward the desired recognition. Complaining alone could not do it, and he knew it. He would not have liked anything that would come easy. Something that even he himself could consider laurels over empty nothingness.

In the family, and personal front, the initial confrontation with his brother had been disappointing but being in New York was very stimulating nonetheless. They have continued to visit each other, but it was not as he would have liked. His wife's way of looking negatively at everything, and being still hurt by what she considered a lack of concern in the part of his brother, did not help the situation at all, but his brother was not contributing to create a better relationship either. During more than two years they had kept political opinions away from their conversations but there was some kind of stress that was visible in spite of being silent. Pandemonium broke loose at a party his brother gave in his house when Miguel Angel and his friends started to discuss politics (when they were celebrating by the bar next to the kitchen of his apartment). Michael had tried not to be involved with it, but some remarks, by one of his brother's friends drew him into the discussions. For a while, he had been handling it well, without getting emotional or antagonistic in any way. .

Someone at the party said, "Have you guys heard Castro's last speech and how he blasted the United States for wanting to overthrow the revolutionary government? He said that many Americans would better be ready to die."

"We finally have a government in Cuba that is doing something, and will be able to change things. No one will be able to stop the revolution like they did in Spain," his brother said.

"Everybody in Cuba was in favor of the Spanish Republic," someone else said and added,. "but the problem was that the communists took control of the republican government and started to eliminate everyone that was not in their favor, and that brought up the Civil War and Franco."

"You are right, that was what really happened. It is the way that any totalitarian regime would do, whether you call it revolution in Cuba, or communists in Spain, or Nazis in Germany. They are all the same. They force their doctrine on everyone and jail or kill anyone who does not agree with them." Michael came to say as he joined the discussion.

"I don't know why you are saying that, Michael," his brother came to say. " . . . You should remember that our father was in favor of the republic, and,, if the republic was communist then he was in favor of the communists, because he definitely was not in favor of the Nationalists."

Michael could not help but get quite upset about the remark and immediately confronted his brother, "The founders of the Spanish Republic were in principle elected by the people and my father was definitely in favor of it like most people with progressive and democratic ideals,. but there came the time that a minority of radical communists started to physically eliminate their political adversaries who did not agree with their ideology, eventually forcing themselves and controlling the republic. They initiated the upheaval that gave way to the bloody Spanish Civil War and eventually to Franco's dictatorship. Our father followed everything that happened in Spain and regretted the terrible events of the war but he was a freedom-loving man who did not agree with any totalitarian ideals of any kind. I can't accept what you are saying about him."

"I don't care if you accept that or not. You can't give an opinion about what he believed in because you don't even accept that Cuba is better with a revolutionary government because you say it is communism."

"I don't care what name they have as long as they are implanting a dictatorship – suppressing free press and jailing anyone who they think is an obstacle to their imposing a doctrine that is totally anti-democratic," Michael said, showing his anger about his brother's remarks, after what he started to get up to leave, but not without blasting away: " . . . You did not even want to listen to me. Me, your own brother . . . You should know that the last thing our father would have done was to support a totalitarian dictatorship of any kind. And that is exactly what I can't accept either. You need to know how many people had been jailed and how many had already been shot in Cuba. I don't have to put up with this. I am leaving." He called his family, got the coats and they speedily left.

Later on, but still angry, he wrote his brother a letter to tell him that he was going to leave New York and regretted that they had not been able to have a better relationship under the circumstances of so much lack of understanding. He ended his letter by saying: " . . . Consider me like if I don't exist. Consider me dead."

The situation had affected Michael so much that he had nausea practically every night. He wake up sweating and feeling very sick and would not feel better until he sweated and vomited. It was like he was going to die every time. He started some prescribed medication but nothing seemed to work. He was hopefully expecting to get a contract to work in the management of a gas company in Venezuela but got frustrated with the delays so he decided to leave New York and go to Miami in November, almost three years after his arrival. Three months later, he was finally given the expected assignment in Venezuela, where he fortunately found a doctor who successfully treated him from the terrible conditions that afflicted him for more than five months. The treatment went well and his health started to improve as he left behind all that was tormenting him in New York. He had found great things in the big city and had enjoyed its culture and the challenges it offered but he had been very unhappy living in the same city as his dear brother and not being able to have a relationship with him. Most painful to Michael was that he could not tell his mother that they were not getting alone as she had always wanted. It was easier to tell her that he was not in New York anymore.

Very soon, the lone exile came to the realization that for Cubans, it was extremely difficult to feel totally at home anywhere they went, particularly during the first five years of their life in exile. He would later realize that not being interested in establishing himself in a Cuban community like Miami, as he was not, was partly because of the realization that Cubans in exile found it difficult to feel totally at home anywhere they went. He however, liked the challenge of different cultures rather than to conform to what could perhaps been an easier path. He and his family spent two years in Venezuela and a year and a half in Guatemala, eventually returning to the United States in 1965, settling for three years in Cleveland, Ohio. They finally moved to Cliffside Park on the west side of the Hudson in New

Jersey, the closest that they could be to the big metropolis he felt so attracted to. This time, the city and its surroundings again gave him the opportunity to continue to develop all his skills, at the same time that his young daughters were getting their education in the way he had wanted – in a free environment, one that they could never have had if they had stayed in Cuba with all that is happening there.

The two girls, by this time were in their high school years and counted on the complete support and dedication of their parents. Michael dedicated all the free time he had to be with them – whether it was in recreation, family activities and school's work. Time dedicated to work on his career as an artist was taking a backseat during that time until he realized that unless he would take time for his art work it will get nowhere. It was then the time that he started to work in the late evenings and well after midnight, as he finally started to give way to the nostalgic feelings that separation from his homeland demanded to be expressed, in the best way he could: through his brushes.

Painting became the sanctuary where he soothed his pain and most intimate frustrations. For years he worked on his paintings from ten thirty at night until three in the morning, and many times, when he could not let go off his canvas, he worked until he saw the first rays of light. It was the only way for him if he was going to recuperate from the lost time. It was the time he needed to catch up with his generation; something that he would also do by competing for inclusion of his work in juried exhibitions, winning participation in many, together with a number of awards. Through many years to come, the activity intensified, bordering on obsession, but it was the only thing he knew he had to do if he was to reach what he would always see as the ever-eluding goal. but, as he told some of his colleagues . . . "When you feel you have nothing to struggle and to reach for, you are artistically finished."

Challenges are something that anyone in exile would learn to live with and work hard to accomplish beyond expectation. It has been the pattern of every migration. In the land of the free, the Irish did it first; later the Italian. It was to be no different for the Cubans. The first wave of Cuban exiles of the early 'sixties was mostly composed of professional people; some of whom had the skills but did not have knowledge of the language. but the dignifying common denominator for all immigration, regardless of its origin, is determination and hard work. The sons and daughters grew with the pressure to excel and gain a career. It was not any different for Michael's daughters. Maggie became the first New Jersey ROTC female college graduate under the army program, eventually graduating with a doctorate degree in Organic Chemistry, after which she was offered a teaching position as an officer in West Point Military Academy which she did not accept due to her decision not to pursue a military career. Maritza, the youngest, also graduated with a master's degree in Art and Education. The father was, of course, very proud of them. When it all happened, part of his mission and dream, when he took them out of Cuba, had been accomplished.

In general, the children that were brought out of Cuba when they were four and six years of age respectively, are already becoming the parents of a third generation of children – not of exiled Cubans, but of native North Americans. A new generation that has continued to fully identify with the cause of freedom for the Cuban people that have already created one of the most extraordinary socio-political phenomena in the hemisphere.

The awareness of the new generation is a promising sign for a future that seems to elude the older Cubans who left with the hope of returning to a free Cuba someday, but instead has become a lapse of time that has turned into a long night. A night that has outgrown many unfortunate Cubans who did not survive the entire length of that long night; a truly sad reality that makes the "Cuban Diaspora" a cruel and painful saga where the only palliative is the persistence of the opposition to the Castro regime and the determination not to let go of the struggle for the eventual re-establishment of the democratic principles in the beloved unfortunate island.

Cubans have yet to be understood by a world at large that does not seem to have awareness of their situation or sympathy for their frustration – all that makes the long night of the exiles much darker, but more dignifying.

CHAPTER TWELVE

A Mother's Adios And Dream Of A Return

Ten years after her son's departure, Michael's mother after her eightieth birthday, finally decided to leave Cuba. Her strength was faltering but she still had good health. Not until 1972 did the opportunity suddenly open up when Cuban and U.S. governments agreed to allow a number of flights and let older people travel outside Cuba to either join or visit their relatives. Michael had tried to get a visa in Mexico for the preceding two years, but the Mexican bureaucracy moved too slow ; even with two trips to Mexico and interviews in the Ministry of Government in search of a visa, the efforts were unsuccessful. Only after having written letters to the Red Cross and Immigration Department did he finally obtain a special visa for his mother. The visa she was given was subject to the Cuban government's releasing and allowing the immigration by number order they called *Cupo*. She had *el cupo* but the number was never called because the Castro government suspended the flights and eventually the program over a dispute with the U.S. diplomatic negotiators. Again, Castro used the switch in policy to benefit his bargaining position, in disregard for the needs of the people of his country. Even the humanitarian Conditions were to no avail whatsoever, spreading frustration and pain once again.

He could never forget the face of his mother pressing against the wire fence near the gate when he crossed the gate to board the Havana-Key West ferry that sunny morning of August 19, 1960. Her eyes were swollen from her sleepless night, with a sad-looking expression on them, as he also remembered her last words.

"Take care of yourself, son. Have faith always. My prayers will be with you at all times, and I know you will be back. This situation can't last too long."

It did last much too long, he thought, forty years later.

The image of his mother would come again and again in his thoughts, more frequently as the initial years passed, and even until twelve years later (still in his exile), that it would become clearer in his mind, as it was evident, that he would not wait any more for his mother to tell him that it was time and that the time has come for her to leave Cuba.

Over and over again in his mind he would see her figure become smaller and smaller in the distance as it was on the day he left Cuba when the boat moved away and she remained without moving a single inch until she could no longer see him. It was the image of the moment when he left his mother sadly looking at the spot where he was, as the ferry boat was leaving the docks of Havana; a memory that had not abandoned him. He remembered when in less than an hour of sailing he only saw the bright silhouette of the skyline of Havana – its Malecon and Morro Castles standing mutely and statically in the distance. Only the waters around him moved with its deep blue and very white surf, making a long funnel of which Michael saw himself helplessly floating in its epicenter. His feelings at the time were struggling between relief and sadness that only be drowned under a feeling of newness and adventure, as well as hope. He sensed, however, that it was to be for a long time, but never did he think that he would not see her ever again.

The memories of his mother's positive character gave him some assurance of her emotional survival. She was indeed a very emotional woman when it came to her two sons' well-being. She was also an individualistic person who could not stand impositions and the typical intrusions of a government that already was trying to control everybody's life with the infamous committees (for the defense of the revolution) that was nothing more than the neighborhood stooges who spy even on their closer relatives (an ominous activity that made the environment of the whole country's life rather oppressive). Traditionally, she followed the family's love of freedom and privacy and Michael considered that situation emotionally explosive for her. "Take care of yourself," he had said. "I will want you to come to the States if this situation continues."

"You go, my son. I will stay here with my familiar things and my memories in this house of ours."

She looked about fifteen years younger than her age at the time of his departure even in her mature state. At seventy, since April of that year, she was tireless, healthy looking, and still attractive.

"I still have my brothers, and my dear cousin Alberta, and of course Mariita," she said with a smile that could not hide her sadness.

Mariita was a blessing; she was a nine-year-old orphan when Maria Antonia Marrero had taken her in her care after the death of Mariita's mother and before her ailing father died two years later. She had married his's cousin Mario a year before he left Cuba, and they lived only two houses away on the same street.

Michael felt good about that because the girl that he grew up with, as if she was his older sister, had come to be a loving woman and a dear companion to his mother. And, although Mario was very much in favor of the Castro government at the time, and had been able to secure a job in the nearby railroad and docks, he was, however, a sensible man.

Now and then, through the years, he could visualize his mother in front of her small altar in a private corner of her room, praying, in her usual devotion and faith, asking for protection for her "children" wherever they may be, as he had seen her doing for his brother Miguel Angel when he had left for the United States in the late 'forties.

If Michael was to relate to his motivations, his constant evocation of the happy times of his childhood was probably much in contrast with the pain of separation from the places and people that he so loved. He was not the only one experiencing these feelings, but in itself, they are the common denominator that Cubans carry everywhere they are. Away from what they love and can't forget and not being able to return to it. It is a different kind of migration, particularly the exodus from 1960 to the "Mariel boatlift" of 1980. That was the exodus of the middle class – technicians and professionals, the poor and not-so-poor (not necessarily rich in their majority), but idealistic and totally opposed to any kind of totalitarian rule, no matter what the circumstances. Love of freedom was the essence of their heart.

Those feeling compounded with the beauty they left behind; the land that Christopher Columbus wrote about in his diary: "The most beautiful land that human eyes have ever seen." he grew up with its light and colors in his eyes and he brought them with him in his mind and retina, sunken deep in his soul, to be forever consoled.

Then there were the loved ones who stayed behind – the ones who suffered the most. It had always been painful for most.

Michael and his mother communicated mostly by mail. He tried to keep her in good spirits, but this was a hard blow, particularly at a time when she had wanted to see her sons, perhaps for the last time for her. His frustration grew, and he found solace in his art, in an intense and steady pace that was accentuated in the 'seventies as if it was a balm for his wounds. The distant and the close by, and the ever-present absence of a kind of love he could not find and substituted for with his love of an unreachable countryside, one that laid close at hand in his mind and heart.

On a nostalgic journey at night in his hotel room during his business travels, he had continued to memorize and draw the sketches of peoples and places he left behind. The childhood memories and visual impressions he had stored in his mind were emerging, and soon he started to paint them on canvas as an outlet for his frustrations. The need to not only retain the beauty of his childhood years and his surroundings in his mind alone, but to put them in art form, became almost an obsessive endeavor.

From paintings of his early childhood memories, one of them was selected for an exhibition of paintings by Cuban exiled artists in Saint Peter's College of Jersey City, New Jersey. His younger daughter Maritza, who was, at one time, an art student in the class of the Cuban master Daniel Serra Badue', had helped to organize the exhibition.

A number of the paintings exhibited expressed the agony of the oppressed Cuban people denouncing human right abuses and their lack of cultural freedom. His only painting in the exhibition was just of a landscape from a childhood memory of the large warehouses by the docks next to the Fesser Railroad Station in his home town.

The New York Spanish language newspaper, *Diario La Prensa*, covered the exhibition widely. A photo of his beloved daughter Maritza and both their names appeared prominently on the press coverage. One of the photos published showed a painting, by one of the participants. It had a Cuban flag with a sickle ripping a bleeding star in pieces. A week after the closing of the exhibition, they received an anonymous letter addressed to his home. The letter defended the Cuban regime as "the legitimate" choice of the people where artists were well appreciated by the regime and had the freedom to produce any art they wanted, and then gave examples of how well Portocarrero and other Cuban artists were treated. The letter was extensive in details and it represented a veiled thread when it ended saying, "Keep working on your art, but remember that its contents will be noticed or taken in consideration." Its intention was to create the sense of being watched. He was amazed at seeing the length by which an ominous regime would go to scare people – even away from their country.

Because the three-page anonymous letter was so well documented about the artists living in Cuba, Michael suspected that the letter had been prepared in the Cuban UN diplomatic mission. being as it may, it was a disquieting situation.

Within less than six months after that experience, He was able to relate the incident with another yet more disturbing one when he received a call from his sister in Cuba telling him that his mother was in the hospital. She had had a thrombosis, she said, and one part of her face was partially paralyzed, but that she was recuperating well.

"When did it happen?" Michael asked.

"Oh, it was already three weeks ago, but she did not want for me to say anything to you until she got better."

"How is she doing now? . . . Can she talk?"

"Yes, but not too well yet. She is doing better, and she may be released soon enough, but she will need more therapy. We were lucky that we took her to the hospital right away. The doctors say that her condition is fair now, but found her too nervous and recommended a lot of rest and to avoid emotional stress."

"What happened?" hr asked, fearing that her conditions may have been caused by being upset about something.

"Well, we didn't want to tell you, but they did a search of the house the day before she got sick. They were three men, but they were not from the town, they must have been from the Seguridad del Estado, the G-2 from Havana. Your mother thinks that the reason was because of her nephew Roberto, who was jailed recently, accused of sabotage in the factory where he used to work in Guanabacoa. but I don't think so because they were looking in your old bookcase and desk and they took a lot of your things."

"Like what?" he asked.

"Well, there were some large rolls of paper, old drawings, I think, and photos. Ah, also your old large leather briefcase that you left with your mother, and other papers you had left in the bookcase."

"Damn it. bastards. It is criminal. No wonder my mother got so upset, and has been hurt." He could not repress the anger as frustration overcame him and continued his outburst of anger as his sister interrupted him. "Michael, let's not talk any more about it please. We have enough trouble as it is."

Michael was so overwhelmed with anguish that he could not say much more about his feelings, but finally managed to say, " . . . Tell my mother not to worry so much, and to take care of herself and avoid getting upset; there is nothing to justify this action, we have nothing to hide. Our life has been always on a clear path, and we have not been actively political. We were not with batista as we are not with this people either." After which, the communication was suddenly cut off.

As he said those few words, he was also thinking that for a totalitarian regime such as this one, all you need in order to be hit was to be not with them.

"Yes . . ." he ascertained in his mind, we have not been actively political in the sense of the word but we have been known in the town for being independent, and freedom-loving people. He remembered when he was fifteen and had a fistfight with a young man of his age whose entire family was militant communists. The arguments that lasted over half an hour revolved around the doctrine of José Martí and the doctrine of Marxism. Michael stressed then that the argumentative youngster would rather honor the USSR flag of the hammer and sickle instead of the Cuban flag and the Cuban ideals of independence from any foreign power proclaimed by the Cuban patriot. The answer was a resounding "Yes", and that was enough to start the fight. Three other youngsters jumped in, one of them holding Michael from his neck, and back but he was able to shunt him over his shoulders with a fast movement, holding his own ground until a few older people who were around the plaza intervened. By the time the fight was stopped, he had been able to hit the other youngster with a few hard blows.

He also remembered the speeches he had written and given during patriotic celebrations at his hometown's Juvenile Fraternity when he was a secretary of the association and later on as its president from the time he was seventeen to his twenty-second birthday. Indeed, he had followed the ideals of his father and uncle about equality and respect for everyone within the frame of independence and freedom,. but he could not even come to wonder how those factors would come to mean anything at such a distant date. The thought came again to the most recent event at the exhibition in Saint Peter's College, and the threatening letter.

It was all happening at the time of the terrible 'seventies in Cuba. Those were the years in which the government of Fidel Castro launched a campaign to discredit and incarcerate any free thinking poet, writer, and artist that showed displeasure with the regime. The year following the infamous *Caso Padilla* or the "Padilla Affair", they incarcerated the poet and author of *Fuera de Juego* ("Out of the Game"), Heberto Padilla, and forced him to publicly declare himself wrong, make apologies, and denounce his colleagues, obviously under enormous psychological pressure to exert from him his "Mea Culpas" – a shameful display of an insane doctrine of paranoia that showed the omnipotence of the most insecure and insufferable regime. To Michael, the incident of the search in his mother's house was just one more of the same, only that the consequences were closer, and he could feel the dagger piercing his heart, even in the distance.

Much more had happened since then. There are just too many years, too many rotten deeds.

He was able to talk with his mother a few times by telephone when her speech got better. but on the following year, she had another attack and she could not speak again. She had a partial paralysis and suffered for another two years and then she died in his sister's arms. He was saddened by the news, which he did not receive until a month later. In a way, there was a sense of relief in his heart because the suffering of his mother had been too long and extremely painful for him too. Her soul was now resting.

He would only be able to see his mother's grave in his hometown cemetery. For many years before her passing, he had always thought that they would be able to see each other again. But, instead, he continued to see her in his mind, as he had done for so many years.

The fall of the USSR at the end of the twentieth century ended the last vestiges of the Cold War. Many freedom-loving Cubans in and out of Cuba rejoiced in the expectation of the proximity of the end of communism in the island. Michael surprised himself when at a dinner, with a few American friends answering the question as to how soon he thought it will be, he said without much thought: "At least ten to twelve years."

"Are you really sure?" He thought for a moment and said, "I don't know. The answer just came that way . . . I hate to think that it will take that much, but somehow, I just do not want to be disappointed with expectations. The situation is unpredictable even when Castro no longer has the shield he availed himself with when he took advantage of the confrontation between the USSR and the U.S.A. to practically perpetuate his dictatorship."

More than ten years had already passed since the fall of the "Iron Curtain" and Castro is still in power. The reasons are many – one of them is the embargo. The European nations do not agree with the U.S. policy and have invested large sums of money in Cuba, primarily on tourism. Like able players, they have made their moves and taken positions. Scruples are not an issue with them. They pay Castro well, and Castro, in turn, pays slave's wages to the Cubans working in the tourist industry. The "Investors", with the complicity or without regulations from their governments, do not pay workers directly; they pay the Cuban government. The wages are way below the standard of some of the worse of the so-called Third World nations. Moreover, Castro has made the dollar the currency of choice, allowing it to be used freely in the country. Cubans are paid in pesos that have a very low acquisitive power; officially, twenty-five pesos would approximately buy one dollar, but in reality, the speculators could get more than that. Most jobs are paid the equivalence of misery, with ten dollars a month. Cubans who are not able to somehow earn a few more dollars from the tourist industry find it very hard to live on their peso earnings. Prostitution has run rampant as a means, and a sad *marches de force* for many young girls, even those holding a degree, not necessarily on the oldest profession of them all. Cubans across the world send millions of dollars to their relatives in Cuba to help them survive and as a result, the regime also benefits from it.

Since 1996, the Cuban government has offered visas to exiled Cubans to visit their relatives and the U.S. itself is also allowing U.S. citizens of Cuban origin to visit Cuba once a year. The result is more dollars come in that help the Cuban regime. All these agreements between Cuba and the U.S.A. came to be conceived since the 1994 crisis with the large exodus of Cuban rafters across the Florida Strait. In a shameless treaty to stop the flow, the U.S. agreed to block access to the U.S. shores by sending back any Cubans who were caught, unable to touch U.S. shores. Under this agreement, many honorable Cubans have been denied asylum and have been sent back to face punishment and disgrace in the island; while a lottery in Cuba selects the lucky few who are allowed to immigrate to the U.S.

More than frequently, the TV cameras showed the shameful and sad tragedies of the U.S. Coast Guards discharging their water hoses on the desperate families to make it impossible for them to reach U.S. shores which, on account of such agreements, no longer looked like "the land of the free" for the families who risked their lives in search of freedom, and were denied it. Many had died on the dangerous crossing, but the world seemed to have become desensitized to tragedies like these.

Michael had grown tired of seeing so much hypocrisy and lack of dignity in the daily tilling of political conveniences, which has been all that really counted in most cases – the particular interest of governments take precedent to any other issue. but no one is going to fight decisive battles for Cubans; they have to do it by themselves, and their only allies are the few institutions and honorable few statesmen who promote human rights and denounce the abuses, and in some way obtain some results, however limited, because that ultimately lies on the Cuban government to implement since they are masters in the game of deceit.

After so many years of the same, now at the beginning of the new millennium, in the midst of so much political maneuvering and seeing how insignificant and ineffective as well as unimportant has been the attitude of most Cuban exiles of not wanting to go back to Cuba until the end of Castro (while many of them are dying before seeing that happen), he decided that he will not be one more on the long list. He will go back to see the disaster for himself. To take the bitter taste of the long and unresolved suffering of its people; to breathe the soft breeze in his lungs that had not forgotten; to feel with its people the oppressive atmosphere that still reigns, and laugh with them about it if he can (as many who stayed behind, including the ones coming to existence during the long process have done, in order to survive and not to surrender their most precious sense of humor and the like). Most of all, he wanted to see the sad faces of children together with the smile in their hopeful eyes, and for him to embrace those who come with love in hand, and not to render tribute to those without a heart.

As Michael will go and walk again over the steps of his younger years to reach his beloved surroundings, he will most of all, miss his mother's kisses – those that mothers always reserve for their returning children. He will feel them in the morning mist and the warm rays of the sun, or the rain that will come to wet his face. He will see her face come away, off the fence that separated them that day when he sailed away, and he will see it come to him and feel again her warm caress. He will stand on that small piece of ground that received her remains, he swears he will, an he will also feel her caress again as he would be there closing his eyes in that sacred place, and in the end

CHAPTER THIRTEEN

Encounter With Arial "The Forbidden Path"

Painting for Beltran was like a way to make contact with his past; not so much the painful, as the joyful one, and more so, the memories of the innocent years – his happy childhood years. He however, found himself entering inside the harsh subjects of the sufferings of the Cuban people. Such was the case when he met the poet Armando Valladares, and his wife Martha in Madrid during his visit to Madrid in 1984 to meet Armando and Marta Valladares. Armando and Beltran, had both, just a year before had received the honors of a meritorious award, granted to each of them by The Cintas Foundation, and both of them were able to celebrate together by meeting in Madrid, for the first time, about a year after the award.

Martha had worked many years to gain international support by calling attention to the poet's suffering, who had been confined to a wheelchair during some final years of his twenty years inside Castro's jails. Her gentle, and persuasive personality, and collected poise carried the voice denouncing the human rights abuses by the regime, and her husband's conditions, making it known worldwide; Martha finally succeeded, when the French Prime Minister Mitterand obtained the release of her husband. The personal testimony which came directly from the poet, stirred anguish and anger in Beltran when he heard the intensely passionate poet, just out of Castro's jails, sitting on the edge of his chair, to narrate the horrors to which political prisoners in Cuba were subjected..

Another disturbing testimony was the one he heard from Jorge Valls,. the almost dogmatic poet and writer who had been in jail almost as much as Valladares.. Within two years of Vall's arrival in New York, the hardly understood ex-political prisoner moved to Miami, where he was harshly criticized by the exile community, for advocating a policy of peaceful civil disobedience, and open communication, or dialogue with Cuba (which was mostly interpreted by the local exile community there as an appeasing policy that could favor more than hurt the Cuban government).

Immediately after his return from Madrid to New York, Beltran depicted the predicament of the political prisoners in a life-size spontaneous oil painting he named *Mud Walls* (*Las Tapiadas*), which is the name given in Cuba to the filthy solitary confinement cells for political prisoners. The cells were blocked from outside light and, in them, the psychological and physical torture given to the prisoners were unmentionable. The political prisoners who refused to wear the regular convicts' uniform and who did not accept the brainwashing rehabilitation were placed naked in such terrible solitary confinement cells, where they shared the tight and crude hole with the rats and roaches, and had to suffer all kind of indignities like being thrown urine and excrements, to make the demonic place even more unbearable. Jorge Valls saw the large painting with the figure of a naked prisoner inside the shameful jail hanging in the artist studio during the only visit he made to the artist, and sat silently in front of the painting, for a while before he was interviewed by the well-known and respected Cuban journalist Aleida Duran (who was also visiting his Ridgefield studio at the time). Aleida had consistently written about the feelings that Beltran expressed on many of his paintings. The interview with Valls, which was later published by the Hudson Dispatch's Spanish weekly, *Ahora*, was the first that the ex-political prisoner gave after his arrival in New York. Jorge Valls was not known to be a man of light talk, but before moving to the table to talk to Aleida Duran, he walked over towards the artist, and said, "Most painters have been known or become notable artists by only one or two pieces of their work. I think that you may have already done yours with these two."

"You may be right about famous painters, but I am far from that and perhaps, my best work is still waiting to be done, if at all. I am glad that you are impressed with them. Thanks for saying that."

"I only say what I see in them, Beltran. You don't have to thank me for it."

The other painting Valls was referring to, and which was next to *Las Tapiadas*, was the *Lapse*, that was done at the same time and with the same dimensions as *Las Tapiadas*, but on a horizontal format. The *Lapse* also contained the expression of despair on two tragic figures emerging from a devastated landscape.

Years later, the visions of the sad subject of many Cubans risking their lives taking to the sea in search for freedom, sailing from the northern shores on makeshift rafts, came to be captured in his paintings. The anguish of his people who die daily at sea in their desperate effort to gain freedom, has been something that could not escape the sensitivity expressed in his paintings. He wondered how much more a country has to suffer for people around the world to condemn the Castro regime for the human right abuses and the totalitarian grip it has on its people. Instead, the blame has been mostly placed only on the so-called embargo by the United States. The embargo that many called "blockade", to inadequately compare it to the harmful "blockade" suffered by Spain, as the result of the Civil War. This, so-called embargo is the biggest excuse that many foreign dignitaries, and some naive, as well as others not-so-naive, but tendentious intellectuals, find to be apologetic towards the ominous regime in Cuba, much to the enjoyment of the man who continues to subjugate its suffering people while shielding himself, and his totalitarian policies behind his favorite slogans and accusations against "Yankee Imperialism" and the inhumane embargo. Yes, the embargo appears to be inhumane, and much of the world is against it. He had been seeing that it had hurt the Cuban people more than it has hurt the regime, had also been skeptical of its effectiveness, and saw it as a poor substitute for what should instead be a different and more effective policy of discrediting Castro around the world; something that had not been achieved by the embargo. He had come to believe that the embargo had not worked at all, except to help Castro to have a good excuse and stay in power while the world felt sorry for the Cuban people, but saying nothing for the fact that the scarcity and anguish suffered by the people in the unfortunate island goes beyond the effects of an unpopular and in many ways unenforceable embargo. It should be made clear to the world that the scarcity and the poor conditions of the vast majority of the Cuban people had long being instituted, among other reasons, by the high cost of maintaining the largest military establishment in the hemisphere after the United States, and the lack of incentive for production in an economy totally controlled by the state.

He had, for many years, kept his opinions about the embargo private, because he had not wanted to offend the sensitivity of so many well-intended friends, as well as the older Cuban exiles, many of whom had suffered many years of unjust incarceration under Castro, and who were mostly in favor of anything that would offer some hope to finish the long Cuban nightmare, as they are driven more by passion rather than reason in the struggle against the regime. but he had communicated with Congressman Torricelli and others about the need to discredit Castro around the world for what he really is, and at the same time he recommended a change to the "policy of isolation" created by the embargo which only helped the dictator and as a result, discredited the United States more than anything.

Politics is something of a matter of convenience rather than a matter of justice for most politicians, and the political leaders of most developed countries are involved in the financial, as well as the security interests of their own countries instead of the morality of their foreign policies. He had come to that conclusion, and had long disbelieved any promises by politicians of any of the major American parties and its candidates in relation to Cuba. Many times he told his friends of the cowardice represented by his having left Cuba instead of staying and becoming involved in an effort to change the course of events, as he feels that Cubans alone have to resolve the Cuban problem. but the Cuban situation under Castro is more complex than that, mainly because from the outset it was turned into a convenient "kick ball" in the international political arena. In the end, only a change of circumstances and general internal civil disobedience and open defiance such as what happened in Romania and also in Poland, and other East European countries, could do away with the current system of government and its rule of fear and institutionalized military power.

In Cuba, the element of political oppression adds dimension to the tragedy, like it does in any migration where the element of fratricidal and power-driven wars are evident, in a world thirsty for peace and respect for human rights. It is not that the Cuban tragedy should be given more attention or be considered more justified than any other. It is only, that it should be better understood and condemned by the international community of nations. Never under any previous governments, including the colonial years under the rule of Spain has the world seen Cubans taking out to sea in such deplorable conditions to flee from oppression.

He knew how strong the motivation was to those wanting to take their children out from under an oppressive system that suppressed the free will of its people – as he himself did with his own daughters in 1960. He was not born with the vocation of a politician but that of an artist, with love for his personal political independence and free will. His works, related to the tragedy of his country, had noted human suffering as a product of tyranny, but have, for the most part, been centered on the beauty of his childhood surroundings and its people. As years passed, the desire of the artist in him to go back and see it again, in spite of the intolerable political conditions, had grown stronger and stronger. He wanted to be able to embrace his sister and her children and see his cousins again and the other relatives and old friends who may still be alive. He longed to see his hometown, and his mother's town of Guanabacoa, and return to Old Havana by his beloved *lanchita* (or whatever they may be using now), to cross the bay under the same sky that no one can change, and see the geography that should still be awaiting any possible deterioration by time and neglect as well as human change to the landscape, and damage caused to the facades of buildings facing the same sun and the same sea. He wanted to reconstruct all of it back in this mind, painful as it may be, to face the harsh realities of his land and his people. He needed to see it under their conditions of despair; the need, at least, to try to spread some love and perhaps find a new understanding of mankind and history in the making; come back if he could, to paint and perhaps to write his impressions in his older age.

He had lived through changing times. The passing years in the last five decades, and possibly the pressures of unforeseen realities in a changing world, had brought about events that he had never thought would come to his personal life and the lives of so many other Cuban exiles. He had seen people die of sadness, as the case of the acclaimed Cuban actor Otto Sirgo, followed by the sudden death of his young daughter and also the death of the most revered comedian actors Alberto Garrido and Federico Pineiro, creators of the beloved characters of "El Negrito" and "El Gallego" who immediately got sick with deep depression and died in Miami within only a year or two of leaving Cuba. Likewise, the many couples whose marriages were broken by the stress caused by political disagreements and by the conditions that they had to adapt themselves to in a foreign environment.

He remembered the time when he coincided with Federico Pineiro on the first trip he made to Key West on the ferryboat in the summer of '57, when the famous actor sat next to him at the boat's cafeteria and bar, when Pineiro asked the bar tender, "Is that the same turkey you have been taking back and forth since last year?" He said, jokingly referring to the sick-looking turkey on the sandwich counter. They both laughed and he got into an uplifting and humorous conversation with the funny and humane actor, leaving him with thethought that for more than forty years, the Cubans have been given the same rotten turkey.

being as it may, as years passed, he had come to believe that nothing happens for no reason at all, and in some way, what is going to happen does happen. However, he did not forget that in his beliefs, there is also the element of influencing events in one's personal life. Negative thought could bring negative adverse events; likewise, positive thoughts would no doubt bring good ones. He also believes in handling your life as if you can change everything you are capable of, but let the events you can't change happen and to work with the resulting situations to make every possible improvement to the conditions created by the uncontrollable events as you strive to change them.

That may all be a very simple philosophy but most people do not realize how many of them knock their heads against a destructive psychological wall, incapable of understanding how and when to make the changes that they can make. but they can't even think of adapting to new circumstances and improving upon them, instead of blaming either their bad luck or other people, without looking for solutions within themselves and their own attitude.

As he was growing up, he had nightmares like the one recurrent bad dream he had during his childhood in Cuba. The bad dream consisted of having to face terrible and unjust accusations. He could not identify what he was accused of, but he knew it was terrible and there was nothing he could find or do to clear himself from it, finally waking up in great agony over the unresolved and ominous situation. The nightmare would recur every now and then until it finally stopped as he grew up. However, he had been so impacted by it that he was never able to forget it, as if it was some kind of mysterious premonition. Later on in his adult life, he would come to find out why.

In his childhood he was not only blessed by having parents that had spirituality in their lives (it showed in the way each one of them believed in a Supreme being and how they were guided by faith, not however, in any rigid dogmatic way). His mother placed her faith in the guidance and protection of the Saints and God from a conventional, but independent Catholic base; his father and uncle were both "Master Masons", who had reached the highest degree of their development in the Masonic Order of Free Masons. They both believed in a Supreme being and the divine nature of men and women as God's design and creation; and they both participated in private spiritual sessions following the recognized scientific methods that were very much in the European culture at the turn of the century. The young Michael was able to read texts by the French spiritualist Denizard Rivail, known as "Allan Kardec", and the studies and findings of Carl Gustav Jung and Sigmund Freud at home in his father's library as he was growing up. On the books, he learned about the practice of bringing spirits through mediums, but he did not agree with the practice; father and son had conversations about it when his father was recommended to consult the spirits about his failing health. He However thought that real and live doctors should be consulted when the sickness was of the body. "Spiritual guidance is something different than physical well-being," he had told his father when they discussed the subject as if he was already a grown man, which he was not.

Three years after his father death, his older cousin Ursula, told him about his father's spirit appearing in the weekly sessions they had (of consulting the spirits) every Friday in his uncle's house. " . . . You should come," she said, "it will be good for you because you will be able to communicate with him. We have seen him appearing, wearing his usual blue denim overalls he liked so much to wear on his job."

He was overcome with a kind of unusual feeling when he heard about it, and answered: "No. I think that I don't like to give his spirit anything to worry about our 'ephemeral' earthy life."

"That is fine, Michael, if you feel that way. It is not that we want to call the spirits to give them our worries. The spirit of our dear ones are restless as they wander very near us on earth before they elevate and they want to give us, (the relatives that they left behind) the necessary faith, and reassurance about the spiritual life before they elevate to reach closer to our Maker. ""That is interesting, cousin, but I will pray for his soul and that is all I want to do now. Thank you for telling me about it anyway."

Years later, he became very close to Ursula. She was already approaching her eightieth birthday and, as a retired professor, lived alone in Miami. She was an extremely independent, and strong in character, with a great education and universal knowledge. Ursula had not only been a very supportive cousin, as well as her other two sisters were, during the painful failure of his marriage and finally the separation that followed, but she was also a source of wisdom that helped him to understand things he would have never thought about.

He has been deeply in pain and suffering from what he saw as an attempt to discredit and separate him from his daughter and grandchildren's love. It was a very difficult time when he saw his intentions to maintain a civilized relationship being thwarted by resentment and ill-founded stories. Considering his loving nature and his most desired wish of keeping close to his daughters and Not far from who was the loving mother of their two married girl,s, . and his grandchildren, the hurtful attitude of the mother unfortunately resulted in a way of punishment and something that brought much anguish and a sense of guilt to his soul. The conversations with Ursula during his many visits to Florida were a source of encouragement and better understanding from a spiritual standpoint.

"You have always been a loving man to your wife and daughters,. Don't let anything bring you down. You deserve to be happy." Ursula would tell her younger cousin, time and again during the most difficult periods of the painful process following the separation, all what caused much distortion and disruption, contrary to his expectation of a loving and more amicable resolution as he had hoped to see. Through it all, Ursula continued to bring him peace of mind and understanding. "You see, there are some people who bring with them a very negative attitude by their own nature. Such people can't be made happy, no matter how hard you try, and they can make others very unhappy, just by not opening up to them. It is a condition they bring in their spirit because of family influences but mostly because of their 'karma', all of what gets more complicated when others, not directly involved family members, are allowed or decide to get actively involved in a negative way as they may have no honest interest in being conciliatory at all.

I can see that all of it has unfortunately happened, Ursula said as she continue to say. I believe that every person has a destiny and a mission. They also have the load they bring from previous lives to contend with and overcome, or improve upon during their life,. likewise, others bring light and happiness. You had been giving everything you needed spiritually to bring happiness to a person. Some people are very difficult to give happiness to. . They can build a castle around them, and not let neither their feelings be expressed or acknowledge that they received any. There is no possibility of spiritual identification, much less joyful intimacy with such souls since they base their existence in the fear they bring or create within them, . I have noticed this a long time ago," she continued: "She was not a bad person, in spite of her apparent inability to enjoy a close relationship with family instead of being so distant all the time, even with you. I never wanted to say anything because everyone has to find his own way according to the

Divine design. As much as everyone has to learn and has his own evolution during his or her own lifetime, no one can force anything unto anyone else, like you can't make anybody love you by force. And everyone should learn to let people find their own happiness, more so when you can't give it to them, no matter how hard you try. When you open yourself to others you can find your own happiness, but when you let insecurity and resentment take over your heart, you can't blame anyone for your miseries. Worse yet, when you spread that attitude to your own children and your children's children."

Michael reflected about all his cousin words of spiritual wisdom, and absorbed it to calm his anxiety and frustrations. He was himself a believer in the will of God, but could not easily understand the forces behind many of his own decisions or why. It was as if he was totally helpless, except, and unless it was by that intimate mysterious guidance that he submitted himself to, time, and again, in prayer in moments of desperation when he did not know what to do, and in moments of meditation when he considered his options in light of his values and the realities he was confronted with. He though himself guilty above all, and he felt the deep pain with the saddening situation that have slowly changed what appeared to be an enviably and apparently happy life in the eyes of many and for many years. He also grew in frustration for not being allowed to avoid much of the anguish his wife and daughters were forced to be in by inescrupulous attorneys, and some other family members, beyond their two beloved daughters.

Maturity had come to his life with a set of difficult circumstances and hard choices. He had been deeply tormented for years, and as time went by, on his two already married daughters' estrangement from him. The situation had continued for more than twenty years There had not been any hope of a change in the painful family situation that would continue to last to no foreseeable end. He has missed the singular personality of his cousin and her spiritual strength. Her stimulating insight was to last him forever.

At this juncture in his life, his convictions had grown stronger in all his beliefs, as he had realized, through his own experience, the..... reassurance that inner spiritual awareness and strength is absolutely necessary to sustain faith and to survive adversities. (Any adversity that all mortals, him included, are confronted with, at one time or another.) Perhaps the confrontations are tests to learn by and grow spiritually, he has come to think; but he also thought that one of the ways to be free, is not to be dogmatic in any religious beliefs and likewise, not to be a fanatic in either religion, or politics.

Approximately a year after his cousin's death, and much to his surprise and amazement, he had a strange but revealing dream. It happened when he was traveling in Spain during the middle of the year 2000.

In his dream, Michael saw himself walking downhill towards his mother's house in Regla, his hometown. It was very early in the morning on the first hours of dawn, surrounded by a dense fog when he heard a familiar voice calling him by his name, he looked back and could see only the bulk of a figure moving through the misty space. No features of the face were visible under the heavy atmospheric conditions. It was the closest he could be to a ghostly encounter but not quite like it. In reality, it appeared to be just caused by the weather, as he could not even see details of his own hands well when he extended his arms towards the person that was calling his name. The figure moved towards him and stopped about four feet away where the face was still blurred but the voice he was hearing again mentioning his name unmistakable brought him memories of his old childhood friend.

"Who are you?" he asked in a shiver.

"I am Arial, and I know you well."

"Arial?" he asked. " That name is somewhat familiar," he said, thinking of the weird and apparent error he continuously made on the keyboard of his computer. Many times when typing the name Eloy, he ended up typing the name Arial when he looked at the monitor.

"Yes, it is my name in spirit. I was Eloy, now I am Arial, which means the 'sun in spring', or the 'sunlight coming from the constellation Aries'. And that is my spirit name. I had wanted to talk to you for a long time but it had not been possible until this moment because it is the first time that you have come visually in my real space. The only other time I was only able to come into your subconscious mind was when you were painting your memory of *El Callejon del Sapo*, the one you called the *Forbidden Path*."

"Oh,. It was a very strange thing," he said, somewhat trembling nervously as his words came surprisingly calm and natural for such an occasion. "I had been doing the painting from the memory of my childhood friend and the faces that I introduced on the ground of the path were intended to be women's faces. Only a few months, after I finished the painting, a friend who was visiting my studio commented something about the face on the central lower plane of the path and that comment kept me thinking about that face. A few weeks later, while I was driving back home and thinking about the face, I came to the conclusion that perhaps, it was like my friend's face. I got home and went straight to the basement where the painting was and much to my astonishment, that face had a great resemblance to your face, Eloy. You mean Arial, don't you? I mean Arial." Well you have to excuse my feeling nervous.

"It was me, Arial. Don't get stifled about that., It was about nineteen eighty-eight when you were working very late at night in your basement studio. Your brother had died in December of the prior year and it was a difficult and confusing time for you . . . when you were becoming aware of how deeply disturbed you were shortly after that trip to Mexico, when thereafter. you suffered because you were still married and you questioned your feelings."

"Yes, those were difficult times. I used to spend many hours painting every night until the early hours in the morning with very little rest."

"but it was more difficult for you later when you realized that you were living a lie, and needed to rectify."

"I became very concerned and tormented by the fact that I was lying to myself, and later to my family."

"Yes, I know. You had been very unhappy after both of your daughters married and left home and you were feeling how empty your life was and how much that sudden and unexpected love was growing while something was dying in you day by day."

"Yes, Eloy..... No, Arial, but those were difficult times. I really didn't know what was happening to me, except that I had been unfulfilled and unhappy for a long, long time before that when all along it seemed to me that I was giving much love and was getting nothing in return. I felt I needed, but it did not seem that the complaints were attended to.. My warning signs were not listened to and love seemed to become more distant from me more than ever. It was like a retreat without return, no matter how hard you tried to change that course, and that was a progressive situation for many years – long before my feelings started to change, long before having met a caring and expressive being who touched my heart. I was not getting anywhere. I was alone most of the time. No sharing of feelings or much else of the simplest things a couple can do together was either possible or enjoyed. I don't think that I was ever selfish but perhaps something was changing inside of me. It was very painful and frustrating, and I was feeling like everything was dying inside of me – as if I was getting very seriously sick. but I would not talk about it to anyone. Eventually, there was not a sense of family or togetherness.. There is no family when your children go on their lives and find no time to come to spend a few minutes with you again. Not even on holidays when it seems that you have to almost beg for them to come, and when they will do it, it is late or not at all on many occasions. I can't blame them anyway. We parents are supposed to give unconditionally, and so I have done it without regret. Ultimately, a couple does not make much of any sense, if they have no cohesion when they are left alone. but even when the family was together, there was invariably a distance in positions, whether psychological or real. I kept taking sanctuary in my art, as my only consolation. Nothing that I tried would work, but a lot of that, through a long time, can make anyone weary, even when there were not many bitter confrontations since appearances were always kept. Maybe, there should have been some harsher ones and with it finding a better understanding and a more loving relationship but neither one liked confrontations. I should be taking the blame anyway. I should have done more to change things or change myself, and be different . . . I don't know what else to say."

"Naturally, they were difficult times," Arial said and kept on talking, even from his blurred state. "I knew how much you were praying. It was quite often and you kept on doing it constantly, even when driving your car. Day after day, asking for guidance when you considered making your feelings known to your wife. You had asked for it to be God's will, and to take you away somehow before you would tell her. You wanted to die first, but you also could not live in a lie, and you were afraid to lose everything – the love of your daughters, the respect of your wife, all of whom you loved very much. You could not do everything. Appear to be a husband and become a liar, a lover, and a cheat."

"Yes, it was a very anguishing and shameful period. Anyone would have to live through it and to know, before making any judgment. but I was not taken away – I didn't die in any freak accident of sorts, that I had prayed for, and I had to confront my reality and set everything on a difficult path of truth. I handled it badly. It was not an easy thing to do, lovingly and gently as I thought I was doing it. but in that tormenting period that I was living, I came to believe that my truth would be acceptable and understood, and that I was going to be able to maintain a civilized relationship and also be able to help in any healing and adjustment process that was surely going be necessary. I didn't want to run, and I wasn't running away from all my responsibilities. I just wanted understanding and freedom to change my life, set it on an honest path and, I was convinced that love, if there was love in my family, would not die completely or be substituted for hate or resentment. I realized that I was totally wrong about that. The message I thought I received as the only honorable solution was not a suicide, and was not an accident that would have taken me away without anyone to be blamed, did not happen. I had to follow my bliss and try to make corrections in my life."

"I am sure you had to." He thought he heard the fading voice saying.

"Yes, but that was nine years ago. That anguish had somewhat been left behind, Arial. I still have with me the legacy effect of being condemned by my daughters – not wanting to see me or talk to me. .

It was something totally absurd, but no one listened to me. My letters were returned in shreds. My calls ignored, and I felt vilified. People who had nothing to do with the family heard horrendous things and fortunately some doubtful ones came to me for clarification, as one of them did during the funeral of my good friend, the poet Pablo Le Riverend in March of nineteen ninety-one. I remember when my old friend Francisco Feito came to hold on to me because I was very pale and with great pain on my chest, as I was overcome with all those negative emotions. the pain in my heart and chest lasted for more than a year before it that eventually and slowly subsided afterwards – thanks to medication and swimming. I know that my small family's pain was as hard as well, I am sure, more so because of the road was conducted towards a bitter confrontation and resentments rather than reason and enlightenment. No opportunity to listen and no allowance for understanding and healing were to ever be given. I had said many things that I thought would be helpful in fomenting a better understanding, but I was a fool by even saying them. There is never a good time for bad news and some things don't make themselves wait, as they are not in your power. I suppose."

"Yes, I know. I know it better than you do because I have followed your path just as when we took that walk along El Callejon del Sapo," Arial said moving closer to put his hand on his shoulder. "I have perceived how badly you have felt about it all, but I also know that you have been happy, long after all that turmoil in your lives had somewhat subsided. You have found your real spiritual self. Not only have you found what you perceived as a more perfect balance in a relationship but also the complete identification of heart and soul. Things have a way to turn for the better for everyone, in the end. Some people find peace and happiness in being by themselves without the fear and the challenge of a relationship, even when pride would not allow them to admit it. Some find happiness in being left alone since, as they bring the people whom they care about closer to themselves, they might cause them the pain that they cry about. Too bad that some people take a long time to see that truth is better regardless of the pain it may generate. It is also true that the cost of that immense and intimate fulfillment of all aspiration of living a true and reciprocal love is high, but the pain for truth in love is well compensated in the long run."

"What you are saying have the wisdom of the heavens, Arial, but we don't always see that clearly because of our earthy nature. Most people in this world are interested in condemnation and punishment rather than understanding and forgiveness. There are deeds of hate and they are a crime but there are deeds that are not created by hate and may have much to do with love. We are not prepared to distinguish between them, and more so if we become overwhelmed by obfuscation and put aside our understanding."

"That is normal. Unfortunately, there are not any schools to teach that during the early stages of a person's education – at least not yet. but I just wanted you to see some of the unseen goodness and to ease the sense of guilt that goes with your situation," Arial said as the figure started to retreat and fade away.

"Wait . . . Wait," "How about my biggest worry now – which is, my sorrow for knowing that those who keep so much resentment for loved ones can't have real peace and can't find true joy in their hearts and souls? I have been praying for that to change. Can you tell me? Can you help? You are close to that infinite wisdom that understands and knows us all, and loves above all, that who knows all the truth. Can we see, as I have asked, the end to the painful journey of those for whom I still have much love in my heart and great concern for?"

"My dear friend, not everything is to be revealed at this encounter we are having, which is probably the only one time that we will communicate in this way, at least about this subject. Your cousin Ursula also had some answers, but not all. The answer is not in any one but in those who want to live in resentment instead of forgiveness. It is a simple case of following the word. Peace and joy is in forgiveness especially on things having to do with love. Truth is hard to accept but, love those who place you in the path of painful and honest truth, because in it you will be blessed. You yourself have also been suffering for the truth. Open up your mind. Forgive yourself. Be blessed, Michael, be blessed . . . !" Arial's voice sounded lower and more distant as the shapeless contour of his undistinguishable figure disappeared, and he was left alone. Michael turned around and started downhill. The fog was lighter and he could see the long stretch of water of the bay at the bottom as he had seen it so many times – before, sparkling in the sunlight. but he would not be able to get closer to it before he waked up.

He could not fully understand if it was a dream or a real revelation coming from the spirit of his childhood friend Eloy, by way of a ghost he could hardly see but hear so well and clear in a dream. He silently thought out some prayer as he turned in his bed and became profoundly asleep again. He waked up the next morning thinking about the experience and feeling that his understanding was enhanced, which comforted him, the more he thought about it. It was significant for him to have such reassuring feelings, but it would not have completely satisfied his desire to see that everyone in his family reach a peace of mind and soul as he was feeling by bringing truth in his life as it would with understanding. Possibly it was too much to expect and the only thing he can do now is to again send his love to all who may still have misgivings or resentments, but most of all to all his dear ones.

The only unpleasant news for that day in Madrid were the ones about the saga of Elian Gonzales – the Cuban *balserito* whose mother had died in the intent to bring the handsome and charismatic boy away from the Cuban tragedy and into freedom, only to find more tragedy befalling on them. Almost the entire world, except for most Cuban exiles, was in favor of the return of the boy to Cuba. International understanding of paternal right laws gave another opportunity to Castro to manipulate public opinion favorably to his interests. Castro had won again, and the cause for freedom of the Cuban people suffered another setback. Michael wondered: "What would Arial's upper-plane interpretation of this be?" but the answers to him and to the world would have to wait.

. . .

Time continued to pass year after year since the momentous dream when he was in Madrid, Spain, by the start of the new millennium, and little that he could imagine then, that a meaningful reconciliation would be yet unfulfilled.

The overriding feelings he felt were indeed harsh, but mostly because of his love of the family being lovely created, since his early twentieth years of age. .It was the feeling of having lost his most endearing paternal caring that has continue to keep alive in him, even at a distance, and he enjoys the unbroken contact with his older granddaughter, and grandson, besides their children who he is happy to be in touch with through many year and beyond, that allowed the expression of love to them, without forgetting the everlasting love for their dear mother, who passed away in 2007, after her seventy seven years of age, when he was away during a personal work exhibition in Zaragoza, celebrating, with his work, the memory of the great Spanish master, Don Francisco de Goya y Lucientes, in the land that saw the birth of the famous painter, he so admired, and also the birth of his own grandfather in the 1840's..

Upon receiving the saddening news, while being still in in Europe; he made his presence felt with his deepest sorrowing feelings for the happening to his dear daughter and family, with flowers, and a letter to his dear daughters,, addressed also to his dear granddaughter Veronica. .... He wrote to them, at the time :

"Oh Merciful God, I beg of you, who know our imperfect human condition, and also understand every suffering; you who know my heart at this and every time, to accept and hear my prayer for forgiveness of my failures and imperfection, and above all to grant my daughters Maggie and Maritza the consolation they need at this sad time of loss, and to grant to the their mother's soul a restful and tranquil place in the light of your glory.

You who know my loving feelings for the ones that I have always love, and my desire for peace and happiness to all, and the end of suffering, and grant us the everlasting expression of love in our hearts., so Merciful God, as it has been for many years now, I continue to ask for your will to be done above all, and I trust in your wisdom and mercy to help us in the family heal, and move forward under your guidance. I ask this in the name of the father, the son and the holy spirit. AMEN" July 1st. 2007

209

"Las Tapiadas'
-(Mud-walls)
(Political prisoner subjected to humiliate in
Castro's jails--Author's oil 66x50 1984

"The Night of the Exiles"
Oil on canvas 60x84 inches – 1988
Collection of The Art Museum of Florida International University
By Elio Beltran at(FIU) Miami collection

"….and the fear was left behind, Oil 48 x 24 inches-1994"'
<Collection of the Art Museum of Florida International Universsity.

"North bound"/ The daring and the carefree.
Oil on canvas 20x24 inches –1994 (FIU Collection)

"Struggling couple"
Oil on canvas 20x24 inches –1994, at (FIU)

"Lost at sea"
Oil on canvas 20x24 inches –1994 (FIU Collection)

"Despair"
Oil on canvas 20x24 inches –1994 (FIU Collection)

"The lost Dream"
Oil on canvas 20x24 inches – 1994 (FIU Collection)

Prayer at Sea
Oil on canvas 20x24 inches- 1094 (FIU collection)

"Reflections of a Rescue"
Oil on caanvas 66x50 inches- - 1995 (FIUCollection)

CHAPTER FOURTEEN

Cuba's Learning Process
(Views From Inside And Views From Outside)

The intense dream Michael had and the impressions received by way of his subconscious mind during the comforting dialogue (he was able to have with his childhood friend) were indeed an unusual experience that made him think about the immense relevance, and the importance of the spiritual world and its relation to every aspect of human conscious life. He did not know, however, how much this apparent revelation from Ariel was to bring peace to his own soul, considering that in all that related to that situation not much have changed for more than ten years. His expectations were not at all optimistic – but to a great degree, he found himself feeling better after having expressed his anguish to his old friend and to hear what was not possible to hear from any ordinary being walking on the same earthy spaces. He returned to New York a few days after the dream.

Michael never mentioned his dream to anyone and among the many thoughts he had after the rare experience was about how much suffering his friend Eloy had been spared when he suddenly died at such a young age, just before becoming a teenager. These thoughts sharply contrasted with the many previous thoughts about poor Eloy having died so early in life and not being able to become a grown man and have a family like he did, and for both of them to enjoy the friendship and association for a long time – beyond the three magical years that it lasted. Hard as it was to see his friend depart so early, the earlier feelings during his own childhood now appeared to be somewhat selfish and caused by his own pain. Now, Michael could only think of all the suffering of the Cuban political process and that of his own life, regardless of all the happiness he himself may have been able to have during part of his own life (yet, he had not been free from the corresponding pains that love can bring) as something that his friend did not have to live through. Eloy didn't have to go through any of that, and neither any of the many of life's disappointments, and failures. Thinking about what was best was not the question now. Each one's life is what it has to be, he would ultimately think, as he obviously considered life as something sacred to live through to the Maker's determined end. He considered it to be worth all the trouble, and accepted it as a necessary part of a grand design he was not able to fathom, but which gave him a sense of self-assurance. In the end, he thought, as his cousin Ursula would surely have said, if she was still alive, that Arial most likely had in his soul all the experiences that was necessary for him to have in the formation of his higher degree of spiritual development.

In this frame of mind, he was walking through the Newark Airport terminal leaving the custom's area when he came face to face with a man he was hardly able to recognize as one of his brother's old friend – Carlos Blas-Alvarez, who was apparently waiting for someone else to arrive from Madrid. He have had only a few casual conversations with the older man but he remembered that he was one of the most quiet and knowledgeable among the group of friends that visited his brother's house in Queens. Obviously, like his own brother and brother's friends, they were all in favor of the Castro government during the early stages of the revolution, but Carlos however, had always been rather tactful on every occasion when they had any conversation, particularly during the night when he and his brother had the hurtful political discussions during the party his brother was giving. A confrontation that marked the long and painful separation of the two brothers.

"How good to see you," Carlos Blas said, greeting Michael with an unexpected and effusive handshake. " . . . I have not seen you for more than thirty years but I immediately recognized you. You look very much like your brother."

"Everybody says the same thing. How are you?"

"Well, I am much older now, as you can see. And I guess, wiser than when we met in your brother's house, particularly after having been to Cuba and having the experience of my life." The tall and bald-headed man said with a broad and emphatic smile. " . . . I was able to open my eyes. I felt bad when your brother died very shortly after my return from Cuba. He was such good friend to everyone. I know that you reconciled with him before his death. It was very good for him because he suffered a great deal about your separation."

After a short pause, the man added: " . . . You know, I was able to have many conversations with your brother before his death and I would like to talk to you about it someday if possible."

"I would very much like that, Alfonso," Michael answered, somewhat puzzled as he tried to relate the man's face and name in his memory of their brief encounters so many years before.

"You mean Alvarez, *no*? . . . That is my name, Carlos Blas-Alvarez . . . You can call me Carlos, or las. Your brother always called me Carlos because he used to say that I reminded him of his older cousin in Cuba. but everybody in that group of friends called me Alvarez."

"You are right, I am sorry. This happens to me all the time. I always change people's name, usually calling them by the name that first comes to mind when I look at them. I knew your last name started with an A but I wasn't very sure."

"That is fine. Look, let me give you the phone number where you can reach me for the next ten days. I am staying with my younger sister in Elizabeth, New Jersey, until I return to Miami. I would like to talk more with you. Please call me."

"I surely will, Alvarez. Thanks. I am glad that you spotted me on this crowd. I will call you soon," Michael said as he placed in his coat pocket the piece of paper his brother's old friend had given him.

The next four days he got busy with all the pending business that as usual had accumulated during his absence. A few days later, he called Mr. Alvarez and agreed to meet him in Elizabeth the next Saturday morning. At the time, over a year after being living alone in his studio of Vernon, New Jersey he had developed a meaningful relationship by letter and by phone with Aurora. A communication that was growing in care since the time they had met in Mexico city, as she lived in Nebraska with the youngest of her three male children.

It was about nine thirty in the morning when Michael arrived in Las Palmas, a Cuban food restaurant in Elizabeth, New Jersey. Carlos Blas-Alvarez was already there having a friendly talk with the man behind the counter. "Do you like some coffee?" He immediately asked.

"Yes, please, a Cuban coffee . . . 'cortadito', please."

"Make it two," Carlos Blas said as he invited Michael to sit by a table near the front window of the restaurant.

"Would you like a cigar?"

"No, thanks. I haven't smoked one in more than thirty years."

"Do you mind if I smoke one?"

"No, I don't. I actually like the smell of a good cigar, for a while at least. I hope that one is good," he said, smiling and looking at the cigar that the slender man was pulling out of his coat pocket.

"It is not Cuban but it is good enough. It is made by Cubans in Honduras where they grow some of the best tobacco outside of Pinar del Rio," Carlos Blas said as he proceeded to light his cigar. " . . . I am glad you came this morning because I have been anxiously waiting to talk to you about your brother since the day I saw you at the airport."

"I am glad to be able to talk to you too. You said you have been to Cuba recently. It will be interesting to hear about it, and of course about my brother."

"Yes, I returned last week from Havana after over a month of staying there. but the trip I wanted to talk to you about was the trip I made during the year before your brother's death in nineteen eighty-seven. I will tell you about my conversations with your brother before he died. I was visiting Miguel Angel, every day in the hospital, and he had told me about your last visit with him on the same day that it happened, which was just two days before he died."

"Yes, I had visited him two times that week after I returned from a trip to Spain and I knew that he was on his last days. It was very sad but at the same time we were able to have some rewarding time together."

"I know all about it." Carlos Blas said, " . . . neither one of you talked about politics when you were there on your last visit, and that is why I wanted to talk to you about – because all the things you talked about then were mostly of lovely remembrances of your mother and father, and the times when you were together in Cuba, and the many good memories you both had. Your brother was not able to tell you about how sorry he was that his political feelings interfered with your relationship."

"No, Blas, at that point, I didn't want him to be concerned with that. I mostly concentrated on making him feel good about the complete reconciliation we were experiencing. It is really surprising to see how small and insignificant political differences become at a moment when love is the only thing that becomes important."

"I know, but Miguel Angel told me about that anyway. He told me how you have been consistent in seeing him at least once a month in New York for almost twenty years just to be together for a while without talking politics. He appreciated that because he knew that you were doing that against his sister-in-law's best wishes."

"Yes, she didn't want to have anything to do with neither my brother nor my brother's wife and children. She was never able to accept anything that had to do with him and didn't want for me to bring our daughters to be in contact with them. The fact is, I should have never accepted that – but I did, and that is entirely my fault for which I have my own regrets. It was very stressful and frustrating, during that time, since I had decided to be in touch with my brother in spite of all that. but I never visited his house either and had not had contact with his wife and my nephew and two nieces for more that twenty-five years. In any, case that is in the past and there is nothing that I can do to change it, but I have been in contact with them during the last eight years, and it is good to see that they all love to see me from time to time. To them, that does not mean that they were right and I was wrong, it only means that we have been able to put any resentment aside and slowly able to rebuild love instead. "I am sorry for bringing you such painful memories with my conversation," Carlos Blas courteously said. " . . . Most of all, I wanted you to know that your brother was really sorry for having been so hard on you about your political views when you left Cuba and for him being so upset and not understanding or accepting your views. He had changed much by the time of his death since he realized what a big lie the so-called revolution has been, and how much the Cuban people have suffered for it. It was very difficult for him to accept that reality, and he could not tell you about it, but he told me. I think that you would like to hear about it, don't you agree?"

"Yes, of course. but I sensed all of that already and there was no need for me to go over that like saying that he was wrong and I was right, or anything of that nature, and there is only sadness in the thought because of all the agony that we went through unnecessarily, when you come to think of it. Families should never allow political ideologies to come between them." "Your brother was idealistic like I was, and like so many Cubans who had been away from Cuba prior to Castro's taking over. We never accepted nor wanted to think that what was happening in Cuba was not good. I had to go there myself and see the disaster, to be convinced on my own, and see the people completely disappointed and with a lack of incentive to do anything constructive. The buildings were falling apart as much as the people, while Castro only cared about keeping his power and the big armed forces well equipped and well taken care of while the rest of the people had to face hardship. It was hard for me to realize all of that when I went there and saw how the young people felt forced to depend on prostitution. It is widespread, when young women with good education and degrees have to prostitute themselves to make a living and help the family. It is disgusting when a government that started by saying that it would eradicate corruption and prostitution would now provoke and encourage it, even exploit it for the interests and benefit of its tourists. It had already started when I went there for the first time ten years ago but it is worse now and it is evident that the Castro government sponsors it to boost the tourism industry. It is shameful.

"It must be a desperate situation for many families. I appreciate what you are telling me about how my brother was feeling at that time because I never wanted to discuss political issues with him ever again, let alone when he was terminally ill. One of the things that comforted me during all the years before our mother's death in Cuba in nineteen seventy-six was the fact that she knew that we were in constant contact after our initial problems. It was something she asked of me and I promised to do when I left Cuba in nineteen sixty. but please, tell me more about your most recent trip there."

"The first trip I made was with the idea of incorporating myself to the revolution as a teacher – considering that I have been a licensed agronomist. I was soon disappointed with all the whimsical and unwise decisions made by the government. They had totally sold out to the Russians. They had even exported to Russia much of the country's good soil and they had cut many of the fruit trees to allow for plantations that were inadequate for the areas and were wasteful and disastrous. Education was based on political grounds rather than technical and logical. I had trouble when I started to argue against some of the projects and I was accused of being anti-revolutionary. It was very difficult to make a contribution and more so to be able to bring the ignorant local leaders to accept any common sense because of the damn political suspicions, constant mobilizations and lack of incentive to work and produce the right results. On top of that, I saw many good people sent to jail on mere suspicions or false accusations and I became very afraid that it would happen to me. Many of the people who were sent to jail became sick and some died due to the mistreatment and abuses they suffered in Castro's jails."

"How did you come out that time?" Michael asked. ",. . . but remember, I am more interested on hearing about your most recent trip."

"The first time I was lucky that I had made special arrangements by going through Mexico. At that time, the Cuban government was encouraging such visits and would not mark your American passports considering such visits of interest to the government. However, they... would force you to update your Cuban passport for which they charged more than three hundred dollars – which is much more that any Latin American country charges for a passport, but that is one of the abusive ways they use to get money from Cubans living in the United States. I always let them know that my visit was temporary and I was allowed to get involved in some of the agricultural projects near my hometown in Santa Clara. I was able to return to the Unites States and get back to my teaching job after my disappointing sabbatical."

"That is interesting, but why did you decide to go the second time?"

You know that since nineteen ninety-four's boat exodus, Castro reached some agreements with the Unites States and President

Clinton's government had allowed Cuban Americans to go to Cuba once a year to visit relatives."

"Yes, I know."

"I had already retired from my teaching job and my younger brother in Cuba was not feeling well. He had been working for the Cuban government as a mechanic in a large rice plantation but he had fallen in disgrace with some of the local party leaders and had to leave the job. And although he was a good mechanic, he could not find a job because everything is run by the party. So he tried to make money by fixing cars in front of his house. I was afraid he was very sick and wanted to be with him once more. I decided to take the opportunity to go and see him before we both got older or worse. I am already seventy-three, like Castro, and I may not live long enough to see the end of the tragedy in our country. So I went there again and was able to see my brother."

"Then you were there when all of the turmoil about Elian Gonzales was going on . . . What did the Cubans over there really think about all that happened?"

"Look, the world had seen one hell of a show by Castro but I can tell you that the majority of the people there including the children, who were dragged to the demonstrations, deep inside wanted the kid to stay in the Unites States."

"It is possible, but from the outside it didn't look like they were dragged. They were all seen happily singing slogans and waving flags."

"Yes, but they were enjoying the outing and being out from the schools. God forbid – for anyone who did not go, and that included all the people who depended only on one employer – the big government, whether to go or not. They all had to, but it was all a sham and a diversion. Even Elian's father actually wanted his son out of Cuba when he let the mother take him on the boat. He definitely knew about it. Everybody in Cuba knows that, but he could not make any move and had to play Castro's game, once Castro turned the case into a very convenient political issue and a matter of state – where he had the opportunity to discredit the Cuban exiled community in Miami . . . Elian's father was so compromised he could not dare say or do anything different once it became a matter of life and death for the regime to win this case. but privately, the Cuban children would sing in low voices among themselves: *'Elian, Elian, consorte quedate en el norte . . . Elian, Elian, amigo llevame contigo'* 'Elian, Elian, my friend stay there in the States . . . Elian, Elian, take me there with you as well.' The older people I talked with felt the same way in private. The majority of the people in Cuba want to be out of the ordeal of this dictatorship and want it to end, but they are all scared to death."

"I was in Spain when all of this was taking place and the public opinion and most of the press was in favor of Elian to be returned to his father. It is a very strong argument in Europe and also for the majority of people in the US, about the paternal rights. No one wanted to hear much about the will of the mother to bring her son to freedom and having died in the intent. Paternal right is considered sacred. No one wanted to hear any logic against it in this case and Clinton didn't want to go against it. They handled the case rather bad from the beginning, including the way they took poor Elian at gunpoint out of the house in Miami. I was appalled when I saw the photo in the front pages of the newspapers in Madrid. That was on top of allowing the case to become a political issue from the beginning and becoming part of Castro's game. I had many discussions with my Spanish relatives and friends about this case. I felt that the U.S. should at least have forced Castro to let go from Cuba the many children whose parents had been claiming them from overseas and are not allowed to leave. The parental rights have to work both ways. If the Unites States took a stronger stand for the case of the mother from the beginning, the world's public opinion would have been different. I am sure of that." Michael said.

"I know, but the interest of the Unites States was not at stake and I am sure that Clinton was afraid of Castro's threats of opening the floodgates again with a 'boat exodus' like in nineteen ninety-four and in the 'Mariel boatlift' of nineteen eighty."

"You are right, Carlos. In any case, I do not believe that Elian's case is over yet. There is something of a premonition I have about Elian – that the whole case, including the mother's sacrifice and the miracle of the boy's survival when all the other eleven people who were on the boat died – is something that signals to something very significant to me. The case for truth, justice and freedom in Cuba would soon come to light and the world will finally understand. People around the world still don't understand the Cubans' suffering."

"I hope you are right my friend…I wish I was that hopeful, but this has been a hard blow to the cause of freedom. I think that there was a lack of leadership in the part of the Cuban-American political leaders."

"I know, Carlos, but don't lose hope. I think that the Miami exile community has lost much on this. It bothered me to hear a broadcaster in Spain saying: 'The Miami mafia has done this and that' . . . just repeating the words of Castro calling every Cuban in Miami a *Mafioso*. It would be okay for Castro to say anything he wanted to discredit his enemies, but for that *'papagallo'* repeating it on the network as if it was his own assertion was very offensive and disrespectful, and I protested about it because the people in Miami are just people who believe in freedom and they are not *Mafioso*. There are many in Miami who are very passionate about their views and can be quite vociferous about it, but many of them had suffered jail sentences and had lost family – not only in Cuba, but also at sea, trying to leave Cuba like what happened to Elian's mother and eleven others on that boat. No one has the right to call them *Mafioso*, and not say anything about the *Mafioso* of them all in Havana – the one disguised as savior behind his anti-imperialistic slogans while keeping the Cuban people starving for freedom under an oppressive and totalitarian system of government."

"I can see how mad that broadcaster got to you, . . . I saw how everything was manipulated by Castro while I was there. He played his usual role of turning this to his advantage with his propagandistic center stage again."

"Since you had been there recently, what do you think are the chances for a resolution of the Cuban situation without bloodshed, Carlos?"

"I don't know, It is very difficult to ascertain. but while I was there, I was able to talk with an old friend whose son is a high-ranking officer in the Cuban Army and he said that Castro's brother Raul has a tight grip on everyone in the armed forces, particularly the officers. His only job is to make it virtually impossible for any member from top to bottom to conspire. Everyone is terrified to talk to even the most trusted friends because of the uncertainty and the fear of breaking the code of expected blind loyalty to the maximum leader. The 'Ochoa Affair' of a few years ago was the best example of the implanted terror within the army."

"Yes, I saw the news documentary of the trial when the accused officers declared themselves as traitors to the dogma."

"Yes, they declared themselves as traitors to the revolution, even when they thought that the drug dealings they were accused of being involved in were helping their government. You know that there has long been a suspicion that the Castro government is involved in helping in the drug trafficking – lending airstrips and secret ports in Cuba for that purpose. Some say that U.S. Intelligence has proof of it, also, that the drug money served to supply arms to the guerrillas and the terrorists in Colombia, who support and run the drug business there – all of what strategically and financially benefits Castro."

"Yes, of course I have heard of it. but why isn't it exposed to the world?"

"Probably because there are other things involved in this issue, most likely, it is difficult to expose the situation for now, but in any case, what you were asking about brings us to the question of terror in the Cuban armed forces. If you saw the documentary, you would remember seeing Castro sitting in the center of a long and narrow table that was spread to form a large rectangle – with all the major Generals sitting around it. I think they were about thirty of them on that table and they were all looking directly at him while the rest of the high brass were sitting in the amphitheater watching over it all. Castro then raised his right hand saying: 'Those in favor of the death penalty raise their hands.' Who was going to dare not lift his right hand? . . . That is control through terror, if you ask me, . besides, by killing his higher and most feared Cuban Army hero, he and his brother also killed any possibility for conspiracy in the armed forces. Then what other possibilities for change are there?"

"Who knows, Carlos? but we have to hope that things will change from within like on many other long dictatorships with a strong figure – like Franco in Spain, for instance, things changed once Franco died. Spain has developed into a mature democracy with good social programs and respect for human rights. The example I see in Spain gives me hope that it will come to happen in Cuba, but God forbid if any one enemy kills Castro and make him a martyr. I just hope that nature or freak fate will take its course instead."

"Yes, but if nature takes a very long course, who will survive the son of a bitch to see it happen? I am getting old, you know . . . Unless he accidentally steps on a banana peel or something like that," Carlos blas said laughing. "but I guess you are right. Look at what happened to Che Guevara – he was made an icon for having been killed. by the way, many people in Cuba think that he was also a victim of the revolution since Castro sent him out to South America just to get rid of him – by putting him away from Cuba. You would remember the disappearance of Camilo Cienfuegos at the early stages of the victory against the Batista regime. No one of the older generation in Cuba thought that he actually died on an airplane crash. In those two cases, just like in the 'Ochoa Affair', they had suddenly and conveniently been put out of the way."

"You are right on that too. They have everything air tight and under control by way of creating fear"

"Let's hope that we will one day know the entire truth about everything . . . Do you remember the group of friends who used to meet with your brother during the initial years of Castro? We were initially, all in favor of the changes taking place in Cuba under the revolution."

"Of course I remember. That was the same way most people in Cuba including myself felt at the very beginning – before Castro started to suppress the liberties by eliminating free press and placing opponents in jail."

"Well, what I mean is – of that group in New York, most of us thought pretty badly of the United States."

"I guess that was understandable, if you were all like my brother listening to all what Castro was saying; that was the party line, so to speak. He is still, accusing the U.S. of everything wrong that happens in Cuba and he still accuses the U.S. of being imperialistic which is a very convenient position and have helped him to keep the sympathy of many European countries. It is a very smart policy. In fact, The U.S. throughout the twentieth century has much to be blamed for, mostly by offering reasons to the enemies of true democracy to justify their deeds. The U.S. should have a policy of solidarity with the oppressed people in Cuba and against Castro by denouncing vigorously the lack of freedom of the press and also the human right abuses in Cuba, as well as the overall suppression of liberties. If they do just that the world would no longer look at the U.S. to blame but to the Cuban dictator. It should be a simple thing for the U.S. to do. In any case none of the European countries respect the isolation of Cuba with the embargo and it does not work anyway."

"Well, Michael, you know that the U.S. government is not going to do any of that and go against the Cuban lobby."

"I do not see that they have cared enough about the exiled Cubans' lobby when they reached shameful agreements with Castro whereby the U.S. coast guards' pursuit any poor Cuban *balseros* coming near U.S. shores and stop them from reaching the land of freedom and send them back to Cuba instead of giving them political asylum here. The scenes the world has seen on TV showing the coast guards blowing high-pressured water against the poor and helpless people on the boats have been deplorable. I don't mean that Republicans would or have done better than Democrats, both parties have just been pursuing the wrong ineffective policies against Castro for too long. Unfortunately, the embargo is doing nothing but help him, but once he has no one to blame for the disgrace of his policies, his possibilities to keep control will diminish and the democratic process would somehow unfold."

"I think that you are dreaming, my friend," Carlos Blas said.

"Not really, Carlos. I think that in general, the U.S. has to find a way to form alliances with the underdeveloped world if they are to successfully promote the democratic principles they profess, and I don't mean to form alliances with Castro but with the people of Cuba. Something that they can do by declaring principles that oppose any form of dictatorship for the suffering people and for Latin America as a whole."

"Let's see what will happen, but I am not that hopeful.

"Well, Carlos, I have to go."

"Why don't you stay for lunch? . . . They have very good Cuban food here."

"No, thanks, I have a lot to do today yet."

"I see that you have not changed . . . No wonder your brother told me that you were always on the go."

"Yes, that seems to be the case. Life is too short and there is always something that needs to be done … Tomorrow may be too late."

He stood up and got ready to leave, thinking that he would not tell Carlos las about his plans to visit Cuba. There is nothing to tell about that for now, he thought. First, I have to see if they would give me a visa, particularly with what they may have on their files about my beliefs and dislike for their ways, to say the least. He looked toward the door of the restaurant and saw a man dressed in a dark charcoal suit wearing a loud and tasteless bright tie that clashed with the rest of the attire.

The man recognized Michael and came towards him with open arms: "*Hola pintor* … How are you? … What brings you to Elizabeth?"

"I am fine, Roger. I am here visiting my friend … Do you know Blas-Alvarez?"

"Of course I do … Hi, Carlos. I see that some people still call you Blas … How did it go the other day after I left the meeting?"

"Oh! … Don't remind me," said Carlos Blas, we were here after a meeting at the Club Cubano in Elizabeth when a discussion started among some of the people there. It was not very good because no one agreed on anything."

"There is nothing unusual about that. One of the problems with Cubans is that we all have a different solution to a problem and we do not easily agree in one."

The flamboyant Roger Rosado jumped at Michael's comments to say: " … You are right. but the truth is there was a lot of bullshit being said at the meeting. Some of those people there think that the Americans are going to do anything for our cause and ignore that Americans are going to do what is best for their interests. Look at what they have done to little Elian, sending the poor kid back to Cuba without concern for the sacrifice made by his mother who died in her intent to bring Elian to freedom. Neither Castro nor Clinton cares about the child. They care only about their damn political interests. Castro has won this time, only because Clinton didn't have the guts to tell the bastard to go to hell and to free every little boy and girl he is holding there, ignoring the many requests made by their parents who are living in other countries from where they have been claiming them. The U.S. government had to ask Castro to free them first before he made a case of Elian's father who in reality would have wanted his son to stay away from Cuba but could not say a word . . . I can't understand why so many Cubans here and in Miami would want to punish Clinton and Janet Reno by voting against Gore . . . That is absolutely asinine. It is true that they screwed up the Elian case but I happen to think that Republicans won't do any better. I will vote for the Democrats regardless because the policies of the Republicans after Regan's presidency had been really bad for the people. They have been opposing everything that may have been good for the middle – and lower-income people. All you have to see is that every country in Europe have been making great advances in social programs and eliminating once and for all the threat of communism because they have nothing to offer anymore. The people there are making progress in many fronts, but not here. I don't see the Republicans doing anything about health insurance and there is a need to solve this problem, but they only oppose it every time without coming up with any better idea. I know I am looking at this from my political views, but the people in that meeting were doing the same. Why would these Cubans want to help the Republican candidates only to punish the Democratic candidate?"

"All right, Roger. You really got carried away and it all sounded like party politics, but even if you may be right in some of what you are saying, don't forget that most of our people are so frustrated that they can't think any different. There had been too many disappointments and too much suffering . . . They can't help it. Remember that in the middle of all the passion for Elian's case in Miami, it seemed to me, at least from outside the country where I was, that the people were united but there was no apparent coordination and no clearly defined leadership among the exiles to deal with this pr oblem and the images that were projected to the world's public opinion were not good."

"Michael is right, Roger. I was in Cuba, and I saw how Castro took advantage of the situation to bring international attention to his benefit, even when the majority of people there were hoping that he would lose the case. Very little attention was focused on showing the world that the Elian case was a product of his disgraceful regime . . .

As for the way the U.S. handled this, it should only signal the Cubans to let go of so much expectations of the U.S. government. What we have in Cuba will not be changed by the U.S., but by our own people.

"Well, I think that sometimes we expect too much from this country, and it may be all right to some degree because this is the land that upholds the principles of freedom and democracy. I love this country for what it represents to us and the world, besides being living here longer than the time I had lived in Cuba. Here we have sons and daughters and grandchildren so we have to defend the democratic principles that we so want for our beloved country of birth, and we should help change this country's approach towards dictatorships and oppression of any kind. We have to bring it to the attention of our congressmen and other people in the government, to keep pressing for human rights and the suppression of freedom of the press in Cuba where Castro is jailing dissidents who had committed no crime but denounce what is a legitimate right to be denounced. but we should insist for the U.S. to do it more effectively and to aggressively promote world support for those principles, not by trying to force policies that no one pays any attention to, but to have a truly acceptable and determined policy that would gain the support of all the free world. That should not be so difficult," Michael finally said.

"I agree with all of that Carlos Blas said. "but I also think that we, the Cubans, have to look back to where all of this mess started . . . We had corruption, and the great desire to finish with all of it, but we felt on the trap of the ones who wanted reforms only to become absolutists, eliminating freedom and progress to impose their own brand of dictatorship."

"I guess we also have to learn from our mistakes."

"both of you are unreal, my friends. I hope your dreams would come true someday."

"I don't see why not, Roger," Michael said. " . . . We are seeing things change already. You have to look at how much the respect for human rights has developed lately, particularly in Europe. The rights of people are respected, and we now see the world bringing people who abused human rights and allowed or promoted the killing of anyone with opposing views to be publicly denounced and be brought to justice, like in the case of Pinochet for instance."

"Come on, Michael, how can you say that? . . . Pinochet's government saved Chile from communism."

"Wait a minute, Roger . . . Don't you think that human life is sacred? It is not a matter of what side are you politically. If your side kills the political enemies, what can you expect when the ball is on the other side? Won't you agree that the world should pass judgment on Fidel Castro for the crimes against his political opponents? . . . Only when that happens would extremists and abusive politicians start to have respect for human rights."

"He is right, Roger. It is ironic that Castro and his brother were pardoned by Batista and were freed and stayed alive within less than two years after they were taken prisoners for the attack on Cuartel Moncada, but they themselves won't pardon anyone who may think of even presenting any form of opposition to them and more so, forget it if anyone would represent even a minor threat to their regime."

"Okay, you guys, I guess I don't have an argument against that. Let's hope for the best but I hope it happens soon."

"It was nice to see you both, but I have to go," Michael said and he started to walk towards his car after the traditional handshakes. He drove away from Elizabeth with his head pounding. "What a big problem we Cubans have," he thought. "Not many people in the world understand us, not even ourselves, but the truth is that we will not give up on our passion and desire for freedom for our people wherever we are, and the world should be better for it."

As he drove away from Elizabeth, he thought about what his old brother's friend blas-Alvarez said about looking into the past and understanding how corruption in politics had opened the road to the worst and longest dictatorship in the history of the hemisphere. It is very possible that the Cuban people, being so anxious to rid itself from the old political ways, had fallen on the trap of demagoguery and away from true democracy. but it has also been in the arms and hands of opportunistic and unscrupulous leaders who had expertly managed a kind of extortion by fear that they mercilessly continued to run and try to justify in the name of anti – imperialism. In the end, finding credible just cause can cover a multitude of sins. Eliminating reasons, the world may eventually eliminate the abuse of power. The collapse of all civil institution when they failed to take a stand on the outset may have contributed to the disaster, but that is easy to say now.

His thoughts came to the gun culture and the power plays in the secondary schools and the universities. It was not apparently a widespread situation but there were a few who knew how to take it to their advantage and there were hidden agendas that offered appropriate ground for a kind of conspiracy for eventual totalitarian control. Havana was a peaceful and safe city if not for the gangs who had surfaced under the sponsorship of some corrupt functionaries during the Grau San Martin government of 1944 to 1948. It was said that it was the way that Grau dealt with pseudo-revolutionaries and troublemakers who made their living as mercenaries and extortionists, hidden behind various make-believe revolutionary organizations that turned to be deadly, mostly to themselves, and to a few who were lured by their gun worshipping and fantasies. Among them, and taking advantage of it, were the infiltrated extremists with a long term agenda for power. Also among them was Fidel Castro, and a few sincerely idealistic students who had aspirations for reforms in government and found themselves involved with the gangs along the way; some never survived the experience.

As a student in those years, Michael remembered the time that Grau San Martin's term in government ended. by that time, most of the gang leaders of the time had eliminated themselves except for a few that included Rolando Masferrer who survived the "Cayo Confites" invasion affair to later on play a mercenary role under batista (who used him to counteract Fidel Castro, who was his ex-university days ally). Masferrer had been looking to eliminate Castro ever since the killing of ex-University Student's Federation leader, Manolo Castro. Years later, Masferrer would be blown away with his car in Miami during the initial years of Fidel Castro's taking power in Cuba. Fidel Castro, who had played the balancing act between the two most powerful gang groups and had silently created his own group, managed to survive the university's gang wars of the 'forties.

All of this could be thought as unrelated, but in his mind, the justification and acceptance of gang activities as a parallel with accepted ideals, instead of treating it as what it really was – an illegal and dangerous practice in need of application of the law in a civilized way, had obviously brought all of what we have seen happening in Cuba during the last fifty or more years. It will be silly to only blame the U.S. for all that had happened. We have to be wiser and find our own way to deal with it, learn from the past and change the future.

He wondered about when and how Cubans would be able to learn from history and the painful experiences that so many generations of Cubans had to live through. He wondered if the future generations would study and learn and be able to build a strong society founded on dignity and with solid civil institutions as the guardians of democratic principles and respect for the law and safeguarding every human right that would make it impossible for the country to fall ever again under an oppressive regime of any kind.

He thought that future generations of Cubans would have to learn to say "Never again" just as the sufferers of the Holocaust did.

After all the discussions in Elizabeth that afternoon, he drove up circling the Great Gorge of Vernon Valley where he met Aurora after a long day with all the usual passionate opinions, of the meeting he had in Elizabeth.

Aurora's uplifting attitude was, as usual, stimulating enough to bring his spirits up. After all, she had been a woman who endured the serious sickness of her deceased first husband before his death in 1985 and when two of her children suffered from kidney disease and the third one got involved in two serious accidents. She eventually donated one of her kidneys when she was already fifty-six years old, when her older son developed a deadly kidney failure. Over all of it, her positive attitude never faltered. At every moment, she maintained her strength of character, joyful and thankful for everyday regardless of the trials, and without a minimal complaint. He soon felt more relaxed when he finally came to her side on the late-afternoon hours.

At dinner the perceptive Aurora asked him, "What is happening? I can see that something is bothering you."

"Oh, nothing really. Only, I am still thinking about the conversations I had today in Elizabeth with two fellow Cubans."

"I can imagine. You people would never change. You get very uptight and down every time you get together to discuss the Cuban situation."

"It is very touchy, you know. I met this friend of my brother who said that my brother had realized how bad the situation was in Cuba before he died."

"Well, I guess you knew that already."

"Yes, I did. but this type of conversation is always sad."

"Yes, I know. I always remember my brother's stories of when he was in the seminary in Camaguey, Cuba in nineteen sixty when he was taken prisoner along with other seminarians and priests by the Castro KGB that they called G-2. To this day, my brother doesn't want to talk about it. He was terrified."

"Yes, but he is a Spaniard, not Cuban. If he was Cuban, he would talk and talk about it to convince the world of the horrors of Castro's rule in Cuba."

"When my brother and his fellow "Seminaristas" were in the Cuban prison, they were put in front of a 'fake' firing squad on two occasions. He thought that he was going to be shot and killed in both cases and he was in total terror because he remembered the stories of the times when priests and nuns were taken from the convents by the 'Reds' in Spain and were tortured and killed. He was eventually set free by the so called 'generosity' of the system in Cuba, but they were in constant harassment until he escaped dressed in civilian clothes and sailing out of Cuba before the end of that year."

"I know about it, and I know that he doesn't like to talk about it, and I respect him for that, but he lives in Spain, his own free country, and he does not have to worry whether his country has freedom or not because he is enjoying all of what a true democracy has to offer. but Cubans don't have any of that. There is no time yet for Cubans to rest and forget."

"What am I going to do with you?" She said, using one of her usual expressions.

"Just love me, that' s all."

CHAPTER FIFTEEN

Singers Of Beautiful Old Songs And More

"I HAVE YET TO SEE A CUBAN WITH AN INFERIORITY COMPLEX"

– Daniel Serra-Badue
Cuban Artist 1914-1997

Placing word by word on a piece of paper to complete a book is like drops of rain that fall in a bucket until it is full, Michael thought, except that rain is a process of nature while words are a process of humans and as such, the end result is not as perfect, and much less would it be as pure. He always detested having to listen extensively to anyone who was constantly talking about himself, raising his or her ego above everything else. It is terrible, because people would always find a reason to have scorn of such aberration, and as a result, he had always tried to exercise prudence in cases where there was no way to avoid being in the middle of the bucket of words. He feels that he would rather drown on water instead.

In any case, there is a story to be told about Cubans as exiles and their idiosyncrasies. As such, some excuses could be granted and hopefully some understanding too. The common denominator for immigrants has always been hard work and struggle to not only survive but to excel. This has not been different for Cubans. In reality, it has been a tremendous incentive and a source of pride in the accomplishments. There has been a sociological need to achieve prestige and worthy notoriety out of the need of Cubans to overcome difficulties and reestablish themselves. Fortunately, there had been good contributions made by Cubans to whatever society they have attached themselves to. To look at only a few of them, we can see the cultural and economic developments in Florida, and likewise in many sectors like the arts, industry, sciences, and sports and wherever other honest activities had seen their dedication.

Still, pride, justified or not, is better, or at least more acceptable to find virtues and merits in others than to force ours on them. And in this spirit, the pure waters falling on the bucket would help clean any excesses in our prose and win true appreciation for it, if at all possible.

Actually, in some way, his own story is not too different from any other story about Cuba and the Cuban Diaspora. being away from Cuba has, at the same time, been painful and stimulating. If looked only at the personal side of it, the journey of up to fifty years has, by necessity, created memorable moments and memorable associations and relationships, as well as disappointments, simply as any other human life, but hopefuly it should not be interpreted by being only words on paper that should be taken just as any other story and not as such in relation to the cause of freedom and the search for understanding and enlightment.

In the Summer of 1980, about thirteen years before his visit with his friends in Elizabeth, was the first time that the world saw a mass exodus of Cuban refugees coming from Cuba on the Mariel boatlift. Castro turned the negative impact of the twelve thousand Cubans who took sanctuary in the Embassy of Peru to his own benefit by letting relatives in the U.S. come with boats to pick them up, releasing in this way, the enormous pressure that the spontaneous act of protest represented for his government. A much larger number of other would-be refugees were also allowed to leave, but among them, Castro diabolically infiltrated a large number of delinquents and mentally sick elements in order to transfer his internal troubles as well as the criminals into the exile community.

Fortunately, the Mariel boatlift also brought many talented artists and writers as well as hardworking people and family members of a good number of Cuban families already established in Miami and elsewhere in America to offset the negative impact made by the ill-intended infiltration.

Michael is no exception and is not alone among Cubans in the quest to achieve; art was to be his most passionate endeavor. by the 1980s, the paintings of his childhood memories had been recognized with various prestigious awards, and he was much in touch with many of the exiled intellectuals and artists in Europe and the United States. but the ones who gave him more pleasure and insight were the ones of the much older generations like Enrique Labrador Ruiz, the creator of the fragmented novel *The Labyrinth of Self* and others which pioneered the touch of the surreal and the beginnings of the magic realism in Latin American literature, and Lydia Cabrera, the internationally acclaimed anthropologist and author of many books related to the Afro-Cuban culture. Others were the poet Eugenio Florit, the retired New York university professor and author of many delightful and uplifting poems, and Pablo Le Riverend, the one-time revolutionary fighter against Machado's dictatorship and allegoric sharp-edged poet of the exiles, author of "A Son of Cuba I Am" and "They Call Me Pablo" and many other colorful but bordering on sadly poignant songs of his old age, but above all, the pains of being away from his beloved Cuba and being old and in exile.

His career as a Cuban painter had been followed by press journalists and art critics, both on the Spanish and English newspapers. Such attention by the news media who covered his participation in awards and juried shows opened a wide avenue for contact with the Cuban intellectual community. All the exhibitions where he participated received coverage by the press and TV interviews through the years contributed to enhance his horizons. The *New York Times* was one of among many English newspapers that had articles written about his works by its art critics like Walter Shirey and others. Other publications and news media all covered his career like the *New Jersey Press, Newark Star Ledger* (with many articles written by reputed art critic Eileen Watkins), Judie Dash of the *Bergen Record* (who interviewed him and who also extensively covered the New Jersey Council on the Arts Priority Fellowship Award); on the Spanish press, Aleida Duran of the *Hudson Dispatch*, Luis Felipe Marsans of *Diario Las Americas*, Hada Rosete, magazine director and publisher, the independent journalists Olga and Adela Oliva, Avelardo Garcia berry founder and director of *La Voz* of Elizabeth, New Jersey and his collaborators art analyst and museum curator Alejandro Anreus, and commentator Roberto Prado. There were also others like Nibio Martinez, director of *La Razon* of Union City, New Jersey, art critic Gustavo Valdes (also the director of *ARS*), independent poet and writer Rafael Roman Martel, and Florencio Garcia Cisneros, founder and director of the New York Spanish art newspaper *Noticias de Arte.*

Following such exposure that included international coverage in some European TV networks broadcasting services in Spain and France, he received a call from a man who claimed to be a freelance producer who was doing a documentary covering the works of Cuban artists including those who were living away from Cuba, as well as artists who lived and worked in Cuba. The man, who introduced himself as Gustavo Martinez from Guatemala, also said that he had just been in Cuba where they had already filmed part of the intended production and he was now ready to film and interview in New York. He also said he had talked to Cuban writer Reinaldo Arenas, and the director of *Noticias de Arte,(the* well-known Spanish art journal in New York), Florencio Garcia Cisneros, who gave him his telephone number. He finally said that the artists he was looking to interview were artists who had won the Cintas Foundation Fellowship like Juan boza and he, beltran, both of whom received the award in 1982-'83 respectively.

He immediately called Florencio Garcia Cisneros to find out about the particular project and the individual in charge of it.

"Yes, I know who you are talking about," Cisneros said. " . . . This man mentioned that he found out about you and your paintings of childhood memories of Cuba when he consulted Columbia University's reference and research department related to Cuban art."

"That is interesting. I didn't know that Columbia University had such records." Michael said.

"The university surely has records of newspaper articles and other news items related to Cubans in the United States, and more so on the activities around New York. I think that man is being paid by the communist government in Cuba to do this project, most likely to discredit the artists in exile. You should not have anything to do with him." Cisneros said in his usual abrupt style.

"I don't know, Florencio. The man said that he would call me again and I will talk to him. I like the basic idea of the project, and I don't want to jump to conclusions."

A week later, Michael received the expected call from Mr. Martinez.

"Hello, Mr. beltran. We are now ready to film in New York. We will do Juan boza tomorrow and we want to see if it is okay with you if we visit your studio the day after tomorrow to do your interview and to film some of your paintings of childhood memories of Cuba."

"You sure can, Mr. Martinez. I will have some of my childhood memories paintings ready and will also have *Las Tapiadas* which is the painting that shows the miseries of the political prisoners who suffered human rights abuses in Cuba ready. My only condition is for you to include this painting in the documentary as you would include my other paintings."

After a brief moment, Mr. Martinez said: "All right, Mr. beltran. We will call you tomorrow to confirm our visit."

Michael never heard from the man ever again. He called Cisneros to talk about the incident and what happened.

"I told you, that man is a communist. You should not even have talked to him as I told you."

"Wait, Florencio. Don't you think that what I did was better? . . . I don't care if the man is or is not a communist as long as he accepted my conditions, which of course he was not able to do if he was really working for the Castro government. In this way, he qualified himself."

The artist had known the controversial Florencio Garcia Cisneros since mid-1970. Cisneros had already founded his newspaper and religiously published it every month. *Noticias de Arte* for a long time became not only the only newspaper that covered every important artistic event in the city but also in the Hispanic cultural world as well, consistently being the best informed. Its publications throughout the years, no doubt, contained important information and articles by Cisneros and many well-qualified independent collaborators who could be worthy of future reference by historians and art students.

Although Cisneros was caustic and prompt to be critical and confrontational in many of his conversations or personal discussions outside his paper and in some of his books, he however, was able to maintain his newspaper clear from such tendencies and was regarded well by most. The prestige of *Noticias de Arte* was never in question. Garcia Cisneros died in 1996, less than a year after he sold his newspaper. Michael had great regard for the poorly understood Cisneros and he had developed a good relationship with him – one that would not be possible unless you were a patient listener and let him vent his opinions and never directly argued against them. Cisneros usual reaction was not always justified but sincere nonetheless.

He remembered how many times Cisneros would not even let him begin to talk when he would say: "You talk too much . . . Don't do that . . . . Listen to me." And then followed his abrupt remarks with some of his own opinions, not stopping to listen as the artist would try again and again: " . . . but let me explain . . . . You are not letting me speak to you as yet, and you say that I talk too much. I don't think so . . . I have not yet even started to say what I wanted to tell you," he would finally say. In that dance of words, they would eventually agree with each other somehow and end with much mutual respect for each other after all. but not many people would be able to reach to that point with Florencio Garcia Cisneros.

The worst controversy that Cisneros got himself involved with was due to his first book about General Maximo Gomez, the Cuban War of Independence hero. It was in that book where Cisneros questioned if Maximo Gomez was a *Caudillo* of the Independence or a dictator and where Cisneros implied that Cuba's highest and purest patriot, José Martí was not protected enough by Maximo Gomez because he left him to stay with a small contingent in Oriente province while he faced great danger for his life instead of keeping him away from it. Cisneros also mentioned other remarks about the death of General Antonio Maceo on the eastern front of Pinar del Rio where Cisneros speculated about the role of Maximo Gomez as a very staunch and harsh military leader who was not concerned enough. The fact is, Maximo Gomez's son, Pancho Gomez Toro, also died next to the famous Cuban warrior Antonio Maceo, also known as the bronze

Titan when they fought against a Spanish column whom they had encountered almost by chance. Garcia Cisneros' animosity earned him so much criticism and even hatred by many Cuban intellectual exiles who strived in the old confrontation between his grandfather, General Vicente Garcia and Major General Maximo Gomez during the ten-year war for Cuban independence at the time when General Vicente Garcia was acting president of the Cuban Republic of Arms.

Cisneros was in the process of writing the second book about his grandfather, amid the uproar caused by his first book when Michael had a dream where General Vicente Garcia, looking tall and handsomely dressed in his uniform, came to him – gallantly expressing his concern for his grandson's books by saying: " . . . My grandson should not include his criticism of General Gomez in the book he is writing about me. It would not do my memory any honor by being bitter and critical of anyone of the men who had struggled for Cuba's independence. He should let me stand solely on my own merits and not attack anyone." Michael woke up, deeply impressed, on account of his surprising and revealing dream. He immediately called Cisneros and told him that he had something very important to talk personally about so he went to see him in the afternoon of the same day.

As he told Cisneros about his dream, he impressed upon the ever-tense friend his deep convictions that it was a serious message from his grandfather and that he should see it that way. The writer became very pale and silent. For the first time since he had known him, Cisneros appeared to be non-argumentative and had no adverse comments to say.

The book that Cisneros finally published about the Cuban revolutionary war hero of Las Tunas, whom the author called "the Tiger of Santa Rita" was not in the least as harsh in criticism of General Gomez as it would have been if it was not for the dream and the artist advice.

In any case, having restrained himself as he surely did, Cisneros could not avoid placing in the book some comments about the documents he thought were significant to prove some of his misgivings about General Gomez.

being as it may have been, Beltran still thinks that Cisneros was honest in what he considered to be the pursuit of truth, nonetheless perhaps deeply immersed in thoughts he gathered from his older relatives who may have been closely related to General Vicente Garcia. Under that scenario or background, and the fact that Cisneros had done a great deal of research, his work merits study, not to discredit anyone's contribution to the Cuban cause for independence but to establish a clear understanding of the human drama surrounding the history.

"If we look for understanding, we will be more apt to be critics of our own republican process and form a higher base of responsible values for a healthier future of our nation," he told some of his Cuban friends who criticized Cisneros. "…We should not be prone to criticize without a mature analysis rather than wanting to keep our history by hiding it, like a child, from the realities of our human nature," he had said and then added: "but unfortunately, there are no assurances that it will be done by honest historians in the future."

Of all the relationships that he had come in contact with during his career as a painter, he very much enjoyed that of older writers and artists – among them, Daniel Serra-badue and Roberto Estopinan. And he relished the conversations he had with them, considering their extensive knowledge and experience. Among the older poets and writers he admired for their work, and most of all because of their great knowledge about Cuban life and culture were Enrique Labrador Ruiz and Eugenio Florit. He particularly enjoyed the extraordinary sense of humor of Labrador Ruiz, and the singular and cultured sense of humor of Serra-Badue.

He had met Labrador Ruiz and the poet Eugenio Florit through his friend from his student days, Elio Alba Buffil, the director and acting secretary of the literary organization Panamerican Circle of Culture of which he was also a member. both distinguished men maintained sporadic correspondence with Michael after they had moved to Miami, and he visited them on the many trips he made there. Don Enrique, as usual, told colorful stories about the people he knew in Cuba during his long career as well as the funny stories he enjoyed to say and did so well. During one of his visits to the old writer in Miami, he had a cold and was coughing when Labrador Ruiz, upon greeting him immediately said, "I will tell you what my uncle said to be the best cold remedy . . . You take a bottle of scotch and a hat, put the hat on the table and start drinking and drinking and then go to bed as soon as you can't see the hat anymore." This was the kind of humor that made the worldly man so animated in any occasion as he always had something interesting to talk about.

"*Hola Iluminado,*" Labrador Ruiz would greet him as usual. "What are you painting lately?"

"Just fine, "Beltran would answer, always wondering why Labrador Ruiz occasionally called him "El Iluminado". The first time Ruiz called him that was in a short letter the old writer sent him, he accepted it as a sign of affection rather than a compliment of any kind since to be called "Illuminated" may have been more appropriate for a visionary, which he was not. but Michael liked to think that it may be because of the light in his paintings and he never asked why Labrador Ruiz called him that way. Considering Labrador's sense of humor, it may have been because Michael had, for some time, worked for a light bulb manufacturer.

The much younger artist that so much enjoyed visiting the talented old writer he liked to listen to all the jucy stories that Don Labrador would tell him about older Cuban painters like the mysterious Fidelio Ponce and the colorist Victor Manuel and the master of transparency and movement, the painter Carlos Enriquez and the many stories of the retired Cuban columnist and novelist's experiences with his lifetime friend, Gomez Sicre (who for many years was the founder and director of the Museum of Art of the Americas sponsored by the Organization of American States in Washington D.C.), a man of immense influence in the development of the careers of many Cuban and Latin American artists of his time.

"You still don't like Picasso?" Labrador Ruiz would ask him, following a previous conversation about Spanish painters.

"Well, you know that I have had misgivings about Picasso's motivations in much of his work. but I have actually come to respect the man because of the fact that I realized that he has made it possible for me to become a painter."

"Oh!, How come?"

"Well, I look at the variety of Picasso's work and how he had gone through different periods until he came to be in total disregard for reality without becoming too surreal. And for a man like me, with works that for the most part have been pegged to the traditional representation of the immediate visual world, his work which also did'n fall all toguether into the abstract, started to stimulate me."

by then, Labrador Ruiz had his usual smile and his sharp and expressive eyes looking at his friend with a hint of wonderment (as the writer usually did when he had something else in his mind about the reply he received at conversations) " . . . Your work is not really a representation of the immediate visual world in the sense that you are talking about. Your artwork is from your memory and more related to your inner visual image from what I saw in the Newark Museum a few years ago, and that is different from what you talked about . . . but in any case, the last time we talked about Picasso, you didn't like him that much and neither did you like Velázquez who is also one of the most revered Spanish painters," Labrador Ruiz said, obviously with his usual intention of bringing out some juicy and analytical arguments he so enjoyed.

"Well, you can see that I am still learning. Actually, what I said that time about Diego Velázquez was that some of his works showed visible corrections that should not be noticed at all but were . . . Have you ever looked at the leg of his horses or at some details of his portraits? . . . In any case, what I had said was that I like Goya more because his paintings are closer to the people and tragedies of his time. All you have to do is look at the *capriccios* collection of his prints and his paintings of the firing squads of May the Second, *Los Fusilamientos del dos de Mayo 1808* and in the *Disasters of War*, and the drama of his *Black Paintings* done near the end of his life."

"Well my friend, you are talking about preference not greatness."
"Yes, it is my preference for Goya's work, with valid reasons. but there is also a difference in the degree of greatness as well, and how greatness is assigned and for what. In any case, as far as the corrections in Velázquez' works, it may very well be the sloppy work of restorers through the years; Who knows? . . . but to me they are disturbing when I see them and even so, those corrections don't take away the glory of

Las Meninas or the beauty of *Venus at her Mirror* which to me is one of the most beautiful nude paintings of all time. but if I were going to find inspiration for my own work, I would look at Goya or Van Gogh and most recently to Edvard Munch. I didn't know much about this painter until someone told me that my painting, the *Lapse,* related much to his expressionist style."

And so was the type of discussions that he enjoyed to have with Don Enrique.

In the case of his visit to Don Eugenio Florit, he enjoyed seeing the gracious poet sit and read his poems. It was also an inspiration to see him reach the age of ninety-five and still writing short and loving letters or sending his latest poems.

besides his admiration for the older generation, he also has great interest in the careers of younger artists. He had been in contact and had developed great relationships with many of his younger colleagues and artists in the art world. He also had enjoyed the stimulating support and advice of young curators who have shown interest in his works, such as Giulio blanc (who unfortunately died when still very young). Others whom he had developed close relationships with were the very active and reputable curators and bright connoisseurs of Cuban art, Alejandro Anreus and Gustavo Valdes Jr., both of whom enjoyed the respect and admiration of the artist. Michael had received great stimulus from Gustavo Valdes Jr. for the development of his works during the late 'nineties. On a much longer term, he also has much to say about Alejandro Anreus' virtues as a young artist and for the valuable advice he had always received from this much younger colleague as a curator and knowledgeable critic through the years, but Anreus, with his reserved and stern character, surely would not appreciate any further ado.

Of all the older Cuban artists he had been in contact with, he had the closest relationship with Daniel Serra-badue (the methodical surrealist painter and accomplished printmaker and professor of art history at Saint Peter's College in New Jersey and the brooklyn Museum) who became Beltran' s mentor and who contributed much to the younger artist's development because of his experience and good advice.

The would-be artist felt a strong attraction for the older, artistic and literary personalities that he came in contact with, ever since the time he spent hours as a child listening in his neighborhood to old Pancho Majagua and his singer and guitarist friends when they were sang to the tunes of old songs by Maria Teresa Vera, Flores, Rafael Hernandez, and other old composers from the times of his grandparents. Other neighborhood kids would laugh and joke around and about the old-fashioned *troubadours* while he was statically watching and listening until the late hours of the night, leaning on the iron railing of his house's front porch. As unrelated as it may seem, it only showed him of his sensitivity since his earlier years. There was something noble in the older generation of artists and writers that made them so attractive to him, the older they became. Perhaps that is why he was greatly impressed by the extraordinary intelligence and personality of the aging Lydia Cabrera when he first visited her home in Miami. Her commentaries about art and the sensitivity so brightly displayed by the grand lady of Afro-Cuban culture surprised him.

Lydia Cabrera liked the portrait of herself made by Wilfredo Lam when she lived in Paris but she criticized the famous Cuban painter for his support of the Castro regime. "He has lived too long in France to know better," she said, trying to excuse the painter. She spoke about the work of Amelia Pelaez and Victor Manuel and in the end surprised beltran when she mentioned some of his own works and comparing it to the works of Carlos Enriquez, another notable Cuban painter of that time. As she turned lovingly to her companion, the discrete and gentle-looking *Tatiana* said: " . . . I can see some of Enriquez' transparency and airy composition in some of your most spontaneous work. Don't you?" The thin and elegantly stylish *Tatiana* (who was quietly seated on her rocking chair, as usual, somewhat distant) showed a lovely smile in response and without saying anything, she again turned to her visiting guest and added: " . . . I particularly like the freshness of your childhood memories paintings because Cuba breathes in them . . . . Don't lose that freshness. I also like that you are apparently not as repetitive as other artists are with their work."

The conversation went on for over two hours during the visit. Beltran listened to Lydia Cabrera's stories of how she had heard many of the legends of African Yoruba beliefs directly from the descendants of the slaves themselves. Those were the stories that so enriched her writings. Then, Beltran also told her about his visual experiences of seeing the rituals of the Abakua, as a child – images that were depicted in his paintings many years after his having seen them. The conversation was a very pleasant experience for both. For the painter, the visit was very stimulating considering the comments she had made. He left that day thinking that it would be the first of many visits that he would make to the impressively charming woman. It was, unfortunately, the only visit he was able to make to the aging lady before she died. He had great admiration for the bright woman who was so revered by Cubans because of her immense contribution to the culture of their country, widely recognized everywhere in the world.

The government ruling the unfortunate island, because of her defense of freedom and human dignity, did not appreciate Lydia Cabrera. She could not live under the oppressive atmosphere of Castro's totalitarian regime.

There was no doubt in Beltran's mind that recognition and appreciation are very elusive and relative issues, particularly when politics play a role since he thought that what is measured in light of political views can be blurred or slanted in the wrong direction at one time or another. Outside of politics, there is also another world represented by the establishment that on very few exceptions is full of "snob-isms" and personal preferences, and is usually plagued with what is considered fashionable at a given time, which may not be necessarily good. Most of the time, greatness needs the passage of time to surface indisputably. Meanwhile, living artist and writers have to struggle with detractions of every kind. The cure for this is to work without thinking on immediate recognition and for the creator of art of any kind to strongly believe in him or herself as being in possession of something worthwhile to give and not to think too much of the if, when, where, and how will it be appreciated. Patience and perseverance are the ultimate words besides working wholesomely with heart and mind was part of his own set of artistic conviction.

"Just as man before a glass can see
A torch that burns behind him, and know it is there before
he has seen or thought of it directly;

And turns to see if what the glass has shown Is really
there; and finds, as closely matched As words to music,
the fact to its reflection,

Just so, as I recall, did I first stare
Into the heaven of those precious eyes
In which to trap me, Love had set his snare."

– Dante's *Divine Comedy (Paradiso)*
Ninth Sphere of Heaven
(The Primum Mobile)

(*   *   *)

At this juncture of the artist's own journey he feels the need of reading himself by exploring the introspective thoughts and emotions that surround his momentous return to his roots.

In "Tales of an Old Man" he finds the means to express his most intimate feelings flowing from inside his poetic expression and as he enters the "Parenthesis" that follows this new chapter in his life he tries to open a window to the Cuban drama and the tragic saga of the Cuban people, both inside and outside of the island, and with it he hopes to be able to expose his most personal motivations for his visit to Cuba in May of 2001.

CHAPTER SIXTEEN

Tales Of An Old Man

An old man with a long white beard came to Michael one day and said:

"Country is not only where you are born, you grow, and live.
Country is more what you grow in your heart,
The passage of time would bring them to your mind."

You are so right. I love this country that has offered me shelter and an interesting life with the enjoyment of the freedom that was not on what I left behind. but I still walk almost daily, if I want, up and down the hill where I grew up under the azure blue skies spotted with big clouds cotton white like. – The same place where rocks used to fly from off the contentions of some child and more of the same from childrens at the other end. The downhills and the hill ups could not see each other well sometimes but it was all like children's play

The hill was full with quartz-like diamonds sparkling in the sun. On one side of it, the blue-green serpentine loose rocks had made a rift where rituals would be played. On the other side, another hill rose to Overlook the bay on the north side. There the Maine was blown long before I was born, but the *Texas* came when I was barely eight, and I saw it when it overflowed the wharfs like if it was a bathtub too small for a fat man. I would go eastward and the town would come towards me with smell of freshly baked bread, right after the smell of molasses would start to fade. All these smells as I imagined rolling over the cobble-stoned stretch to soon reach the pier where the *lanchita* would take me to the trolleys at the other end which would then take me to pass colonial buildings standing mute, as they seem to lean over the Old Havana streets.

I shall then return, in the real me, to see the saddest of the sweet, regardless of who would be watching over me. I will miss the days of my free will, and I will silently recall the happier days when the engagement of smiles and the carefree exchange of eye's loving caresses flowed over anyone who would have cared to set the sight on them. Don't tell me that young hearts still would do the same, even to this date. Somehow, I find it hard to think that with so many reins, it can yet be the same. There would be the casual and the obliged concern for all – that happiness should really represent. The old, the ones who passed this way when life was gay, would more than understand that it cannot just be the same. What you have not lived or enjoyed not would ever leave the flavor on your tongue.

I will then walk south from the same hill and would probably see that there is not the same farm where I ran free. The same place where my father used to buy or, in those times, beg for a quart of milk in the depression days to bring his sons the necessary daily fresh regardless of the scarcity or of what was needed to give in exchange, except for blessed good respect, and generosity confronting the starvation threat.

It didn't last too long, thank God! I didn't know, as I was too small, but in time, I was told. Respect my father always won

As I will continue to walk by the same road along the farm going east, up to the point where the cattle used to be brought at the end of the same alley-el callejon – where us kids used to run behind and then in front of the big bulls. It was so much the real fun, but I will not find them anymore, those things have gone. I will be left to stand alone among new things that may have been built, as some also most surely destroyed to cover up the same geographic place where I will pass again with a magnifying lens, to see if at all, is mine to stretch beyond the corners of my mind.

My walk will take me, after a short ride, to the town where my mother saw the first light of her colonial land – Guanabacoa, and its high and low silhouettes so near my own town, where my grandfather rolled the first trolley car seen by anyone in those early realms. Regla, with its hard working class and colorful *diablitos* dancing by and with the *bata* drums (brought from Africa by the Abakuas, Yoruba pure, distilling the music that would come behind. I will come back to where I started my walk a while back and go to where I have been following my own tracks. A little bit to the southwest, I will cross the railroad tracks that may still be on the same place. I will try to find the mangrove trees, and the marshes with its low bushes, if they have not been yet obliterated. I know, at least, I will reach the water by the outer banks of the Martin Perez . . . Perhaps I will see the million little crabs still running away from my path towards the sands. I hope to find at least, some grains like shining salt, and see some birds along the way with their green feathers and red or yellow necks . . . The *tomeguines* will sing once again, and I will be ecstatic as I would hear them. Very close, by the waters of the bay, it would be shallow where the tide runs away towards the riverbed. From the small, old wooden dock I may be able to spot some old and even new colored fish. The ones that came to swim near the surface or still clearly visible to reach well near the bottom, not farther than four feet away. It will be like ever spring when the thousand butterflies would come alive to blind the passerby with a storm of color and their up and down flying. I will see children playing on the streets, and that will be all I want to really see, as if I blind my eyes from the sadness of the miseries of man, except for the ones that I would not pass, which are the ones with a kind word or humble charm who would come to say . . . "Don't worry about these times. We have so much that no one can take away, or hide. I am with you regardless of how far, regardless of how much it will take for freedom to arrive."

The old man was right about country being not only where you are from, but much more than just that. The strength of country feeling is where you find your heart; and so, I find it not only in the distant past. It is here crossing my front door and everywhere the taste of being in a dear country comes to mind, like the day I came to find it was like that on:

New York, St. Patrick Day, of 98 . . . .

Rush, rush, rush . . .
        Fifth Avenue, Sixty-seventh Street and down
They are coming now
I hear the bagpipe's tunes resound,
I already see the plaid skirts and tall, feathered black hats
Moving forward with a martial graceful
glide, I can see them close now
Drums and pipes with such intense impact
I can't hold back the emotion that overcomes my mind
"Am I Irish, if not for the color of my
eyes?" Yet, my heart pounds and tears
seem to want
To show their glow and shine,
As if I am aroused in the longing of thy land.

My land for freedom badly fights
And here is the almost similar
regard, but today I come to realize
In thirty eight years . . .
This land! NEW YORK
! Is also my dear one.

Shamrocks all over the large crowds
Piccolos reverberating in a spark to tell
– "You also here belong
More than your mind can promptly recognize
The years gone by have melted the fiber of your heart.

"Over there . . . Over there . . . Over there" tunes
Penetrating ... penetrating
The pores that years have opened
To bring the values of belonging deep inside
Telling me in no uncertain strain,

"You are not an absent outsider in your exile
You have arrived to riches unsurpassed,
When without losing what you cherish of your past
You gain the blessings of all lands
To feel the freedom and its plight."

Hear "When Irish eyes are smiling" With the sounding
of the band
Feels like if dancing in the throbbing of your veins
   ... To say,
"I am the same in the longing
Of an island ... far away and left behind."

NEW YORK March 17, 1998

A LETTER FROM SAN DIEGO BAY

Six o'clock and the sun is going down
    over San Diego bay
The haze spreads over the horizon hills
    and Coronado Island,
And I, a lonely witness
    from my hotel window on the ninth floor,

Thinking of how this beauty would have been lost
without mankind's enjoyment,
    should there not be one, to see the sun
Small boats lay over the
still waters on the right,
A few buildings
Between me and the waters.
The sun keeps sinking getting closer and closer
to kiss the edge of the land I see,
and then ... to disappear behind.
The noise of the thousand cars over route
    five become more noticeable
      as the sun finishes
        the ritual, of its daily life.

but this time, October 17, 1996 I saw it
as no other time before, Since timeless past, I saw it
and felt alive and thankful . . .
For this miracle to touch my mind and eyes, while I
miss you.

SAN DIEGO
October 17, 1996

Traveling to Omaha, Nebraska on June 11, 1994 to be at the opening of an exhibition and a reception honoring the memories of Cuba paintings being exhibited. It was very early in the morning when the plane made a scheduled stop in Chicago:

THIS MORNING AT O'HARE

This morning at O'Hare
Like any other Saturday of the
nineties, The casual appearance of
the travelers In silent dialogue with the eyes
Of early risers – most of them, longing for a pillow,
Or for a quick boarding and departure.

Suddenly widened my awareness
Or perhaps narrowed it,
To the corner at the end of that brook
Where multiple-colored fish
Feeling my sight would move or swim
To hide, behind a rock,
Or up, or down where more likewise
Would do it, at the same time. Was I also asleep, or what?

My eyes closed, tired of the distance,
To see and feel the paradise that was . . . And still in my
mind is.
Running barefoot – stepping on the puddles
Or feeling a tap swirling in my hand yet to be tried, Or the
warmth of our sun melting in the rain.

Where else this miracle repeats ?
In spite of time, but in a child's fortunate life
And yet, it stays alive today
In all that still remember
How it was in children's eyes.
Flesh still to be tired or dismissed

At the due time
I wonder if it could ever die,
Eloycito, or Arial would know – I know today, This
country side of mine will come alive again Perhaps in
Omaha or any other place.

CHICAGO 11, 1994

Las Vegas has become one of those unforgettable places, but:

IN BETWEEN THOUGHTS

All the glitter and lights of Vegas
All the shine of silver and gold
All the promise of fortune men hold
None of them are in my heart and my soul

Not as the tears of love
And the joy of feeling blessed In some special way . . .
Embracing the shine of our eyes
And the promise of love that we have
Elio Beltran

LAS VEGAS, NEVADA April 18, 1991

"Ah me! for aught that I could ever read, Could ever hear
by tale or history,
The course of true love never did run
smooth; . . ."

– William Shakespeare
A Midsummer Night's Dream

I found the old man again another day coming across my path to say: "Have you found the love you meant to have?"

"I don't know. I thought that love is every gift you have and you want to give . . . I have given more and more, but I seem yet to be looking for what I have not."

"The search," he said, "is always because of thirst. You thirst because you have not been given what a soul should share instead."

I left the old man, not without asking: "What about the loved ones who don't offer what I don't demand? . . ."

With a smile, he said: "Go forward with your quest. There is nothing you can do to get away from your own self."

I went forward as he said . I eventually found that I could not only run away, but what I found was unexpected and with revealing strength. No logical understanding could simply explain to the heart or mind how much my senses became trapped on the web of my own making. I blamed my adventurous or my eccentric leanings. I feared of losing in the end what I found and whatever that I may have been given.

My prayers were for guidance and for wisdom. None I thought I had for months of daily introspect and longer wait. In the end it was all clear, the truth had to come first.

Selfishness may be called against me. Incapable as I am, to change the destiny of my hands and heart. I took a one lifetime love that came imposing its demands of happiness, and so it went when I found the wise old man for the third time. He said:

"Why are you suffering in spite of having what your thirst has claimed and you could not deny?"

"To give joy, I feel I was born to give, but none is drawn from my coffers by the ones that let my love run by the side. Some just don't forgive and impose their verdict of guilt and do not accept God's will."

"I am today with someone who shares my final times without remorse, without regrets. She is the surest bridge to heavens and the softest breath of tender care. She is passionate and she is mild, strong, demanding, and in love at the same time.

She is totally attentive and with a positive mind. She follows my steps and leads if my intuitiveness goes wane. I don't think what else to want but to keep her by my side. What else can I say, old man? This it is not a whim and not a passing fad. She has been with me ten years passing. Let anyone be assured that I still love without exceptions the ones who have stayed on the sides. No doubt that my love they have, but distance, and more than regrets, does not allow them a change of heart. I ask for their forgiveness herein and all the time, and I trust that in due time with the help of the Almighty, I will find it along the way before I leave this realm."

"Let no one misjudge and criticize without first having tried the shoes that were so tight. And let no one feel scorn for those who love the truth to come forward instead of hiding it and pretending it does not exist while they fool all themselves and everyone to keep appearances and the like," said the old man as he went on looking for new desperate ones to help in their quest for the light.

THE ALMOST IMPOSSIBLE DREAM:

The phone rang and I answered. Your voice, same as ever,
Caring, soft, and close to my senses. I almost knew it was
not true,
but I believed it
I wanted to cling to it and didn't say a word. I only heard,
and then I knew
It was indeed not true.
I waked up knowing it was a dream but dreams are also
true . . .
And more beautiful so.

In dreams we die and wake up alive
In dreams we lost a precious star . . .
but in it we have known of its wonderful light.

Then we forget the harsh disquieting pain, in haze, And
turn awake . . . to retain . . .
The invaluable loving feeling, That one which otherwise
We would have never had.

March 1992

To my daughters Maggie and Maritza

Castles in the sand
Are built by children
With an everlasting dream.
They may be taken away by water or the wind,
but their love remains
As strong as steel.

And so remains my silent longing
For the time to see
The castle of your love Withstand the test of time, Storms,
and myths.

Your father
August 1, 1977

THE **B**RIGHT PERMANENT SIDE

Today I think of things permanent: The things mostly
ignored.
The things indifference have made seem lost.
The mist over the lake, overlapping the mountainside.
The snow on the untouched mountain top.
The sun shining on places I do not walk any more,

but ran one day under the rain.

The father hands and arms.
The shining armor and the sword,
Protector of loved treasures.
The little girls that were and are no more,
but permanently in my heart stay.
The forgetfulness of blinding hate.
The un-forgivingness of those who have not learned

That life is more than useless regret.
The precious blessings of thanksgiving

For things that only seem to hurt,
but build character instead.
Our priceless joy of understanding.
but, have I said before?
Permanent things that most don't know
Or want to see, I want to note herein . . .
And in them reinforce my spirit more,
First on the things that cannot ever be lost, and yet,
Why am I thinking of those things that can be changed?

> Like hate for love,
> Resentment for repose.

Only because I do not see, The intent to change
Of those who fear some other pain?

The fear of pain is not worse than not giving rein
To comprehend, and test the benefit of turning a dark page
And look for the bright side that always waits.
> It waits to greet all those
> Who dare to search

I know now why this sad tale does appear where I look
To find the joyful permanent.
It is that bright side that permanent remains For all to
find, either now, or at the late end. Sorry for those that it
may never learn.

> Vernon, New Jersey
> December 17, 1995

Resentment for repose.

It waits to greet all those
Who dare to search

I know now why this sad tale does appear where I look
To find the joyful permanent.

It is that bright side that permanent remains For all to
find, either now, or at the late end. Sorry for those that it
may never learn.

Vernon, New Jersey
December 17, 1995

PARENTHESES

Suddenly, like in a surreal painting, I stand here forty-one
years later, after leaving Cuba for my exile, overlooking a long and
complicated landscape. With Fidel Castro still in power, as frightened
as ever, playing two ends against the middle, as usual, possibly fearing
his physical death more that his necessary final judgment that he most
likely does not believe in.

How it did happen may not be consequential now although it
is important to know the process which made it possible in order to
learn from it.

In my mind, Castro has just played the same game of survival
and manipulation under the guise of being the preacher of a social
revolution and the discredited Marxist-Leninist doctrine but basically
singing the same old song of anti-Imperialism. "Fine," but while the
Cuban people has more necessities as a whole, it becomes easy for the
leader of that disaster to blame it on the United States and ultimately on
an embargo that has not worked except to give him more ammunition
to sustain his longevity as the longest-lasting dictatorship in the world.
I see many poor Cubans who took to exile and have been waiting and
hoping for Castro to fall or die, and instead, they are the ones dying
every day in Miami and elsewhere, away from Cuba, without being
able to go back and fulfill their dreams of seeing their country again.

To many of them, it would have been too painful to go back when
he is still there, and all you will be able to see is the misery that he and
his gang had created, which is everywhere visible. Not only on the
deteriorated walls and dilapidated buildings but also in the shattered
hopes of the people whose only aim is to survive day by day and
whose most precious virtues are their gentleness and their patience,

and fear is their most hated curse; the fear that feeds and maintains an ominous regime.

Well, this should be enough for what some may want to see as a tendentious statement, or as a big jump to conclusions, but there should be more to it than that. whose cowardice prompted them to sacrifice a whole country, kill and jail their opponents, and yet believe that their doctrine will succeed in the long run.

Would they be left believing that faulty as their doctrine is, they are ideals nonetheless, and that even crime is It is too simple, and still it will leave the creators of this nightmare, the ones justified for them to reach their goal regardless of the consequences to innocent others alon the way

No, this can't and will not happen!

There are yet many people around the world who only apparently see a charismatic figure but not the monster behind the mask, and thus, remain unconcerned, and even unsympathetic, primarily because they have not suffered the oppressive feeling of a tyranny. Worse yet, do not see him rule under a guise of paternalism.

Many have told the tragic stories, but not many have listened to them. Perhaps their testimony may not even come close to make the seemingly indifferent people everywhere in the world to understand and be compassionate enough towards the sufferers of such disgrace, let alone to vigorously condemn the false hero once and for all – or at least not to give him and his gang credibility and validation. This would open, at least, the possibility that people across the world would not allow themselves to be fooled and fall on the same disastrous fate.

Let's not make any mistake. The intentions in this story is not to favor any political side of any kind except the dignity of mankind, and for any man or woman to look at the alternatives of love and respect for human rights instead of domination by terror and hate. You will recognize the parties mentioned herein not by their apparent ideals but by their own rotten deeds.........

Michael's story should be seen away from the fringes of any political motivation. It has been intended to exalt beauty – the beauty of a country and its freedom-loving people. A beauty that is recoverable whenever men and women of good will want to revive and preserve it.

The last unwritten chapter to the story, will be on being back to Cuba, regardless of the sadness of the experience, regardless of the consequences.

Michael will see his land and the people he left behind again, and the experience of being back for a momentous visit will contrast with the experiences of having been there before, and even now with Castro still in power.

Perhaps in that parenthesis lies the clarity that he has tried to find and the clarity he may be able to offer for those who care to pay some attention. but, all in all, for the possible enjoyment that knowledge can bring as well as a definite conviction that there is beauty in loving – this big love of wet grass under your feet, and salt from the surrounding sea on your lips, and the splendor of standing on the grounds where you ran on as a child for whatever it lasts, under the rain or the shining free sun will become forever.

The Author

(*　*　*)

CHAPTER SEVENTEEN

Cuba – Forty-Two-Plus Years Since

The descent of the 727 jet chartered by the Cuban government was approaching the José Martí airport in Havana as it was flying over the overwhelming number of palm trees gracefully waving as they stood high in clusters like the never-changing icons they are on the familiar Cuban landscape; a sight that emotionally struck Michael who could not retain a tear from rolling down his check. The emotion deepened when he noted the glittering shine in Aurora's eyes as she stood to take a shot with her small camera. by this time, they had almost forgotten the upheaval at the Miami airport where the Cuban government representatives handling the boarding proceedings had made every passenger stand in line for three hours since five in the morning for screening and also for eventually collecting an ominous unexplained fifty dollars' tax for each one of them in spite of already having collected the highest fare per flying mileage that anyone has to pay anywhere in the world, at \$375.00 for the 190-mile round trip paid by everyone of the passengers on the crowded aircraft. Not even counting the one hundred and fifty dollars Michael paid for his Cuban visa and the typical twenty dollars they would charge for airport tax before the return flight.

It was all expected by the couple, when they decided to take the trip under the American government program that allowed American citizens of Cuban origin and their spouses and close relatives to visit family in Cuba for humanitarian reasons once a year. There were more unappealing things to be confronted by the travelers who brought gifts for their loved ones. They were told that they would have to pay one dollar for every dollar value of the gifts that they brought with them (including any medication or prescription drugs) for their needy relatives in Cuba.

"Let me answer the questions that the custom authorities would ask." Aurora said as they walked into the terminal building. "You heard what the other people boarding the flight said that you have to declare an amount of money for such gifts upon arrival," she continued.

"Yes, I know. They said that if you declare at least about thirty dollars they may or they may not search you, but if they search you and they estimate that you are actually carrying more than two hundred dollars, as most people do, you would have to pay that much money and as you know it is a totally unfair tax."

"You should not talk at all because if they should detect your Cuban accent they will search us. I will speak for both of us."

"That is right. They would love your beautiful Castilian accent." Michael said with a smile as they approached the inspectors who were roaming like hungry buzzards among the disorganized bags that were scattered all over the floor of the baggage claim area.

"We are Spaniards. We do not carry any gifts."

Her forceful straight answer to the standard question raised by the inspector was apparently enough.

"*Muy bien,* continue ahead towards the exit." The thin and long-faced man who was not wearing any uniform said as he signaled to the only wide door at the front end of the old terminal building.

They proceeded rapidly towards the door with their two large bags loaded with gifts, medicine and clothing that they would eventually leave in the island. The gifts included many toys and candies that Aurora and her sister had bought for every child that they would encounter anywhere they went while in the island, whether family or not.

The encounter with his sister and his cousin was an emotional one that morning of April 29, 2001. Mariita's hair was totally white and it looked nicely groomed although loose and not too short, just slightly above her shoulders. Her freckled face and wide smile as well as her permanent innocent expression were a real delight to Michael and which also captivated Aurora. Mario was slim as ever and now also had white hair over his perpetual tropical tan, looking somewhat older than his age but still very agile and animated. Soon they met all the children and grandchildren, including the most recent addition of twins who are now three years old, full of energy and childhood mischievousness. It was a preliminary family gathering that was to be followed by many more as they kept meeting more unknown family members during the nearly two weeks that followed. but they had to leave from that first meeting during the mid-afternoon to check in at the Plaza Hotel in Havana and be ready to receive Aurora's sister Camino, who was to arrive from Madrid later that afternoon.

The five-story hotel, with its high ceiling and beautiful stained-glass windows had been the pride of the new independent republic that had inaugurated the hotel in May of 1902. Now, it has been restored by foreign investors associated with the Castro government to operate it for the tourist industry.

Aurora's sister had made reservations from Spain on their behalf, and it included breakfast and dinner which was a convenience considering that it was not easy to find adequate places to eat and they did not want to venture out and look for a place to eat in a city that had changed much since the years when it was still a model city in every respect.

Michael knew that eating in the hotels was best, and he was not disappointed. The dinner that night consisted of a buffet with abundant choices that included beef, pork, rice and fish, as well as pastries and assorted fresh tropical fruits as dessert. It was an example that the tourists had to have the best of treatment, and for the hotels to have abundant and good food supply which unfortunately was not the case in any ordinary poverty-ridden Cuban household.

The afternoon still reserved an unexpected surprise for Michael. They closely watched from their hotel penthouse and terrace next to the dining room an extraordinary tropical storm with a magnitude that he had not seen in more than forty years (and not as spectacular as this one was to be). It was like a feast to the eyes and ears with not only the torrential rain flowing with the winds all over the roofs of the nearby buildings, but also the almost constant lightning thundering loudly as it illuminated the walls and roofs of the surrounding buildings of Old Havana. Michael was delighted with excitement as he called Aurora to join him at the hotel terrace. The rain was suddenly blowing hard into their faces, making all the other witnesses to this majestic display of impressive fearsome force to take shelter behind the louvered and classic high French windows that adorned the hotel's dining room by its terrace.

He stayed at the edge of the terrace until the rain and lightning practically blinded him while Aurora forcefully pulled him into the dining room from where they kept watching the storm for the entire forty minutes that it lasted. To him, it was like the island was giving him a significantly charismatic reception with the greatest display he had ever seen in a tropical storm. Nothing equaled this one; he was now sure that he would not be able to see anything like it again for the rest of his life.

Suddenly they both became worried about the flight from Madrid, which was to arrive just at the time of the storm. but after a long wait at the hotel's lobby, Aurora's sister, Camino, arrived in one of the chartered buses servicing the airport, exhausted but happy to be there. They all went to sleep after Aurora's sister was given a room at the end corner of the fourth floor, about five doors from the couple's room. For Michael, it was the first night he that he slept in Cuba since August 18, 1960.

They met for breakfast and laughed loudly at Camino's story that she had a sleepless night because of the roosters singing almost every hour from a roof across the street. They went to look from the terrace and saw an open terrace two floors below where there were chickens and one small pig in some kind of improvised corral. It was the first example of Cuban improvisation where the poor people living in those Apartments make do with the best that they can in order to provide food for the family in a kind of clandestine environment. The apartments did not even have any window shutters, as if it had been yanked out, and where water obviously went shooting from side to side of the floors during the heavy rain of the night before. It was a sad sight that can be seen in many of the deteriorated buildings all over the city.

Poverty never mean uncleanliness in Cuba. For Michael, who had kept the memories of his childhood surroundings at the highest ideals of beauty (on every corner of the places he once walked and around the hills and every bend and depth of a landscape which was like a magical playground for him and his friends, as well as his memories of an exciting, clean and vivacious city by the sea with its Malecon and uniquely well-manicured architecture ranging from the Colonial to the Art Deco styles) his return to Cuba and seeing the dilapidated facades and filth surrounding almost everywhere in a life of widespread poverty with survival as the rule to live by, was perhaps the most shocking; but it was all expected. Also expected was the sense of oppressiveness that he felt. Not expected however, was to find his people enduring so much suffering in silence, and yet they were still so gentle and patient people, so sadly betrayed and so strongly surviving in a hopeful and unspoken desire to see the end of a terribly long ordeal without them showing any hatred for it.

No hate towards the U.S. for the embargo was ever mentioned by anyone, yet he would privately hear much carefully expressed resentment for the prolonged imposed misery they had continued to endure in the name a of a revolution that has totally lost its meaning except to its irrational leaders. Some young people said that since they know that the miseries they are enduring are absolutely not due to the embargo, they could not care less if it was lifted or not. This was a surprising find for Michael but somehow it corroborated his belief that the embargo was not hurting Castro but instead serving as an excuse for him to keep rallying the people and using it as the best excuse for all the poverty and misery visible everywhere. He had given a great deal of thought to the dilemma of the Embargo. During the last three years, his views had been that the embargo had not been effective in changing the political scenario in Cuba. In any case, he is aware of the many reasons the U.S. government has in keeping the pressure by means of the embargo, as he has discussed this issue with some of the Cuban-American leaders both in and out of the country. The greater reason they said had been to make sure that Castro did not get the benefit of credits. Michael had stressed that the embargo's credits could be maintained while other restrictions limiting the bare necessities of the Cuban people could be lifted on a humanitarian gesture towards the Cuban people at the same time that the U.S. would make very clear to the world a declaration of principles in favor of the poor and suffering people in the island and set out on a campaign to internationally discredit and denounce the Castro regime more vigorously and effectively.

Some restrictions had been lifted judging by the fact that the U.S. under the current law allows for Cuba to buy in the United States as long as the regime pays cash for it. Castro has ignored this opening but not for long, for he would take advantage of it, if and when it would be convenient to him, but not necessarily to the Cuban people.

The fact about the credits is that Castro would not pay anyway and there are more countries around the world today who have no desire to continue funneling money to the dictator without anything in return, except perhaps the Chavez government in Venezuela who is seeking payment from Castro by borrowing trained militia, teachers, and agitators as well a experts in fighting street demonstrators and in organized repression Castro style in order for Chavez to emulate Castro and subjugate the Venezuelans and bring them to unlimited suffering like the one endured by the Cuban people. Free oil from Venezuela and the misery of the Venezuelan people is the price and the payment by Castro.

Michael was impressed with the unusual quality of endurance of the Cuban people that was evident in the common people in the streets during his visit; he could see them without showing any visible resentment. A quality that is also accompanied by incredible dignity, without arrogance; a humble, and frequently even humorous attitude in spite of the struggle for survival using their demonstrated unrelenting imagination to make do with incredible ability, evidenced in many ways, one most noticeable is how they managed to keep old cars running, like in the case of the vintage 1953 Pontiac that took them away from the airport that morning, even with its overwhelming fumes filtering most likely from rotten exhaust pipes underneath the leaky floor of the old car; very remarkable indeed for a car that old in a country without adequate supply of spare parts. Overall, most impressive is the Cubans' ability to make things work by finding creative ways to manage with little or nothing at all.

He saw the abject visible poverty in every house of his hometown, and also in the entire country, except in the hotels and resorts for tourists where Cubans are not even allowed to enter without finding security guards to chase them or even taken them in custody for interrogation, or worse. All in all, a kind of depravation surrounded by poverty not blamed on the U.S. embargo by the Cuban people but on a lie that cannot be attacked by their sufferers, nor expressed publicly, due to the fact that Cuban life has, for many years, been founded on fear (because fear is the bedrock of a totalitarian and undemocratic rule that does not allow for individuality and freedom for anyone to develop and prosper, let alone express themselves in public).

While in Cuba, he concluded that Castro wants generalized poverty as his best ally and for that reason, he is the major contributor to create such a state of affair since it benefits his hold on the entire country, as long as everyone depends on his government for their meager survival.

It was hard and unfair to tell the common Cuban, whether on the street or in private, about his impressions because it would bring uneasiness above and beyond what they already have. Therefore, Michael reserved any such comments with them while in the island. He did, however, enter into some discussions about the Cuban situation with a group of Spanish friends in Madrid, at his return. Michael found it necessary to discuss such issues with them because of the prevailing misinformation that most people had in Spain about the realities in Cuba. . They also feel that Castro has done well in providing education and health care to the people.

"Not so," he told them. "Health conditions are awful. The Cuban government runs many laboratories and ship medication as an export commodity. It even sells the expertise of medical professions to people who would be able to pay for it and to come to Cuba for the treatments. but there is no medication available for the Cubans when they need it."

"You do not want to see how much the embargo had to do with it because you, like most Cuban exiles, do not want to accept that," most of his friends in Madrid argued.

"Look, as a matter of fact, most Cuban exiles feel that the embargo is good because it helps the cause against Castro. So if that is the case, they would probably be happy if it was actually working but instead they are frustrated because there is no apparent effect so far after so many years, considering that Castro is still in power."

"Well, Michael, we actually see that there is everything in Cuba, every time we had been there and we did not see people in misery so the government must be doing something good after all."

"You do not see the terrible poverty of the people who do not even get paid any decent salary for what they do. The Cubans working in the hotels are paid miserable salaries while the government gets a higher rate for each worker they provide to the foreign-owned hotel chains. You do not see the misery because when you go as tourists from Spain to the resorts run by the Melia chains of hotel and to the different resort areas, you only see the abundance presented on the buffet and menu of the hotels, and at cheap prices at that. but the average Cuban finds it hard even to serve one meal of rice and beans a day. You also are taken to nightclubs and to the few streets and restaurants located in areas exclusively reserved for tourists and which are off-limits to Cubans who are not allowed to enter even if they could afford it to go there anyway."

"Still, without the embargo, the Cubans would be better off, Michael." Some of his friends insisted.

"Maybe so, because Castro would then not have any more excuses for the poverty he likes to have because it is exactly that poverty which keeps the Cuban people to be dependent on his government for the misery it provides to them. My sister-in-law used to think the way you all do, but she came with us to visit the real Cuba and saw how people really lived there. She is now happy that she was able to see the reality and you should hear all she has to say about her findings."

"I tell you more," Michael said. "I do not think that the Cuban government cares about providing any relief from poverty to the Cubans. My belief is that if you give people freedom and opportunity to achieve prosperity and progress then they will undertake a strong initiative and individuality and with all of that, they will have the foundation for democracy. Castro is definitively opposed to these principles and so he is a totalitarian leader who claims to defend the poor but contribute to nothing except to their continued impoverishment in order for him to perpetuate his hold on power with his hypocritical and demagogic argument that his system of government is in defense of the poor. The poverty that he is not in the least interested in eradicating because it will mean his demise. The worse of these facts is that such leaders, besides wanting impoverished subjects generally depend on their use of terror and fear to sustain their power."

"Furthermore," Michael added "you all know by what Spain, together with other European developed countries, have been trying to do since approximately nineteen eighty-five, which is about fifteen years ago, regarding the help they are trying to give to the third-world countries so that those countries can improve their economic conditions. All of that effort is just because the majority of the industrialized, rich and democratic countries have started to realize that the generalized poverty in the so-called third-world countries is becoming a threat to the freedom and prosperity enjoyed by the stronger economic powers.

The discussion among friends finished amicably as usual and perhaps with more insight for everyone.

During his visit to Cuba, Michael had given much thought to the realities confronted by the Cuban people, and at the same time, he had been able to equate them with his experiences during his visits to Western Europe, mainly in Spain, which is one of the developed countries who had made greater progress in their democratic principles during recent years and as a result, being a country who had achieved great economic progress.

He had seen Spain as having demonstrated great concern for the underdeveloped countries by becoming more involved in helping them. He has also seen the immigration problems faced by Spain with the *magrevies* and the exodus from the South Sahara areas in Africa as well as the immigrations problems of the United States. In all of these experiences, he has come up with his conclusions about the confrontation between progress in one hand and a tyrannically created poverty on the other.

It is pitiful, however, Michael maintained, that the involvement of Spain in Cuba since the early 'nineties has apparently been more for financial gain than with the idea of eradicating poverty. He has also told that to his Spanish friends when he told them: "The Spanish enterprises pay the Castro government in good hard currency while Castro turns around and pays miserable salaries to the Cubans working in such Spanish ventures. Yet Spain somewhat feels pity for the Cuban people and many Spaniards continue to blame the United States for the poor situation in Cuba. The fact is, helping to eradicate poverty may very well be a priceless price to pay for us to be able to see the end of undemocratic tyrannies that disguise themselves as victims that is what is happening in Cuba. Helping to eradicate poverty however, should not mean helping the tyrants, and it should not mean forgetting the people either since tyrannies control by using terror and fear. Effectively helping to eradicate poverty may also help to see the end of terrorism." His friends stayed silent and he continued to make sure that his points were well understood.

He insisted that promoting private enterprises is an effective way to fight poverty but how can the industrialized world do it when they have to deal within Castro's manipulative ways?

"You can see how the Spanish enterprises are forced or agree to accept associating themselves with the Cuban government as the only alternative and thus, end up like the resort hotels that the Spaniards and the Canadians have opened in Cuba, which in the end has become another way for the regime to exploit its people. The free world, after so many years of the same has not yet learned to deal in this case because all that Castro does is to set his conditions and the only thing that has to be done is for the free world not to accept them without at least some meaningful gains for the cause of freedom and some prosperity for the sufferers of the system, but Canada and Spain, to name only these two countries that are involved mostly, but, not exclusively in the tourist industry have only given in to the demands and are paying the Cuban regime and in turn the regime pays miserable salaries to its people and continue to harass and incarcerate the opposition, thereby Democracy and freedom takes a set back again and again,"

Michael had been able to see what was happening in Cuba now and for a long time and had concluded that the intent of the government there is not to fight poverty. He also said in his arguments: "As another example, the so-called *Paladares,* started to appear in and around the city as private enterprise restaurants that Castro allowed shortly after the demise of the Soviet Union in order to help his regime to survive by promoting tourism. However, once the small enterprises started to prosper somewhat, he would start to tax them out of business with taxes ranging up to seventy-five percent in the recent years. On the same vein, if small farmers are allowed occasionally to bring their produce to sell at the edge of towns and cities, such ventures are not allowed to last long because they would then be accused of price gauging or undue speculation. A typical excuse or reason the regime would particularly give once the small businesses started to proliferate and present the beginning of a possible buoyant-free enterprise inside the regime's tightly controlled system where no private enterprise would be allowed to exist and much less to prosper even when such small businesses are welcomed by the Cuban people as a relief to some of their hardships. The whimsical cancellation of the little freedoms the government had occasionally given to the poor farmers and also the heavy taxes imposed on small restaurant operators obviously show the aim of the government of keeping the people down as submissive as they could possibly be in the name of a revolution that no one believes in anymore, except those who had lived from their wasted stories."

For Michael, the terrible conditions that he found in Cuba was not much of a surprise when he started to see the harm done to the people as compared to the physical appearance of almost every building. Everywhere he looked he was not even able to recognize his childhood surroundings, as if geography had also been forced to change. He was however, able to discover that the few recognizable landmarks gave him a sense of perspective. He found that his mother's house, the same one where he and his brother had been born and grown up, was still miraculously standing alongside the ruins of most of the surrounding houses. The tall Corinthian columns were still proudly holding the roof above, even when many tiles, as well as almost the totality of the four-feet-high walls around the open terraces above the roof had almost totally disappeared. The terrace's side walls had suffered a kind of vandalism which was apparently created in part by the need to take the bricks out in order to make vital repairs or additions to other neighbor's houses. Most of the houses of such type, with about sixteen feet high of stucco ceiling construction (located in the same block where his first home was) have added or inserted a middle floor between the floor and the roof that the Cubans call *Barbacoa*.; the inner structural innovations are typically built by the people to add additional living space for their growing families or to house additional families who can't find anywhere to live, given the institutionalized poverty of the Cuban people who still have to pay rent to the government. Needless to say, no additional sanitary facilities are added, and the living conditions are less than adequate to say the least.

As he moved around his hometown and by the streets of Havana, he could see garbage and debris piling up without being systematically collected. He saw garbage floating over the small Tadeo river running between Guanabacoa, and Regla his hometown, the same river that once ran cleanly and beautifully among the low bushes (typically planted to surround the thin strain of water). He saw garbage even floating in the waters that surrounded the famous La Fuerza Castle, located just on the area of Old Havana (which has been the most refurbished area, something that has been done with money from the United Nations agency UNESCO) near the Ernest Hemingway hideout of La bodeguita del Medio and Ambos Mundos Hotel, a mere handful of blocks in downtown Havana which is the area mostly frequented by tourists. Most streets elsewhere are full of holes where filthy water remains stagnant alongside the debris falling from the deteriorating buildings.

There is no running water most of the time. Sometimes, water service is only available for a few given hours during the week. The Cuban people still manages to have their house's interiors as clean as they can possibly have them under the circumstances. They have always been known for their love of cleanness in their homes, regardless of how poor they may be. He saw how much effort the people in Havana did to bring buckets of water up the four or five floors to their apartments every day when there is water running at any of the nearby public faucets, four or five blocks away from where they lived, or when the water would be delivered to the neighborhood by a cistern truck, which does not happen at a pre-programmed frequency.

The physical changes he found everywhere he looked was only the sign of deeper decay corroding not only the facades and the infrastructure of buildings but also the souls of people who have been forced to live in miserable prospects of decay rather than being given progressive means for a more hopeful condition which is not possible within the system due to the lack of any significant incentives that the limitation of freedom has created.

The generalized decay is visible all over the country. To Michael, such condition is the highest cry of protest and dissent that every corroded facade in the dilapidated cities and towns are throwing in the face of those few who have immersed this country in such kind of misery in order to perpetuate their domination, taking advantage of the people's dependency on a falsely portrayed paternalistic, and so-called socialist regime acting in the name of unrealistic and anti – imperialistic postures used to serve their ambition and their sick power-driven totalitarian rule.

Terror is the base of power to those who create a doctrine of thinking and of imposing the thought of being representatives of a better class that should rule all others. Such is a policy of terrorism that marks every soulless demented demon, whether they are called Hitler, Stalin, Castro, or any of the emerging fanatic terrorists of the modern world. It is just the same doctrine of destruction by hate and domination by instilling fear.

Michael had this notion very clear in his mind and needed not to dwell on it particularly during his visit. He avoided talking about it with his relatives and friends as he saw how the people lived and how afraid they all were. He went to visit the old lady who now lived in the house he had built for himself and his family in the early 'fifties which is the same house that he had to leave when he took the ferryboat to his exile in 1960. He was delighted to see the house again. The tiles he had placed with his own hands to finish the bathroom and the kitchen area were still intact and shining just as new, as also were the tiled floors except for three – or four-odd ones that replaced the originals at the entrance of the living room. He was happy to see and talk briefly with the little old lady who had recently lost her husband. but he saw how her expression turned to fear when her neighbor from across the street, a wretched-looking man of about sixty years of age came to alert her to be careful because he, Michael, the old owner, had come from the U.S.A. to take a look at his old house and to later claim back his property and take it away from her as soon as Castro was out of power.

Such kinds of thought were something unfathomable in his mind, since for him that would be out of the question. but nonetheless, the poor woman was made to believe of such nonsense anyway. That is the case of many poor people in the island who have been brainwashed to believe that they would be thrown out of their houses and into the streets by the old owners, should Castro fall. When the reality is that, most Cubans who had left their properties are not even considering such aberration. There may, of course, be some exceptions among the exiled Cubans, but even in those few possible cases, there would have to be legal procedures similar to those instituted in Eastern Europe after the fall of Communism whereby the people would be protected from any kind of injustice, based on the studies made by prominent Cuban-American economists working in Washington D.C.

Brainwashing and indoctrination is a way of life for the regime in Cuba. Michael saw how it worked not only in the case of the poor old lady but also on the many other people in the same situations. A few days before the incident at his old home, on the first of May celebration in Havana, while the Cuban government was celebrating a usual rally in the Plaza de la Revolucion, the old Pontiac that was lent from a friend so that they could be taken to their hotel in Old Havana was stopped by the police two times, and in both occasions they were questioned about why they were not at the rally. After a very annoying delay, Michael had to interfere in behalf of the driver and the companions by saying that the driver came to receive them at the airport. After inquisitively looking at the documents, they were finally allowed to go on their way. It was obvious that there was pressure for the people to go to the rallies that, of course, were not attended just voluntarily.

During the several days that they spent in Havana, Michael noted that many idle men were sitting on the sidewalks, mainly around the center of the city where the Central Park and the Capitol building were located. "There is nothing to stimulate the people to go to work," he was told. "They would be paid by the government about two hundred and fifty Cuban pesos which is only about ten dollars a month. In which case, they would rather sit down and look for opportunities to make money by getting closer to the tourists." A very peculiar way of vagrancy, Michael thought.

It was true; they could not walk two blocks away from the hotel without being swarmed by men and by young girls trying to get something – from a tooth brush to an aspirin, or anything one could spare. And in many cases, it could be noticed that it opened the possibility for prostitution as could be easily seen almost everywhere in the tourist areas of the city where it takes place, in exchange for anything at all and for money too. Sadly enough is that many of the young girls particularly had graduated from some practical and meaningful career that would have made a decent living for them and their family if they had been living in any other country of the hemisphere. In a personal sense, there is no practical use for a career in Cuba. One of the nieces in the family had a pharmaceutical degree but the only job she could get was selling flowers to earn only about ten dollars a month. by the time she figured the cost of transportation and dressing for the job plus the prospects of the degradation and filthy mode of transportation available, she would rather stay home.

How can a government that proclaimed to end corruption and prostitution, and everything that they said was wrong in the country when they seized power, was now the promoter of a much more miserable degeneration? An activity which is known to be systematically promoted internationally in order to attract a large number of male tourists with hard currency, produced by a prostitution which is much more widespread than ever before in the history of the country. Such indignities struck the visitor in the face but did not blind him to see the goodness and gentleness of most of the simple Cuban people he found on the streets and everywhere they went.

He made an effort to forget so many signs of decay in the current society and went about in his search for brighter things, or at least the things that can't change, like the ones that could be found in nature and in the qualities in the noble fabric of most of the suffering Cuban people. He finally stood by his mother's grave with his sister, who brought him there with tears in her eyes, and then his father's at the Masonic Mausoleum, and later to sit for a while by the place where the body of his childhood friend, Eloycito, was laid to rest. It all gave him the gleaming feeling he came to find. A sense of love, and a sense of connecting, and not necessarily closure, if you will, but most of all, a perspective on life's meaning from all dimensions, even enhancing his conviction that hardship and death itself would not terminate the blessed spiritual values of the experience of life, and that of established human relations even under apparent casual or any imposed separation. A necessary feeling of being there in the flesh, touching the ground where forty-one years had gone by without him being there, and yet, if only for a short time before he would return from it, and before he would part, that time forever from his beloved lands.

The journey to follow his childhood steps through his long-memorized paradise was to be an exciting rather than a frustrating event, which was the most likely thing to happen to anyone without Michael's level of perception to detect every area and map out the absurd changes. He found some added tracks on the proximity of the old Fesser railroad station in front of his mother's house in Patilarga, for the whole length of La Calzada; tracks that took the place of the old frame houses that used to be aligned across the street, none of which exists any more. A barbed wire fence had substituted what once was the entrance to such houses making it impossible to enter the railroad yard and reach the areas where the mangrove trees were so abundant during his childhood and where he enjoyed so much hiding on the encampment that he and his friends constructed at the end of the various tunnels within the thick brush and bushes; tunnels that connected their hideout spot from the west edge of the railroad rails and also from the spot nearer to La Loma Blanca and another near the secluded Arenal by the old docks of Arellano y Mendoza at the edge of the Martin Perez river where they played many of the memorable baseball games, and yet another near the spot by the riverbank where thousands of minute crabs would be running to hide under the sand all at the same time, like an army, each of them carrying his largest claw up in the air as a menacing weapon, or otherwise as thousand ballerinas towing away with their right arms above their heads at full speed and with their similar rhythmical grace.

He could still see them, but unly, in his mind, right where it used to happen as a daily ritual of sundance, just as he could still see the many butterflies flying in an undulating parade of color, up and down in what looked like a million of them in a fabulous and flickering flying cavalcade of a beauty contest between a great variety of beautiful monarchs, and the most common orange or deep yellow *Charitos*, among a few sporadically mingled custodian dragonflies, or *libelulae*, popularly know in Cuba as *Caballitos del Diablo*, or Devil's little horses; insidious as they were, the people there also gave that name to the motorcycled police which showed the Cubans' imaginative side.

He knew the absence of all those signs of life that were marvels of an unrepressed natural phenomena of the area during the short springtime which was not necessarily that wild, but which offered, during his childhood years, such unusual gift to the eyes and senses for anyone who would be fortunate to be there during the most intense period of three or four days that it happened. The joyful game of monarch-catching he played with his sister Mariita and the neighborhood kids did not come now like a wave to blind the passerby, as it literally happened in those wonderful years. What a shame!, he thought, when his sister had written him in answer to his question about the memorable butterfly events by saying:

"There are not any more butterflies under these Cuban blue skies. No more butterflies flying free across the street."

Again, in springtime, but this time in 2001, he stood in front of the imposing fence that impeded his stepping into his old paradise of his early years and he could see the sharp contrasts between both periods in life that now more than ever shows the change not only of the surroundings but also of Cuban life as a whole and the least, the changes at this point in time are totally negative. He was now able to note the absence of all those signs of life as it used to be. The entire surrounding habitat had been destroyed in an exchange for useless development meaning – a seemingly totally abandoned terminal where he saw no trains moving and no mangroves in the distance. They have been substituted by a large esplanade by the empty docks, supposedly cleared for containers but are now also as empty, and next to it some dead Russian cranes that had long been idle apparently for lack of repair and maintenance, but most likely because of the absence of business. Michael had heard about them from different people in town, when he asked, and they responded:

"All those large cranes you see by the many empty docks did not move since the most part of the mid-'eighties. And the ships anchored at some of the docks, southwest of the harbor are idle as well. The ships are part, if not all, of the Cuban merchant fleet, one of the pet projects of the 'Comandante en Jefe' that had also resulted in failure."

"Could it be the result of the fact that the Soviets ceased to use Cuba as a base of operations since the fall of the communis t regime in the Soviet Union, or is it on account of the embargo?" He asked, but got no direct answer, and only a gesture that could have meant, "Who cares."

Some in Cuba say that although it was bad enough then, the situation has worsened since the downfall of the Soviet Union and the inability of the Castro regime to let go and allow the country to turn into a democratic society. Instead, he has tightened the grip at all levels with his never-ending tirades that hardly anybody in Cuba believes anymore except to know that they have to endure and survive it somehow.

The tourist industry does not need cargo ships and cranes, he concluded. Tourism that uses prostitution and creates a sub-economic system that incubates a widespread person to person acceptance of corruption at all levels of a society that struggles to survive, day by day in the prevailing miserable standard of life.

Michael could feel much sadness about the life conditions he encountered and his preference was not to discuss his impressions with family and friends; he then decided to keep greater attention on visiting and reminiscing about every place that brought him so many dear memories of his happy childhood.

He went to visit the old colonial House of the Pirates and the surrounding citadel. The place has also changed with some of the frame's structure substituted by stucco towards the front and the porch area with new floor and roof on them. but he could see that the backside and the entrance to the citadel still had the old Spanish flat bricks visible under the half-fallen stucco, showing the structure of the upper arch threshold of the colonial years. He found out that one of his older cousins was living in the house and he went to visit him. As he entered the reconstructed living room coming from the old vestibule behind his cousin Luis, he saw that there were no furniture at all in it, but only an altar on one of the walls painted in striking silver with an statue of Saint Lazarus in the center with his crutches and his two accompanying dogs, dressed under a white cape but still showing his bare legs filled with the bleeding sores that identified the legendary leper who appeared to be humbly looking down into the eyes of everyone who entered the empty room. Two adjacent and very French-looking wall chandeliers adorned the otherwise empty wall except however for the majestic and sturdy figure. The suffering and miraculous saint for whom there is great devotion in Cuba presented a very unexpected and most impressive sight.

After a short spell, Michael said: "This is quite a change for this room as I remember it when I used to play right here with my friend Julio while his very old grandmother was seated on her rocking chair which was the only piece of furniture in the room. Later on, Julio disappeared overnight when he was about nine years old. Do you remember him?"

"Of course I do. Everybody thought that he was dead until he showed up in the neighborhood about eight years later and told the story of his adventures of the time when he disappeared and secretly went to live and work on a farm near Santa Maria del Rosario. Later on, he became a fisherman and sailed most of the time off the coast of Yucatan, Mexico. Last time we heard about him, he was living in Venezuela with his older brother Arturito, who as you would remember was a great baseball player."

"That is an interesting story of those years because it was a mystery how he suddenly disappeared, as was the mystery of the ghost of the wooden -legged pirate who used to roam around this house. I remember when I heard the ghost walking and rolling his chains as he moved around the wooden floor that was badly sagged on the sides and had a high lump right here in the center of this room. It was all very eerie." Michael said standing in the center of the room, as he asked:

"Whatever happened to the ghost? Do you still hear him walking around at night dragging his chains?"

"Not anymore, since we dedicated this room to the saints and placed the statue of Saint Lazarus on that wall, ." his cousin said without blinking an eye.

"When was that?" Michael asked.

"Oh that was in early nineteen eighty when we did the last repairs to this house."

"Oh, no wonder that there were some reports of a wooden-legged man with a patched eye arriving in Miami on a boat during the nineteen eighties 'Mariel boatlift' of refugees." he said with a smile and a wink as he looked to the surprised cousin Luis.

"Anything can happen these days. Who knows?" Luis said, lifting his shoulders up to the height of his protruding ears, looking like if he really believed that it could be an acceptable end to the pirate's story.

Michael continued to walk around the hill where many small houses had been built during the forty years of his absence. But in general, he could still identify with his surroundings with the exception of the panoramic view of the horizon that was sadly changed. There was no more the dairy farm in the distance with its blue grass and three eucalyptus trees that were the real landmark of the farm days; he also walked through La Finca de Vicente and the side of La Calzada where the *Aguinaldo* flowers covering all the fences along the road made you believe that snow had fallen on the early mornings of late December and early January (when he walked with his friend Eloy and his dog Sibiri cutting through the morning mist towards their usual rounds around El Mangle and La Loma blanca where they used to place their hunting traps).

Turning back by the Hill of the Hermit where the old park still stood, Michael passed briefly by the same spot where Eloy had challenged his baseball teammate, the big and black Alfredo, to a fistfight, just the same day when they had first met on a more than memorable marble game. On his way down the west side of the hill he saw that the beautiful and big **"*mamoncillo*"** tree that the Taino Indians called "*kenepa*", as well as the taller and very larger *ceiba* with its protruding all-around thick and bare roots were not standing and offering its comforting shades anymore; also non-existent was the spot by the south side of the hill where the *Diablitos* of the Abakua celebrated their secret initiation rituals of Afro-Cuban tradition that he and his friends witnessed one night, as scared intruders that they were, when they watched, hiding behind the tall, grass by the rocky blue "serpentine rocks" cliff overlooking the entrance to El Callejon del Sapo by the old slaughterhouse that was also no longer there. but there still was the entrance to El Callejon, now badly paved and full of holes, and still a narrow road surrounded by poor housing in both sides, instead of the thick brush and bushes that used to look like a long tunnel during the happier childhood years when they used to run in it with the fearsome bulls as if they were in a Cuban kind of the Pamplona, Spain feast of San Fermin. No more was he able to romanticize the beautiful surroundings of his youth when he looked at what is there now but seeing the changes resulted worthwhile, in spite of the obliteration suffered and the change for nothing comparable, by far, in beauty and worthiness. At least until this moment in time,. melancholic as it is, all that he have left behind was in reality acquiring much more value and significance in his mind, as he still dreams of seeing the return to beauty once hate and fear is substituted by reconstructive love.

The rushing memories and the old names of places that no longer existed as such, came hurriedly into his exhilarated mind as he looked over all the panoramic view that was no more except in his inner vision.

Walking along the north side of the hill, he found that the large and tall warehouses with its yellow frontage that used to stand by the peaceful and shaded road passing in front the Fesser terminal docks and which have come to life in so many of his paintings have been substituted by low-level warehouses that ran deeper into the extended docks (that had been apparently expanded to house larger cargo ships which however were no longer seen as the docks showed no activity whatsoever).

The place was surrounded by a fence that did not allow anyone to pass as he has hoped to be able to do, and therefore, no one could get closer to the edge of the bay that he liked to do during his growing years when he used to go fishing with his father or play and swim and watch the many colors of the tropical fishes under the small wooden dock his father had built and next to where he had buried the remains of his beloved Sibiri after the already blind fifteen-year-old dog that had been his and his friend's childhood companion, was struck and killed by a truck in front of his mother's house. Not being able to reach to all the places he so wanted to get close to was a disappointing experience but as it was by then, he was well prepared and not at all surprised by his findings. The fences and the badly design layout of the entire area as everything else suffering deterioration in Cuba is all part of the same demoniacal design of domination, limitation and destruction imposed without regard for anything but Castro's worthless ambition.

He was frustrated that he could not step into those areas anymore, but he was glad that he was there again and he still could see the ever-free and unchanged blue skies and breathe the spring air as he traced his steps over those grounds overlooking the entire piece of geography he knew and loved so much. In his mind, it had not changed at all.

The idleness of the docks and the many scattered cranes around the bay literally resembled the idleness of the perfectly healthy, young and mature men that Michael saw sitting on the sidewalks all around the center of the city at all times of the day as if there was nothing else to do. Some of those men may have been waiting for the "Camellos" – the long, rectangular boxes that are used for the miserable, uncomfortable, and mostly standing-room-only public transportation cargo trailers with a humped roof that them the nickname of "Camels". The stinking "Camels", where anything can happen within its crowded bellies, according to the many despicable stories they heard, are pulled by a tractor truck much like an eighteen-wheeler, connecting every neighboring town and some farther areas to the inner city, transporting people much like cattle (that occasionally can't avoid doing their natural necessities in such smelly quarters).

The cost of such transportation is cheap (just as crossing the bay is to and from Havana and Michael's hometown of Regla) riding or rather sailing now on a motorized barge with floors, walls, and ceilings of heavy iron sheet metal (where riders are boxed in), with a compartment that had a few and rather small glass windows measuring about 2 x 1 feet in height and neither did they have any seats; a far cry from the old *lanchitas* he so romanticized on many of his paintings. The small windows did not offer the open view of the bay and the city, as did the old fifty-feet *lanchas* with their twelve or more 6 x 3 feet windows.

What a contrast! He thought as he compared it to the old "*lanchitas*" that carried as many passengers as these drab barges did. They both could carry as many as sixty passengers, but the "*lanchita*"s, as the towns people lovingly called them, not only were clean but shiny as well. The inside wood work was shining bright with fresh marine varnish which included the wooden and elegantly designed benches lying along both sides of the boat where more than forty people could sit comfortably. The wood cover of the diesel engine was clean and shining as well, and all the metals on the boat were made of bronze and were always kept sparkling like when they were new. Such was the loving care that the operators had bestowed on them.

Nowadays, the passengers enter the dirty and hateful boxes. First to enter are the ones with bikes (usually sixty percent of the passengers), followed by the people without bikes. Michael saw all of it on the two occasions he jumped inside the depressive sailing cages. All the passengers were standing up. No seats anywhere. They would not talk, and none would look at anyone in the eye; most would steadily look sadly to the floor as the barge would sail away with what looked like a cargo of zombies (which they are not) but a load of broken and saddened human beings (which they are).

What a difference! he thought. During his days, almost everyone on the boat talked to someone else or participated in animated chat within a group, whether they were students or workers, professional or not; they all enjoyed the ride as a pleasant social gathering.

Today's fare is less than five cents in Cuban currency which is really nothing and which represents the "benefits" that the government's subsidized transportation; possible only by paying the lowest salaries to any of the workers in the third-world countries of Latin America. The average salary of the workers who travel on them is not much more than the equivalent of about ten dollars a month paid by the only employer – the Cuban government. It will be all they get, unless they are able to work within the tourist industry and be able to get a few dollars in tips. Aurora let a little old lady go ahead of her when she went to pay the fare to cross the bay and was surprised to see that the lady turned around and gave her a boarding ticket for the ride, with a sad smile and without saying a word. She tried to strike a conversation with the woman but found that there was no interest from this poor lady to start any kind of conversation, and instead, she entered the depressive – looking sailing box and stood with a somber look in her eyes as she leaned against one of the walls of the boat.

The tourists coming to Havana can use any of the thousand taxis that crisscross the city at all times; taxis that the Cuban people can't afford. They are not to service the Cubans who are not allowed in the hotels. The taxi drivers have to be paid in dollars. The fare is relatively low at ten dollars for a metered trip to the airport and about three to five for a metered ride within the city, except if the trip would take you to the outer burrows; but the tourists are usually generous with their tips.

On two occasions that Michael ventured in a conversation with some of the taxi drivers, they privately and individually told him that the various and different fleet of taxis are managed by a high-ranking military official, most likely a colonel, who dressed as civilian and to whom the drivers had to give at least seventy-five dollars everyday out of their tips on the runs they were able to make without the meter running, which they occasionally do unofficially. The driver would keep the rest of the tips that they got, which would not be much under the circumstances. It was hard to believe, particularly about the amount of money involved in such scams, but there is no doubt about the resentment felt by the drivers. Their salaries are only about fifteen dollars a month, and they work more than ten hours a day almost every day of the week. One of the drivers was saving money to go to Mexico where he had some friends. He was hoping to earn visas from the visa lottery that the government runs.

All the taxi drivers are extremely bitter. When he asked one of them privately if there was any prospect for the regime going down with little or no bloodshed, the young man said: "There will be a lot of it. There is no way that no bloodshed would happen because there is too much abuse, too much frustration, and too much suppressed hatred, and too long of being controlled by fear."

The sadness in most people is noticeable by their apprehensive demeanor. Michael saw it as he watched people in their workplace, at the hotels and other establishments and offices. Although courteous, he noted that they are mostly taciturn and dispirited. In addition, he could also see that out of five or six people in a workplace, there was at least one hard-faced person with an authoritarian attitude who watched all others. They are the so-called members of the *vanguardia* or members of the committee for the defense of the revolution who are nothing more than the resentful stool pigeons of the workplace, such as the ones who acted in the same manner in the neighborhood where they lived. He was saddened to see that although a minority among many (that probably amounts to less than five percent of the entire population) they serve as the pedestal where a lie is supported and perpetuated against a suffering majority.

As a price, the government gives to the "vanguard people" and their close family a few days or a weekend vacation in a secondary hotel in Havana or in Varadero beach, giving them free lodging and two hundred and fifty pesos to spend, which is the equivalent to twenty-five dollars. A miserable price for a miserable job of being indoctrinated stooges.

Although a minority, it is very sad to see its existence and the fact that there can be people who lend themselves to such denigrating activity, particularly supporting a worthless cause for a miserable reward. Perhaps this realization in itself was one of the greatest disappointments that hit him the most – because he could not conceive to be part of (what he had seen on a small part of the Cuban people) their low self-esteem and little shame. A blemish that he would have rather not seen and that which he hoped would disappear by their own kind of self-cleaning when it is no longer justified or sustained by fear, or better yet, when pride, truth, and courage become their greater qualities.

He preferred to think about qualities and some of the qualities of the Cuban people have been used to impress with the government's international propaganda. but as he discussed with his friends in Spain, even some of the most boasted so-called accomplishments by the Cuban regime, which are not virtues of the system at all, are sometimes widely accepted by many foreign people who do not get to see or know the truth. During his visit, he liked when he saw how clean and nice the school children looked in their uniform, and he admired the parents who made quite an effort to show their pride in sending their children clean and neat looking, with their freshly ironed clothes. A sight that can be seen practically all over the country and which he remembered was always the characteristic of the Cubans (to do just that), no matter how poor they may be.

There are more children now, of course, as the population has grown; there is as well, no doubt that it is in the best interest of the government, to showcase the children as one of their accomplishments. but there is also no doubt that the so-called better education really means brainwashing and indoctrinating them into a culture of hate, primarily towards the giant of the north, and to use the children in all public demonstrations organized by the government in order to impress and show off a false popular support.

Other claims of accomplishments are with the health care and the virtues of the medical field in the island. The biggest truth is that even during the colonial years, Cuba has been able to produce good physicians, many of them internationally recognized. It could be said that it is in the genes of Cubans to produce good doctors in medicine, and surgeons and scientists in the medical field since Dr. Carlos Finlay, who contributed to the discovery of the mosquito being the cause of malaria during the construction of the Panama Canal. Since long before the revolution, the Cubans made the birthday of Dr. Finlay in December 3, the day to honor all physicians every year. There have always been good surgeons and clinics in Cuba long before Castro. In addition, Cubans, long before Castro, had one of the best health care systems in the hemisphere which they inherited from the Spaniards who established the hospitals and private clinics that were accessible and at practically no cost to the poorest of people. The tradition continued during the years as an independent republic and it was the pride of every Cuban, so there is not much to show for now as current accomplishment.

He always remembers one of the greatest surgeons that Cuba has produced: Dr Jose Iglesias de la Torre who created the world-recognized procedure of colostomy to operate colon cancer. Dr. Iglesias operated Michael's mother in 1951 of a large and deadly cancerous tumor when she was sixty. His mother survived from it and lived for another twenty-five years free from any reoccurrence and the operation cost him nothing at all. Dr. Iglesias took exile in the U.S. during the early 'sixties where he taught his techniques and currently where many older generations of surgeons still remember him with great regard.

A great number of physicians have left the island to try their fortunes elsewhere as they did not find the right environment to use their skills under the existing situation in Cuba.

The government assigns a doctor to every ten or fifteen square blocks in every neighborhood to take care of consultations and attention to minor emergencies. These doctors are paid an equivalent of twenty-five dollars a month and they are assigned a less than adequate living quarter where they do not have running water most of the time and from where they have to render their services. Michael spoke with some of them in the capital and during his visit to Pinar del Rio and saw that the doctors were overwhelmed with work, any hour of the day or night, averaging about fourteen hours of work every day. They are constantly frustrated because of the lack of appropriate medication and basic medical supplies. Anyone would think that it is to be blamed on the U.S. embargo, and very few people ask why the regime does not seem to lack the supplies of military weapons for their armed forces which cost much more than any medical supply. besides, according to the U.S. government, there is no embargo on medical supplies to Cuba.

The greater virtues are on the people who survive all the hardship as stoically as they can since there does not seem to be any relief from it. The worse is that they have to hear all the time like a broken record that it is all in the name of a freedom that they don't really have at all. One of the problems is that a large part of the population which is now in their forties and fifties do not know anything other than Castro and his regime and do have neither a point of reference nor been given any honest sense of history, except that most young people know that what they have is anything but good. The desperation have caused many to venture into the high seas in whatever way possible to flee the island, and countless have died in the intent.

When you visit a Cuban family, poor as they may be, they make all kinds of efforts to make visitors feel welcomed and who are greeted with even a modest meal (for which they may not have the proper utensils to serve and eat it with). Michael asked for a knife to cut a piece of the traditional '**lechon asado**' and he was presented with a large kitchen knife to cut the roust pork. He was somewhat embarrassed. It was not a large gathering but they have to sit only four at a time at the table and take turns to eat and enjoy not only the tasty Cuban food but also the loving atmosphere where they give you everything they can.

You will love them for it, and you would want to give them everything you brought – your money, your clothes, whatever you have with you even down to your toothpaste. And you will feel sorry that there was a limit in what you can carry for your trip and the things you have brought for them.

He would try to put all the indignant things aside and behind, including the way he was harassed by the "Seguridad" del Estado at the Melia Hotel in Varadero, as well. He had spoken with the waiters at the cafeteria and they noticed his Cuban accent (that he has not totally lost in spite of his forty-one years away from the island) and since that moment, he was watched at all times because ordinary Cubans are not allowed to even walk in the lobby of the hotel unless they are conducting business authorized by the government. Most tourists at the Melia Varadero are from Spain just as his wife and his sister-in-law (who came from Madrid to join them). Finally, on the second of the three days they were to stay in Cuba, he was sitting in the lobby waiting for Aurora and her sister when one of the bellboys came looking for him.

"Sir?" he said. "You are wanted in the security office." "Who me?" he asked incredulous of what he heard.

"Yes, they have asked for someone matching your characteristics. Would you follow me please?"

At that moment, Aurora had just arrived and questioned the man about what was going on.

"They don't want you, they want him. You can wait here," the bellboy told Aurora.

"No, I won't., wherever he goes, I shall go too." And they both followed the tall and heavyset man through the inner corridors behind the lobby walls, all of which looked terribly dreary; a far cry from the elegant lobby area.

They were finally guided inside an almost empty room except for a desk where a small-framed man in his forties, sporting a well-trimmed moustache, dark and straight abundant well-groomed hair, wearing a long-sleeved shirt and a brown tie was sitting behind the desk. He asked Michael to sit at the only chair that was right across and closely in front of his desk and told Aurora to sit on a separate chair near the door. The only thing on the wall was a large photo of Che Guevara. It all gave him the oppressive feeling of having entered an interrogation room of the KGB, although in this case, it was the infamous G-2.

Aurora pulled her chair closer to Michael's and although silent yet, her Spanish temper was already boiling.

The man took the phone and seemed to call for a woman named Margarita to come to his office and join him. For a long ten seconds, the man looked into Michael's eyes until Margarita entered the room and stood on the right side of the man. She was a very thin and tall woman dressed very plainly and without a smile on her face. She looked like the typical, resentful, and long-faced watch dog of the revolution. She stood there without saying a word, only to be a witness, as it was probably the only reason she was called in, Michael thought.

"Can you tell me why I have been called here?" he asked.

"It seems that you fit the description of someone who had gone without paying the bill," the man said.

"How can it be?" Michael said as he totally disbelieved what he heard. And then he remembered he had some coffee and pastries at the coffee shop that morning, and got tired of waiting for the waiter who had apparently disappeared so he went to the casher instead and paid there.

"Wait a minute," he said. "In the first place, I have not come here to go away without paying anything and this is very offensive for me. In any case, I was served by someone different than the person I paid to this morning at the coffee shop. but I can't believe that you called me here for that. I feel that I am being harassed for some other reason."

Aurora, who was holding back from saying anything until that moment, almost jumped out of the edge of her chair to break the unsavory dialogue:

"Yes, that is right! We are tourists who came to spend money here and thought that Melia was a trustworthy hotel to come to. but this is unbelievable. Judging by what we see here, Melia has accepted having this kind of police stay inside their hotels to harass the tourists." Aurora furiously complained.

"Wait a minute, Aurora. Let's get to the bottom of this." Michael told her, trying to calm her down. Looking at the commissar he said: "That's all we can say. There is no such case of leaving without paying this morning. We can go to the coffee shop and I will tell you to whom I paid to and then you can leave us alone. We are very upset about this as you can see."

"No, the report is that it happened last night, not this morning." The man who had stayed very quiet throughout the couple's outburst said, while the woman just stood there like a standing broomstick silently overlooking everything from her outstanding height.

Michael looked at Aurora as he asked: "Last night? What was last night? Ah! I know. We were at the hotel's nightclub watching the show."

"Yes. We only asked for three beverages and you paid right away when they served them."

"That was all we had, and we were asked to pay as we were served. That's all." Michael said as he looked into the man's eyes and added: "There is no reason for this. You must give us an explanation of why we had been bothered for no reason at all."

"Do you carry an ID with you?" the man asked.

"No, I don't. but my wife has my passport with her in her purse. Please, Aurora let me have my passport."

Still red in the face, Aurora pulled the distinctive blue American passport from her purse and handed it down to the man, who looked at it intently and returned it immediately saying:

"We are sorry for the inconvenience."

"No. I think that you should bring here the person who served us last night and clear this matter up once and for all because there should not be any doubt. but we will complain to the Melia organization in Spain because we feel that we have been harassed unnecessarily and we have never seen this type of treatment anywhere in the world where we have traveled," Aurora added with her sharp and assured Spanish accent.

"The man is not here at this hour but I do not think that is necessary. It must have been some mistake and we are sorry for it. You can go," the long and sour-faced commissar finally said.

They left to meet Aurora's sister and tell her about what had happened.

Michael made a comment about how soon the commissar changed his attitude when he saw his American passport. He then said: "There is no doubt in my mind that they just wanted to check on me because I look very Cuban here and they just wanted to let me know that I am being watched. I am sure that it was all they wanted to do."

"That is possible. but I feel very uncomfortable and uneasy about all of this, so we should leave today rather than staying here another day as we had thought of doing. I know you wanted us to see and enjoy Varadero and it is beautiful, but not this way. We should leave today."

The two sisters were rather upset and so was he, although he was taking it more like a part of what he thought he would find at some point during his visit, (but not while staying on what was supposed to be an international hotel chain). He had rather expected that kind of problem as he roamed around his hometown taking pictures and filming. Yet nevertheless, he was not bothered at all. He finally convinced them to stay for that one more night which they had paid for since the time his sister-in-law reserved the rooms in Spain. They left the next day to go and visit the Vinales valley which was the other Cuban natural jewel he wanted them to see on the most occidental province of Pinar del Rio.

The experience was not only offensive but it was also a reminder of the oppressive atmosphere that he remembered living in in the early 'sixties before he left for his exile. In any case, he knew that it was expected, perhaps he even expected worse, but he had decided to come back at least once to see his sister and the rest of the family, and walk again around all the places where he grew up – from Regla, to his mother's hometown of Guanabacoa, and to Hemingway's beloved fishing village of Cojimar.

In spite of the apprehension while he was visiting those cherished places (where he truly expected to be either harassed or watched intently but to his surprise none of it happened) he was able to enjoy and look into every cardinal point and every corner of all places; identifying what have not changed and exploring to see what the changes have been. He entered the shell of the ransacked Cojimar Yacht Club building which was a beautiful as well as unusual with its Art Nuovo structure which was a sort of a mix between Contemporary and Colonial styles – a spacious and elegant place prior to the revolution. It was of a very attractive architecture, however simple,, with gracious high-ceilinged salons for social events. It also had an Olympic-size swimming pool on the grounds that overlooked from its high grounds, the beautiful *rada* of El Cachon and the silvery, shining Cojimar River. Michael remembered when he and his brother used to come to participate in swimming competitions right there, where now there is no pool but only a lot of indescribable rubbish.

The institution was a model of middle – to lower-income private social organization open to all during the old years but now, it was only a very dirty and abandoned shadow of a building, abandoned after being used for only the first two decades of the revolution as the headquarters for the Association of Women of the Revolution. Nowadays there are no building, no women, and no revolution except for the generalized destruction in the place. More sadly, nothing of the happy and peaceful days at a time when it was an exemplary role model of a progressive and free society open to all, without hate or fear.

The three travelers drove away on the compact car rented from one of the government-run tourist agents. Their destination – the valley of Vinales, one of the most beautiful spots in the island that Michael remembered dearly from his excursions of his school years.

They missed the main road going to Pinar del Rio and ended up traveling around the countryside towns of rural Havana. It was like a blessing in disguise because they were able to see real country roads and the small towns of Alquizar and Ceiba del Agua, driving on sugarcane plantations on both sides of the road and areas of very red soil with clustered royal palm trees that made the ride a very attractive one. The blessing was evident when they had a flat tire before they got to the busier road. It was a front tire that was obviously a defective one since it blasted and totally peeled away (showing wires that burst coming out in all directions). Luckily, it did not happen when they were on the faster central highway, something that would have put them in great danger. The main concern was that the tire was in such state of deterioration that having it in the car was an invitation to disaster.

He felt that he should have checked if before getting on the road but he had been too used to get rental cars anywhere in the world without worrying about the tires not being in perfect conditions; that is not the case in Cuba, of course. At the moment, at least, they were able to use the spare tire and enjoy the rest of the drive. The complaints would come later in Havana when they returned the car they had rented for their tour outside of the city. The situation was just another example of the deficiencies, and this time the neglect for the safety of the tourists by a state-owned operation which leaves a lot to be desired, as they would later tell the perplexed commissar on their vigorous complain (a government functionary who does not normally expect being called irresponsible and neglectful in an environment that most people are afraid of harshly expressing any criticism of a government-run entity.

They arrived to the valley with very dark and low clouds pouring the thickest of rain almost at the edge of evening; but suddenly the rain stopped and a bright late afternoon sun illuminated the entire area as if by magic, night was pushed away another hour. It was enough for the travelers to be able to see a beautiful tobacco plantation spreading like a green carpet as they rode downhill. On the right side, Michael identified a large barn as that of a typical Cuban barn used to dry the precious tobacco leaves. He had to stop because seeing how the leaves are hung in the barn is like seeing a work of art, as he remembered from the few times that he had the opportunity of visiting a Vega so many years before, and he wanted to show Aurora and her sister something that was so real and, so unchanged since the colonial years.

He parked the car in front of the large barn and next to the small cottage in front of which a few children were playing. Aurora and Camino stepped down and talked to the children and the mother who was folding tobacco leaves on a small table under a small roof that ran along the left side of the cottage. They soon gave some small toy cars and candy to the one four-year-old boy and dolls to the three – and five-year-old girls respectively who first ran away, looking shyly from a distance but later came closer as their mother greeted the travelers. After a short while, they asked for permission to look inside the barn and a young man guided them inside where they found two older men dismounting the already dry leaves from the long bars where it hung in small bunches. Many of the barns that stood from floor to the twenty-foot ceiling were still full of tobacco.

It was interesting to see that the two men inside the barn were dressed in white and with the typical Cuban farmer's hats. The hours working inside the barn had tainted their hats up to their shoes in a monochromatic light brown, yellowish color which blended them to the hanging tobacco. Their gentle smiles and quiet moves as they caressed the leaves in their hands were more than eloquent in terms of their love for the trade. They were both very thin, which makes them look somewhat taller than they actually were. The two brothers have been working in La Vega for more than fifty-five years, first with the original owners and now producing for a government-controlled operation.

After thanking everyone for their gentle attention during the short visit, they continued down the road. About a mile away from the plantation, a man in his forties standing next to a bike, signaled to them from the roadside. Michael decided to stop momentarily and the man came to his side of the car to talk to him: "If you are going to stay in a hotel, can I recommend a house instead"

"What is it?" Michael asked.

"There are a few in the valley, and I know the best of them. You can also eat the nicest fresh lobster tonight for only ten dollars each, three doors up the road in my mother's house. She cooks very well and likes to attend to the tourists."

"We are going in the direction of El Mirador Hotel, but would like to see the house if it is nearby."

"You can follow me and I will take you there right now."

"Okay, let's go," Michael said.

It was not raining any more when they started up a dirt road following the man on the bike, but by the time they reached the house where the man stopped, water was running downhill like an overflowed wild brook. Aurora and Camino were not happy about the idea of staying in a house instead of the hotel and as such, they did not go down to look. He had to step on some rocks so as not to get too wet as he jumped over the overflowing ditch to get on the front porch of the house where he was greeted by a middle-aged woman who invited him in. On the porch, an old man was sitting on a rocking chair reading a newspaper. The lady showed Michael a very clean bedroom with a queen-sized bed and another smaller room with a regular bed and the bathroom in between them. He was pleasantly surprised to see how clean everything was and also how comfortable the beds were.

"The three of you can stay here for twenty-five dollars a night. We offer you breakfast in the morning. We do not offer dinner but there is a house up the hill where you can have dinner. They cook very well." "Yes, I know. The man on the bike told us about it. Do You have running water here ?

"We have plenty of water in the cistern tank especially today with all the rain, and we provide hot water with an electric heater."

"Oh! Really? Let me see it." Michael said.

"That is it." The woman said as she signaled to what looked like a three-by-ten-inch pipe connected to half an inch of pipe coming from the wall near the low roof of the shower area of the bathroom. It had a homemade sprayer at the end which made Michael think that of an improvised electric water heater that heats the water as it runs through a resistance built inside the thick "nipple pipe". He was amazed to see that such ingenious and almost primitive gadget would work without getting anybody electrocuted.

"Do you actually have electricity here?" He asked.

"No, but we have a small generator that works with gasoline and we let it run in the morning for hot water, and that is all we use it for, because we use kerosene lamps at night since gasoline is very expensive and the motor that runs the generator is very old and we can't use it for long periods."

He stepped towards the back and saw that the small house had a yard where a few chickens and hens were eating fresh corn under a tin roof that protruded, as if to make a shaded dirt floor back porch. Suddenly, he saw the most beautiful rooster he had ever seen. It was so large and its feathers were so bright, with the colors so incredibly intense that it seemed totally out of the ordinary. The impressive rooster became even more extraordinary when it ran fast to mount one of the hens. The move caused quite an uproar in the open henhouse and the noises brought Michael memories of his grandfather's backyard behind his unusually large *bohio* in the outskirts of Guanabacoa. He came outside and enthusiastically said to his two surprised companion. "Let's stay here tonite, wont you?"

So it was at the valley one night:

It was dark when he came by the front of the small hut converted as an inn for the night.

Some candles and kerosene lamps dimly made more shadows than lights, moving like flickers as the old man was softly rocking away when he gently greeted his guests for that night.

"Did my daughter tell you that I am not very old? Did she?"

"No, we just did not talk about any of that, my good man," he replied.

"Well son, I am only sixty-one. It is just that I fought in La Sierra, if you want to call it a fight. I got hurt after my third year there when I fell off a cliff on the mountainside when I was jumping for joy when Batista had decided to part."

"Oh, is that so? You have much to tell, I am sure of that."

"Well, being in La Sierra was easier than most would surmise, because many more risked and lost their lives in the cities than fighting up high in the mountains, where life was placid and the war was mostly a propaganda farce. I did not shoot a single shot, although I could have done better than many of my counterparts."

"Today, I am a half-disabled man, and I see the truth in so much as we struggle to survive and get nowhere most of the time . . ."

"We struggle with trying to get by, by hosting the people when they pass by. Nothing is easy, even by doing that. My father did better when he was a farmer in some other people's farm. He raised six children, of which I am the younger one."

The few moving lights came on his deep and wrinkled face while he didn't show neither sorrow nor a smile as he continued to say:

"I enjoy the life passing just by looking around the beauty of these parts."

"I can understand it," Michael said as he sat down next to the man. He listened to more of the stories of a war that was not even that, and of the man's disappointments for two of his children who

Were, instead sent to die in Angola and Ethiopia. A far away war that brought nothing but misunderstood pride.

"My wife died of sadness, and for a foreign interest in exchange for a help that no one was able to extract."

Michael saw the sadness when the words sounded harsh. He decided to signal a kinder recount that would calm the man's anguish, as he moved to say: "I like it better when you say that you enjoy your surroundings – the sparred mounds or *mogotes* as they are here called, the half-bluish mountains scattered around in its static erected stance where time itself seems to have never passed. Timeless is the word that I am trying to find."

Continuing to add: "The many birds flying, with the song of the breeze and the incredible softness of the morning lights, the conversation of crickets, with noises of the summer nights or the tingling drops falling from the tin roofs of the porch out in the back, when it rains in spurs, and later stops, leaving the most peaceful feeling to take charge of your sleep like no other place has."

The morning was rising slowly afar as the shadows of hills dressed with the morning mist unique to Vinales, were starting to lift.

Not too far the roosters were singing their peculiar call as it could be heard from distances afar, and the rooster who was nearer would answer like saying to all:

"This is my country forever here free, where no one comes to limit, or change anything that is moving on the narrow paths well near the mogotes, where a man on a horse can be seen really far, down the valley passing by those tall barns."

You can see miles apart, as the white herons suddenly take off from the extended lawns that nobody has planted in and where they looked like snow on the first morning light.

The rooster was singing when he was awakened and called to run to the porch of Hotel Mirador, and to look at all the white birds flying like a cloud just across, like a large blanket, all so neatly and so grand that there can be no doubt it is one of the spots where God has placed His mastery hand.

It was all but a dream that Michael have had, because he would have rather stayed in that house by the road where rain water was

Flowing, and where the rocking chair man as he sat in his porch had so much to tell him. But there was no agreement, to stay other than where it was then considered to be a safer place, which they decided was to be one of the two main local tourists hotels.

His feelings were that he knew his own countrymen well and how good they could be, as well as how he saw them to be at the little country house that was so appealing to him – how clean and how good what they offered was right, but majority rules and they stayed at Hotel Mirador and what he really had was only a dream of what could have been fine for that memorable night.

Again, when they paid their hotel bill, the electronic equipment for the credit cards did not work well so they had to pay cash. It was the pattern in many hotels. There was the obvious intent to force the guests to pay in cash rather than through credit cards.

Having to pay cash was a great inconvenience because they wanted to reserve the cash to give to his needy relatives and his old friends before he was to leave the island. The U.S. government allows the citizens visiting relatives in Cuba to spend at most, about three thousand dollars during their one-time visit per year. Therefore, the more they had to spend in cash, the less money they have left to give his family. He had been saving that money for three years with only that in mind, but the way the Cuban system runs limited their ability to use the money as they had planned. Finally, they were able to pay with cards when they said: "We do not carry cash, so you better fix that machine or write the charge by hand if you want us to stay here." Such strong stand worked most of the time, and they continued to use that technique as the only way to counteract what they saw as the government functionary's intent to handle the tourists' cash.

Michael also decided to leave the island five days earlier from the original planned date because of some very serious circumstances one of which was to have more money available for his family before the return trip, and the second reason was to avoid anticipated difficulties and even possible detention by Castro's G-2 police at the airport. They had already been the targets of frequent harassment and the watch seemed to be closing in on them while in Havana more and more, representing a threat to their safety return. Aurora feared the G-2 was

Trying to find reasons to take Michael into custody and whatever else at any moment. It had become more evident during the last few days in Havana.

Havana, as any other large city is full of shadows at night and towards the last few days of his visit, he felt as if he was not being watched as much on a personal basis or at least less obvious for a while, if nothing else,. but he still saw the hidden cameras everywhere, not only in every hotel lobby but also in the streets of Old Havana. The feeling did not last much when he suddenly noted signs of a search in their hotel room when he found some of his personal notes and papers mysteriously misplaced in two different occasions. During the same week, he met someone he thought was connected to the government. He had accepted to take some money from a relative in Miami to give to a man in his mid-thirties who worked with one of the Cuban government agencies that deals in tourism. Michael did not feel comfortable with such contact from the beginning, more so, when he noted the man come to the hotel one night parking his car on a prohibited spot near the entrance of the hotel. Michael could discreetly see from the far side of his right eye that there were three other men inside the car with a suspicious appearance, like that of the usual plain-clothed "Seguridad del Estado" personnel of the ominous G-2. Michael acted very carefully during his conversations with the man but he was surprised when the person unexpectedly advised him, as he handed him a letter for his relative back in Miami:

> "Let your sister-in-law take the camera you have been filming with to Spain since they may take the films away from you at the airport when you are ready to depart for the United States. She would have no problem, as she is considered to be a tourist, but you are not. You should also arrange to leave earlier than your anticipated scheduled departure date."

"Why do you think that changing the date of departure may be necessary?" he asked.

"There had been cases when people who had been filming all over the place, as you have, were later detained at the time of departure with any excuse, even if you may not think of any reason for it, you should not forget your condition as a person who had left the country because of your beliefs and your disagreements with the system, in addition to being an artist who has expressed your denunciations in some of your works through the years." The man said as he leaned closer to Michael, as if to show that he wanted to pass on an important piece of private information, and then added, as he looked towards the entrance door in the main lobby: "Advancing the departure day will throw off the rigid data system of controls when anticipated expectations for specific action are changed outside the system of controls."

He saw the logic and felt confident that the advice he was given was in his best interest, and did not give the Cuban government any opportunity, to harass them or even detain him before he could leave the island and so, made the decision to leave earlier. He let his sister-in-law, Camino to take the camera and the films on her return trip to Spain the day after receiving the advice. On the same day, he and Aurora went to the official agency to make the changes on their return flight to Miami. They paid seventy-five dollars each to advance the date of departure, and went on to do the few things they had reserved to do for the end of their visit. At their return to the hotel, Michael turned on the TV set. He had already noted that the hotel room was fitted with cable TV only after six p.m. It allowed them to keep track of some of the news back home, in the U.S. and the rest of the world, but during the day, while the service personnel are still working, there were only government-controlled stations being aired. He realized that the government does not want the average Cuban people to see any foreign broadcast while they are at work. They can only see and hear programs of plain brainwashing and indotrination which is also what they can see at home all the time if they are able to afford a TV set.

Fidel Castro had gone on a tour of Eastern European countries during that time, and the Cuban station's broadcast was centered on everything he was doing (which is what it is airing all the time

Anyway – Castro here, Castro there, for hours every day). Michael was able to see the segment where Castro was cheered by Iranian students and fundamentalists when he gave a speech at the Teheran University campus when he implied that the U.S. is the common enemy, whose power has to be destroyed. Castro said: "Iran and Cuba, in cooperation with each other, can bring America to its knees." A very revealing and hateful statement of a man who would be an ally to any enemy of democracy and to any advocate of terrorism against America and the free world's civilization anywhere in the world. It was said just four months before the criminal terrorist attack against the United States, perpetrated in New York City and Washington D.C. that took the life of nearly four thousand innocent people and changing life in the planet forever. In the days that followed the tragedy, the threat of biological weapons also became of great concern considering the fact that there are many countries that have experimental labs. That could be developing such weapons and place them in the hands of terrorists or also they could be used by unscrupulous heads of government with criminal tendencies.

On May 8, 2001, a day before Castro's conference at the Teheran University, Michael was reading the Cuban government-controlled newspapers in Havana that published photos and reports of the warm welcome given to the Cuban dictator by the president of Iran, Mohammad Khatami. The paper signaled to the solidarity of both governments in the struggle against the economic sanctions of the United States against them, all with words of both their country's solidarity, and prominently mentioning the cooperation of Cuba on the construction of a biotechnology complex which, as they significantly boasted: "Will be the most modern in the Middle East." biological technology that could be placed in the hands of fanatical terrorists against democracy anywhere and more imminently with the intention of bringing America to its knees as Castro affirmed in Teheran a day or so after the publication.

On the last day of his stay, Michael went back to his hometown. One of the things he wanted to do was to find old friends but he was disappointed when he was told that the few who were still alive advised that it was better if they did not see him. He could not readily understand but he was later told the reasons why by another old friend who was very ill when he went to his house to visit and confort the poor man who was obviously on his few last days.

"Don't feel bad, Michael. You see, they are afraid to be seen with you or receive your visit because they have been obviously involved with the government for a long time and they are afraid of being signaled as dissidents. Most likely, they are afraid of suffering some reprisals."

"I see. I have been naive not to think about that. I have wanted to also see Carmen Fernandez who lived next door to me during my childhood years. She was the one who bought me a set of oils and brushes so I could start painting with oils after I agreed to paint a dress for her. I found out that her younger sister had died and I want to also express my sympathy."

"Well, Michael, I am about to die and I am not afraid to tell you that it is to be expected that she won't see you. Particularly in her case since she has been one of those people in town greatly identified with the regime. She and her husband had been to Russia on special government projects a lot of times and they think that they are part of the elite in the system where they have, you may say, very compromising relationships. The same thing may be happening with the rest of the people you would have wanted to see again anyway."

"I will not worry about this anymore because, under the present circumstances, no one knows what everyone's agenda is. I always give people the benefit of the doubt, at least until something else becomes more evident. Whatever it may be," Michael said as he wished his old friend well and tried to psychologically ease the pain that his friend's sickness was causing. He finally left his friend's house to continue on his last walk by the 'Hill of the Hermit'.

From the top of the hill he could look again in all directions and into the bay and see the reflections of the waters that he had visualized so much in his mind which all became alive again on his paintings during his long absence. Now, he could still see part of the bay, but as he looked southeast to the old panoramic view, he was not able to see the same things he left behind so many years before because much has disappeared and the open areas of the old farmland that was like his playground had been filled with poorly constructed houses and some gas tanks in the far distance where La Loma blanca used to be the silent witness to his childhood adventures. He could remember how he and his friends used to get some the grazing horses, strap them with only a rope around the mouth and ride them frantically, sometimes dangerously over the many railroad tracks that ran alongside the farm.

As he started to walk towards the other side of the hill near the street that he would have to take to go towards the town cemetery, he saw a not-too-tall man of fair complexion who started to walk slowly next to him. The man, who may have been just about Michael's age, wore a clean shirt with small checkered squares and old khaki pants; he was wearing no hat and his abundant white hair was nicely groomed. His face was clean shaven and somewhat rosy with a few freckles all of which gave him a gentle expression and reassured by his bright brown eyes under wide eyebrows. A few soft wrinkles adorned his calm appearance. His black shoes looked white with dust, possibly for having walked over unpaved roads for some time.

"Good morning," Michael said as the man moved by his side.

"Good morning," the man answered with a smile. "You are not from here, aren't you?" He asked with a sure and penetrating wise spark in his eyes.

"No, I used to be, but now I am only visiting the town," Michael answered.

"Yes, I know. You are obviously from another country, most likely from the U.S.A."

"How can you tell?"

"Oh, I only have to see the way you dress, it is easy. I have also been looking at you for a while as you walked by the edge of the hill and approaching the street from where I was a while ago."

Michael felt intrigued by the man, and was also amused by his clear intuition and gentle manner.

The man continued: "You see, I can tell you that you are looking at everything as if you are trying to see behind every rock, through every fence, and every wall, and far beyond every roof. I could also tell you that you are like walking in a dream."

"Yes, I am, Sir. I used to run all over this hills, when I was growing up, since I lived down there by La Calzada," he said as he signaled towards the area. "Perhaps you know someone in my family."

"No, I don't. I came here only for a week to visit my younger sister and my father who is ninety-five years old and is very delicate at this moment. In any case, I feel as if I have known you for a long time," the man said.

by this time, they have both stopped their walk momentarily and they were both facing each other.

"I also feel as if I have known you for a long time," Michael said. "Yes, I know. I'm sure you do," the man said. "You see, I grew up in the countryside of the city of Cienfuegos. The people from that area are country men like me and we know many things about the land and about people and I can tell you much about yourself even without having known you and your family."

"Oh! My childhood friend Eloycito was also from Cienfuegos, and he used to live in that house by the edge of the hill," he said as he pointed to the blue house that could be seen from about one block away. "I was there three days ago visiting his sister and to see if I could talk to his father who is also ninety-five years old and very weak. Unfortunately he could not remember me."

"You mean Arial, don't you?"

Michael's jaw dropped when he heard the name Arial, as he remembered the dream he had a few years earlier when his childhood friend Eloy presented himself as Arial on what became a revealing and inspiring experience.

"What do you know about Arial?" Michael asked.

"Well, the name just came to mind. This happens to me sometimes. It is as if I get some kind of unknown bliss to communicate with others in a way that I do not understand, or realize and it is only until later that it becomes more clear."

Michael felt a rare sensation as he heard what this strange man, whom he had just casually met, was saying.

"In the same way that the name came to my mind, I now feel the urge to tell you many things that seem to be galloping into my mind

Right now without any of them making much sense at the moment," the man said.

He suddenly felt very intrigued by what the man was saying and said:

"I would like to know what you have to say. Why don't we sit there for a while?"

There was an old park bench next to the veranda that overlooked the bay, and they both sat down.

From the bench, they had an overview of the town's roofs and a good part of the bay with the skyline of Old Havana in the far distance, as if they were viewing some of Michael's paintings of that site.

"You have stood in this bench many times during your youth, to watch the dancing *Diablitos* and the crowds that followed them during the town's traditional celebrations. And in that part of the park there was almost a fight that you were able to stop."

"Yes it was the time Eloy challenged Alfredo, one of my baseball teammates to a fistfight. but how did you know?"

"I do not know, It just came to mind when I thought of the name Arial while I was looking in that direction a moment ago. You, see these are some of the things that happen to me sometimes, although not very frequently, thank God.. Sometimes, it is so mysterious that I get scared of it, particularly when it does not come with a clear justification of the reasons, as to why it happens. Afterwards, I would feel very tired and weak, so please do not leave me now. Stay a while before you go on your way."

"Of course I will stay. I am amazed and very interested in whatever you have to say."

"Well for now, not much. Only that I should tell you that you are a very fortunate man in spite of having suffered with your separation. I do not know if it is a separation of country, or from your children, but I know that you didn't leave your children here when you left for the U.S.A., and although they may not be very far from you, they are not close to you."

"How can you be so right? I wish I knew when this estrangement would end," Michael said sadly.

"There is nothing that you should worry about," the man, who suddenly looked as if he had aged almost instantly, said. After a short moment continued:

> "No one we love is ever away, and nothing is lost in
> the heart of those who love above all. Much is lost by
> those who keep resentment in their hearts."

"That part worries me", Michael said. "I wish that those who may feel resentment within the family would feel love instead, and enjoy the happiness that it brings and not the loss that keeping resentment represents."

"Well, I can tell you that it is not resentment that puts you at a distance. It is mostly fear. Fear is as destructive a feeling as any other negative one. When you let fear run your life, it can destroy as much than hate and that is why those who want to control use fear to do it and in the process, destroy not only love itself but even the strongest of things. You can just look at the decay in the facades of buildings all over Havana and in this town and except for the old fortresses that seem to endure it all, there is much destruction everywhere. You have to be just like those old fortresses, and I feel that you can be."

"No, I don't think so. I know that I am strong, but I am afraid to die before I could see the end of destruction and the lack of love, at least of those things and people that I so love," Michael said.

"Well, we are living in difficult times, and it is not going to get better for a long time in the world. Not only here, because the same forces of hate and ambition to control by fear will bring about terror in many parts of the world, because there are more and more people who ignore the basic wisdom of generosity and love, and the principles of respect for the rights of others. There will be those who will abuse the power, and there will be many who are not allowed to prosper in freedom. And there is much to be changed in the world in the next twenty years," the man who suddenly exuded so much wisdom told Michael who was static while intently listening.

After a moment, Michael appeared to be more worried as he said: "You don't mean that it will all take twenty more years to have a change here, do you? If that is the case, we will not survive and live to see it."

"No, I don't think so. You may see some changes start here before we part, but not on the upheavals to come from other places because of the inequities in one hand and the ignorance and evil-minded fanatics on the other, . but we are not going to get stifled about that now."

"That expression sounds very familiar to me. I now feel as if I have known you at some point in time. What is your name?" he asked.

"My name is not important. I am as any other old man you may have found earlier in your life. Your name may not be important to me either, but I know you as I have known Arial, I guess."

"My name is Michael Beltran. How have you known about Arial?"

"Yours is more related to something else, I think rather than related to the first name of the famous artist Miguel Angel or perhaps to Michael the Archangel for what you tell me, but it is not, you like that name much for other reasons. I do not think that you are trying to hide from any painful realities with it but at the same time, I do not think that you should be shy. Modesty is confused with timidity more than with shyness sometimes. In any case, who you are, is who you are regardless, and what you really are meant to be is what is important,. But most people do not see that. Names become important when people get to know what your life means for them."

"That sounds too complicated. You remind me of Shakespeare. Are you sure that you have been in Cienfuegos' countryside most of your life? Please, don't get me wrong. I know for sure how smart the Cuban "Guajiros" can be. I somewhat consider myself to be a *guajiro,* in many respects too, but I wish I have one-half of your perception and wisdom. I guess that, on the surface, you do not consider names to be so important, and apparently, the question is in being or not being." Michael said with a smile and without waiting for an answer."There are times when knowledge of something, that may have to be learned in your lifetime, or in school is not learned that way, but you are able to know perhaps by intuition and then you come to know.... more than what you thought you knew. I believe in the subconscious mind, and some people believe in knowing from having lived previous lives."

"I know,. My cousin Ursula believed in that, as the buddhists do – that they are traveling towards Nirvana. I still have my doubts but sometimes it makes sense. We all need to progress spiritually and in knowledge. A lifetime alone may not be enough," Michael said, and immediately added: "I still would like you to tell me how it is that you know about Arial when I have only talked to you about Eloy."

"There is much that is learned anywhere you are, and there is much that you do not even know on how you learn it. To me Eloy and Arial are the same one, just as you and your chosen name are not. but you have not yet reached your friend's stage. You are still here in the flesh and your name has more to do with the sun."

"The more that I hear from you, the more puzzled I am," Michael said as he instinctively bowed his head and scratched the hair over his right ear. "You must be some kind of wizard to come and mention the sun in relation to my name, my mother had told me the same thing about my first name when I was a child. I think that you must have actually known me and my family from the time we lived here many years ago."

Michael noted an unusual depth in the man's eyes, as he looked directly at them, as he was finishing his last remarks. Wisdom, he thought, is what those shining eyes revealed, but also some kind of familiar warmth that he wanted to know more about.

"No, my friend, at this moment, I do not remember to have known you, or your family,. but who knows? In any case, as I have told you already, many things have come to my mind while I talked to you. Things that I have not known anything about. I can tell you more now – the important things that may have happened in your life, as well as what will come to happen in your future are already well-established, and there is nothing you can do about it. The more you try to change things, the less you will accomplish them because you may be trying too hard and thus create a lot of resistance around you without realizing it. Just let go; you have worked very hard to reach everything that you have accomplished. And yet, you still feel that you have not reached the peak you envision for yourself. Let go of it, but keep doing what your heart tells you to do, without expecting much in terms of immediate recognition. It is not for you to force anything, as I said. What will be, will be no matter what you do now or later to have it go your way. Just be patient and persevere in what you do and what you believe is good, and do not push it. You could come to see surprising things happen if you do just that. . Follow your instincts and do not look for anything outside yourself."

Michael was speechless for a few seconds before he was able to speak again after the man finished talking in what seemed like a very long minute.

"Well, I guess I had to come back to Cuba to hear you tell me all that you are telling me now. Who are you, really? How do you know so much about me?"

"I do not know myself, but it seems that I was placed on your way because there was a message. Someone someplace wanted me to give this message to you based on what came to my mind the moment I met you a while ago. I hope it means something to you."

"Yes it does, my good man. It really does! Actually, I feel very fortunate to have met you as I was going on my way."

The man leaned forward and took a solitary flower that was growing next to the veranda and extended it to Michael and said: "Please place this flower on your mother's grave when you get to the cemetery. Do it with a prayer for her and for Cuba in Arial's name." He smiled, showing a sense of accomplishment. He got up and then walked away.

Michael took the flower, started on the opposite direction for a few seconds and turned to look back, just before the man could get to the end of the park; but the man had already disappeared from view.

A strange, lighthearted feeling overcame him as he continued his long walk to the cemetery at the edge of town at a fast pace.

Two days later, the Cuban chartered jet took off from the José Martí airport in Havana. Michael and Aurora sat tightly next to a window where they both looked out in silence as the plane lifted away. His heart pounded, as hard as it did during the first day of their journey, but his mind was with a feeling of gladness in the midst of sadness. As he saw the many royal palm trees sinking in the distance, he also saw the island he so loved sinking in a cloud of uncertainty. In his heart, however, there was a strong feeling of future liberation. . . .

CHAPTER EIGHTEEN

Revelations From Arial (The Sun In Spring)

The jet plane that Michael and Aurora took from Havana landed in Miami where they were to stay for a few days before continuing their journey to Spain. They had remained silent during the flight. both of them kept the thoughts deep inside themselves without wanting or being able to break the spell of feelings, and memories that had so impacted their hearts and minds. He was overwhelmed with the images of the impoverished nation submerged into a decadence unsurpassed by anything imaginable; the product of the inadequacy and total failure of a system, not the cause of an ineffective embargo. He was very sure of the fact that Castro did not want Cubans to be prosperous at all. Castro is not interested in having the embargo lifted. He knows that if Cubans are given total exposure to the opportunities opened to a free flow of all that makes a free society, he would no longer be able to control the Cuban people any more. Cuba would change so rapidly and radically that there would be no way to continue an absolute totalitarian rule over its life.

The more that Michael thought about the conditions of the country, the lack of freedom that people had endured for so long, and the saddened faces of everyone they saw everywhere on the unfortunate island, including those that have succumbed, per chance or lack of alternative to servicing the corroding Cuban system of government and its infamy, the more he thought of the need to expose all the undeniable facts to whomever would be willing and able to listen to the manifestation of his thoughts and personal testimony for whatever it's worth without expecting anything in return except the feeling of giving an opportunity to the truth with the hopes of it becoming a worthwhile contribution to the causes of freedom and the democratic principles that will sustain it, as well as the future long-lasting happiness of the Cuban people.

In some way, Michael feared that some of his thoughts may not be appreciated by many of his fellow Cubans, if they did not in any particular case fit the usual pattern, particularly in Miami, the bastion of Castro's opposition, where the struggle is passionately played day by day, by the most combatant of freedom-loving Cubans anywhere, however he also thought that the truth, as he may come to see it, had to be said regardless if he comes to be convinced of it being worth, while for the cause of advancing the cause of freedom.

. What would his thoughts be able to do? What would his thoughts do for Cuba? He did not know, but he will write them with the hope that they will be understood and eventually appreciated. Back to Cuba contains the history of how he saw and lived through all the process from the pre- revolutionary fortieth to the fiftieth anniversary of the, so called, revolutionary government. History that he hopes will be helpful to the younger generations of Cubans anywhere.

Upon writing his own story, Michael sees himself, almost unwillingly, but by necessity being immersed into the subject of the Cuban struggle for freedom, just for having been born in Cuba and being sensitive enough to feel the pain of its people, he has an unavoidable concern. He has been an artist that has been greatly motivated by his childhood memories of Cuba. Always Cuba as the common denominator of his work as an exile, and now suddenly he decides to visit the island to check and to recoup the elusive images of yesterday trying to find landmarks, and he finds a world of flattened hopes and people like misguided robots struggling for any meager sustenance. A saddening situation, far deeper and far beyond the imagination from anything the country had ever seen before, even in the worst times in its history. All of it happening under the same beautiful sky and undeniable beauty of the common people and the bids of untouched landscape, and all that has been touched by unbelievable decay that he still was able to uncover and admire looking at the old facades of building its contours, texture and beauty that still breathe in them as the very essence of its noble pass and legacy waiting to be awakened like the princess of a fairy tale. He knew that all of it was to be expected of his visit after so many years since he left in 1960. Many years of being absent from the island; he knew that there was fear as there is in many like him living outside the imprisoned island, fear to confront such harsh realities and looking at them directly in the eye and feeling the pain for the suffering right where it happens day by day. but such feelings and the visit that he thought necessary in his case should not say anything about, or be equated to a political motivation, if any of that, at all.

The artist in him started to paint and has continued painting his childhood memories of more than sixty years before, and also, the lot of the political prisoners and the saga of the "'*balseros*'" struggling to reach freedom for many to find death (as it happened to Elian González's mother and the eleven other freedom-seekers, companions and many more throughout the years at the immensity of the deep blue waters surrounding the unfortunate island, without such paintings being neither politically nor commercially motivated; neither does he feel that all his art work should be treated as commercialized commodities, even if some could become one. He had been able to keep his art free from such motivations; most of his work had been depicting the times of a happy Cuba – the one he remembered as a child, not the one he remembers of the sporadic corruption, and gang activities permeating the political landscape of Havana of the forties and fifties; the one that he and all sensible Cubans sadly saw during his years as a student in a struggling society trying to find a way for progress, away from the seemingly corrupt ways of the time. The times when Cubans like himself, when living in the island did not feel fear for, nor did they see in America the strong enemy of the north as the threat to their freedoms, neither did they saw the United States as the ruling power

That would try to impose its will and control the destinies of the Cuban incipient democracy of those years. There was a lot of admiration for the American way of life, its democratic principles and history as well as the music and the quality of products the giant country produced and exported to the largest of the Caribbean island.

During the years after his return from Cuba, many things had come to happen that could not be ignored or brushed aside, but needed to be seriously considered for inclusion on his book as they are crucial to comprehend the way history comes finally to make sense and to signal like a compass. by its nature, every happening comes together like lost pieces in a difficult puzzle when time itself seems to have run out of solutions.

From the American perspective he has seen that in recent years, according to the established policy, the emphasis has been to place conditions to the government in Cuba for the lifting of the embargo, as it is, for instance: For the Cuban government to free all political prisoners, and also to allow true free elections to take place, but those noble conditions have never been accepted by Castro and it is the policy and strategy followed by his closest collaborators in power.

A strategy by the Cuban regime that will continue as they only seem to care to demand an unconditional move by the US, and the European developed nations, while in reality what they want is for nothing else to change and to keep absolute control and obtain or continue to draw the benefits of their stubborn strategy as their most valuable propaganda tool towards the world at large and continue to extract other benefits derived from anything the counterpart would be willing to give and they can keep developing associates and followers all across Latin America as it is already happening with Chaves and others that are following Castro's technique to perpetuate his rule for the perpetual misery of the people while they also make believe that they are the only 'saviors' of its people.

In the US, the voices of a few powerful U.S. legislators were being heard in Congress to advocate the lifting of the Cuban embargo, unfortunately not for humanitarian reasons, and not to counteract Castro's claims that allow him to keep repeating over and over his accusations about imperialistic aggressions he has so well uses to prop his otherwise wasted regime with his old broken record of a rhetoric that he wants to be able to continue playing and that he may soon not be able to justify doing it anymore.

Shortly after a new era of terrorism has been opened on the outset of the twenty first century when ominous and criminal weapons used against the civilized world at large, and particularly against the United States of America began with the senseless attack on the World Trade Center twin towers and Washington D.C. last September 11, 2001 which had created the need for action in a priority sense, by necessity becoming the concern of every lover of freedom and respect for human life around the world. In the wake of this new dangerous time, there could be no exception and no rest in the scrutiny of friends and potential enemies of the democratic principles that need to be protected now more than ever before in the history of the civilized world.

In the Cuban front, manipulation of the international public opinion continues in the press as it is directed from Cuba with orchestrated statements. One simple example of it was brought to Michael's attention by Aurora; it was the news on page 4-A of the Sunday edition in Spanish of the *Miami Herald* on October twenty under the heading: "Cuba admits to have kept links with the Pentagon spy Anna Belen Montes." A report about comments by the Cuban chancellor coming from Agency France Press where the Cuban regime spying in the Pentagon is depicted to be justified morally and not necessarily being sponsored by the Castro government, based on declarations given to the French press by Castro's Exterior Minister at the time, Mr. Pérez Roque.

Other news spread all over the news media was about the October 2002 visit to Cuba by the old guard at the helm in the U.S. government agencies and the State Department during the Cuban missile crisis of October of 1962. Castro has been seen again playing his usual "innocence game" on such a serious scheme when on various interviews about documents showing that he had asked Nikita Khrushchev for a pre-emptive nuclear attack on the U.S. The long-lasting dictator in Latin America was looking for ways to justify his dubious motivations and trying to downplay the seriousness and the grave implications of such an attack if it would have taken place.

Fortunately also for the Cuban people in the island who would have certainly entered in a perilous stage that could have had catastrophic consequences for them as well, at a cost of many innocent lives, was it not for the fact that Khrushchev was actually gambling in order to place strategic pressure on the U.S. to negotiate the dismantling of American missiles in Turkey.

On the rebound of such negotiations, Castro gained a commitment by the U.S. not to invade Cuba, and in addition the U.S. government became the guardians against any kind of anti-Castro invasion attempts by organizations operating in the United States; a commitment for the time of the crisis and thereafter. A concession that is kept alive in the minds and hearts of most exiled Cubans since it added bitter resentments to the already unsavory withdrawal of the promised U.S. air cover to assist on the failed bay of Pigs invasion of 1961.

Documents related to the 1962 missile crisis revealed Castro's desires and intentions to see the U.S. suffer a pre-emptive nuclear attack. A horrendously criminal intent and outright request to his bosses in Russia which the dictator was trying to let the world interpret to his favor through some totally baffling remarks when he is trying to explain the inexplicable, giving his very irresponsible motivations and intent, that without a doubt places him among the masters of terrorism. He actually thought nothing of using nuclear weapons on the United States according to historic issues and documents discussed at the interview Castro gave to Barbara Walters from ABC in October 2002. His cynicisms to some degree match the terrorist leanings and tactics he uses to keep control of the Cuban people, all that is evident throughout the entire history of his dictatorship.

With all these developments taking place, the fact is that it is time that the Cuban people are given support in the building of their moral strength in order for them to undertake an effective civil disobedience against a government that should be constantly discredited in the eyes of the world and of his own people so that they can be stimulated and work to ultimately free themselves from the totalitarian rule. Unfortunately. The fact has been, and continue to be, that the majority of the Cuban people are terrified because of the tight surveillance and constant repression they are subjected to, besides being totally dependent to the government as the only employer and absolute dictator of their very own life, with the honorable exception, among the sufferers of such calamity, are the many political prisoners and a small but growing number of dissidents in Cuba.

In New York City, April 12-2003

I was reading the New York Times headline on page A-2:

*"CUBA EXECUTES 3 WHO TRIED TO REACH U.S.
IN A HIJACKING"*

It should have read:

*"CASTRO AND HIS HENCHMEN CRIMINALLY
AND WITHOUT DUE PROCESS OVERNIGHT
EXECUTE 3 WHO TRIED TO REACH FREEDOM IN
A HIJACKING"*

The Article by David Gonzalez also mentions the *"harsh sentences"* of a week before handed down to 78 nonviolent dissidents receiving prison terms ranging up to 28 years.

News like these may be diluted and practically unnoticed within the overwhelming reports of events surrounding the war in Iraq. Castro knows it and is timing himself again, like in all his inhuman and desperate acts he criminally commits to terrorize the Cuban people and to irritate and make the exile opposition the way he wants it: totally frantic. The angered reactions by the exile community, particularly in Miami, are and should be totally acceptable and look upon with sympathy and understanding by the world at large, but unfortunately only few voices will be raised anywhere else to vigorously denounce the tyranny.

The window of opportunity for solidarity with the oppressed Cuban people is not at all closed, as it may seem. Gestures to help and bring closeness instead of isolation to that people was not only necessary when the dissidents were starting to be heard and the tyranny appeared to be softening its grip; it may be more than ever necessary now. History has a way with twist and turns, and so it has happened with the war in Iraq changing the scenario again, but in its latest outburst of cruelty and terror he has recently and again perpetrated against the Cuban people, Castro may very well have miscalculated the tolerance of the world at large for the merciless ways he uses time and again to terrorize and impose his ominous regime on the Cuban people, in an act that has brought repugnance and disgust to even his traditionally apologetic sympathizers around the world, perhaps with the exception of opportunistic politicians and some shamefully ingratiating partisan positions taken by a handful of political leaders in some world capitals with unscrupulous leaders, mostly preoccupied with a political agenda rather than taking a just and dignifying position showing indignation against the bloody dictator in Cuba.

At a time like this when Castro has so callously demonstrated his true evil nature with his latest executions unjustifiable to the world is the moment when, we should expect that the US political leaders starting with the Cuban American congressmen representing, and in the position as the undisputable leaders of the exile community, should have decisively take the case outside the traditional Miami deadlock with the local political interests and, beyond and in spite of that, go to bring their word and plea, personally, to every democratic capital of the world starting with Europe and Latin America in representation of the true people of Cuba to convince everyone including old Castro's sympathizers and world leaders to gain momentum to expose and isolate a regime who's time has come to be despised by every freedom loving people around the world. Unfortunately, when it comes to governmental, as well as Miami local policies has continued as usual for more than five years after the infamy.

Perhaps the most eloquent plea has been made by the renown novelist *Mario Vargas Llosa,* with a manifest that was presented to the multitude by the well known philosopher and writer *Fernando Savater, in spite of his long lasting sympathy with the Cuban regime,* appeared at the concentration to denounce the crimes committed by the Castro dictatorship, in Madrid on, April 26, 2003, where over three thousand people including not only Cuban exiles, but also Spanish writers, journalists, and politicians of both major political parties in Spain gathered, after a gray and rainy morning, under the many signs with slogans denouncing the recent acts by the Cuban dictator and proclaiming that the time for action against it has come.

The entire Spanish media, covered the event and many newspaper editorials of different political perceptions denounced the crimes of the many years of the regime in Cuba, emphasizing like never before, so vigorously, the intolerable and disgusting act by of the recent unwarranted and criminal use of the firing squad by Fidel Castro as well as the imposition of long sentences to close to eighty peaceful dissidents in the island in an effort to repress and terrorize the Cuban people.

Vargas Llosa, among other significant things said the following in his manifest: *"In light of the recent events, it is vital, that the democrats of the world manifest its vigorous condemnation of Castro's repressions but for solidarity and respect of the Cuban people",* adding that *"All rational persuasions being already depleted after thirty diverse international attempts to reduce the rigor of that regime, it is fundamental, as punishment, that the democratic governments make the decision to substantially reduce the diplomatic presence of this dictatorship in their countries and expel the Cuban government from all international organisms where they still have a sit; the presence of the Cuban government in them is a collective embarrassing situation to the Countries participating in organizations like the "Latin American Parliament", the "Ibero American Summit", the Cotonou Agreement" and others".* And he adds, *"It is not a case of punishing the Cuban people with new embargoes and blockades, they in itself have suffered enough by its own government, but instead the tyranny should be thrown out from all forums and organizations where they are represented",* Vargas Llosa coincided with the editorial of La Razon of Sunday the 27th of April 2003 on its page 4, where the following was written: The *Castro regime, has demonstrated that they only understand using violence by the use of firing squads and should be given the same treatment of isolation done to Pretoria, in its time; lets repeat it confronting the Cuban dictatorship with what the world did with great efficacy against the racist regime in South Africa".*

There isn't much more that could be added after such intense and asserted manifestations made by this prominent intellectual, who is not Cuban but understands the suffering of the Cuban people except to underline the sentence *"It is not the case of punishing the Cuban people"* and what the democratic world should do at this juncture, only concluding now by stressing again the most important point to the Cuban exile leaders, that the time has come to take the oppressed Cuban's agenda to the world beyond Miami and the USA pleading for the actions expressed by this eloquent manifest.

Arial's vision, expressed in *Back to Cuba,* for the kind of action needed by the exile leadership still holds true in spite of the apparent setback recently infringed to the struggle to end the nightmare in Cuba. He would give his encouraging remark again. *"Let's not get stifled about that"* and insist to the exile leadership to act effectively in the most noble ways denouncing the despotic ways of the regime in Cuba while helping the suffering people and holding high the hope for a bright future with freedom for the Cuban people. We can think now and easily hear and keep hearing his logic forever more.

At a time when all of the new signs and cries for change are sounding loud right inside and outside of Cuba, particularly in Europe, for the Cuban exile community, the need for better understanding and unity of effort is more evident than ever before, all what makes Michael think again about Arial's remarks when he said as usual his "Let's not get stifled about it", the need for unity and effective leadership is now. It is more than ever a mandate for the elected leaders of the community regardless of party or local politics of any kind, all and anyone capable of such leadership have to act now in order give the right steps to create the right atmosphere, and to rise to the occasion to implement sensible actions to attain a successful end against the regime and to help in the beginning of an orderly escalated transition towards democracy in Cuba avoiding the chaotic and disastrous situation that could otherwise arise in the very immediate future.

Let the struggling, the oppressed, and the impoverish people of Cuba know now that we are all with them and not against them as the regime tries to scare them to the contrary all the time, unfortunately with a considerable degree of success so far.

While approaching the end of the final chapters of *Back to Cuba* with its hopeful promise of a proximity to freedom and happiness symbolized by the metaphorical *"Return of the butterflies"* one can't help but harbor a sense of loss or like if something has again been stolen in the process, yet an apparent setback to the cause of human rights.

The just aspiration of people to be respected in its basic dignity have suffered many setbacks throughout the history of the world; setbacks caused by the imposition of unacceptable irrational repression by a tyrant who's time comes to be dismissed as in so many other occasions in history. Such is the case with the Cuban despotic rule of fifty years, represented by lies that have been imposed in the name of ideas that have already been proven inhuman in its practice anywhere; false lures in the promotion of ideas that have only serve to enslave and destroy the most basic and noble of human aspiration which is the dignity of man and the right to live in freedom.

Reviewing promising hopes and signs revealed by history are a necessity to survival. On a related effort to understand and mark the paths to be taken in the pursuit of freedom one can get perhaps involved in what may seem to be speculative considerations. Dialogues often times become a defining journey as it happens in any written story and it is not different in *Back to Cuba,* a story that in spite of the harsh nature of a sad narrative of a journey that include so mucho painful events, is however in the entire journey, a love story, that can, in itself, be perceived when, love of the strength of the concerns for a suffering country, and in essence, a\ love manifested from the outset, in every turn of fate, of the narrative, including the love for, and by the people that live confronting so many difficult, and painful alternatives than had, at times alone it all, to be soothe in joyful memories and reminiscences of happy times and life as it was in Cuba during the nineteen thirties and fortieth, however touched by spurs of unrest that was a prelude of worse times to come, yet the best being still remaining alive in our hearts and minds.

The author had no doubt that all the time the current dictatorship has lasted, and what will continue to last for Cubans to endured as they have, is the worse time that Cubans have ever lived, not-withstanding, the times of Major General Valeriano Weyler who mercilessly directed the Spanish army against the Cuban population causing starvation and thousands of death with the infamous concentration camps in which. he converted every city and rural town in the island with the purpose of isolating the Cuban freedom fighters in the countryside during the long war they fought for their independence; a war that started in 1868, known in history as *The ten Years war.*

The main dialogues that appear, as the *BACK TO CUBA* story unfolds, throughout its eighteen chapters, take place between Michael and his mother, and also with his friends and family members amidst the anguish created by imminent separations from country and love In spite of all difficulties and the relentless repression, there is obviously some light at the end of the tunnel, considering all the dissident movements struggling against all odds.

His spirits were lifted when he received a letter from his sister in Cuba.

** (The letter from his sister has, in some unexpected way, broken the magical spell of his being at a vantage point in writing" *Back to Cuba/The Return of the Butterflies",* where the name of his beloved father and older brother Michael was used to keep himself, if at all possible, away from the center of the story.

> September 13, 2002
> Dear brother Elio,
>
> Always wishing you and Aurora to be well. We are all well here. First of all, I want to thank you for the money that you and Camino sent me last week. I was able to buy a few things that we needed, and also to fix the part of the Roof, that had fallen down during the heavy rains brought by the many storms of this summer and, as you know, because of the ongoing deterioration of the roof as a whole. Fortunately, there was no one hurt when it came down and has now been fixed thanks to you, Aurora and Camino. She also sent me some photos of your recent visit to Spain and we are glad to see all of you looking really good in them.
>
> The other day was visiting my daughter Consuelo and we saw a butterfly flying by. It was very unusual because as I had told you a long time ago, we don't see many butterflies around here any more. I was able to get the

butterfly very easily because it kept flying around me while I was thinking about you. I am going to send it on a small envelope inside my letter. Let's hope that it will get to you, if it does, because I don't think that it can fly much more. If it does get to you, keep it inside a book as a memory. Elio, I hope that you are in a better state of mind and no longer down as I noted on your last letter remembering your visit here. Let me know if you are back to painting again ...

Well, give my regards and a kiss to Aurora and for you a big hug and a kiss from your sister,

Mariita

The butterfly arrived somewhat damaged, and deteriorated, just as the walls of Old Havana buildings are now. but likewise, showing the blemished but enduring beauty of a glorious past still stretching beyond comprehension in spite of the punishment they have suffered and the obvious neglect. The unusual soft, green-wash color like a sweet and ripe honey dew on the front of the wings still glowed with the gold-like lines decorating its edges in its peculiar way as veins spread from the fragile body gave the entire expanse a most luscious and delicate crystal-like effect.

As he looked at the beauty that was still alive in what was left of the butterfly's wings, he tried to recall every butterfly he remembered seeing in those childhood years when life, in spite of the aftermath of the depression, was like a pleasant ocean breath surrounded with the colors and flavors of the peaceful, unforgettable kind; when poverty, although sometimes saddening, was never suffocating and offensive, because dignity was not abused and growth was still possible to whomever had the talent and the drive regardless of the conditions. So it is not all about butterflies that does not fly in an overwhelming quantity as they used to, except for this one that Providence presented with a sad cry of decay that arrived to bring yet a message of hope.

This butterfly he received from his sister – ... is indeed a unique butterfly, he thought. A gleam of hope that is not dead. A hope that is at every corner, even when the faces of much discouraged people sitting or standing bewildered on their idleness' and lack of incentive except for survival does not readily show it. All of them silently waiting for the ominous city buses, or 'Camellos', all over Havana, or waiting patiently for nothing at all and going nowhere fast because there is nowhere worthwhile rushing to go to without freedom and it seems that it is as elusive as ever under the present circumstances.

Florida, November 11, 2002
To Mariita
Dear Sister,

I received your letter with the butterfly and you do not imagine what it brought with it, so timely, as if it was a message from the gods to the ancient Greeks. It seems that butterflies will soon be flying again along "La Calzada", as it was during our childhood days, with all their splendor, and with the promise of a return to the happy days when they used to fly in such tumultuous abundance that gave to our lives and to light, the sense that make them vibrate. It is in itself a good omen in difficult times, telling us that not all is lost, nor it evanesces indefinitely. The colors of this butterfly, so providentially, in spite of having arrive with its wings semi pulverized in some of its contours, just as the old Havana buildings they still let us note their recoverable original beauty. I can see in its delicate glow of its turning light green with its bordering edges of the finest gold that could only be a nature's gift as virtues considered by many, with much reason, as being a free gift from the creator of everlasting goodness.

Our mother would have said 'color verde esperanza'. (the green color of hope) I have placed the butterfly inside a book, as you told me on your letter. It is very interesting to me, the way that the butterfly came to you just at the time that you were thinking about me. It is something to be well appreciated and for us not It is something to be well appreciated and for us not to forget its symbolism, particularly for those who do not forget the happy childhood days so far from the preoccupations of the times in which we are now living. Let this butterfly and its promise of joyful life to be fulfilled in abundance, and for us to be able to see it. I have included with my letter a photo that will bring you memories of those days and the time when the roof tiles were not so destroyed as they are now. (You, me, and our dear dog, Sibiri, look so very good in it, back in 1945 he looks as if he is smiling)

I am glad that you were able to fix the part of the roof that fell, and I am glad that no one got hurt when it happened.

Your letter is beautiful and it will also go inside a book with the hope that it will, if possible, immortalize your Noble feelings; feelings that deserve and will surely have God's blessings.

Aurora sends you her love also. I hope you will soon be receiving this letter and that all will be well. Give my regards and a big hug to Mario and everyone in the family as well as all the friends that would remember me, without exceptions.

Your brother, with love.
Elio

A hope for the return of many butterflies happily flying again along "La Calzada ", and in every sunny road and field that run across a beautiful island represented by this single butterfly that came from so far and in such a long and significant flight.

A butterfly with its promises of a return to abundance of the right and noble kind, far from the impositions of fear and the reign of lies shall arrive at long last.

Elio F. Beltrán

Reaching for *"THE END OF A LONG NIGHT"*.

For many years, there have been many signs that appear to signal to the end to the Cuban nightmare. In November 1989 with the fall of the berlin wall followed by the subsequent transformation in Eastern Europe, and the end of the ruling of the Soviet Union by the Communist regime, there was a widespread expectation and hope that the Communist regime in Cuba would also follow the pattern, however, knowing how tight the regime has all the strings of repression over the island, I was personally skeptical of any quick development of a change towards any significant transformation.

For this Second Special and Updated Edition, for the final pages I am adding the following analysis that I call: :

Synthesis

CUBA, AMERICA, Europe

The World

For the After Words, from the First Edition of 2003, up to the Special Edition of 2011, the emphasis, on all the historic developments, was mostly related to the painful saga of a country suffering from a prolong, and infamous Communist dictatorial status, where, among other textual expectations, or perhaps, "predictions", was for an eventual forthcoming generational process of changes that would ultimately generate the demise of the shameful and miserable totalitarian status.

At this juncture, seven years later, after a necessary, historic, and dramatic account of events, enmeshed in my life as well as that of millions of Cubans, for more than fifty year, I frankly express my sincere apology to my readers.

Now, having, concluded, that for this "AFTER WORDS", to outline a " Synthesis " of what is now, seen nearly reaching the first two decades of a, more than challenging, politically, as well as. environmentally, worry some 21rst Century..

The News, From Cuba, in April 20, 2018 was that Cuban dictatorial regime is preparing for the end of the Castro era, with Raul Castro, announcing the naming of Miguel Diaz Canel, to become president of the Cuban Council of State, and Council of Ministers, and that Diaz Canel, would succeed him. "Raul Castro" as head of the Communist Party, when he steps down from the post in the year 2021 .

While I can't call this a truthfull "generational change", it may be however, the first sign before the long lasting nightmare is already moving into an evolution towards, at least, the first manifestation of the demise of the historic cupula, that should in time, bring in a more real generational change with the crumbling old structure, of such a long nightmare for the Cuban people.

As it is well known, the Castro's regime, through the years, has gone beyond experimentation of the spread of the totalitarian system of government rule, that started to spread in Venezuela with Chavez, after having started by initial elections, and backed by his military powers, that later ended with Nicolas Maduro, backed by the Cuban regime, and falsely, and systematically blaming the USA, with every conceivable means, to hide the inadequacy and failure of his government, that has caused inflationary rampage, and also serious scarcity of food and needed fundamental staples, that has created great political crisis and population unrest, and most recently causing the painful and saddening exodos of millions of its peoples into surrounding countries like Colombia, Brazil, and also many arriving in the US, with a proportionally large majority in Miami, and also in Spain during the last few years; besides Venezuela with Maduro, there is a serious situation in Nicaragua, with Daniel Ortega, in power for an extensive number of years since his start as a guerrilla leader, over 35 years ago, and most recently, as acting president during a long subsequent periods, that, has reached with great crisis, and bloody confrontations with its people, with many dead protesters.. There is much political unrest in many of the other Latin America countries, in addition to other countries in Central America with the spread of dangerous gangs involved in drug trafficking, that has created a sudden large exodos, now mostly to Costa Rica, and for manty years traditionally to the US.

The USA is also confronting a very polarized scenario, into the second year of the Donald Trump presidency, half way into 2018, with the slogan of a nationalistic " America First", showing to the European allies, as well as, to Mexico, Canada, and China, a new trend by the lifting of Trade Tariffs, and showing other manifestation during NATO meetings, starting in Canada, and later with the traditional allies in Europe, that may signal to a rocky road ahead, and not very well received abroad, not mentioning a very apparent show of personal friendly trends towards adversaries like Russia, particularly shown, in recent personal Summit, with Putin, at the start of 2018; all of what is to be measured in terms of a "worrisome immediate future", adding to the current trend towards Nationalism, in our own country, as it has recently been a political trend, in a few of the European countries, as well, in some measure, being a serious concern in the USA as well, considering, the very divided political situation in our own country, that in itself is, altogether a worrisome development, with the noticeable advent of such tendencies implemented by Trump within, very controversial moves that he has made during the start of his tenure, that are reaching more than great concern for the country and its allied countries.

In general terms, The world is not in the best of stages, since the end of the year 2017, and I feel oblige, here in, to give testimony about my observations, regarding the serious contemporary ills, that, with senseless treatment, can create a very lamentable situation for all, the, USA, Canada, and European, Middle Eastern, and Asia, considering president Tromp recent, push with the increase in trade tariffs, causing an unexpected competition with China's growing economy, in critical confrontations with the US, considering how it is already starting to create potential hardship, for US farmers, plus the possibilities of inflationary trends that will surely affect prices, and the budget of innocent consumers at home itself, who will end paying the price for these daring moves, that separately, are also bringing up a serious confrontation with North Korea, if no sensible and serious agreement, with avoidance of a devastating war with weapons of mass destruction in the Asian Continent; hoping that some common sense prevails an proper personal consensus with traditional allies, that may be needed, as a part of the panorama for the immediate future, and beyond,

It is not joyful at all, having to express, at this time, these concerns as a Citizen, in a non- political basis, but on the basis of observations, that can easily be perceived, and surely noted by many other concerned citizens, politically or not, of our beloved United states of America, but just for the logical analysis, of the current circumstances, and situations, that are very visible, and logical, to surmise.

The need now is for the use of well-intended and guided diplomacy first, and fairness always, with the proper mutual respect, if not cooperation in the avoidance of malefic unfounded, and unfortunate developments, for the world at large..

Other problems, like the spread of Terrorism, looks like it is, apparently starting, somewhat recently to be in some control, possibly due to the better cohesion, and more concerted connection with the European Union Countries, and the US after a more critical period that started in 2001, with 9/11, followed by attacks in Madrid, Spain, Paris, and Nice, and later on in Barcelona, and New York, as a lesson being learned, however not totally vanished, and in need of a more effective constant improvements of a united counter-terrorism agencies, and systems.

Separately in another very serious threat is the worsening Global Warming, Trump's current policies have only shown a detachment from the Europeans, and world council agreements, particularly at a moment when it is evident that the climatic conditions is fast deteriorating at great speed in the last decade, and now causing major damages, with increasing force with greater than usual devastation, noted Just looking at the last 2017 disastrous effects the Hurricane Maria, caused in Puerto Rico, and now in this month of September 2018, we are experiencing enormously, major floods caused by the landing, in North Carolinas, of a Hurricane converted into a tropical storm Florence, followed also, in the same week, with equally, excessive flooding, in Oklahoma, causing great damages also across the adjacent States, in the West, and in Canada, not only with great unusual flooding, but also generating, never before seen in such extreme happenings, across the entire world, during and before this century, including violently destructive fire tornadoes. How much proof is there to be?, without the US, not attending to the evident warnings, and still being separated from the needed attention, in concert with the rest of the world, in the struggle, and formulation of measures to stop the progress of such a threat of eventually risking a near total extinction, that needs preventive work, and joined global policies, in an effort to protect the survival, of life in our planet. These steps are extremely necessary, and at this moment; I also need to stress the importance of the needed care with the proper attention, not only to the horrendous possibilities of devastation, in any war with arms of mass destruction, but right here, in our country, to put a stop to the mass killings of innocent people, including little children, such as on the saddening criminal events in Sandy Hook, Connecticut, already a number of years ago without proper legislation to avoid the use of assault weapons of war.

The level of violence in our beloved USA, has reached more than unacceptable levels, contemplating that, since six years ago when we saddening saw the sad massacre of children 6 to 7 years of age in the Sandy Hook Elementary school in Connecticut, still we are without proper legislation, and it has continued with more such events with massive criminal event in Orlando, Florida, and in Las Vegas Nevada, followed by the recent Parkland School in Florida, yet, again, sorry to say, still without proper legislation being even considered by the politicians controlling Congress. In conclusion, it is not a matter of the Second Amendment, that was not created by our founding fathers, to be used for the proliferation and free and easy access of such criminal assault weapons of war. That should not be allowed to be able to continue to happen.

In closing, if at all possible, wishing for reaching of a happier ending, of this chapter in history, I can only be praying for the end of the insensitivities that has created it. That is just one of the most important things that should be expected to change for the better, for our beloved America,

"Among the worrisome signs already mentioned on this Synthesis
At this date on July, 23rd, of 2019, are the serious emerging confrontations
Currently developing in the Middle East, surrounding Iran..
All of what should all be hopefully, and sensibly avoided."

Elio F. Beltran

And now also going to "Back to Cuba"/The Return of the Butterflies"

Just a few months ago, I had the interesting, and fortunate privilege of meeting a number of young Cuban American architects, engineers, and economists, as well as students of those, and other important disciplines. In that occasion, I meet and spoke with many of them at a Florida International University, gathering in Miami; I was impressed with the knowledge and enthusiasm of these valuable young professionals, and the promise, and willingness to participate in the forthcoming restoration, and reconstruction of Cuba, once the nightmare ends there, making way for such noble desires to finally become possible.

It is a very hopeful promise that shows the value of the new generations that are willing, and will be able to contribute to bringing Cuba back to what it has meant to be; a bright and shining star illuminating and upholding the respect of human rights, among the community of freedom loving democratic nations of the Western Hemisphere, and the world, a very welcome sign of the metaphorically anticipated "Return of the butterflies".

As I was writing the AFTER WORDS for the final remarks for Back to Cuba/The Return of The butterflies, in Spain, Aurora tells me: "Why have you turned a story that started as an account of beautiful images of happier times, and as a real love story, into what will be perceived as a political endeavor in your part? After all you are not a politician!

"Yes, you are right. I started by bringing out the beauty of our Cuban surroundings and ours customs during happier times and all the memorable loving experiences, as well as the struggle, and the suffering, for love itself, but you have to remember that it is inevitable for a freedom loving Cuban, to forget, or ignore the suffering of his oppressed people, and that, my dear Aurora, is also a real love story".

Elio F. Beltran

Author of this Updated Second Special Edition of "Back to Cuba / The Return of the Butterflies".

ABOUT THE AUTHOR

The author was born in the colorful town of Regla, across the bay from Havana in 1929. His childhood was filled with images of urban and countryside landscapes enmeshed with the interesting people he grew up around in the peaceful innocent years in the aftermath of the depression.

As he grew up in Havana, he lived the experiences of his formative years as a student, in pre- revolutionary Cuba during times of political uncertainties where gangs were used as a crucible for future political power without regard for life or death in the process. within that environment, he had a brief uneventful but revealing encounter where he confronted the then emerging student leader Fidel Castro.

He left Cuba for his exile in 1960 and became an American Citizen in 1968, Back to Cuba /The Return of the Butterflies, is part of his recollections that, in essence, have evolved to become a true account of the history he has traveled through the last sixty plus years, with many revelations as well as a surprising insight into what may come in regards to the anticipated, and much desired process, for the return to real democracy and freedom, by and for the Cuban people, and the possible roll of the US, Government and how its polices could change in tune with the transformations of the Cuban political scenario as the historic leaders of the revolution would necessarily give way to the new generations that will undoubtedly emerge.

Elio F. Beltran has received many awards; among them from the NJ. State Council, on the Arts, The Institute of International Education, Cintas Award. The Silver medal award, by the French Academy of Arts Sciences and Letters in Paris, France, as well as having been nominated Artist of the year by The International Biographical Center in Cambridge, England in 2004, celebrating fourteen oils related to his "Balseros",, (Cuban Rafters) series of oils that are part of the art collection of Florida International University, in Miami, since the 1990's, also receiving many other honors for his "Back to Cuba/ The Return of the Butterflies" book, and for his Childhood Memories of Cuba Paintings. The Author/Artist also continues to pursue his career endeavors in Andalusia, Spain, and in the United States, where he continues to live with his Spanish American wife Aurora A. McIntosh-Beltran, Since 1994.

* * * * *

A significant part of his art work collection, has recently, in 2018, found a permanent home, being added to the Florida International University (FIU's collection), in Miami. The same year that he received The Marquis Who's Who Lifetime Achievement Award.

Just, at the time of my having also finished the final review of this new special updated edition of **"The Return of the Butterflies/ Back to Cuba",** with the many events about the Cuban saga, since its beginning of December 31st of 1959, it will incredibly reach its 60 years anniversary at the forthcoming December 31th, of 2019, and, as per the actual facts, and turns of history, towards the end of this work, and moving into what is currently happening, not only in Cuba but in our current environment in our beloved USA, The Americas, as almost, the entire world, which has been commented under the heading **"Synthesis"** following the **"After Words- Reaching the end of the Long Night",** I could not avoid writing an added analysis of what this moment in history looks like, without any pretention, except to express honest concerns, about this moment in history, on an easy to understand format, with the hope to be able to add, if possible, some enlightenment, over much of what can currently be perceived as serious concerns for the future, ahead of these times, and beyond the Summer of 2019.

Honestly, I would have rather keep the focus on some of the beautiful childhood memories of the many happy times, that have inspired me, throughout my entire life, particularly in My hometown of "Regla", across the bay from Havana, and its memorable and beautiful surroundings areas that saw my student years, that also started my witnessing, the many historic events, in which I grew up, and later from my new beginning as a USA citizen starting in 1968, that stimulated my career as an artist with my childhood memories of Cuba, that later found an extended meaning, in both, painting, and writing history, and with both vocations, able to participate in many important cultural endeavors, both, in Europe, and The USA. I should add, how much of a blessing it has all been, even when, there has been many saddening instances, in the story of Back to Cuba, I am still looking forward to what, on the book I name it **"The Return of the Butterflies"** which I envision as a renaissance for our beloved Cuba, as it was inspired by the letter received from my dear sister, appearing close to the end of the last chapters of the book.

I am leaving therefore, some of the happy memories of Cuba, surrounded by the bright deep blue and light transparent colors, that so exuberantly blended the Atlantic and the Caribbean waters, where I learned to swim, and fishing, as well as navigate on a 16 feet boat build by his uncle, who also added an old cranky, but effective motor to be used for a special adventure, that this very young nephew, adventurously took on, with a few of his school friends, sailing out from the Havana bay to explore, a little known cave, that they knew was hiding between exuberant thick bushes, aligned by the top of the hills overlooking the small, but beautiful beach cove named **"Bacuranao",** in those years, hiding on the t north ester coast, at about 15 Kilometers, east of Havana, the Capital of Cuba.

In sum, It seems that the colors of the, ever moving, Cuban surrounding seas, made very definite long lasting impressions on my retina, and on many of these paintings, which will also be added to the collection of the Florida International University, in Miami; paintings that show how much, such memories of the impressive waters, surrounding my birth place, have influenced the, at times, mysterious forms within the painting's ever moving waters, in which unexplained visions, may appear floating on a mix of little understood shapes, within, those memories, and significant inspirations, up to the most recent, Oils named; **"Lets love and save our Beautiful Planet"**

"Author in Cuba before his exile".